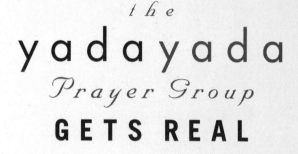

the

yadayada

Prayer Group

GETS REAL

a Novel

the yadayada *Prayer Group* GETS REAL

a Novel

neta jackson

INTEGRITY®
PUBLISHERS

Nashville

THE YADA YADA PRAYER GROUP GETS REAL

Published by Integrity Publishers, a Division of Integrity Media, Inc.,
5250 Virginia Way, Suite 110, Brentwood, TN 37027.

HELPING PEOPLE WORLDWIDE EXPERIENCE *the* MANIFEST PRESENCE *of* GOD.

Published in association with the literary agency of Alive Communications, Inc.,
7680 Goddard Street, Suite 200, Colorado Springs, CO 80920.

Scripture quotations are taken from the following:
> The Holy Bible, New International Version. Copyright © 1973, 1978,
> 1984, International Bible Society. Used by permission of Zondervan Bible
> Publishers.
> The New King James Version, copyright © 1979, 1980, 1982, Thomas
> Nelson, Inc., Publishers. Used by permission.
> The King James Version of the Bible.

This novel is a work of fiction. Any references to real events, businesses, organizations,
and locales are intended only to give the fiction a sense of reality and authenticity.
Any resemblance to actual persons, living or dead, is entirely coincidental.

Cover design: Brand Navigation, LLC | Deanna Pierce, Mark Mickel, Terra
        Petersen | www.brandnavigation.com
Cover Photo: Steve Gardner | Pixelworks Studio
Interior design: Inside Out Design & Typesetting

Library of Congress Cataloging-in-Publication Data
Jackson, Neta.
The yada yada prayer group gets real / by Neta Jackson.
   p. cm.

ISBN 1-59145-152-3 (tradepaper)

1. Women—Illinois—Fiction. 2. Female friendship—Fiction. 3. Christian
women—Fiction.   4. Chicago (Ill.)—Fiction.   5. Prayer groups—Fiction.
I. Title.
PS3560.A2415Y337   2005
813'.54—dc22   2004022323

Printed in the United States of America
05 06 07 08 09 DELTA 9 8 7 6 5 4 3 2 1

To all the

"Yada Yada Prayer Groups"

and praying sisters

springing up around the country—

Remember:

Pray like Jesus

Serve like Jesus

Love like Jesus

Prologue

CHRISTMAS DAY 2002

*T*he lean, wiry woman let the door of the central dining room bang behind her, taking in big gulps of clean, cold air. Not a moment too soon. If she had to listen to the kitchen "super" gripe about one more thing, she might do something that would land her in solitary. *Nag, nag, nag—that's all she ever does. I cain't do nothin' right.* It'd be easy to take down that cow, big as she was—but she couldn't go there. Had to stay cool.

Four months down . . . 116 to go.

The woman hunched her shoulders against the sharp bite of the wind, wishing she'd put on a couple more layers—but it was sweltering working the big steam dishwasher in the CDR kitchen. Digging in a pocket of her jean jacket for a cigarette, she turned her back until she got the thing lit, then she leaned against the building, blowing smoke into the wind, watching it get snatched away.

Beyond the squat, two-story "cottages" sprawled in an awkward line from the CDR to the visitors' center, she could see the ten-foot wire fence rimming the perimeter of the prison yard, topped by rolls of razor wire like a great, wicked Slinky toy. *Humph.* That fence might keep them *in*, but it sure didn't keep the bone-chilling prairie wind *out*.

She switched the cigarette to her left hand so she could warm up her right one under her armpit inside the jean jacket. *Christmas Day . . . so what?* Not enough to do. Any other Wednesday she'd be in the prison school. She was going to get her GED if it killed her—not that it would. Maybe college too. If she could survive an addiction to the lethal Big Four—heroin, methadone, vodka, and Valium— surely algebra and Illinois history weren't going to waste her.

And "Christmas dinner"—what a joke. Yeah, they'd been served slices of pressed turkey, blobs of mashed potatoes covered in greasy gravy, sweet potatoes smothered with melted marshmallows in big metal pans on the steam table, along with "the trimmings"—jellied cranberry sauce, Jell-O salad, rolls, butter pats, and canned cherry cobbler. Okay, it was one step up from the usual "mystery mess" and seasick-gray canned vegetables. Still, the long tables of sad women hunched over their trays, spearing food with plastic forks, served as a painful reminder that they weren't home for Christmas.

Only two food fights had broken out, though—chalk that up to the holiday spirit.

"Wallace!" A sharp bark from inside the CDR caught her like a watchdog on the prowl. "What makes ya think we done with these dishes? Get yo' butt in here, or I'm gonna cut yo' pay hours."

The woman named Wallace deliberately took a slow drag on her cigarette before dropping it on the ground and grinding it out with her Nike. *Cut my pay hours—big deal.* At fifty cents an hour, it wasn't a big loss. Still, the job added to her credit in the commissary and helped fill the hours. But she was going to quit this lousy kitchen gig—tomorrow, if possible. Already her hands looked like pale pink prunes. Even piecework in the factory would be better than this. Maybe they needed somebody to shelve books in the library . . . or do garden-and-grounds. Yeah, that was it! Garden-and-grounds. Physical work. Outdoors—

"Wallace!"

Well, come spring, anyway.

FINALLY RID OF HER SOAKED APRON and the sour-hot breath of the kitchen supervisor, Becky Wallace made her way back to C-5, one of the minimum-security cottages at Lincoln Correctional Center, a cement-and-wire fortress sitting on the Illinois prairie. The rec room on the lower level of the CDR was open seven to nine tonight, like most evenings. But maybe the pileup at the pay phone in the cottage had dwindled. She fingered the scrap of paper in the pocket of her jean jacket, making sure it was still there. A phone number . . . some woman up in Chicago had sent her a number last week. She'd been afraid to call, afraid to hear the voice on the other end. Afraid not to.

Today, though, she was going to suck up the courage. Surely her baby's foster parents wouldn't refuse to accept her collect call on *Christmas Day.*

A Department of Corrections truck sat in front of the door of C-5, piled with parts of the standard-issue metal bunk beds and a stack of narrow mattresses. She peppered the truck with a string of cuss words. Were they sticking *more* new arrivals in her cottage? The dorm on the first floor was already packed to the max. Maybe they were going to double-up the single rooms upstairs. Her name had moved up on the list for the second floor. Man! She'd give anything for a single. Yet if she had to have a roommate, that'd still be better than sleeping like cordwood in a woodpile.

Even walking to the bathroom was like playing Russian roulette, never knowing who was going to hit you up for your last cigarette or bust you one for "dissin'" her in the food line. And just when she got everybody figured out—who to watch out for, who to stand up to, who to give a wide berth—they stuck in some newbie who upset the whole social order.

The TV was babbling in the day room, and a game of Bid Whist was going on at one of the card tables. But the phone in the hallway was free, screwed to the wall facing the front door of the cottage like a one-eyed mole planted there to spy on their comings and goings. Behind that wall—squeezed between the day room on the left and the dorm on the right—was a small kitchen with a hot plate and a fridge, and an even smaller room with a washer, dryer, and ironing board.

Becky stood looking at the scratched-up black phone a moment. Finally she picked up the receiver and punched zero, then the numbers on her scrap of paper. *One ring . . . two . . .*

"Operator. How may I assist you?"

"Wanna make a call. Uh—collect."

"State your name, please."

"Becky Wallace." *Andy's mommy,* she wanted to say. But didn't.

The line seemed to go dead. A long stretch of silence. Had she been cut off? Two men in service uniforms came clattering down the stairs, followed by a female guard, arguing about the double bunk that had just been delivered as they went out the door, leaving it standing open. Becky slammed it shut with a well-aimed kick, then she turned back to the phone as a tinny voice spoke in her ear. *"I'm sorry. That number does not answer. Please try again later."*

Becky swore, fighting the urge to rip the phone right out of the wall. *Not home?* Where *were* they? Didn't they know how much she needed to talk to her baby? On *Christmas,* for—

"Hey, Wallace!" A tall girl the color of light caramel came in the door. "You got a package." She held out a brown box, neatly taped.

Becky stared at it. "Ain't no mail call today. It's a holiday."

The girl shrugged. "Musta got lost in the mailroom. Somebody asked me to drop it off." She grinned. "Maybe it's food."

Not likely. "Thanks." The tall girl was all right—kept her nose clean. Athletic. Maybe they could form a volleyball team when the weather loosened up. But the girl was too nice. She'd have to make sure she covered the girl's back if anybody ever messed with her.

Becky took the package and headed for her bunk in the dorm room. A quick glance told her that five women were already sitting or lying on their bunks, ready to be done with Christmas Day. Kneeling beside her lockbox, she twirled the combination lock and dropped the package inside. *Later.*

THE LIGHTS-OUT ORDER HAD BEEN GIVEN; the front and back doors to the cottage locked. Muffled snores slowly coursed through various parts of the room like belly rumbles after a meal of chili beans. Still Becky Wallace waited. Finally, she slid a hand under her pillow and drew out the package. She sat up, slowly, quietly, so as not to wake her bunkmate above.

Light filtered in through the barred windows of the dorm room from the floodlights in the prison yard, and she peered at the sending company: *Estée Lauder.* What kinda business was that?

The tough packing tape had been slit open for inspection and retaped with ordinary office tape, which easily gave way under her sharp thumbnail. A whiff of something fruity—melon?—spilled out of the box as she lifted the lid. In the dim light, she felt inside the box. Nestled in a bed of shredded, crinkled paper lay long plastic tubes of various sizes . . . a small round jar . . . a spritzer with liquid inside. Carefully she lifted out one of the plastic tubes, unscrewed the lid, and squeezed. A delicious squirt of creamy silk fell cool and soft into her hand.

Hand cream. Rich, velvety hand cream. Slowly she spread it over her hard, cracked knuckles and worked it into the chapped skin on the backs of her hands. Then she silently began to weep.

1

CHICAGO—NEW YEAR'S DAY 2003

*T*he call of nature—Willie Wonka's, not mine—got me out of bed at the bleary hour of seven thirty, even though the New Year's Eve party upstairs had kept me awake till after three. *Three a.m.!* But Willie Wonka's bladder was on dog-time—*old* dog-time at that—making sleeping in on holidays a moot point. Stuffing my feet into my scuffs and pulling Denny's big terry robe around me, I stumbled out of our bedroom mumbling thinly disguised threats at our chocolate Lab as he led me to the back door.

Coming into the kitchen, I caught a glimpse of pale blue sky and the rising sun bouncing off a row of windows at the top of a nearby apartment building like golden dragon eyes . . . and for a nanosecond I entertained the illusion of a blissful day in Key West. But when I opened the back door to let Willie Wonka out, a wall of icy air killed *that* pipe dream. I slammed the door after Willie's tail and peered at the little red needle on the back porch thermometer.

Brrr. Ten degrees.

Then I smiled. Add the windchill factor, which was sure to kick up by noon, and surely the Uptown Community Church youth group would cancel the so-called Polar Bear Plunge they had scheduled for today.

But by the time Denny and the kids wandered out of their bedrooms around eleven o'clock, the thermometer had inched up to almost twenty degrees, and everyone looked at me stupidly when I asked if they were going to cancel. "Mom," said Josh patiently, pouring himself a heaping bowl of oat flakes and raisins, "it's a Chicago tradition." As if that explained anything.

"Happy New Year, babe," Denny murmured, wrapping his arms around me from behind—and the next thing I knew he had untied the belt, snatched his robe off me, and disappeared with it into the bathroom.

"I was just warming it up for you!" I yelled after him, scurrying back into our bedroom in my pajamas. Time to get dressed anyway.

"Mo-om!" whined Amanda, wandering into the kitchen ten minutes later while I was making another pot of coffee. "I *really* need a new bathing suit. This one is so . . . so *babyish*."

I turned and eyed my fifteen-year-old. Apart from the fact that it was absurd to be talking about bathing suits in the middle of a Chicago winter, there was nothing "babyish" about this busty teenager, who was indeed filling out her one-piece bathing suit in all the right—or wrong—places. I declined to comment. "Go get some clothes on before you catch cold," I ordered. But I grinned at her back. I'd make some hot cocoa and take it along—that'd be a big hit after "the plunge."

The phone rang at 11:25. "Jodi!" said a familiar voice. "Are these *bambinos* still going to do this craziness?"

I allowed myself a small grin as I cradled the phone on my shoulder and stirred the pot of hot chocolate. "I'm afraid so, Delores. And not just 'bambinos,' either. Denny's got his bathing suit on under his sweats, in case he gets brave. Is José coming?" Like I couldn't guess. Delores Enriques's fifteen-year-old son had been showing up rather frequently, trailing Amanda like Peter Pan's shadow. Or was it the other way around?

"*Sí*. Emerald, too, but just to watch. Edesa and I are coming up on the el with them. This I've got to see for myself."

Two more phone calls followed in quick succession from Yada Yada Prayer Group members. Florida Hickman wanted to know what elevated train stop was closest to the beach where the Polar Bear Plunge would take place; Ruth Garfield grumbled that only love for Yo-Yo Spencer and her brothers would get her and Ben out on New Year's Day for such craziness. "But what can we do? A car they don't have. We'll be there at twelve. Then straight to the doctor so they don't die of pneumonia. *Oy vey*." A *click* told me the conversation was over, and all I'd said was, "Hello?"

THE SMALL CROWD GATHERED AT LOYOLA BEACH along the bleak lakeshore of Chicago's north side, wearing ski jackets, knit hats, and fat mittens, looked oddly out of place tromping over the sand. Even more so because a mild December had delayed the usual buildup of ice and frozen spray sculptures that usually marked Lake Michigan's winter shoreline. The lapping water looked deceptively harmless.

"Going in, Jodi?"

I squinted up into the face of Uptown's lanky pastor, who could easily have played Ichabod Crane in community theater. Widowed and childless, Pastor Clark *was* Uptown Community—a mission church that stubbornly hung out its shingle in Rogers Park, Chicago's most diverse neighborhood. Today he was bundled in an outdated navy parka with a snorkel hood, a long hand-knit scarf wound around his neck, hands shoved in his jacket pockets.

"Me? Not for love *or* money!" I held up the armload of beach towels and blankets I was carrying. "I'm here on life support."

He chuckled and trudged on to greet others gathering to witness the Polar Bear Plunge. The crowd was growing, and I saw Leslie Stuart's silver Celica pull into the beach parking lot. "Stu" had been attending Uptown Community for several months, ever since we'd met at the Chicago Women's Conference last May, even though she lived in Oak Park, on the west side of the city.

"Hey, Jodi. You going to take the plunge?" Stu's long blonde hair and multiple earrings were hidden by a felt cap with earflaps. She was grinning, flap to flap.

"Don't think so. Calendar says January."

"Ah, c'mon. You know what Oliver Wendell Holmes said: 'You don't quit playing because you get old; you get old because you quit playing.' Hey—there's Delores and Edesa!" She waved both arms in their direction.

I bit my tongue. Stu was probably in her midthirties—not *that* much younger than I was. But she didn't have to make me feel like an "old fogy" just because I was smart enough *not* to jump in the lake.

"Ack! I left something in the car." Stu ran for the parking lot, passing Delores Enriques and Edesa Reyes as they headed my way, bundled against the stiff wind adding whitecaps to the choppy gray water. I dumped my load of blankets and towels so I could give them each a hug.

Delores and Edesa were members of a Spanish-speaking Pentecostal church and had attended the same conference that had brought women together from various churches around the city. None of us imagined that the prayer group we'd been assigned to for the weekend would take on a life of its own. But when Delores got an emergency phone call that weekend saying her son José had been caught in gang crossfire in a local park—well, no way we could stop praying after that, just because the conference was over.

"Where are Emerald and José?" I asked.

Delores jutted her chin in the direction of the knot of excited teenagers gathering at the water's edge, still bundled in their winter coats. "Such antics!" The forty-something mother wagged her head. *"Mi familia en México?* They will think we have all gone *loco."* She rolled her eyes. "But whatever Amanda and Josh do, Emerald and José want to do it too."

"Don't mind Delores, Jodi," Edesa said cheerfully. "Underneath all that fussing, she's happy José is *alive* and can *do* something fun and crazy!" Edesa's dark eyes danced in her warm mahogany face. Edesa—college student, baby-sitter, and "big sister" to the Enriques children—wore her African-Honduran heritage as brightly as the neon-orange wrap that held back her mop of loose, nappy curls. And she'd rescued Amanda's grades last spring tutoring her in freshman Spanish.

"Hey, Ben! Over here!" I heard Denny's voice hail Ruth and Ben Garfield trudging over the hard-packed sand like two refugees trekking out of Siberia, following Yo-Yo Spencer and her half brothers, Pete and Jerry. The boys ditched the adults and joined the teasing, shoving group of teenagers at the water's edge, as Ruth and Ben stopped to talk to Denny.

"Hey." Yo-Yo nodded at Delores and me, then arched an eyebrow at Edesa. "You gonna take the plunge, 'Desa? Jodi? Anybody?"

"Are you serious?" Edesa shook her curls and laughed.

Yo-Yo grinned, reached inside her overalls and bulky sweatshirt, and pulled out a swimsuit strap. "I dunno. Thought I might if some other adults did." She tipped her spiky blonde head toward Ruth and Ben, who were still talking to Denny. "Didn't tell Ruth, though, or she woulda given me a nonstop lecture all the way here. Didn't tell Pete or Jerry, neither. Ya know them two—they think you're dead meat if you're over twenty."

I hooted. Yo-Yo "dead meat" at the ripe old age of twenty-three? Ha!

A flurry of activity near the shoreline caught our attention as the teenagers and even a handful of brave—or merely foolish—Uptown adults started shedding coats, sweatshirts, sweatpants, shoes, and socks and dumping them in piles on the beach. "Oh, good grief," I sputtered. "Denny is really gonna do it. Stu, too."

The Polar Bear Plungers formed a ragged line, backs to the water, facing the huddled onlookers. Bundled up as I was, I still felt the bite of the wind nipping off the lake, making my eyes water. Denny was jogging in place, trying to keep his blood going, while the younger set hopped up and down from one bare foot to the next. Josh—the oldest Uptown youth at eighteen—held up both hands like a prizefighter, dressed only in his swim trunks, complete with shaved head. "We who are about to freeze," he yelled, grinning defiantly, "salute thee!"

The Polar Bear line went crazy, cheering and yelling like gladiators about to enter the arena.

"Hey, wait for us!" somebody yelled. I glanced over my shoulder and saw Chris and Cedric Hickman—Florida's boys—running toward the line of half-naked daredevils, leaving a trail of their clothes and shoes on the sand as they stripped to their swim trunks. Behind them, Florida was hustling in our direction, picking up clothes as she went, trailed by a tall black man carrying a young girl piggyback.

"Bless You, *Jesus!*" Delores breathed. "It's Carl Hickman! And Carla. The whole family!" She winked at me. "Now maybe that's worth coming out today to see."

I felt torn between wanting to greet Florida and her husband— it *was* a first, Carl showing up at an Uptown event with his family— and not wanting to miss The Plunge. Just then the ragged line broke ranks and ran into the water, yelling at the top of their lungs. Beside me, Yo-Yo kicked off her shoes, dropped her denim overalls and sweatshirt, and ran toward the water.

"What? Yo-Yo's going in? That girl, she is crazy, yes?" Without turning my head, I knew Ruth and Ben had joined our little cluster. "And Denny! A heart attack he is going to have."

I was trying to keep track of my kids in the water—Amanda was still wearing her bright red knit hat—to make sure they came out again. But I couldn't help laughing at Denny, lifting his legs high and waving his arms, looking for all the world like a marionette pulled by invisible strings. A majority of the teens plunged headfirst into the numbing-cold water, then came splashing out, still yelling and dancing up and down. Denny, probably figuring he'd gone far enough proving his manhood, turned when he'd waded in up to his waist and splashed back to shore.

I rushed forward with my armload of towels and blankets, trying to locate my shivering family. "You're nuts," I told Denny, throwing an

7

old quilt over his shoulders, but he just grinned, as proud of himself as if he'd climbed Mount Everest. Josh ran up, grabbed a towel, and ran off again to pose with the youth group for somebody's camera.

"Here, Yo-Yo," I said, handing her an extra beach towel, as we rejoined the group of Yada Yada sisters and the ragtag assortment of husbands and younger kids. "Hey, Florida. Carl, it's great to see you . . . and Carla!" I grabbed the eight-year-old and gave her a hug. "You guys coming to the Warm-Up Party at Uptown? Pastor Clark drove the church van here to give a ride to anybody who needs one."

Carla hopped up and down in her white pull-on snow boots, tugging on her daddy's hand. "I want some hot chocolate!"

I bent down to her level. "I've got some in the car. Yours will be the first cup when we get to the church."

"No! I mean over there!" The little girl pointed and all heads turned. Sure enough, Stu—back in her sweats and felt helmet—was passing out Styrofoam cups of hot chocolate from a huge Igloo cooler to a cluster of grateful teens. Right on the beach.

"Sure, baby. Come on," Carl murmured, as she pulled him away.

I groaned inwardly. Upstaged again. *God, why do I always feel like this around Stu?* Then I scolded myself. *Suck it up, Jodi Baxter. Who gave you a patent on bringing hot chocolate?* I looked at Ben and Ruth. "You guys coming to the Warm-Up Party?"

"Don't look at me," Ben Garfield groused. "Ask Ruth. I'm just the cabbie."

"Of course we come," Ruth announced. "We didn't drive all this way to just watch these young people catch their death. Though the purpose of such nonsense, I don't see." She looked this way and that. "Where's Avis? Doesn't she go to your church?"

"Ha!" I snorted. "You're not going to get Avis out of the house to watch a bunch of crazies dip in the lake in midwinter—not unless it was a baptism or something."

"Well, now, see?" Florida grinned slyly. "I been prayin' that this here Polar Bear thing be like a prophecy, an' someday we gonna see all these kids come outta that water washed in the blood of Jesus."

Yo-Yo had one leg back in her overalls and one leg out. But she froze in midhop as if someone had yelled, "Red light!" in the kids' party game. Her blue-gray eyes widened. "Whatcha talkin' 'bout, Florida? Washed in *what* blood?"

2

I laughed aloud at the look on Yo-Yo's face. Poor kid. She had barely stuck her toe into "this Jesus gig," as she called it, since coming to the Yada Yada Prayer Group, and she was still trying to figure out what she'd gotten herself into. "Uh, baptism," I said. "You know, to show we've died with Christ and . . ."

I stopped. Her round eyes and mouth were obvious clues that I was talking gobbledegook. "Never mind. We can talk about it later." *Avis can explain it later* is what I meant. *Or Florida.* Somehow my churchy clichés didn't communicate to Yo-Yo, who wasn't that long off the street and out of prison.

By now, most of the Polar Bear Plungers had wiggled themselves back into their clothes and were making a beeline for cars in the beach parking lot. Seeing Josh in the driver's seat of our Dodge Caravan, Yo-Yo's brothers piled in along with José and Emerald Enriques, so Denny and I hailed a ride with Pastor Clark and the Hickman family in the church van. Fourteen-year-old Chris muttered darkly about having to ride with the "old farts," which got him a slap upside his head from Florida.

The spicy smell of homemade chili greeted us as shivering bodies crowded through the door of Uptown Community's storefront on Morse Avenue. I shanghaied a couple of teenagers to haul my picnic cooler of hot chocolate up the stairs to the large multipurpose room on the second floor, set it on the pass-through window from the kitchen, and began filling cups with the sweet, hot liquid.

"Ooo, girl, this stuff is good!" Florida drained a cup and held it out for a refill. "You use real chocolate to make this?"

"Yeah. Cocoa, sugar, milk, cinnamon." I felt mollified. Stu might have won points by being Johnny-on-the-spot with her hot chocolate on the beach, but even Jesus saved the best wine till last when He partied.

The bathrooms were busy for a while as the Polar Bear Plungers got out of their wet swimsuits and damp sweats and back into dry clothes. The rest of us sat on folding chairs in little clumps, sipping hot chocolate and filling our bellies with bowls of thick chili. I could hear the electric hand dryers going nonstop in the women's bathroom. "Makeshift hair dryers," I murmured to Florida—or tried to—but I'd just eaten some crackers and it came out, "Mathift hay dryerth."

Florida snickered. "Oh Lord, I'm glad somebody else feedin' my kids today! These holidays take a big bite outta money we don't have." She cast a roving eye around the room. Satisfied that her kids were both eating and behaving, she craned her neck again. "I don't see Stu. She didn't drive all the way from Oak Park just to jump in the lake for two minutes, did she?"

"Two *miserable* minutes," I added.

Florida snickered. "Ya got that right! But if ya ask me, it's time that girl quit talkin' 'bout movin' into the city and do it. She's puttin' a lot of miles on that fancy lil' car of hers, traipsin' back 'n forth ever' Sunday for church and Yada Yada too."

"Yeah, I know. She talks about getting out of real estate and back into social work. . . . Maybe she wants to, maybe she doesn't."

Ruth sat down with a *whumph*. "What? A new job Stu has?" Florida and I quickly shook our heads, but Ruth was already shooting her marbles down another alley. "When is Nony coming home? Doesn't school start next week?" Ruth fanned herself with an old church bulletin she'd picked up and sighed. "I suppose we'll be hearing 'South Africa this' and 'South Africa that' once she gets back."

Nonyameko Sisulu-Smith—another Yada Yada sister we'd met at the conference last spring—and her two boys had been in Kwazulu-Natal ever since Nony's mother had had a stroke last November, yet she'd been taking her own sweet time coming back, much to her husband Mark's frustration. He had finally joined them in December "for the holidays," but Nony's absence had left a big hole in the Yada Yada Prayer Group for too long. "Last e-mail we got from her said this weekend," I said. "Didn't I forward it to you, Ruth? They thought her mother wouldn't survive the stroke, though it looks like she's recovering bit by bit."

"E-mail, she-mail," Ruth muttered. "Haven't looked at it since Christmas. A favor that woman should do, die decently and let Nony come home to her family."

Florida and I looked at each other. That sounded terrible—but we both knew what Ruth meant. We all thought Mrs. Sisulu would "pass," and then Nony could wrap things up with her relatives and be able to be "at home" here in the States with her husband. Yet I had my doubts that her mother's death would change anything for Nony. It was South Africa that was in her blood, not just her extended family.

"So, a man she has now," Ruth said.

I stared at Ruth. "Who?"

13

"Avis! Last time Yada Yada met, teasing her you were, about some man who showed up at church with her. Church dates—sounds serious to me."

"Ruth!" Trying to follow Ruth's jumps in conversation often left me spinning. "Yes, I was teasing her, but I hardly think it's serious. The guy knew Avis's husband before he died—an old friend, I think, who moved here to Chicago on business and looked up Avis since he didn't know anyone."

"Mm-hm." Ruth just fanned as if she knew better.

"Hey, guys." Stu was one of the first ones out of the bathroom, her still-damp hair falling over one shoulder as she pulled up a chair to join Ruth, Florida, and me while balancing a bowl of chili, a napkin, and a plastic spoon. "Anybody know of any apartments for rent? Not you, Ruth—I don't want to live out in Lincolnwood. Somewhere in the city. Here in the Rogers Park neighborhood would be great."

Florida and I exchanged a tiny glance. Stu hadn't overhead us, had she? *Nah.*

"So." Ruth nodded knowingly. "You are no longer selling houses? Back to social work, eh?"

Stu wrinkled her nose. "Got an interview at the DCFS office here in Rogers Park next week. Probably have to start at the bottom again, but I'd like to work with foster care."

Ruth flinched slightly. Foster care was a touchy subject, ever since the Department of Child and Family Services had taken away a foster daughter she'd wanted to adopt and sent the child back to her mother—after the girl had spent five years in Ruth's home.

"Don't know any rentals offhand," I said hastily. "I'll keep an eye out, though."

"Uh, Señora Baxter?"

I jumped. José Enriques stood behind me, smiling big, his wet black hair slicked back from his forehead. *Gosh, he's good-looking.* Too good-looking for only fifteen. No wonder Amanda was smitten.

"Could I speak to you and Señor Baxter a moment, please?"

Me *and* Denny? My systems went on red alert. He sounded too serious, and he was smiling too big. Ruth fanned her bulletin really fast now and stared at José. Florida studiously looked the other way and—*dang it!*—was trying not to laugh.

"Uh, sure, José." I reluctantly stood up and looked around for Denny. I handed my empty chili bowl to Florida but kept my cup of hot chocolate. I had the feeling I was going to need *something* to hang on to.

Denny was talking to Carl Hickman and Ben Garfield, which made an odd trio. Ben was sixtyish, short, wide waisted, and crowned with a surfing wave of silver hair on his high forehead. Carl was twenty years younger, tall and thin, his pecan coloring setting off his salt-and-pepper moustache and tuft of hair under his bottom lip. Denny was solid, given his job as a high school coach. He had flecks of gray in his brown hair, too, but his clean-shaven face couldn't hide the big dimples that creased his cheeks or the laugh-wrinkles around his gray eyes, making him look like an overgrown kid.

I caught Denny's eye and crooked a finger at him. He excused himself and met us in the middle of the room. "What's up? Hi, José. No frozen toes?"

José grinned. "No, Señor Baxter. But the girls"—he waved toward the women's restroom, which still buzzed with high voices and the electric hum of the hand dryers—"are creating their own sauna, yes?" He laughed.

Get to it, José, I muttered to myself. My anxiety was popping out like pimples on prom night.

As if reading my mind, José suddenly sobered. "Señor and Señora Baxter, I would like to ask your permission to give Amanda—"

My heart lurched and I sucked in my breath, ready to scream, *"Not on your life, buster!"*

"—a *quinceañera.* It is a special party when a girl turns fifteen. I have talked it over with my mother, and she thinks it is a wonderful idea."

I just looked at him stupidly. Amanda had turned fifteen last August. Had Amanda put him up to this? What was Delores *thinking,* giving *my* daughter a birthday party, a . . . a *quince*-something. Whatever. Sounded like something from their Mexican culture. The Baxters, however, were anything but Hispanic. Ordinary Midwestern white-bread. That was us.

"Hm. Sounds interesting, José." Denny gave me a quick glance to be sure I wasn't about to fall out on the spot. "You do know that Amanda already turned fifteen last summer?"

José nodded. "*Sí.* But we were not yet friends till you came to visit us at Iglesia del Espirito Santo, so it was not possible then. Now that we are friends, it seems a shame that a wonderful girl like Amanda should not have a *quinceañera.*" He smiled big again. "It does not really matter if the time is exact. It can be for her fifteen-and-a-half birthday!"

Which would be—I counted quickly in my head—February. Next month.

I took a quick glance around the room. Where was Delores? Why didn't she say something to me earlier? She should have warned me, given me a heads-up . . . there she was. "Just a moment,"

I murmured and headed for Delores, who was retying Emerald's hair ribbon and laughing with Edesa.

"Excuse me," I said, firmly taking Delores by the hand. "Can you join us, please?" and I dragged her across the room to where Denny and José stood talking.

"Now." I put on the best smile I could manage. "José informs us he wants to give Amanda a *quin*— . . . uh, a *quin*—"

"A *quinceañera. Si!*" Delores beamed, her round cheeks still glowing pink from our foray out by the lakefront. "A wonderful idea, yes?"

I still didn't have a clue what a *quinceañera* would entail, but it didn't really matter. "Well, yes, of course—maybe for Emerald. She'll be fifteen in a few years, and I'm sure it will be lovely. But . . ." I looked at Denny for help; he looked at me as though curious to know what I was driving at. "But . . ." *Oh God, help. What am I trying to say here? I don't want to hurt Delores's feelings—or José's either, for that matter. But . . .*

Okay, I was going to be honest. "But it feels awkward for *you* to give our daughter a birthday party." I could feel the color creeping up my neck. "As if . . . as if we fell down on the job, didn't celebrate her birthday adequately." Personally, I thought Amanda had a very nice birthday, though admittedly just a family dinner with Edesa Reyes and Emerald as special guests—her "big" and "little" sisters. We'd even redecorated her bedroom—well, we'd given her some sunshine yellow paint and a new comforter.

Apparently, though, that was B.J. *Before José.*

Delores opened her mouth, then shut it and wrinkled her brow. She looked genuinely puzzled. Suddenly she laughed and clutched me in a big hug. "Oh, Jodi, Jodi. You think too much!" She let go of me and grabbed one of Denny's arms and one of José's, like they were going to do the cancan. "We love Amanda too—Amanda the 'lovable,'" she teased, playing on the meaning of Amanda's name. "You must share her with us, not keep her all to yourself! She is becoming a young woman—that is the purpose of a *quinceañera*. Like a . . . what do you say in English?"

"Like a debutante ball or 'sweet sixteen' party?" Denny said helpfully. I stared at my husband. What did he know about debutante balls? Not in *our* income bracket.

"*Sí!* That is it." Delores beamed again.

Over Delores's shoulder I saw Amanda coming out of the women's bathroom, her butterscotch hair twisted up in a butterfly clip. "Just tell me," I hissed, "have you mentioned this to Amanda yet?" If not, no harm done if we said no.

"No, I don't think so," Delores said. "José?"

José shuffled. "Well, kind of."

Great. I turned to Denny. *Now what?*

Delores was unperturbed. "Jodi, just think about it, okay? It could be fun. We could do it together." She beamed. "Another Yada Yada party—Mexican, this time."

"Sure," Denny said. Denny the Amiable. "We'll think about it. But it depends—how much it costs, things like that. We couldn't let you pay for something like that."

Amanda headed for us like an arrow toward a bull's-eye.

"Yes, yes, we'll think about it," I said hastily. "And . . . it's sweet of you to think of her. Just don't say anything more to her right now, all right?"

"Hey! What are you guys talking about?" Amanda eyed her father and me suspiciously, then darted a questioning look at José.

18

"How long you *señoritas* take to change clothes, is what!" José joked. "I am being a gentleman, waiting till you are finished to get some food—but I am starving! Come on." He grabbed Amanda by the hand and headed for the kitchen pass-through.

I heard Denny chuckle. "Nice save, José."

3

e stayed to help clean up after the Warm-Up Party, so it was nearly four by the time we pulled into the garage behind our two-flat. The kids scrambled out of the minivan and hustled toward the house. "Josh! Take Willie Wonka out, okay?" I yelled after him. "He hasn't had a walk today."

Josh's stride stuttered just long enough to tell me he'd gotten the message—long enough to probably roll his eyes too. "What's his problem?" I muttered, hauling the damp towels and blankets out of the back of the Caravan. "It's his job to walk the dog."

"Rose Bowl," Denny said, grabbing the sport bags with the wadded-up clothes and making his own shot put for the house.

Sure enough, the TV was on by the time I got inside, and both Josh and Denny were engrossed in the pre-kickoff interviews and commentary. "So what do you think Oklahoma's chances are of taking home a win today?" . . . "Well, Bud, we've had a great season, the team has worked hard, and we're ready. Don't tell Washington State, but we plan on taking home that trophy." Mutual grins and laughter.

Sheesh. Do they bag that stuff and sell it by the pound? I stood in the archway between the front hall and living room, debating whether to put my foot down and send Josh out with the dog or give up and take the dog myself. Josh looked up. "Mom! I promise to walk Wonka at halftime, okay? Just let him out in the yard for a few minutes—he'll be okay till then."

"Well . . . all right." As long as he wasn't ignoring me. I shed my own winter wraps, let Willie Wonka out, gathered up the damp towels and blankets, and headed for the basement to toss them into the washing machine. Josh seemed different lately. Not bad or anything, but less predictable. Like shaving his head last fall and leaving a long topknot—dyed orange!—just before his grandparents came to visit. *My* parents at that. We all survived, and the topknot, thank goodness, had eventually gone the way of all his other hair. But the bald head had stayed like a permanent light fixture.

And then there was the college application to the University of Illinois in Champaign—due January 1. Yet when I checked on it after the Christmas hustle-bustle, Josh hadn't even started! He barely got it in yesterday's mail so it'd be postmarked December 31. What was *that* all about? Last year he'd been so eager about going to college.

I set the washing machine temp to Hot, let it start filling, and filled the cap of the detergent bottle with blue liquid. *At least he's not into drugs or pierced body parts—thank You, Jesus!* I opened the lid of the washing machine to toss in the detergent—and realized with a start that the machine was already full of washed clothes. My upstairs neighbors'! *Oh God, don't let them come down here till I spin the water out of there.* I quickly hit Stop, reset the machine to Spin, and bundled my armload of towels and blankets back up the basement stairs. Didn't want them to know I'd even been down there!

Back in our first-floor apartment, I dumped the laundry on the kitchen floor and collapsed on a stool. Saved! What if I'd dumped that detergent on top of all their clothes? I'd be in deep suds then. But as my thudding heart slowed, I thought, *This is so stupid! We've lived in this two-flat for a year and a half, and we still barely talk to our upstairs neighbors.* Rose and Lamar Bennett, an attractive African-American couple, held professional jobs, and we hardly ever saw them unless the furnace went on the fritz or Willie Wonka accidentally left a pile on the sidewalk. DINKS, Denny called them— Double Income, No Kids.

It bothered me that we had so little interaction with the Bennetts. I wasn't sure what I'd expected when we'd moved into the city from Downers Grove, but I'd imagined we might become friends, or at least friendly neighbors. Didn't happen. We were more like cold sides of beef hanging side by side in a frozen-food locker.

I got up from the stool and turned on the teakettle. That was one reason it had meant so much to me when Avis Johnson—my African-American principal at Mary McLeod Bethune Elementary, where I taught third grade—had invited me to that Chicago Women's Conference last May. Avis was also a member of Uptown Community Church, even before we started attending, so I knew her two ways: "Ms. Johnson" Monday through Friday, and "Avis" on Sunday.

I'd been in awe of her at first, never imagining we'd become friends as well as co-workers. Avis was so classy. She had a calming, upbeat presence, both at school and at church—and she looked mighty good for fifty-something too. Yet we'd gone to that women's conference together—urbane Avis Johnson and hick-chick Jodi

Baxter from Des Moines, Iowa—neither one of us dreaming we'd come home with a prayer group as jumbled as a drawer full of mismatched socks. Not only Florida Hickman ("five years saved and five years sober—thank ya, Jesus!") and Ruth Garfield, a Messianic Jew; but Hoshi Takahashi, brought up by Shinto parents in Japan, who'd met Jesus at the home of Nonyameko Sisulu-Smith when Nony's very American husband—a professor at Northwestern University—invited his students for an authentic South African meal.

And that was only the beginning. There were twelve of us in the prayer group, though for several months last fall we were only eleven when Adele Skuggs, owner of Adele's Hair and Nails on Clark Street, boycotted the group because—

The teakettle whistled.

I shut off the flame on the stove, batting back sudden tears. *Oh God, we've been through so much mess this past year. I could really use some peace in this new year—even dull and boring would be nice!*

I grabbed a dishtowel, overwhelmed as fresh memories flushed out along with the tears. *Denny on his knees at Adele's salon, asking forgiveness of poor, confused MaDear Skuggs for a crime he didn't commit, yet owning the legacy of sin that had created so much rift between us . . . the heroin-crazed woman who had robbed the prayer group at knifepoint in this very house . . . and the face of the young teen boy, caught in my headlights just before my car hit him, that still haunted my dreams.* I gave up, slid down the kitchen cabinets until I was sitting on the floor, and had a good bawl.

With that sixth sense of dogs, Willie Wonka wandered into the kitchen and tried to lick my face. "And that," I said, blowing my nose into the now-damp dishtowel, "is why I didn't even *try* to write the annual Baxter Christmas letter this year, Wonka. Not that you care." Or could even hear me, for that matter. Yet in spite of being almost stone-deaf, Willie Wonka was a patient listener.

I got off the floor, splashed water on my face, made a big mug of hot tea, and grabbed the phone out of its cradle. I had a sudden urge to talk to Avis. She hadn't been at Uptown last Sunday, and with this being a school break, it felt like a *month* of Sundays since I'd even seen her, much less had a good talk with her.

The most comfy chairs were in the living room, but it was obvious that only football aficionados were likely to enjoy them until January 2. After peeking in on my family—even Amanda was sprawled on the couch, her feet on her daddy's lap, yelling for Oklahoma—I headed back down the hallway to our bedroom at the back of the house, punching in Avis's home number as I went.

She answered on the fourth ring.

"Avis! It's Jodi." I kicked off my shoes and flopped down on the wedding-ring quilt covering our bed. I could hear a TV in the background—sounded like the football game. Stereo football—my house, her house.

"Hi, Jodi. Just a minute." I heard the phone muffle but could still hear her say, "Turn the TV down a little, will you?" Then she was back. "What's up? How was the Polar Bear Plunge?"

Turn the TV down? Who in the world was at Avis's apartment? No one was ever at Avis's apartment when I called. She was a widow and lived alone. Had a married daughter on the south side, another in Cincinnati, a third in college. Maybe Natasha was home for the holidays. "Got company?" I asked casually.

"Oh, Peter Douglass came over to watch the bowl games. Apparently that's a tradition for him, but he doesn't have any football buddies here in Chicago yet."

And you *are a football buddy?* I wanted to say. Avis had never shown the slightest interest in football since I'd known her. "Hey," I said lightly, "we should've invited you guys over here. Denny and Josh and Amanda are glued to the tube."

"Oh. Well, he wanted to see the Cotton Bowl, then the Orange Bowl, now the Rose Bowl." She laughed—and didn't seem the least bit annoyed at all that football. "Now tell me how the Polar Bear Plunge went! Did you go in?"

"You know better, Avis Johnson! But Denny did—along with Josh, Amanda, and a bunch of other teenagers. Oh yes, and Stu and Yo-Yo!" I ticked off the Yada Yada sisters who had come to the beach, bringing their kids—or kid brothers, in Yo-Yo's case. "We went back to the church for hot chocolate and chili—it was kinda neat to have Ruth and Ben there. Ruth didn't come when Yada Yada visited Uptown that time."

"Well, you wouldn't get me out on the beach in the middle of winter!" Avis said. "It's wonderful that Josh and Amanda keep including Yada Yada's kids in Uptown's youth activities. Especially Yo-Yo's brothers, since they don't go to any church. Real missionaries, your kids are."

"You think? They've both been a little weird this fall—we had to ground Amanda for two weeks, remember? For sneaking off to the Mexican Independence Day parade with José and lying to us."

"Well, they're kids, Jodi. Good kids, though. You ought to be thankful."

Well, I am—most of the time.

"You gonna be at church this Sunday? Didn't see you last week, so I wasn't sure if you'd gone out of town . . ." I was fishing shamelessly, and I knew it. Avis never missed church, but she hadn't mentioned anything about going away for the holidays.

"Oh, sure. I'm leading worship. Peter's been church hunting and wanted to visit some churches in the area. So I took him to First Church of God up in Evanston. I used to go there before I came to Uptown."

I had a slow, sinking feeling in my gut, like a blob of mercury sliding back down to zero in the meat thermometer after pulling it from the roast turkey. It had never occurred to me that Avis might go to some other church—though I sometimes wondered why she came to Uptown in the first place. For all Pastor Clark's good intentions of growing a diverse congregation, we were still pretty WASP-ish and rather slow to warm up to Avis's free style of worship and prayer. Florida showing up—and staying—had been a lot of support in that department, at least.

I heard Peter yelling in the background—and the Baxter trio yelling in stereo down the hall. Must've made a touchdown. "Oh, stop," I heard Avis say, and she laughed. "You're nuts! Stop it." And she giggled. "Peter is doing his own version of the end-zone dance. At his age!" She laughed again.

I couldn't imagine the distinguished black man Avis had brought to Uptown a month ago—clean-shaven except for a neat moustache, comfortable in a suit and tie, dark hair with only a hint of gray on both sides above his ears—doing the "touchdown stomp." There was no doubt about it, though—a male voice was *woo-hooing* in Avis's living room, and Avis was giggling like a sixth-grader.

"Well, guess I better let you go since you've got company." *Oh, grow up, Jodi! You sound like a kid who has to share your mommy's attention.*

"You all right, Jodi? Didn't ask why you called."

"Yeah, I'm okay. Had a good bawl a little while ago, just thinking about the trauma we weathered this past year. Glad I didn't know

27

last New Year's Day what God was going to take us through. And I was kinda missing you. Just wanted to hear your voice."

"It *has* been a while, hasn't it? When did Yada Yada last meet? Before Christmas anyway. I'm so glad you called, Jodi. It was a tough year but a good year. God gave us the Yada Yada Prayer Group—who would've thought? And we've all learned a lot about God's faithfulness to us in the midst of all the . . . *stuff* that went down."

A feel-sorry-for-myself lump gathered in my throat. "Yeah. I was just telling God I wouldn't mind a few months of 'dull and boring' right about now."

Avis laughed. "I'll stand in agreement with that! Let's all pray for 'dull and boring—'"

Blaaaaaaaaaat.

"What was *that*, Jodi?"

I sighed. "Back door buzzer. Front doorbell has a nice *ding-dong* to it—you know." I clambered off the bed and headed toward the kitchen. "Guess I better get it. Talk to you later, okay?"

I hung up the phone in the kitchen and peered out the glass window in the top half of the back door. *Good grief.* It was my upstairs neighbor—Rose Bennett. Had she figured out that I almost rewashed her clothes in the machine? She couldn't have! I'd covered my tracks . . .

I put on a smile and opened the door. "Hi, Rose." Her slim shoulders were hunched inside a sleek white jogging suit, her hair tied back with a black silk scarf—not her usual dressed-for-success attire. On a gentler day, I would have stepped out and just talked to her on the back porch. But that wind was nasty. "Come in before you freeze."

The woman hesitated then stepped inside. "Jodi, isn't it?"

To my credit, I did not roll my eyes. We had only lived in the same two-flat for a year and a half. "Uh-huh. Jodi Baxter. What's up?" Did I really want to know?

"Lamar is being transferred to Atlanta. We'll be moving as soon as we find someone to sublet the apartment."

"Oh." I blinked a couple of times. "Okay. Thanks for letting us know. At least it's warmer in Atlanta." I smiled helpfully.

Rose Bennett didn't even say good-bye. She just nodded, slipped out the door, and walked up the back stairs.

I shut the door after her and leaned against it. The Bennetts were moving! Was that good news or bad news? They certainly hadn't been very friendly. On the other hand, they hadn't been any trouble either—except for that late party last night. Maybe it'd been a good-bye celebration with their friends.

My brain was suddenly crowded with awful possibilities. What if a family with five noisy kids moved in upstairs? Or members of a heavy metal band who needed space to practice? I groaned aloud, imagining green spiked hair, black leather, and metal chains. "Okay, God, what's up with this?" I ranted. "What part of 'dull and boring' don't You understand?"

4

*T*he last few days of winter break, my kids acted like caged monkeys with bellyaches. Every time I asked Amanda to do something around the house, she wailed, "But I only have three more days till school starts!"—making it sound like these were her last days on earth. And Josh found some reason to be out every night till midnight, his non-school-night curfew. Funny how popular he was now that he had his driver's license.

"Can't we set a limit on how many midnights per week?" I fussed at Denny. "I never go to sleep till Josh gets home, and this is getting ridiculous!"

Frankly, I was glad when Amanda was invited to spend Friday and Saturday with her best friend in Downers Grove, taking the Metra train out to the southwest suburbs. Patti Sanders and Amanda had gone through elementary and middle school together, Awana Club and summer camp too. But the hour-plus drive on traffic-glutted highways between our Chicago neighborhood and Downers Grove meant that the girls hadn't seen each other that often since we moved. "Have fun, honey," I said, giving Amanda a kiss at the Rogers Park Metra station Friday morning. *Go, go,* I thought. *Drive somebody else's mother crazy.* And then I immediately had an anxiety attack when the train pulled out. She had to change trains at the Metra hub downtown. What if she got on the wrong train? What if Patti's mom wasn't at the station to pick her up? What if some maniac saw she was alone and . . .

Get a grip, Jodi, I scolded myself as I drove back to Lunt Avenue. *Haven't you learned anything about trust this past year? Didn't God protect Amanda and you and Denny and all the Yada Yadas when we got robbed last fall? Didn't God bring Hakim back to your classroom after his mom yanked him out?*

I grabbed one of the worship CDs we kept in the car, stuck it into the narrow slot, and punched through the selections till I found the song I wanted: "God is in control! This is no time for fear . . ." By the time I turned into our alley and clicked the garage opener, I was belting it out with Twila Paris: "God is in control! We believe that His children will not be forsaken!"

I came in the back door still singing—"He has never let you down; why start to worry now?"—but was immediately drowned out by an awful racket blaring from the stereo in the living room. Josh was in the dining room playing games on the computer but looked up when I tapped him on the shoulder.

"Oh good, you're back." He headed for the living room yelling, "Dad! Mom's back!" And suddenly the racket went dead. I shook my head to stop the ringing in my ears. Blessed tranquility.

Denny appeared in the dining room archway, shrugging into his winter jacket and carrying his sport bag. "Where's the car?"

"Oh. I put it away. Sorry." I knew Denny had to coach a basket-ball practice today at West Rogers High, just forgot in the heady praise trying to drown out my anxiety about Amanda. "Uh . . . what was that on the stereo?"

Denny grinned and pecked me on the cheek. "A CD Josh wanted me to hear—a demo of a punk rock group called Head Noise." He waggled his eyebrows. "Jesus People. You wouldn't like it." He yelled down the hall toward the bedrooms, "Josh? You coming?"

I already knew I didn't like it. I mean, gospel groups like Radical for Christ or Kirk Franklin were one thing—loud, but at least you could hear the words—but heavy metal? punk? It might be *Christian*, but it didn't qualify as real music.

Josh appeared, jingling his own set of car keys. "I'll drive."

I raised an eyebrow at Denny. "Josh going to work with you?"

"Nah. He's going to drop me off, then pick up some of the guys and go down to Jesus People to hear this band. They've got a couple of gigs today." Denny winked at me and followed Josh out the back door.

I looked down at Willie Wonka, who was sniffing the back door as though checking for positive ID of who'd just gone out. "Well, looks like it's just you and me, Willie," I said and headed for the computer. I had a few things I needed to do, and a quiet house with nobody needing clean socks or help with homework was an unex-pected bonus.

I checked e-mail first, deleted half of the new ones, scrolled past messages addressed to Josh or Amanda, and opened one from Hoshi Takahashi.

To: Yada Yada
From: Htakahashi@nwu.edu
Re: Mark and Nony

Dear Sisters,

Just got an e-mail from Dr. Mark and Nony. They are leaving Johannesburg today and will be arriving home tomorrow, Saturday, Jan. 4. Nony says hi and she's missed everyone so much and has lots to tell us.

    I am also so happy to see them again! This house is not the same without Marcus and Michael.

Love, Hoshi

Bless Hoshi! Mark Smith had asked if she'd be willing to house-sit the fish tank, geckos, and houseplants when he left to join his wife and sons in South Africa a month ago. It actually worked out for Hoshi, since the dorms at Northwestern University closed for winter break. But it'd been pretty lonely too. Most Northwestern students went home for the holidays; "home" for Hoshi was Tokyo—and Hoshi's parents hadn't called or written since their disastrous visit last September.

My heart squeezed. A lot had happened since that crazy woman—now in prison at Lincoln Correctional Center—had sliced Mrs. Takahashi's hand during a robbery at our house. The doctor who stitched Mrs. T's hand had assured Hoshi that her mother's wound would heal quickly. Yet the deeper wound to Hoshi's family was still open and raw. *"This is what happens when a daughter is disobedient and forsakes her religion!"* her father had fumed.

I made a note to call Hoshi. What time were the Sisulu-Smiths flying in? Was anyone picking them up? That'd be fun—maybe Denny and I could do it. We'd still have room for their family of four in the Caravan, though luggage might be a problem.

I called up Google and typed "quinceanera" into the search line. Wow! Lots of hits. I poured myself a cup of the coffee still sitting in the coffeemaker—ugh! Too bitter. I made some fresh coffee and settled down to read up on the party José wanted to give Amanda.

I was not happy at what I found. I mean, it sounded practically like a wedding, with a fancy gown, a special mass—which was a problem, since we weren't Catholic, and neither was the Enriques family, for that matter—and maids of honor and *chambelánes,* for Pete's sake. Not to mention food, favors, a live mariachi band, and a huge birthday cake for the "hundreds of guests."

Good grief! *What is Delores thinking, encouraging José in this crazy idea?* Well, there was no way Denny and I could afford such a celebration. Sometimes this multicultural stuff went too far.

I printed out some articles to show Denny, then I went back to Google to search for information on learning styles. Hakim Porter might be back in my classroom, but his mother was still opposed to testing him for a learning disability. And maybe the problems he was having weren't a learning disability at all. Avis seemed to think it could be related to posttraumatic stress after his big brother was killed . . .

A familiar wave of nausea sent me to the bathroom. I rarely threw up, but the feeling was so strong I sat on the side of the tub for a few minutes just in case. It still seemed like a cruel cosmic joke that the little brother of the boy I'd hit with my car last June ended up in my third-grade classroom—unknown to either his angry, grieving mother or me. Not till that awful day we'd faced each other at the first parent-teacher conference.

No, no! I know You're not into cruel jokes, God! God had to have His reasons, didn't He? *God is merciful, full of grace and truth . . .*

Trust. *"This is where trust comes in, Jodi,"* Avis had said. *"Trust that God has your good at heart—and Hakim's good, and his mother's too. Even if you don't understand it right now. Or ever."* Which was certainly true; I *didn't* understand it.

I splashed cold water on my face and returned to the computer. Avis had promised to see if she could arrange counseling for Hakim with a school social worker. The loss of a sibling was reason enough, but Avis suspected that having no father in the home compounded Hakim's loss. And I was following a hunch. Hakim was obviously no dummy—he'd proved that with his math skills when we'd used a balance scale to find the missing addend. But he absolutely bogged down when it came to reading and writing. Not to mention his defiance and lack of cooperation when it came to group work.

Whatever was blocking him, I needed to find a key to teaching this kid. I wanted to see the triumph in his eyes again, like when he'd put the exact number of weights needed on the scale and said scornfully, "Didn't you know that?"

BY THE TIME DENNY GOT DROPPED OFF by one of the other coaches, I'd printed out a bunch of articles to help me brush up on various learning styles. One phrase leaped out at me about "the logical learner," described as capable of abstract thinking at an early age, able to compute math problems quickly. That sounded like Hakim. I needed to read more about that.

"Hi, babe." Denny kissed me on the back of the neck. "Did Amanda get out to Patti's house okay?"

Amanda! She'd never called—and I'd been so engrossed in my searches, I didn't call her either. I nearly fell over Willie Wonka in my haste to get to the phone, but a quick call to the Sanders home assured me that she'd arrived safe and sound and the girls were now hanging out at Yorktown Shopping Center. "Want me to have her call you when they come in? Though I don't expect them for an hour or two. They wanted to see that Tim Allen movie. *Santa Clause 2*, I think. Hope that's all right."

"Oh. Okay, thanks. Yes, have her call." *Grrr.* Amanda was supposed to check out any movies *before* she saw them, not after. She'd argue that she knew this one would be okay, but still.

When Denny got out of the shower, I followed him into the bedroom, reading from my printouts about the Mexican *quinceañera* while he got dressed. "See? It *is* the Mexican version of a debutante ball, except it's focused on just one fifteen-year-old. A huge fiesta, with fancy dress, gifts, food, musicians, dancing . . ."

"Sounds like fun." Denny was splashing on some aftershave.

"Denny! There's no way we can afford something like this for just a birthday party! Maybe when she gets married in ten years, Lord help us."

"I thought José wanted to throw this party. Let him pay for it."

I stared open-mouthed at my husband, who must've gotten beaned on the head by a wild basketball today. *"Denny!* We can't do that! That's like . . . like admitting they're a serious couple. Besides,

José is only fifteen himself. Where's he going to get money to do something like this?" I stopped, suddenly realizing that Denny had dressed in black slacks, a teal shirt, and black cardigan sweater instead of his usual around-the-house jeans and sweatshirt. "Why are you so dressed up?"

He grinned. "Because. Both kids are gone. The house is empty. *We* are going out to dinner. And then . . ." He waggled his eyebrows.

Had he listened to anything I'd been saying? But his grin was irresistible—and going out *would* be nice. It'd been a couple of weeks since we'd had any time together. "Wait a minute. Amanda's supposed to call. And doesn't Josh have the car? When is he going to be back?"

Denny shrugged. "By his curfew, I guess. He said don't wait up. We can take the el up to Evanston. They've got a lot of good restaurants. And Jodi . . ." Denny leveled his gaze at me. "Amanda can leave a message."

"Well, okay." I headed for the shower. I'd be stupid to turn down a dinner date with my husband. It seemed weird that our teenager had the car and his parents had to take public transportation, but it didn't seem to bother Denny. Okay, it might even be fun. Still, I didn't care how good he looked and smelled—we *were* going to talk about this Mexican fiesta thing.

5

I totally forgot to call Hoshi Friday night to find out when Mark and Nony were arriving at the airport. Just as well. Denny would *not* have been happy with me making Yada Yada phone calls after we got home last night, because after a great dinner at Thai Soukdee in downtown Evanston, we were definitely "in the mood"—though riding the el home with the temperature in the teens almost put a chill on it, along with the fact that Josh would be coming home sometime before midnight.

Before? *Dream on, Jodi.* More like five minutes after. By then Denny was snoring softly, but I was still half-awake, with one ear tuned to the noise of a key or footsteps in the hall. Josh knocked on our bedroom door to say, "I'm home," but I could almost bet he'd be asleep before I would.

The next morning I dialed the Sisulu-Smiths' home near Northwestern's campus around eight o'clock, hoping it wasn't too early. Hoshi answered on the second ring.

"Yes, Jodi? . . . Oh, Dr. Mark and Nony arrive at 11:52, South African Airways . . . No, they plan to take a taxi."

That sounded like Professor Mark Smith. Not the type to ask somebody to pick them up. Yet Hoshi thought the idea of going to the airport sounded like great fun. "We'll surprise them! Yes, I'd love to go. You can pick me up?"

I wished the entire Yada Yada Prayer Group could go to the airport to give them a welcome home, but that wasn't practical on such short notice. Hoshi and I would have to do—and Denny, too, if I could sweet-talk him into it.

He emerged bleary-eyed but still looking yummy about nine o'clock. It took a few chugs of coffee to get his brain cells moving before he answered my query about the airport. "Why not let them just take a taxi home, if that's what they usually do?" he reasoned, refilling his coffee mug. "Mark can afford it on his salary."

"That's not the point. Nony's been gone over two months! I'm sure they'd be pleased if we showed up to meet them, even if they'd never ask."

Denny drained his mug and shuffled toward the front door to get the newspaper. "But if Hoshi's going, you don't really need me," he called back over his shoulder.

I followed him toward the foyer. "I know. I just think Mark would feel more comfortable if there was another man." I batted my eyes at him. "I'll make cheese omelets for breakfast if you say yes."

He swatted me with the newspaper. "That's shameless bribery. And it's my last free day before school starts on Monday."

Yet the cheese omelets worked, and Denny pulled into the parking garage at O'Hare Airport at 11:45, close to Terminal 3. I thought they'd be coming into the international terminal and have to go through customs, but it turned out they'd landed in Atlanta that morning and had done all that. The last leg on South African Airways was a domestic flight, operated by Delta.

The three of us made our way to the baggage claim area, carrying the winter coats they'd left behind—Hoshi's idea. "Wish we could meet them at the gate," I said, remembering how much fun it used to be to meet people as they spilled out of the jetway from the plane. But a world full of terrorist threats had changed that forever. There wasn't even a place to sit down while we waited.

We saw them before they saw us. Ours weren't the only heads that turned as the Sisulu-Smith family made their way through the press of people searching for their baggage carousels. Mark Smith came first, wearing a royal blue dashiki with gold stitching around the neck and wide sleeves, and carrying two small carry-on bags. In the wake he created, Nony moved right behind him, holding both Marcus and Michael by the hand, the boys looking like clones of their father, including the royal blue dashikis. A stunning black and yellow dress of geometric patterns wrapped around Nony's body down to her ankles, stopping just above the gold strap sandals that cradled her slim, brown feet. A head wrap in the same African print covered her hair, except for the two large hoop earrings that dangled on either side. Definitely dressed for a South African summer.

"Uh-oh. They're going to get a rude shock when they step outside," I murmured, following Denny as we pushed our way toward the bright splashes of colorful dress brightening up the drab baggage claim.

Denny reached them first. "Can I help you with those bags, mister?"

Distracted, Mark Smith shook his head. "No, thank you . . . what?" His mouth broke into a wide grin, spreading his thin moustache that dropped down and outlined his chin in a carefully sculpted goatee. "Denny Baxter! Jodi . . . and Hoshi! You too?"

A sudden flurry of squeals and hugs took over the conversation as the seven of us greeted each other. The boys hung back, as though not sure they remembered these people after their two-and-a-half-month absence. I hugged them anyway.

"You look very African for a man born and bred in Georgia," I teased Mark, as we waited for the carousel to start spitting out luggage.

He actually blushed. "Well, you know Nony—we *all* came home with at least three new outfits, all traditional South African something. Had to buy another suitcase just to bring home all the extra stuff."

"Oh, stop." Nony rolled her eyes. She leaned toward me. "He bought his share of souvenirs—carved wood, brasswork, stuff for the walls."

"Well, sure. It was my first trip to Africa."

"Hopefully not the last," Nony murmured.

I eyed Hoshi with the slightest lift of my eyebrow. Well, Mark and Nony were back, along with the ongoing diplomatic standoff: "Your country or my country?"

Mark was right about one thing—they had a *lot* of luggage. Even with a cart, we all had to carry something, and we filled up an entire elevator, what with seven people plus cart plus stray bags. We got out on "Da Bulls" level—Marcus and Michael wanted to stop at all the parking-garage floors so they could hear all the different sports theme songs, but their father threatened bodily harm if they

hit the buttons—and Denny trotted off to get the car since Nony
was practically barefoot in her thin sandals. But even the short dash
to the car from the elevator foyer must have been a shock to the system by the time we slammed all the doors after cramming everybody plus luggage into the Caravan.

I was glad Hoshi climbed into the third seat with the two boys
so I could sit with Nony in the middle—Hoshi, after all, would get
to visit with them once they got back to the house. I asked the top-
of-the-head questions: Did you have a good flight? How is your
mother doing? Are the boys glad to be home? "There's not enough
time!" I moaned. "We'll have to invite you guys over for dinner so
we can hear everything about your trip."

Nony nodded wearily. "Yes. Maybe later. I need some time to
reflect, to ask God what it all means before we tell you about it."

"And develop our pictures," Mark tossed from the front seat.

The sky was spitting snow, and Denny had to turn on the windshield wipers. Lake effect? Or a big storm? I'd forgotten to check
the weather.

"Jodi?" Nony's low voice seemed meant for my ears only. I leaned
closer. "How is Denny—after MaDear's terrible accusation, I mean?
While I was in South Africa, seeing the still-painful struggle my
country is going through after the end of apartheid . . . I kept thinking about Denny and MaDear, aching for them both. And praying
for them, praying for all my brothers and sisters, black and white,
weeping for all the hurts still quivering in a million hearts as we take
stumbling steps forward—praying that forgiveness and God's love
will one day prevail."

A lump gathered in my throat. *Nony doesn't know.* She'd still
been here when Denny had walked into Adele's beauty shop to pick

me up on our anniversary, provoking a tirade from Adele's confused mother, who thought my husband was one of the men who'd lynched her brother when she was only a girl of ten. Denny had wanted to clear things up—he wasn't even born then! He'd grown up in New York, for Pete's sake! Yet the incident had thrown up a wall between Adele and us. Citing a lot of painful stuff her family had had to deal with over the years, Adele had dropped out of Yada Yada, leaving us feeling guilty and not knowing what to do.

I took Nony's hand in mine. "Thank you for the prayers," I said. "God did something amazing around Christmas—but first we had to ask, 'What did Jesus do?'" It sounded trite the moment I said it, like the WWJD catch phrase that ran rampant through Christian pop culture a few years back. I meant it, though. Not, "What would Jesus do?" but "What *did* Jesus do?"

Nony's eyes glistened. I think she knew. When I had a chance, I'd tell her about Denny's decision to ask MaDear's forgiveness—as though he really had committed that sin against her. *"Because,"* he had explained to me later, *"she needed to hear someone say, 'I'm sorry.' And because I'm not guilt-free."*

Nony looked away and I heard her murmur, *"Yes,* Lord! You said you came to heal the brokenhearted and proclaim liberty to the captives, to make the blind see and set at liberty all who are oppressed!"

I grinned and squeezed her hand. Nony was *definitely* back.

Forty minutes later we pulled into their driveway on Evanston's north side. As the guys unloaded the luggage, Nony sat for a moment just looking at her house—a red-brick two-story, pretty even in the dead of winter with bare ivy creeping up the brick and framing the windows, and wheat-colored decorative grasses waving gently in the chilly breeze. She sighed. "It's good to be home." Then I realized how tired they all must be after their twenty-four-hour journey.

"I thought about making Japanese lunch for welcome home," Hoshi said shyly. "But then I thought, Marcus and Michael would like something truly American."

"Pizza!" the boys yelled in unison.

"You didn't." Nony rolled her eyes.

Hoshi nodded with a guilty smile. "With do-it-yourself toppings, all lined up on the kitchen counter, ready to go."

Denny and I were invited inside to partake of the do-it-yourself pizzas, but we declined, knowing it took energy to chat, even with friends, and they all probably needed a good nap. Amanda was a convenient excuse. "We have to pick her up at the Metra station," we said, giving everybody one last hug and climbing back into the minivan—leaving out the itty-bitty detail that her train didn't get in till almost five.

AMANDA POPPED OUT OF THE METRA TRAIN, lugging her backpack. "You *both* came to pick me up?" She seemed highly amused. "Good grief. I was only gone one night."

"Two days," her father reminded her, taking the bulging backpack and giving her a big squeeze. "Two long, gloomy days. The house was quiet, the phone never rang, no snack dishes stacked up in the living room, no undies left in the bathroom—"

"Dad!" she screeched, but he made her laugh.

I opened the sliding door and climbed in the middle seat so Amanda could sit up front—a ploy Denny and I once figured out if we actually wanted to talk with one of our offspring while in the car. "Did you have a good time with Patti?"

Amanda shrugged and looked out the window. "I guess."

That got a sidelong look from Denny. "You guess? I thought you girls were best buddies back when."

Another shrug. "Yeah, guess so. Once."

This wasn't what I expected. "Did something happen, honey?"

"Not really . . ." Her voice trailed off, and I thought she was going to leave us guessing. But suddenly she whipped her head around, eyes flashing. "It's just . . . Patti and her new friends are so . . . so *ignorant*. They were, like, telling me all about the cute boys at school, and all the R-movies they sneak into, and they asked if I liked anybody, and I said kinda and told them about José—"

I pressed my lips together.

"—and they, like, got all weird because he's Hispanic and started asking all sorts of embarrassing questions, like if we'd, you know, done it yet, and what's the matter, don't I like white boys anymore? And is it true Latino guys just want weird sex—"

"Amanda!" My mouth flopped open in spite of myself. "Patti said things like that to you?"

"Well, not exactly Patti. It was some of her friends we met at the mall. And she laughed, too, and didn't seem to get it. I mean, I tried to tell them he'd been shot last spring—and right away, they started making jokes like, 'Ooo, Manda's sweet on a gangbanger.' They made me so *mad!*" By now Amanda was practically yelling. "So I just walked away. Who cares about them, anyway?"

Denny pulled into the garage from the alley. "You walked away? What did Patti do?"

"She, like, ran after me, and we took a bus home. But I think she was upset that I'd made her leave her friends. Later she tried to ask me about José—trying to make it up to me, I guess—and I *really*

46

wanted to tell her how he told the drug dealers to butt out of the park that day so his kid brother and sisters could play, and he plays a tight set of drums at Iglesia, and he wants me to have a *quince-añera*, and that he's one of the sweetest guys I've ever met." By this time Amanda was climbing out of the car. "But it felt like . . . like throwing pearls to the pigs. So I just told her to forget it!"

She slammed the car door. A second later she opened it again. "Oh. Thanks for picking me up." And the door slammed again.

Denny slowly turned his head and looked at me. I know my mouth was hanging open. And for once Denny was speechless.

6

*D*enny and I just sat in the car for a little while, sorting through our thoughts. Finally he said, "Did we want to know all that?"

I snorted. "Well, yeah. Not knowing would be worse. The way those girls talked! It's more than ignorant. It's . . . it's . . ."

"Slander. Bigotry. Spreading rumors about an entire ethnic group."

Well, that too. I was going to say crude. Vulgar.

"I'm proud of her, standing up for herself that way." He chuckled. "Feisty gal, isn't she? Must get it from you."

I let that one go. Not sure it was a compliment. I get feisty, all right—dumping on my husband and kids when I'm upset. Yet not always feisty when I should be, reluctant to make waves in the teachers' lounge when they're gossiping about someone or when the politics get hot. But Amanda had walked out. *Ha.* I could just see her. Not slipping away demurely, either, but probably storming through the mall like her hair was on fire.

"Denny, what do you really think about José and Amanda? I mean, she talked like José's her boyfriend—and she obviously knows he wants to throw her a *quinceañera*. Kinda surprised she hasn't been bugging us about it."

"Yeah. Give her points there." Denny scratched his chin. "I think she's too young to date, and we can set some limits there, but we can't dictate her heart. And if she's going to 'kinda like' a guy, José Enriques is pretty good news. We know his mother, he goes to church, and he's been hanging out with Uptown's youth group."

I agreed with all that. Yet I hated what I was thinking: *I don't want my daughter swept off her feet by a "Latin lover." Would he follow in his dad's footsteps—end up a high school dropout driving trucks?*

"But as far as this *quinceañera* thing goes," Denny continued, "it depends. An informal Mexican party? Sounds fun. The whole nine yards? I agree—it'd feel awkward to have José and his family throw a big shindig for our daughter. Sounds like a lot of money we can't afford—and I don't think the Enriqueses can either. Still . . ."

"Still . . . what?"

Denny looked at me with a funny expression. "It kinda fits Amanda. Who she is. Who she's becoming. I mean, she came back from that mission trip to Mexico last summer soaking up the culture. Her Spanish has been improving by leaps and bounds. Huh! Remember a year ago this time? She was making Ds and Fs. This year? As and Bs. And it's not just José—she's crazy about the whole Enriques family, especially Emerald. And Edesa Reyes too."

"I know. I just . . ."

For some odd reason, the song I'd been listening to in the car the other day popped into my head: *"God is in control."* Did I believe that? Or was I always going to approach problems the Old Jodi way—stewing and fretting till I'd wrestled them to the ground? No! My Yada Yada sisters had been teaching me to "go to the top" on the first round, not the last. Not just to believe *in* God, but to *believe* God.

"Denny, why don't we pray about it and ask God what we should do?" And then I giggled. "Good grief. I sound just like my dad. I used to hate it when he said that!"

FOR SOME REASON, praying with Denny about the *quinceañera* was like pricking my anxiety with a pin and letting all the air out. Not that I was clear what we should do. So why not call Delores and talk it over? Tell her our reservations; ask more questions. Why not?

Yet when I called Saturday evening, Delores was working the late shift in pediatrics at the county hospital. *Doesn't matter,* I told myself as we four Baxters climbed the stairs to Uptown's meeting room the next morning. *I'll call her when we get home from church.*

Avis was already there, talking to Pastor Clark. They made a funny contrast. Pastor Clark, pale, thin, and gawky, dressed in his "Mr. Rogers" sweater and slacks that looked like they needed a good press. And Avis, tall for a woman, her cocoa-brown skin smooth and unlined even though she had already passed the big 5-0. She had a new hairstyle since I'd last seen her—braided all over her head and tied in a knot on top—and she was wearing a smart black and tan tunic slit up at the sides over a pair of wide-legged slacks.

Both Pastor Clark and Avis had lost spouses—funny, I'd never thought about that before. Widower and widow . . . except now there was Peter Douglass, Avis's new "friend," sitting by himself about two-thirds of the way back, a lonely island in a sea of empty

51

folding chairs. The only African-American male, he wore a black sport coat, gray dress pants, and a gray and red tie—a little over-dressed for Uptown's casual garb. But he did look *fine*. I liked the touch of gray to his close-clipped black hair.

"Denny!" I whispered, giving a short nod in that direction. "Go say hi."

Denny obediently walked into the row of chairs just in front of Avis's guest and extended his hand. "Peter Douglass, right? Denny Baxter. And my wife, Jodi."

Peter Douglass stood, an impressive three inches taller than Denny. "Yes, I remember," he said, shaking both our hands, smiling politely.

"Mind if we sit?" Denny peeled off his bulky winter coat. "Hardly need this today. Can you believe this mild weather for January?"

I was hoping we'd get a chance to talk a bit, even if it was just the typical dance around jobs, sports, and how Chicago weather compared to Philadelphia. But just then Avis gave the call to worship: "Praise the Lord, church! If you have your Bibles, please turn with me to Isaiah 43." I dug into my tote bag, but Avis was already into the Scripture, reading strongly into the hand-held mike: "Fear not, for I have redeemed you! I have called you by your name; you are Mine! When you pass through the waters, I will be with you; and through the rivers, they shall not overflow you. When you walk through the fire, you shall not be burned, nor shall the flame scorch you. For I am the Lord your God, the Holy One of Israel, your Savior!"

I expected the music group to launch into the first song, but Avis held up her hand as though to put them on *pause*. Instead, she picked up a copy of the *Chicago Tribune* and said, "I don't know how many of you had a chance to read the paper yet, but there was another suicide attack in Tel Aviv this morning."

Murmurs of "Oh no!" and "Lord, have mercy" spun around the room. I flinched at the picture of carnage I could see on the front page even from my seat. The news from the Middle East was so disturbing lately, I could hardly read the newspaper anymore.

"This is the first Sunday of the New Year," Avis continued, "yet we are reminded with painful reality that we still have the same old problems infecting our world, our nation, and ourselves. And yet, brothers and sisters, we must not behave as though we have no hope. For our God is a *mighty* God—"

"Thank ya, Jesus!" No mistaking that voice. Florida must have come in. I twisted in my seat to catch sight of Stu, Florida, and the three kids sitting toward the back. Stu must've picked them up. No Carl, though.

"Even though the nations rage, we can trust in God—Father, Son, and Holy Spirit—who is not only Redeemer and Friend, but Lord of the nations. One day we will see His glory in its fullness—yet even now, we, His people, must reflect that glory by abiding in His truth and pouring out compassion for all who are caught up in endless cycles of violence and revenge. For our God is not only a God of justice, but of mercy, forgiveness, and grace. Our challenge is to let His light shine through us to all the world—beginning with our own neighborhoods right here in Chicago."

"You preach, Avis!" Florida called out—and to my surprise, Uptown's mostly white congregation actually clapped, with a few amens, hallelujahs, and several chuckles thrown in. But Avis was done. She walked away as the music group launched into one of Uptown's favorites, "Shine, Jesus, Shine." The words had special poignancy after Avis's call to worship for the new year: "Flood the nations with grace and mercy . . . let there be light."

On the other side of Denny, I saw Peter Douglass's eyes follow Avis as she walked back and forth off to the side, giving herself up to worship with raised hands and tears while the music group of guitars, keyboard, drums, and vocals plunged forward with song after song of victory and praise. A small smile tipped the corners of his mouth.

And then it hit me. *That man is head over heels in love with Avis!* I was so taken aback I hardly knew what to think.

But my thinker was pulled back to the service when Pastor Clark began his sermon. All over Christendom, he said, churches were celebrating Epiphany—the visit of the wise men to the child Jesus. "It's an old, old story. Yet it's a story that's still being written. Wise men and women—children too—are still bringing their gifts to Jesus."

And then he told the familiar story of the boy who came to hear Jesus teaching in the countryside one day, bringing along a lunch his mother had packed for him—five small loaves of bread and two dried fish. And he gave them to Jesus. "Jesus used that little gift," Pastor Clark said, "to feed and bless and refresh thousands of people who were hungry and tired. A miracle, we say. But Jesus is still waiting for *us* to bring *our* gifts to Him, so that He can continue to feed and bless and refresh a hungry and hurting world. That is the question I'd like each of you to ask yourself as you head into this new year: 'What is the gift that's in my hand? Am I willing to give it to Jesus?'"

Being the first Sunday of the month, the service ended with a simple communion. After I'd taken my piece of bread and sipped from the goblet of wine, I closed my eyes, thinking about Pastor Clark's question. Did I have any gifts in my hand? I couldn't think of any. Certainly not like Avis, who had the gift of worship . . . or

Nony, who seemed to be a wellspring of memorized scriptures that came pouring out in her prayers. All I could come up with was teaching third grade at Bethune Elementary. *That's it, Lord? My job?*

WELL, YEAH, I thought, as I dumped my tote bag on the teacher's desk in my third-grade classroom the next morning and changed out of my walking shoes. *I'm a teacher, so guess that's what I've got in my hand.* But how could I give my teaching to Jesus? I certainly couldn't talk about God in a public school! *So? Just be a good teacher,* I told myself. Yet sometimes I felt as if I was barely hanging on with my fingernails. This school was better than a lot of Chicago public schools—especially with Avis Johnson at the helm—but I still felt overwhelmed by a classroom so diverse, English was the second language for almost half the children. And the parents! Back in Downers Grove, my classroom had thrived with lots of parent involvement and support. Here? I *still* hadn't met some of the parents, even on report card pickup day. And some kids got dropped off at seven in the morning and didn't get picked up till six at night, like the school was expected to provide breakfast, childcare, after-school supervision, discipline, healthcare, and—oh, yes—the ABCs too.

And then there was Hakim. Correction: Hakim's *mother.* She hated me—with good reason. I'd killed one son in that auto accident; why *should* she let me teach her other son? Was she still trying to get him transferred? I didn't really blame her. And now that I knew Hakim's identity, it wasn't easy to see the personification of my guilt staring back at me every morning in the classroom when he took his seat.

About once a week I felt ready to pack it in and try waitressing.

I took a deep breath. Almost time for the bell to ring. *Okay, God. It doesn't feel like much to me, but it's all I've got in my hand right now. A new year . . . one teacher scrabbling for a foothold . . . one troubled boy who needs redemption . . . and thirty other squirrely eight-year-olds. If You can do anything with that, it's all Yours.*

7

We'd packed the Christmas decorations over the weekend, but I still lit a group of pillar candles on the dining room table as I called Josh and Amanda for supper. It felt good to be back on some kind of schedule after the holidays—maybe we'd even sit down at the dinner table all at one time. At least soccer was over and Josh had a couple of months before baseball practice started at Lane Tech. Right now Denny's after-school schedule was the wild card since he was assistant coach at West Rogers High for several team sports—soccer, basketball, baseball. But I expected him any minute.

Sure enough, Denny walked in just as we were serving the scalloped potatoes and leftover ham. "Hey! Candles! What are we celebrating?" He tossed his jacket on top of Willie Wonka, dumped his sport bag in the corner, and planted a kiss on my forehead.

"First day of school in 2003, what else?" Amanda smirked, beating me to the punch. *Hmm.* My kids knew me well.

"So. What's new at Lane Tech?" Denny piled the creamy potatoes on his plate and sprinkled them with grated cheese. Ever the optimist. Whenever I asked that question, it was like talking to empty air. How could a whole school day be summed up as "Nothin'"?

Amanda shrugged. "Not much. Oh. I joined the Spanish club. Meets on Thursdays after school."

Denny and I looked at each other. Why weren't we surprised? "That's great, kiddo," he said.

"Just so you don't have to come home in the dark," I added.

Amanda gave me the "look": *Parents. So predictable.*

Josh helped himself to seconds. "What about you, Josh?" I asked, trying not to notice how the candlelight danced on his shaved head.

He chewed thoughtfully a few moments. Then . . . "What do you guys think about the death penalty?"

I blinked. "What?"

"You know—it's been in the news a lot. Governor Ryan's just about to sign a bill turning over the verdicts of everybody on death row. All the kids are talking about it at school."

"He's gonna let them all out?" screeched Amanda.

"Yeah, and they're all going to come after *you*, Piglet."

Amanda swatted her brother with her napkin.

"That's enough," growled Denny. "Not 'turning over' the verdicts, Josh. 'Commuting their sentences'—probably to life without parole. I think a moratorium would be good; there are too many holes in the system. If you've got the money for a big-name lawyer, you're not going to end up on death row. The whole system needs an overhaul."

My mind scrambled. I did remember hearing something about the debate going on in Springfield—especially after a couple of verdicts got overturned when new DNA evidence proved the guys were innocent. "I . . . don't know what I think. Someone like John Gacy, who killed all those teenage boys?" I shivered. "He was a monster."

"Yeah, well, who are we to take someone's life?" Josh's voice raised a notch. "That's playing God, don't you think? It's pure and simple revenge—an eye for an eye. I agree with Dad. Life without parole is sufficient to protect society from people like Gacy."

"I don't *disagree*, Josh—"

"Anyway. The debate club at school is looking for new members to debate current events. I signed up to support doing away with the death penalty, period." He gathered up his dishes. "Can I be excused?"

I stared at my son's back as he took his dishes to the kitchen and then disappeared in the direction of his bedroom. When did Josh Baxter suddenly get political?

Denny corralled Amanda to help load the dishwasher, so I commandeered the computer to check e-mail while I had a chance. I scrolled through the list—aack! I hated all that spam!—till I came to one addressed to "Yada Yada" from "BlessedRU." Ha! That was Nony.

To: Yada Yada
From: BlessedRU@online.net
Re: YY at my house?

Dear Sisters,

THANK YOU to everyone who has called or e-mailed a "welcome home" since we've been back. Sorry I haven't been very good about contacting you all individually. There's SO much to do after being gone for two months!

But how about having our first Yada Yada meeting of the New Year at my house this Sunday? I brought gifts for everyone—smile.

Love, Nony

Gifts? Yum. Anything Nony picked out would be fabulous. As for Yada Yada meeting at her house . . . I racked my brain. For the life of me, I couldn't remember if someone else had volunteered. Better check with Avis; otherwise, why not?

I skimmed through the rest of the Inbox till I found one addressed to Baxter Bears—Denny's too-cute "addy" when "Da Bears" were actually playing good football—but who was m-smith@nwu.edu? That wasn't Hoshi—oh, wait. Mark Smith! I clicked it open.

> To: BaxterBears@wahoo.com
> From: m-smith@nwu.edu
> Re: Nony's birthday
>
> Dear Jodi,
> Thought Yada Yada might like to know that Nony's birthday
> is coming up January 20, two weeks from today. She'll be 37.
> (I'm in trouble now!) I know she wants the prayer group to
> meet at our house this coming Sunday—that's a week early,
> but thought you'd want to know.
>
> Mark Smith

I grinned. That was cute—Mark letting us know about Nony's birthday. It fell between two Yada Yada meetings, but why not celebrate at the first one? Kind of a "welcome home" and "happy birthday" rolled into one!

I forwarded Mark's e-mail to everybody else on the Yada Yada list, adding, "Why don't we surprise Nony with a card shower? Anyone want to volunteer to make a birthday/welcome home cake? She won't be expecting anything since we're meeting at her house." I hit Send.

"Mom? You done yet? I want to research some stuff about the death penalty." Josh loomed over my shoulder.

"Give me five more minutes, okay? Sheesh."

The Hulk disappeared, muttering under his breath. I sent the spam e-mail to oblivion, called up the Internet, and clicked on Favorites. There it was . . . my "Meanings of Names" Web site. A brief search found nothing even close to "Nonyameko." Figured. Maybe I could Google it—why not? I called up the search engine and typed "South African names female." Sure enough, there it was. Within a few seconds, I was looking at the meaning of Nonyameko Sisulu-Smith's name:

"Truth and Justice."

Ohmigosh. Could anything fit Nony better than that?

"Mom!"

"Okay, okay." I shut down the window and turned the computer over to Josh, an idea for Nony's birthday already percolating in my brain.

BY MIDWEEK, Chicago's temperatures hovered in the midfifties. Unbelievable! It felt like spring. I almost expected to see tiny lilies of the valley or crocuses peeking out of the grass as I walked to school each morning. Then again, Chicagoans had a pessimistic attitude about their weather: "Wait five minutes; it'll change."

But the unseasonably warm weather quickly lost the contest for shoptalk by the end of the week with headlines that trumpeted: US TROOPS DEPLOYED TO THE GULF and ILLINOIS GOVERNOR COMMUTES SENTENCES OF 167 ON DEATH ROW. Josh could hardly talk about anything else.

For some reason I felt heavy in my spirit as I drove to Nony's house late Sunday afternoon to meet with the Yada Yada Prayer Group. It sure felt like the country was gearing up for war—and Josh was eighteen. What if they reinstituted the draft? Or what if he joined the army? He'd teased us about it when he turned eighteen last September. But with the possibility of a real war on the horizon, it wasn't funny.

Oh God, I'm not ready for my kids to grow up! I moaned as I parked the van along the curb in front of Nony's house. Several cars were already there, and the el was just a few blocks away for those without wheels. Then I noticed a car I hadn't seen in months: Adele Skuggs's blue Ford Escort.

Adele had come back to Yada Yada! We'd only had one meeting in December and still no Adele—probably too soon after our reconciliation with MaDear. But seeing the blue Escort lifted my spirit. I wanted to shout, "Thank ya, Jesus!" like Florida, right there on Nony's front sidewalk. I settled for a whispered, "Thank You, Jesus," as I rang the doorbell.

Within twenty minutes, everyone had arrived and we were talking nonstop like a bunch of windup toys. When I saw Delores, I suddenly remembered I'd never called her to talk about the *quinceañera*. "Gotta talk to you," I buzzed in her ear, "about . . . you know."

Delores beamed. *"Sí.* Anytime. I'm home by three o'clock this week."

"Hallelujah!" Avis said, finally calling for attention. "Look at this—all twelve of us!"

"Like de twelve *dee*-sciples," Chanda George cracked, generating a ripple of laughter. Her Jamaican accent was always fun to decipher.

"Adele, we are so glad to see you again." A chorus of "Mm-hm" and "Yes!" met this statement.

Adele's bulk was parked on a straight-backed chair from Nony's dining room, arms folded across her chest, the gold hoops in her ears dangling as she nodded her short, reddish, natural 'fro. "Didn't plan to come back," she shot back, "but guess God had other plans." She grinned, revealing the little space between her two front teeth.

My heart squeezed, and I suddenly felt close to tears. Would I ever really understand the miracle that had taken place when Denny asked MaDear—poor, confused MaDear—to forgive him for something he hadn't done? Except . . . Denny had meant it. The reconciling power of owning the sins of our people. White people.

Before we do anything else," Avis said, "let's give the Lord some praise for bringing us all back together again, and for all He's done to sustain us in these past few weeks." Without missing a beat, she began to praise. "Yes, thank You, Lord Jesus, for coming to earth as a little babe, knowing ahead of time what it was going to cost You—humiliation, suffering, your very life. Thank You, Jesus, *thank* You!"

Others joined in, Delores breaking out in Spanish, Chanda babbling something—speaking in tongues or just a heavy dose of patois from the Islands, I couldn't always tell which—and Nony turning something from the Psalms into her own prayer of praise.

I pinched my eyes shut. *Oh God,* I prayed silently, *it's so good to be back "home" with Yada Yada. Though I'd still like to put in a petition for a couple months of "dull and boring"—*

A sharp poke in my side brought my eyes open with a start. "Psst. They want you," Florida hissed in my ear, jerking her head toward the doorway that led from Nony's family room into her kitchen. Yo-Yo and Ruth were beckoning at me behind Nony's back. I got up from my end of the couch as quietly as possible and tiptoed out.

"There!" Ruth said, indicating a large, rectangular bakery cake sitting on the counter. "A good job Yo-Yo did, yes?"

I stared at the cake. Yo-Yo worked at the Bagel Bakery, and I'd shanghaied her to see what she could do with my idea for Nony's birthday. Nonyameko's name was written in beautiful green icing across the top. A fairly decent "drawing" of Lady Justice in flowing icing robes, blindfold, and holding a black balance scale—*Black icing? Cool!*—took up most of the cake, with two words on either side: *Truth* and *Justice.*

"Perfect," I murmured. "Nony is going to be *so* surprised."

"What are you sisters up to?" A deep male voice made me jump. Mark Smith, dressed casually in sweats, poked his head around the corner.

"Shh. Nony's cake." I grinned. "We're celebrating her birthday early. Thanks for the heads-up."

Nony's husband, smiling big, walked over to the counter and looked at the cake. His smile faded. He pinned me with his dark eyes. "What's this?"

I was so startled, I almost couldn't find my tongue. "Uh . . . Nony's name. What it means: 'truth and justice.'"

"Really." His eyes drifted back to the cake a moment. Then he walked out of the kitchen, pausing to say flatly, "You're only encouraging her, you know."

8

*Y*o-Yo frowned and stuck her hands into the bib of her denim overalls. "What was *that* about?" I had a pretty good idea what it was about—but was he serious? Or just joking?

"Men, schmen." Ruth waved her hand as though brushing Mark's words out of the air. "Who knows? Half the time what they say makes no sense. Jodi, did you bring candles?"

Ruth's question shook me out of my stupor. "Yes . . . oh, rats. They're in my purse in the other room!" I pulled open one drawer after another along the kitchen counter till I found what I was looking for: a kitchen junk drawer. Aha. There they were—birthday candles. The skinny, sparkly kind. I quickly stuck about eight of them in various places on the cake, and Yo-Yo was right behind me lighting them with her cigarette lighter.

I suppressed a giggle. Smokers had at least one redeeming quality: a ready light.

"Come on, come on," Ruth hissed, standing ready to open the door to the family room. "The praise time is pooping out."

This time I *did* giggle as the three of us pushed through the door with the tall, skinny candles spitting sparks in every direction. "Happy birthday to youuuuu . . ." we began singing, a bit off-key, and stopped in front of Nony, whose large, dark eyes widened as the rest of the Yada Yada sisters chimed in. "Happy birthday, dear Nonyyy . . . May Go-od bless youuu."

"Oh, my sisters," she sputtered. "It's not even my birthday yet—oh!" Her eyes read the cake. "Truth? Justice? What's this?"

I felt a flush creep up my face, remembering Mark's reaction. But I plunged ahead. "It's what Nonyameko means: 'truth and justice.'"

Murmurs of "Oh" and "That figures" and "Amazing" mixed with smiles, hugs, and general laughter as Nony digested this information.

"Blow! Blow!" bossed Ruth, setting a stack of little paper plates, napkins, and plastic forks alongside the cake on the glass coffee tabletop, which rested on a graceful sculpture base. "Just don't spit on the cake—I want to eat some of that truth and justice."

Nony blew, which got her nowhere, and she finally had to pinch out the sparklers. "Will I still get my wish?" She smiled, looking amazingly girlish in her simple rose-colored tunic top over black velour pants.

"Me bet she does!" Chanda crowed. "A winnuh-woman." Her grin widened in her plain brown face. "Lak me, when me lucky numbers win de Lotto dis year."

I thought I heard Avis heave a big sigh.

Ruth deftly cut the cake. Yo-Yo passed paper plates around as Avis said, "Why don't we go ahead with some personal sharings or prayer requests while we eat? We have some catching up to do and don't want to go too late because—"

"—tomorrow's a workday," sang out three or four voices. Avis *was* pretty predictable.

The next half-hour skimmed past like an express commuter train. Nony jumped up and passed out the gifts she'd brought back for each of us—long hand-dyed silk scarves in amazing bright colors, no two alike. For a few minutes, we all tried tying them around our hair, draping them around our necks, or using them like a sash. Yo-Yo sat looking at her yellow and green scarf a long time, then finally tied it around one strap of her overalls and let it hang down. I wasn't sure whether to laugh or cry. Not exactly a fashion statement—but Yo-Yo was actually an attractive young woman underneath the spiky hair and shapeless overalls she always wore. It was almost as if she *hid* herself inside her dreary wardrobe. Was she afraid to be pretty and feminine?

Florida said it was Carla's ninth birthday next weekend—the first birthday they'd celebrate with her since she was two years old . . . and Florida couldn't remember if they'd even celebrated it back then. "Lot of stuff I don't remember from those days." Her mouth twitched, overtaken with a momentary sadness. Then she flashed a grin. "But this year I'm goin' to give her the best party I know how to give. Because—oh, thank ya, Jesus!—God has been so good to bring her back home."

Stu, who had helped find Carla in the foster-care system, leaned over and gave Florida a quick hug.

"Chanda, can you bring Cheree and Dia? Carla likes your girls. Thomas too. My boys will be there . . ."

After Florida got promises from several of us that we'd come to Carla's party, Avis moved us on. Delores said things were pretty much the same at the Enriques household, meaning her husband Ricardo was still looking for a job—"Yeah, throw Carl in that pot, too," Florida muttered. Edesa and Hoshi were both back in the thick of university classes.

When it was Ruth's turn, she said, "Ben got a big kick out of seeing all those youngsters do the Polar Bear Plunge on New Year's Day—though he'd never admit it, big grouch that he is." She laughed.

"Youngsters!" Stu protested. "What about me, and Jodi's husband, and Yo-Yo?"

"Oh, *you.*" Ruth tapped the side of her head and shook it slowly back and forth as if breaking bad news. Even Stu laughed.

"Hey. That reminds me," said Yo-Yo. "What was you sayin' that day, Florida, about being washed in the blood of Jesus? I've been wonderin' about that."

Florida nodded, suddenly serious. "See, it's like this. I saw all those young people going in the water, going down, coming up, yelling all excited—and it's like I had a vision that it was like a baptism, and one day all those teenagers, or some of them, or most, were goin' to be wading into that water—oh, help me, Jesus—to be washed in the blood."

"Mm! I stand in agreement with that," Avis said, and for a few moments, she and several others broke out in some spontaneous hallelujahs.

Yo-Yo was still frowning. "But . . . what's *blood* got to do with it?"

The group was suddenly still. When we first met Yo-Yo—brought by Ruth Garfield to the Chicago Women's Conference—she had declared she wasn't into "this Jesus thing," though she was "cool with it" for the rest of us. Then a few months ago, she'd started asking a lot of questions about what it would mean to be a "Jesus follower." As far as I knew, the Yada Yada Prayer Group was as close as Yo-Yo got to going to church, because she worked at the Bagel Bakery, which closed on Saturday for the Jewish Sabbath but was open all day Sunday.

"That's an excellent question, Yo-Yo," said Avis. "Next time we meet—do we know where we're going to be? Jodi, your house, isn't it?—let's talk about that very thing. In the meantime, Yo-Yo, I want to give you some Scripture passages to read."

Yo-Yo squirmed. "Uh, I don't really know how to find stuff in the Bible."

"So? I'll help you," said Ruth, and that was that.

"Anyone else before we begin our prayer time?" Avis asked.

Stu tossed her hair back and leaned forward. "Uh-huh. Two things. Have we heard yet from Becky Wallace? I don't know if the box I ordered from Estée Lauder got to her at the prison." She looked around. I shrugged and shook my head; other heads wagged no. "Well, anyway, I still need four dollars each from some of you—but if it's a problem, just let me know. Not a big deal." She sat back against the couch.

Florida poked her. "You said two things."

This time Stu grinned. "I've got a praise report." Her smile widened, as though she'd been sitting on good news that couldn't wait any longer. "I got the job! With the DCFS office in Rogers Park! I—" An outburst of general whooping and handclapping cut her off. I was impressed; after all that talk, she'd finally done it. When the noise and high-fives died down, she said, "I start the first of February. I need to take some classes to renew my social work license, but . . . it's exactly the job I wanted!" Then she made a face. "Big cut in pay, though, from selling real estate."

"You go, girl!" said Florida. "If you ask me, DCFS *needs* a burr under their saddle like Leslie Stuart."

That got a laugh. *Yes,* I thought wryly, *Stu could definitely be a burr under someone's saddle.*

"But I really don't want to commute from Oak Park every day, so I'd like to relocate by the end of the month—in Rogers Park would be ideal. That's only three weeks, so, *please*, if you know of any apartments for rent, let me know, okay?"

Adele spoke for the first time. "I don't know, Stu—people don't usually move this time of year. It'd have to be a sublet or something. Hard to find."

Sublet . . . Suddenly I squirmed inside. My upstairs neighbors were moving and needed to sublet. But—maybe they'd already found a renter. Probably had. I better not say anything till I know for sure. Wouldn't want to get Stu's hopes up, raise false expectations—

Oh, right, Jodi Baxter. Get real. You don't want Leslie Stuart to move into your house because she'd drive you nuts. Admit it.

I swallowed and looked around the room, wondering if anyone else had heard the words in my head. Yet the sharing had already moved to Nony, who was saying, "—to pray for the families of murder victims, who are having a difficult time with Governor Ryan's decision to commute the sentences of those on death row."

"Why?" said Yo-Yo. "Killing the perp won't bring the murdered person back. What do they want?"

For half a second—like the instant before you know your car is going to crash or a fuse is going to blow—there was a deathly silence. And then the room erupted. Everyone, it seemed, had an opinion—a *strong* opinion—about what the Illinois governor had done in his last few days in office.

"Why they making criminals' rights more important these days than victims' rights?" . . . "So? That's what democracy's all about—everyone's rights." . . . "Now you *know* you more likely to die in the 'lectric chair or however they kill ya these days if you *black* than if you white." . . . "Look at those guys who spent ten years on death row and they were innocent!" . . . "Well, they got out, didn't they? The system works!" . . . "Huh. Not always."

This was going nowhere. I half-expected Avis to interrupt and tell us the best thing we could do is pray about it. Though oddly enough, Avis was staring at the wall as if she wasn't even listening.

During a brief pause, Delores said quietly, "To me the issue is not only taking a life, but what solving problems by killing does to *us.*"

Her observation seemed to plug the gushing comments. Something clicked for me. "Oh, Delores! I've thought the same thing about abortion—wondering what it does to our collective spirit as *women,* that so many women are aborting their babies."

"Oh, good grief!" Stu's angry outburst shot me down like a heat-seeking missile. "Easy for *you* to say. Most women who have an abortion aren't thinking about 'our collective spirit'—they're . . . they're frantic, don't know what to do."

I pressed my lips into a thin line. It was the only time I'd opened my mouth during the entire discussion—if you could call it that—and Delores's comment had made me think.

"Sisters! Sisters!" Nony spoke up. "Please. I did not mean to begin an argument. I only wanted to ask us to pray for the families of murder victims—I did not mean that we should not also pray for the men and women on death row."

Quiet Hoshi spoke up. "Do you know a family for whom this is true, Nony?"

Nony hesitated, then shook her head. "Not here in the States. But these are troubled times all over the world, and God has laid it on my heart to include the newspaper headlines in my prayers." She looked at Avis. "Should we begin our prayer time, Avis?"

Avis slowly pulled her gaze away from the wall. "Of course. Go ahead and lead us out, Nony."

And so Nony began to pray. "Oh, Lord God! You have told us in Your Word that even when we are troubled on every side, we do not have to be distressed. We may be perplexed, but we do not have to despair. Yet it is not for ourselves only that we pray. You have comforted us in our afflictions, so that we might be able to comfort others in their troubles . . . "

The prayer itself was comforting, promises from Scripture to help us focus beyond our own opinions. "Thank ya, Jesus!" came from Florida's corner, and *"Venido, Dios Santo!"* from Delores. I peeked through my eyelids. Most everyone had their eyes closed, a few hands were lifted, and several murmured in agreement as Nony prayed. Stu, however, was busily digging in her purse for a tissue, the muscles in her face tight. And Avis just sat quietly with her head bowed, her forehead resting on her hands, her eyes hidden from view.

This wasn't like Avis. Not like Avis at all.

9

What is it about Mondays? You'd think that after a weekend to get all the kinks out, the kids would be ready to settle down at school and learn something. Yet it seemed like every Monday I had to "reeducate" my entire third-grade class about the rules and break up at least three fights—okay, scuffles. At least I was still bigger than they were. Denny told me that last fall at West Rogers High, a student attacked one of the English teachers and broke her nose for telling him to "shut up and sit down."

The student got a one-day suspension. The teacher got reprimanded for not keeping her class under control. She quit.

But I was learning—learning to cover my classroom in prayer every Monday before the kids even got there. Which is what I was doing the next morning after our Yada Yada meeting at Nony's house. *God, I can't believe I ever thought I could do this job by myself.* I dumped my tote bags on my desk, pulled off my walking shoes and thick socks, and slipped my stocking feet into a pair of comfy leather clogs that I kept at school.

The new year has barely begun, Lord, and already I feel like I'm playing catch-up with the kids. I have no idea what some of the family situations are like or what happened at their homes this weekend . . . but You do! Oh God . . . I started walking around the room, touching each desk in turn. *I pray for Kaya and her struggles with reading. I need some new ideas, Lord! . . . and Jade. Thank You for her sweet spirit . . . Ramón—he's got a long way to go controlling that temper, but he's made some progress, so thank You, Lord . . . LeTisha . . . D'Angelo . . . Hakim . . .*

I stopped by Hakim's desk. A long, jagged line, like a lightning bolt, had been scratched into the top of the wooden desk. When had he done *that*? With what? Had he smuggled a knife into school? How? We had metal detectors at the school doors, for heaven's sake!

A dozen angry questions piled up in my brain, like so many cars colliding in a fog bank. But as I stood there looking at the disfigured desk, the most important question of all rose to the top.

Why?

I SOMEHOW MADE IT THROUGH MONDAY, with only relative chaos reigning after lunch when Cornell yelled—right in the middle of our science lesson on renewable and nonrenewable energy sources—"Hey! It's snowing!" The entire class rushed to the windows, and a few even climbed up onto the wide windowsills, tipping over the sweet-potato plants we'd started in Styrofoam cups.

I picked up the still-whirring table fan—"wind power"—that had been knocked over in the mad dash to the windows and wondered feebly how I could turn January's first snow into a lesson on the different forms of H_2O. *Maybe tomorrow,* I thought, peeking over the heads of nearly thirty bouncing short people at the snow flurry blowing outside. *See if enough accumulates to bring some inside.*

So far, I'd said nothing to Hakim about vandalizing his desk. If it was a ploy to gain attention from the class or get a rise out of me, I determined not to fall into his little trap—though I was sorely tempted to screech at him like the Wicked Witch of the North to put a little terror into the hearts of any other would-be desk carvers. When the final bell rang at 2:50, though, I simply pulled Hakim aside and leaned close to his ear. "Wait in your seat a few minutes. I need to talk to you."

Immediately the dark eyes grew wary, but he sat, glaring out the window.

When we were alone, I came to his desk and pointed to the jagged scar. "What's this?" No answer. "Why did you damage your desk?" No answer. *That was a dumb question, Jodi. Did you really expect an answer?* "What do you think we should do about it?" Still no answer.

I suddenly felt incredibly awkward. Was anybody watching me? What if Hakim's mother came to pick him up and walked in? I was not only a white grownup standing over a black child, but I was the grownup who'd robbed *this* boy of his only big brother. What right did I have to—

Stop it, Jodi! You're a teacher. Hakim's teacher. He needs you to be firm and clear about acceptable behavior.

I held out my hand. "Give me your knife." He mumbled something. "What did you say?"

"Ain't got no knife." The back of his hand brushed across his eyes and came off wet, but his face remained closed, distant.

Don't be fooled by the tears, I told myself. "Then how did you do this?"

His pause was so long I thought he was again refusing to answer.

Then I heard, "Paper clip." To my surprise, Hakim put his head down on his arms and began to sob.

Baffled, I reached out and rested my hand on his back until his body stopped shaking. Then I said, "Hakim, I don't know why you scratched your desk. That was wrong. It ruins your desk for you and for the next child who uses it. I'm going to have to tell your mother and work out some way to—"

The moment the words were out of my mouth, I knew them for a lie. No way was I going to call Geraldine Wilkins-Porter and tell her she had to pay for this desk!—or whatever the school policy was. I'd pay for it myself before I'd voluntarily get into it with the woman who already hated me.

But my words acted like an electric prod on Hakim's body. He jerked upright and stared at me. "No! Don't tell my mama! She be sure an' take me outta this school then." He sniffed, and I handed him a tissue from the pocket of my denim skirt. "I'm sorry, Miz B. I jus' felt mad an' . . . di'nt mean to ruin the desk. Please don't tell my mom."

My own eyes threatened to puddle. "Thank you, Hakim. All right. Maybe we'll talk later—you and me, okay?"

He nodded, then grabbed his coat and knit hat and ran out of the room.

For some reason I felt strangely encouraged. Hakim had said, "I'm sorry." That was a breakthrough, wasn't it? But, he said he did it because he "felt mad." Mad at me? Mad about schoolwork? Did he even know?

I changed my shoes, gathered my tote bags, and headed for the school office, determined to ask Avis about some counseling for Hakim—could we do that without his mother's permission?—for posttraumatic stress or whatever it was Avis thought accounted for Hakim's behavior.

Avis was in her office, but the school secretary informed me I had to wait because another teacher was already in there. Finally, she waved me through the door that said *Ms. Johnson, Principal.*

Avis usually enjoyed wearing bright colors, though today she had on a black blazer, black trousers, and white silk blouse. Then again, she didn't seem her usual cheery self. I stuck to business, telling her about the damaged desk and what had happened when I confronted Hakim. "He needs help, Avis. He's up, down, all over the place. You know *I* can't talk to him about . . . about what's bothering him. Not if it's related to the death"—I swallowed—"of his brother. But he's wound so tight, I'm afraid one of these days he's going to explode."

Avis sighed. She looked distracted. Had she even been listening to me? Finally she said, "All right. I'll talk to the school social worker and have her talk with Hakim. Do you mind if I fill her in on the background?—confidentially, of course."

Oh, great. Of course, anybody who read the papers last summer probably already knew about the accident in which thirteen-year-old Jamal Wilkins—Hakim's brother—had been killed running across Clark Street during a thunderstorm. And that Jodi Baxter of Rogers Park had been behind the wheel. The charges . . . the indictment . . . the dismissal. All public record, if anybody cared.

I cared.

"Is that it?" Avis rose. "I have some work—"

"Uh, one more thing," I blurted.

Avis looked at me, her eyes heavy-lidded like she hadn't slept much last night. "Yes?"

"Avis, I know this is personal, but . . . what was going on last night? When Yada Yada spun out with this death-penalty thing, you kinda faded away and never came back."

I saw her flinch, as if I'd pinched a nerve. Then she sighed and sat back down. "Close the door."

Uh-oh. Did I just open a can of worms? Should I apologize? Back out? But I was more curious than I was chicken.

"I'm sorry, Jodi. You're right. I checked out—that particular topic is a hard one for me. I was hoping it wouldn't come up. Of course it's all over the news." She paused and stared at the wall, just as she had last night.

I waited.

She blew out a breath. "I have a cousin on death row—his name's Boyd. Not here; in South Carolina. Though I wish to God he *were* here. The governor's action would be the answer to my prayers, because Boyd was framed. He didn't do it; I'm sure of it."

My insides kind of collapsed. "Why didn't you just *tell* us? Sheesh—all the stuff people said . . ."

Avis shook her head. "Didn't trust myself. I can get very angry about it. And to tell you the truth, Jodi, I'm tired of praying about it. I've prayed and prayed for years that justice would be done, that someone would tell the truth, but it's like all my prayers hit the ceiling. *Bam, bam!* They fall back flat on my face."

My jaw nearly dropped. I wasn't sure I'd heard right. Avis was always encouraging the rest of us to "press on through" in prayer, regardless of the circumstances.

"I . . . wasn't going to say anything, but you asked."

I didn't know what to say. "Maybe other states will follow suit and put a moratorium on executions . . ."

Avis flinched, and I wished I could rewind my thoughtless word. *Executions.*

"I'm not holding my breath," she said flatly. "In fact, I don't even pray about it any more, because I *expect* God to answer—some way, somehow—and when He doesn't . . ." She smiled ruefully. "My whole life would fall apart if I gave in to doubt."

I reached across the desk and laid my hand over hers. "Avis, I'm so sorry. Sorry we were so insensitive last night."

She shook her head. "You didn't know. No one did."

"But you should tell Yada Yada! Don't carry it by yourself. You're always telling us to bear one another's burdens. Let us help carry yours."

She leaned her elbows on the desk and massaged her forehead with her fingers. "I don't know . . . Some things are just private."

I thought about her last words as I trudged home through the snow, which was sticking to the sidewalks, trees, and rooftops like a thin layer of vanilla frosting. *Private?* What did she mean by that? True, Avis didn't talk about her personal business very easily. Yet she'd told us about the death of her husband from prostate cancer . . . and even the hilarious story about the scar from her lumpectomy looking like an old man with no teeth and a protruding red nose. We'd all howled till we couldn't laugh anymore. It was *so* unlike Avis to be telling jokes about breasts, but she'd been laughing too.

So what was so private about her cousin being in prison, even on death row? Yo-Yo had been in prison—for forgery, admittedly, nothing violent. Still . . .

And then it hit me like a snowball in the face. What was private wasn't the fact that her cousin was in prison.

Avis had doubts about God.

10

We didn't get that much snow after all, but at least it stuck to the ground, looking like a group of cosmic third graders had smeared the sidewalks, cars, and rooftops with a thin coat of white paste. *Knowing Chicago, we'll probably have the Big Blizzard in March,* I thought, waiting for Willie Wonka to finish watering the snow in the backyard after I got home from school. Glancing up the outside stairs to the second-floor apartment, I saw several stacks of empty boxes on the landing.

The Bennetts are moving . . . Stu needs an apartment . . .

I sighed. I probably should run upstairs right now and ask if they'd found someone to sublet yet, but it wasn't like they'd asked *me* to look for a renter. In fact, it wasn't really my business to make sure they found someone to sublet—not even my business to find Stu an apartment, was it?

You're stalling, Jodi Baxter. Just ask.

By that time, Willie Wonka was done with his business and waiting eagerly with his nose to the back door, begging to be let in. I shivered inside my thin sweater. *Better get my coat before I run upstairs.*

No sooner had I dried off Willie's cold toes and grabbed my jacket, however, than the phone rang. I picked it up.

"Jodi? Delores. Got your message yesterday, but I had to work. Can you talk now?"

"Sure, Delores." I tossed my jacket onto a dining room chair and wandered into the living room to sit in the recliner near the front windows. "Nobody's home from school yet—Amanda joined the Spanish club, and Josh has discovered the debate team. Don't really like them getting home after dark, but guess it'll work out as long as Josh can walk her home from the bus."

"Spanish club?" I could hear the pleasure in Delores's voice. *"Muy bueno!* She'll be bilingual before you know it, Jodi. A lot of service jobs want someone who can also speak *Española.* After all, Hispanics are the fastest growing minority in the—"

"Yes, I know." I tried to focus on the reason I'd wanted Delores to call—and on my resolve to talk honestly about our concerns. "Delores, could we talk about José wanting to give Amanda a *quinceañera?* Denny and I have been thinking about it . . ."

"Oh, *si! Si!* He is so excited about it and has so many plans."

I stifled a groan. This was not going to be easy.

"That's what I'm afraid of, Delores. He really needs to *not* make any plans until Denny and I can make a decision. That's why I need to talk to you."

"Ah. Of course. I understand. Tell me what you need to know."

I took a deep breath. "Well, I did read some stuff on the Internet about the background of the Mexican *quinceañera,* and all the traditional ways to celebrate a girl becoming a woman—but of course you know all that."

Her laugh tinkled in my ear. "Oh, *si.* My *quinceañera . . .* so special!" And for the next few minutes, Delores chatted on and on about the fiesta her parents gave for her fifteenth birthday in Colima, Mexico. "Except my parents were Pentecostal, not Catholic, so we modified the religious service."

"Really? I mean, you can do that?"

"Sure." Delores chuckled. "Of course, the *abuelas y tías*—grandmothers and aunties—rolled their eyes and beat their bosoms. 'What? No mass? No veil?' For the old ones, it has to be 'just so'— meaning just like their own *quinceañera*. They are . . . well, never mind."

"What?"

"Nada, nada. I mean, it's a long story. The tension between traditional Catholics and the 'new Protestants' in Mexico has broken apart many families. I . . . my *abuela* hasn't spoken to me since I married Ricardo in a Protestant wedding."

"But Ricardo . . . is he . . . I mean, he doesn't attend church with you at Iglesia."

"He used to . . . but you know how it is. He had to drive the trucks on Sunday. Then José got shot, and Ricardo's angry at God. Then he lost his job . . ."

I'd only met Delores's husband one time; he was sitting like a bump on a log in José's hospital room last May, barely speaking. "Oh, Delores. I'm sorry."

"Just keep praying for Ricardo, Jodi. Now, where were we—oh, *si! La quinceañera* for Amanda. For you it should be easy! She is the first one in your family, so there are no traditions, no expectations you have to live up to."

"Except José's," I grumbled.

Delores laughed. "Oh, don't worry about José. He just wants to get a band together and play Latino music and dance with Amanda."

"That's it? Play music and dance? What about—"

At the other end of the house, I heard the back door slam. "Mom! We're home! What're all the boxes doing on the back porch?"

"Aack! Delores, I can't talk now," I hissed into the phone. "The kids just got home. I'll call you when the coast is clear, okay? I've got some more questions."

I pressed the Off button and hustled toward the back of the house. Maybe—just maybe—this *quinceañera* thing would be do-able after all.

TO MY CREDIT, I DID TRY a couple of times in the next few days to catch my upstairs neighbors at home to ask if they'd found a renter, but it was Friday evening before we actually connected. It was one of those nights the Baxter family galloped off in all directions: Denny had to coach back-to-back basketball games at West Rogers High; Josh picked up Yo-Yo's brothers and took them to the game on Denny's pass; and Amanda was baby-sitting for one of the Uptown families. That left Willie Wonka and me to fend for our-selves with a big bowl of popcorn and a video of *The African Queen*.

Just as well. Whew! What a week. Avis and I barely saw each other at school except for a brief stop in the hall, when she told me she'd talked to the school social worker about some sessions with Hakim. "But we do need to get parental permission," she'd warned. "So keep praying, Jodi." So . . . I'd been praying. Praying for Avis too. About the pain she carried for her cousin in prison, for her private struggle with God. I wanted to tell other Yada Yada sisters to pray too—but I put a lid on it. Avis's struggle was hers to share . . . or not.

I'd eaten to the bottom of the popcorn bowl when I heard enormous thumping, like rugs had been rolled up and furniture was being moved across bare floors. *Yikes!* The Bennetts were moving out, and I hadn't asked if they'd found someone to sublet! "I really would like to know who's moving in," I muttered to Willie as I put the video on Pause, stuck my feet in a pair of scuffs, and grabbed my jacket from the coatrack. The dog followed me to the kitchen, his tail drooping like a limp noodle as I unlocked the back door. "Don't worry!" I said, bending down and giving him a smackeroo between his wrinkled brows. "Be back in less time than it takes for you to chew up a newspaper."

I scuttled up the outside steps leading to the upstairs apartment and almost fell on my face on a treacherous icy patch. "Should have taken the front stairs," I grumbled, pulling myself up gingerly by the handrail. When I got to the top, the kitchen curtains had been taken down and bright light spilled out onto the small porch. I rapped tentatively on the window in the door. Nothing. I rapped again, louder. Someone peered into the kitchen, disappeared, then what seemed like a full minute later, Rose Bennett appeared wearing old sweats and a bandana around her hair and unlocked the door. "Yes?"

I was sweating inside my jacket. Guess she wasn't going to invite me in. "Uh, hi, Rose. I heard you packing and, uh, wondered when you guys were actually leaving for Atlanta."

"Is there a problem?"

"No, no! Just didn't want you to leave without saying good-bye." Well, that was kinda true. Even if we hadn't been cozy neighbors, we could at least have a decent farewell. "Did you find someone to sublet your apartment?"

"Huh! Unfortunately not. And the movers will be here Tuesday, and we're going to end up in Atlanta paying double rent till our lease runs out if we don't find *somebody*—Jesus *Christ!*"

I cringed . . . but decided this wasn't the time to ask her not to vent on God's name. *At least she's not mad at me.*

"I'm sorry, Rose. I was hoping that would work out for you." Should I say, *"I know someone who needs an apartment"*? But what if Stu had already found something this week? Then Rose *would* be mad at me for getting her hopes up.

"Yeah, well, if you know anybody needing an apartment . . ." She closed the door.

Yeah, well . . .

I gingerly made my way back down the icy stairs and locked our back door behind me. Willie Wonka stood right where I'd left him, his tail waving big-time now. He followed close to my heels as I made myself a cup of mint tea and returned to my movie in the living room.

Somehow, Katharine Hepburn wading through the swamps pulling *The African Queen* while Humphrey Bogart smirked at her had lost some of its mesmerizing power.

Just call Stu and ask if she's found an apartment yet.

Sheesh! Pinocchio had nothing on *my* Jiminy Cricket.

So what if she hasn't? I argued in my head. *Then I'll have to tell her about the one upstairs! And, okay, I don't want Leslie Stuart living next to me. Is that so bad? She'll find something—this can't be the only sublet in Rogers Park! And then we'll both be happy.*

Willie Wonka nosed my hand. Why did the dog always sense when my hackles were up? "What do you think, Wonka? Why should I deliberately invite Stu to move in one short staircase from me? Look how she shot me down at Yada Yada last Sunday. And whenever I toss out an idea, Stu's always got a better one. Maybe she doesn't do it on purpose, but I end up feeling like two cents anyway. If she moves in here, she'll probably rearrange my kitchen, tell me how to teach third graders, and become 'Cool Aunt Stu' to my kids, in whose eyes I'm slipping anyway. Grrr!" I threw a small pillow across the room, startling the chocolate Lab, who scrabbled after it and brought it back to me.

"Huh. Thanks." I took the pillow and hugged it a long time.

I WOKE UP EARLY THE NEXT MORNING—early for Saturday— and let Willie Wonka outside while I started coffee. All was quiet upstairs, though the thumping had gone on till almost midnight. All was quiet downstairs, too, which was fine by me. Amanda got in at eleven thirty, and Denny and Josh came in around midnight after taking Pete and Jerry home. *Let 'em sleep.* Saturday was about the only day I got any morning time to read the Bible and pray. Even then, I had to fight with my mental to-do list.

Settling down in the recliner with a mug of coffee, I opened my study Bible to the purple ribbon, which marked where I'd been reading in the book of Isaiah. I was determined to become more familiar with the Old Testament books Avis and Nony quoted from so often. At least I'd made it to Isaiah 43, which was fairly familiar.

As I started to read, I felt as if I'd been slapped upside the head. "Fear not!" the very first verse said. "For I have redeemed you; I have called you by name; you are Mine!"

Fear not . . . Inside my head, a little voice seemed to say, *"What are you so afraid of, Jodi?"*

Afraid? I'm not afraid.

"Yes, you are. You're afraid to let Stu into your life."

Oh, that. I'm not afraid, just—

"Yes, that's fear. Fear she's going to melt you down to size."

So? Why should I put myself in a position where—

"Position? I have redeemed you! That's your position! I have called you by name! You are Mine!"

Even though I hadn't moved a muscle, I felt like I'd fallen flat on the ground and gotten the wind knocked out of me. *Called me by name*... With stark clarity I remembered what I'd discovered about the meaning of my name: "Jodi: 'God is gracious.'"

"That's right. I am gracious—toward you! And Stu . . . And the Bennetts . . . But you need to get out of the way. Stop protecting yourself. Let Me be gracious."

I did not like the way this conversation in my head was going. Doggedly I read on, determined to finish the chapter. But words kept leaping off the page: "Since you are precious in my sight ... Do not fear, for I am with you ... Behold, I will do something new ..."

I shut the Bible with a *thump*. All these verses were prophecies for Israel—not Jodi Baxter, Lunt Avenue, Chicago, Illinois, in 2003. Besides, didn't good fences make good neighbors? Wasn't that in Proverbs or something? Keeping your boundaries clear was just common sense, not fear.

Brrriiing! The ringing telephone at my elbow made me knock over my coffee cup, balanced precariously on the arm of the padded chair. I punched the On button before the phone could ring again and wake everybody up. "What?" I snapped, trying to mop up the spill with a wad of tissue before it soaked into the rug.

"Jodi?" The voice on the other end sounded confused. "Am I callin' too early?"

I winced. "Florida! Can't believe I answered the phone like that. Sorry. It just startled me."

"Oh. Okay. Listen . . . you comin' to Carla's birthday party today?"

Carla's birthday! I smacked my forehead with the heel of my hand, still holding the soggy tissue. I'd completely forgotten. "You bet. What's the time again?"

"Two o'clock. Do you have some small paper plates and plastic forks I could borrow?"

I giggled. "Borrow? Sure. Just be sure to wash the plates before you return them. Anything else?"

"Smart aleck. Oh, yeah, do you have some crepe paper streamers I can *have*? And can Amanda come? She's so good with the kids—she'd be a big help. But I'll only *borrow* her—you can have her back."

By this time both of us were laughing.

"Not sure. I'll have to ask when she wakes up. Sorry—we didn't talk about it."

"Okay. See you around two, then."

"Wait! Florida?" I had no idea why I was doing this, but I blurted, "The apartment upstairs is being vacated. Do you . . . do you think I should tell Stu about it?"

"Do I think . . .? What's the question, Jodi! Of course you should tell her about it! Thank ya, Jesus! What an answer to prayer!"

I sighed. "That's what I thought. See you at two."

I hung up and stared at the phone in my hand for a full minute. Then I dialed Stu.

11

Stu answered on the fourth ring, just as the answering machine kicked in. *"Hi! Sorry I missed your—"* "Jodi? Wait a minute . . . how do I turn this darn thing off? . . . There. Okay. Kinda early for you, isn't it? Anything wrong?"

I rolled my eyes. *Mental note: never get one of those videophones.* "Hi, Stu. Hope I didn't get *you* up. I thought you might be interested to know that our upstairs neighbors are moving on Tuesday. They need someone to sublet—"

The shriek on the other end made me hold the phone at arm's length. When I brought it back, Stu was babbling. "For real? When? How soon could I move in? Is it like your apartment? What kind of shape is it in? Is it too early to call? I don't want to miss them . . ."

I glanced at the clock. Seven forty-five. Still kinda early for Saturday. But I gave Stu the number—let her figure it out.

Denny poked his head into the living room. "Done with the phone? Carl Hickman said he might come to the men's breakfast at Uptown if I picked him up."

Men's breakfast? Oh yeah. They were doing it every third Saturday of the month now. But if Denny took the car . . . I shook my head. How was I supposed to get Carla a birthday present with no car?

As it turned out, I got the car after all. Carl had begged off because of "gettin' ready for Carla's birthday," so Denny decided to go for a run and end up at the church in time for the breakfast. I could tell he was teed off. "Always some excuse," he muttered as he went out the door.

What was *he* so huffy about? Carla's birthday seemed like a good excuse to me.

To my surprise, Amanda said she'd love to go to Carla's birthday party—she even wanted to go shopping with me to pick out a birthday present.

"Yeah," I ribbed. "Anything to get out of cleaning your room." I hugged her just the same.

SINCE DENNY LET ME HAVE THE CAR in the morning, Amanda and I took the el down to the Hickmans' that afternoon, lugging a shopping bag with snack-size paper plates, plastic forks and spoons, rolls of yellow and green crepe paper, and two gifts for Carla. I'd wanted to get a "chapter book" for her to read but got discouraged wandering around the Barnes and Noble bookstore. All the books for children of color seemed to be biographies of great African-Americans or historical fiction about slavery or recounting the Civil Rights struggle. Important stuff—but heavy. Where were the books young girls liked to read about school friends and annoying brothers and mysterious disappearing cats and begging to get their ears pierced—ordinary books with children of color as the main characters?

I wavered between a couple of Coretta Scott King Award books:

Almost to Freedom, a clever story of the Underground Railroad from a rag doll's point of view, and a rollicking tall tale about *Thunder Rose.* Which would Florida want Carla to read? One was historical, hopeful, and sad at the same time; the other just for fun with a dynamo young black heroine. "Mo-om!" said Amanda, pulling me toward the cashiers. "Just get both."

I'd thought we were done, but Amanda insisted we also had to get something fun and girlish. So we ended up at Target for bubble bath, nail polish with glitter in it, and some colorful barrettes. Sheesh. It all added up. But then . . . this *was* Carla's first birthday party since she'd come home to her biological family.

Every time the el made a stop and opened its doors, the heat seemed to sneak out among the disgorging passengers, leaving plenty of room to trap the blast of arctic air blowing off Lake Michigan as the doors closed. "It's really getting cold, Mom," Amanda grumbled, putting up the hood of her ski jacket until only her nose showed. Fine by me. I didn't like the looks of that young man with all the tattoos and a ring piercing his lip who kept leering at her. *Lord, give me strength!*

We got off at the Bryn Mawr stop and hustled the few blocks to the Hickmans' apartment building. It *was* getting colder. Amanda pushed the buzzer labeled HICKMAN, and a few moments later a voice cackled on the intercom. "That you, Jodi? Get up here. I need some help!" Amanda grabbed for the door handle as a loud *blaaaat* filled the foyer.

Florida had her door open by the time we climbed the stairs to the second floor, a cigarette in one hand, urgently waving us in with the other. "Crepe paper! Did you bring some? Gotta get it up quick!" She waved smoke away from the air space between us.

"Sorry about the cig. I'm so nervous I can't even spit. Hey, baby! How ya doin'?" Florida gave Amanda a big squeeze.

The apartment was silent except for our footsteps as we walked down the long, dim hallway to the square room that served as eating, study, and play space. "Where are the kids? Where's Carla?" I dumped the contents of the shopping bag on the round table in the middle of the small room.

"Carl took Carla out, and I tol' him not to bring her back till two thirty—give folks time to get here. But that man—he could show up any minute. Hey! Yellow and green! That's real nice."

"Well, it's great he could get her out for a while." Amanda and I taped yellow and green streamers to the light fixture in the center of the ceiling, then twisted and strung them to various corners of the room. "Denny called him this morning, wanted him to go to the men's breakfast at Uptown, but he said he had to help with Carla's party."

"He said that?" Florida muttered something short and *not* sweet under her breath as she brought out a pretty grocery-store cake with *Happy Birthday, Carla* in pink icing script. "Huh. Had to drag that man out of the bed at noon and practically dress him myself so he could take Carla out for a while. So help me, Jodi, that man gonna land on his butt outside this door one day." She arranged the small party plates and plasticware around the cake.

"Sorry about the blue flowered plates, Flo," I grunted, trying to reach the corner of the room above the computer desk. "Didn't have any to match the crepe paper." With a last stretch, I smashed the piece of tape on the end of the streamer to the wall.

"Oh, that don't matter. They're pretty—yikes!" The door buzzer made us all jump. "Hope that ain't Carl yet."

Chanda and her three kids trooped up the stairs . . . followed in short order by Edesa with twelve-year-old Emerald in tow. "Mama had to work today," Emerald explained, immediately attaching herself to Amanda, who was filling paper cups with jellybeans and cellophane-wrapped suckers for party favors.

"Amanda." Florida stood over the two girls, scratching her head, which was covered in springy corkscrew curls. "Do you know any party games? We ain't got much room up in here, but it's too cold to go outside."

"Um . . ." Amanda flashed me a *Help!* look but said, "Uh, sure. Emerald and I'll think of something. Hey! Can we use these suckers for a candy hunt?" Suddenly all business, she pointed at Cheree, Tia, and Thomas. "Mom! Keep Chanda's kids in the kitchen for a few minutes till we get these hidden."

Florida grinned as Amanda and Emerald headed for the front room with handfuls of suckers. "Knew that girl would pull it together."

Two kids who lived in the building—a boy and a girl—arrived at two ten with a gift wrapped in used Christmas paper. At two twenty, Cedric—Florida's twelve-year-old—came barging in the back door, jacket unzipped, shoelaces untied, a basketball tucked under one arm. "Where's Chris?" Florida demanded, glancing at the clock.

Cedric shrugged. "I dunno. He went off with some guys." Rolling her eyes, Florida marched him to the bathroom to wash up.

Carl and Carla finally walked in the back door at two forty-five. "Surprise!" we all yelled, clustering around the Hickmans' table. "Happy birthday, Carla!"

A brief smile flickered over Carla's face as she took in the motley crew of kids and adults all grinning at her. Her hair was done like her mother's—short, bouncy corkscrews all over her head. Her eyes swept up to the crepe paper streamers, and her face clouded in a pout. "That's ugly. I want *pink* streamers!" Crossing her arms across her flat chest, Carla glared at her mother accusingly. "I *always* had pink streamers at my *other* mommy's house."

"Ah, I'm sure ya did, honey." Florida tossed an apologetic glance in my direction. "But we have pink roses and words on your birthday cake, see?" She raised her voice. "Okay, all the kids in the front room! Amanda and Emerald have some games for you."

I gave Florida a quick hug in passing as she shooed the younger set down the long hallway. She made a face at me as though to say, *"I'm hangin'."* Then she slipped into the bathroom and stayed there for five minutes before reappearing. Her eyes looked red.

Squeals from the front room, then kids darting into the bedrooms and back to the dining room, hunting high and low, was evidence that the candy hunt, at least, was a huge success. Amanda insisted on giving each child just one sucker from the stash, then she handed me the rest to divide out between the paper cups of jelly-beans. By the time I was done with that, she had all the kids lined up behind a broomstick in the front room, trying one by one to toss a bag of pinto beans from Florida's cupboard into a plastic bucket. Even the big boys—Cedric and Chanda's Thomas—wanted a turn, so Amanda pushed the broomstick starting line way back.

"Look at that," Florida murmured, as the two of us peeked into the front room. The kids were jostling each other for another turn. "Don't know what I woulda done without Amanda and those games. Saved my butt."

Carl holed up in the bedroom while Chanda, Edesa, Florida, and I chatted in the dining room, accompanied by rhythmic clapping at the other end of the apartment as the kids hollered, "Who stole the cookie from the *(clap)* cookie jar?" The door buzzer went off during an alphabet game, and Florida yelled, "Carl! Get that, will ya?" while she refilled our coffee cups. But he came back alone and disappeared into the bedroom again. "Musta been a wrong buzzer," Florida cracked, then excused herself to the back porch for another cigarette.

Chanda shook her head. "Dat woman, she one nervous wreck."

When Amanda finally herded the kids back to the dining room for cake and ice cream, Florida lit the fat candle in the shape of a 9 and we all sang "Happy Birthday." Even Carl came out of his self-imposed exile—though I didn't blame him, since he was the lone adult male in a house full of female hormones and kids with big lungs.

"Okay, baby." Florida stood poised with the knife. "You want the piece with your name on it?"

Carla shook her head. "Don't want any. Wanna open my presents now."

"Don't want cake and ice cream? It's your birthday, baby."

Carla shrugged. "Daddy bought me a shake and fries at Burger King."

If looks could kill, Carl Hickman would have been dead on the floor right then and there. I'd never seen Florida so mad! Tight-lipped, she cut the cake and passed paper plates to Edesa, who was dipping ice cream. I noticed that Florida set aside the piece with Carla's name on it.

Carla ripped into her gifts, which included a bubble-gum bank from the kids downstairs, a birthstone locket from Edesa and Emerald, a dollar lottery ticket from Chanda and a white plastic purse on a long strap from Chanda's kids ("Ina case you be a winnah, girl!" Chanda giggled), the books and bubble bath from us Baxters, and a Black Barbie in a fake-leather pants outfit from her mom and dad. Most of the gifts got tossed aside two seconds after opening, except for the bubble-gum bank and the Black Barbie, which held her interest for several minutes. But suddenly Carla stood up and looked around. "Where's the big present?"

Cedric snorted. "What big present?"

"The big one! From my other mommy and daddy! They said they were gonna get me a Barbie bike for my birthday." She stamped her foot. "Where is it?"

I could see Florida struggling to keep her cool. "Honey girl, we don't have a Barbie bike—"

Carl cleared his throat. "Uh, actually, there's a big box out in the hallway. Got delivered 'bout a half-hour ago."

Squealing, Carla ran down the hall toward the front door of the apartment and out into the hallway, followed by every single kid. Within sixty seconds, they were back, pushing and pulling a big, long box—just the size of a girl's bicycle. "I knew it! I knew it!" crowed Carla, hopping up and down. "I knew my mommy and daddy wouldn't forget!"

I never did see Florida again. Carl opened the box—sure enough, a pink Barbie bicycle, with only the handlebars to be screwed in place—and Carla insisted on riding it up and down the narrow hallway. Chanda took her kids on home to get them out of the way, Amanda and Emerald played video games with Cedric, while Edesa and I cleaned up after the party. I knocked on Florida's bedroom door on our way out but got no response.

All the way home, tears for my friend blurred the brick facades lining the el tracks. Even Amanda rode home in silence, staring out the smudged train window. As we walked up our block, Amanda suddenly pulled on my jacket sleeve. "Hey, Mom! Isn't that Stu's car parked out front?"

12

tu! I'd completely forgotten our phone call that morning, and I did *not* want to talk to her right now. After what happened at Carla's party, I just wanted to have a good cry in my bedroom. But she was probably upstairs talking to our neighbors about the apartment. Maybe we could just slip inside unnoticed.

Wrong. Stu was standing in our living room, talking in excited rushes with Denny and Josh. A basketball game flickered on the TV behind them, the volume turned down. "Jodi!" Stu whirled as Amanda and I came in the front door. "I got the apartment! Can you believe it?" Her laugh followed, like a shadow on speed. "The Bennetts are *so* happy you referred me."

Denny scratched his head. "I didn't know Stu was looking for an apartment." He narrowed his eyes at me slightly as if I'd been withholding information. Well, okay, I had. But—

"You're going to live upstairs?" Amanda grinned. "How cool is that!"

"Yeah. Especially if you make more of that cranberry bread you brought for Thanksgiving." Josh smacked his lips.

Stu laughed again, giddy with success. "That's a deal. Soon as I unpack."

I swallowed. *God, this is what You wanted, right? So help me here.* "That's great, Stu. Uh, when do you move in?"

"Next weekend. The movers are coming for the Bennetts' stuff on Tuesday—that gives me a few days to do some painting up there. Not much. You guys wanna help? Oh!" She held out a bunch of mail she'd been clutching in one hand. "Here's your mail—I grabbed it on my way in. Something there from Lincoln Correctional. Open it!"

This was too much! "Uh . . . later. I've gotta . . . I've . . ."

I grabbed the bunch of mail and fled to the bathroom. Locking the door behind me, I turned the water on full force in the sink and bawled into the closest towel.

TEN MINUTES LATER, I heard a gentle rap at the door. "Jodi? You okay?"

Grabbing some toilet paper, I blew my nose and unlocked the door. Denny was leaning against the doorjamb, his eyebrows arched in little question marks. I sighed. "Yeah. Sorry about that. I need some coffee—no, make that some tea. Something calming."

Over mugs of chamomile, I told him it wasn't so much Stu moving in but what happened at Carla's party. "Carla was an absolute brat, Denny! Florida is so hurt. And Chris never did show up . . . I know Florida's worried. What is he—fourteen?" I shuddered. "She knows better'n anybody the dangers out on the street for kids that age."

Denny didn't look one whit surprised when I told him Carl had slept till noon—not exactly "helping" with Carla's party. He cursed, slapping the table and making our mugs jump. He looked at me guiltily. "Sorry. I'd like to shake Carl—or kick him in the butt. That man's gonna lose his family *again* if he's not careful, but . . . feel like I gotta be Mr. Nice—you know, the white guy/black guy thing."

"Maybe Pastor Clark could talk to him."

Denny threw up his hands. "Sure he would! But he's white too. I don't know if the trust is there. Maybe I should talk to Mark Smith."

I nodded—though two African-American men couldn't be more different. An academic professor and an unemployed ex-addict? One other drawback: Mark and Nony didn't attend Uptown Community. Well, Carl didn't either, but at least his wife and kids did. That placed their family under Uptown's pastoral care.

I sighed. This diversity business was complicated. What did we know? Not much.

We could hear the TV back on in the living room. Denny got up. "Guess I'll catch the tail end of the game. By the way, how come you didn't tell me Stu wanted to move to Rogers Park? Or about her new job? You usually give me an earful about all the Yada Yada doings."

I shrugged. "Sorry." I could barely explain it to myself, much less Denny. My reasons sounded so . . . petty, so small-minded. I was a big girl, wasn't I? Why did Stu always catch me off balance?

Denny disappeared into the living room to join Josh in front of the TV. I wanted to call Florida to see how she was doing, but decided to wait till later that evening. "Better start the laundry," I muttered to Willie Wonka, "before the Bennetts tie up the machines with last-minute stuff." Wandering into the bathroom to unload the hamper, I saw the mail I'd dumped on the floor and bent to pick it up.

There it was. Postmarked Lincoln, Illinois. A letter from Becky Wallace.

Slitting it open with my thumbnail, I pulled out the sheet of lined notebook paper. The letter was short, the scrawl now familiar.

Dear Mr. and Mrs. Baxter,
Don't know who to send this to, but I still have your address from last time. Got the package of nice hand cream and stuff. The card inside said, From the Yada Yada Prayer Group—guess that's you guys. Tell all the ladies I really appreciate it. It was the only Christmas present I got.
    But tell the lady who sent me a phone number, I don't get no answer. Maybe it's a wrong number. Could she help me contact my boy? I miss him so much, I think I might go crazy.

Respectfully,
Becky Wallace

I read the letter again, then slowly folded the sheet of paper and slid it into the envelope. I should probably apologize to Stu for not opening the letter while she was here—after all, she was the one who'd ordered that Estée Lauder stuff on Yada Yada's behalf . . . and got the phone number. I sighed. Great way to start off our new relationship as "housemates"—me eating crow.

THE MOVING TRUCK MUST'VE COME AND GONE while we were all at school on Tuesday, because that night everything was silent

104

upstairs. Until Stu arrived, that is, cheerfully lugging in buckets of paint, rollers and brushes, disposable paint pans, and even a short stepladder. For the life of me, I couldn't figure how she got a stepladder in that sporty little car of hers.

We never did get to say good-bye to the Bennetts. They were just gone.

I sucked up my courage and told Stu—and the kids—they could help her paint *after* they got their homework done. I had to do lesson plans. Didn't much matter, because Denny gallantly offered to help and stayed up there till eleven o'clock, scraping and spackling. I took up a plate of taco salad left over from supper, and Stu acted as though I'd brought up caviar and prime rib. "Mm! I'm so excited about moving that I forgot to eat lunch!"

I showed her Becky Wallace's letter and apologized for the other day. "No problem," she said, spooning globs of black-bean salsa all over her taco salad. "Amanda said Carla's birthday ended in a big upset—was sorry to hear that. I'll call Florida and tell her not to get discouraged. Reuniting a family takes time."

I hesitated a nanosecond, but the words popped out of my mouth. "Easy to say; harder to do—not get discouraged, that is." Then I left Stu and Denny to their scraping.

I had tried to call Florida Saturday night, but the line had been busy—or off the hook. And neither Florida nor the kids had come to church the next morning. I was really getting worried. I'd tried again Sunday afternoon and Chris had answered the phone. *"Ma! It's Mrs. Baxter!"*

After what seemed long enough to grow tomatoes, Florida had come on the phone, her voice flat. "Hey, Jodi. Whassup?"

"What's up? You tell me! I see Chris got home."

"Yeah. An' grounded till they put a man on Mars."

"Huh. Don't blame you. Are you okay?"

The phone seemed to go dead for a moment. Then a sigh. "All right, I guess. Just, you know, wanted to do a nice party for Carla. Ended up wantin' to wring her sassy little neck. Carl and Chris, too, for that matter."

I stifled a giggle. "I know. I would've gladly helped you. Might as well throw in Carla's foster parents too."

"For real!" Now Florida snorted, and we'd both started to laugh. That was Sunday. At least she'd talked about it. But I knew she still felt hurt. Had to admit, though, when I got a little distance from it, I couldn't really blame the foster parents. This was Carla's first birthday *not* with them—after five years. Like all absentee parents, they were trying to make up for their loss with expensive gifts.

But it had sure done a number on Florida's soul.

BOTH MY KIDS SEEMED ELATED that Stu was moving in upstairs. They even hustled their homework so they could go upstairs and help her paint. Stu's idea of "not much" paint expanded to include nearly the entire apartment. Her choice of colors knocked me over till I got used to them: melon and lime in the living room, sea blue and lavender in the kitchen, seashell and burgundy in her bedroom. It was kind of fun seeing the former beige-on-beige rooms burst into life, like a garden of perennials. I even tackled the pantry myself with two brushes, one for each color.

On Wednesday night, Denny and I excused ourselves from the paint party to attend Bible study at Uptown. Pastor Clark had been teaching on the parables of Jesus since the New Year—a lot more appealing to me than that "end times" stuff he'd tackled last fall.

When we got home, loud music pulsed through the floor from upstairs, and the phone was ringing. "Don't tell me Stu likes punk rock too," I groaned, rolling my eyes as I grabbed the phone.

"Doubt it." Denny wandered off to turn on the evening news. "She's just tolerating the kids' music 'cause they're helping her paint. The honeymoon will wear off."

"Soon, I hope!" I yelled after him, covering the phone. "Stu hasn't even moved in yet, and already we have our own episode of *Upstairs, Downstairs*—Hello?"

"Upstairs, downstairs?" said a familiar voice. "I may have the wrong num—"

"Delores!" I laughed. "Sorry. I was still talking to Denny. It's a little crazy over here—did you hear Stu is moving in upstairs?"

"*Sí!* She called me a couple of days ago—called everybody, I think. Anyway, Jodi . . . I know it's late, but José keeps asking me if you and Denny have decided if we can go ahead with a *quinceañera* for Amanda."

Oh, brother! How long had it been since we'd talked? Denny and I really did need to give the Enriqueses some kind of answer. "Delores, I'm *so* sorry. Have to admit, I've been a little slow on this one. Denny and I still have to talk about some stuff, but"—I went out on a limb—"I think we can pull something off, if we can keep the expenses down."

"Oh! Wonderful! Amanda is such a special girl. We can plan it together."

"Okay, Delores. I'll call you by the weekend, okay? Wait a minute—hold on." Out of the corner of my eye, I saw Denny waving his arms in the doorway.

"Is that Delores?" His voice was anxious. "Don't let her hang up!"

I covered the mouthpiece. "What is it?"

He pointed back toward the living room. "Isn't her family from Colima? I just heard on the news—there's been a huge earthquake there!"

13

I let Denny break the news to Delores—then I got on the phone and called everybody on the Yada Yada list to pray for the safety of Delores's and Ricardo's families. When the kids came downstairs, they said Stu had just left, so I had to call and leave a message on her voice mail at home.

Home. That would soon be our address after this weekend.

"Denny," I murmured, when we finally got to bed and the house was settling into a creaky silence. "How bad was the earthquake?" I snuggled under his arm and laid my head on his chest. I could hear the slow beating of his heart.

"Mm . . . they're saying it registered 7.6 . . . a lot of damage." I could tell he was drifting off. "Don't know how many fatalities yet . . ."

A low moan from the wind chased down the alley outside our bedroom window. It'd been getting colder each day. Real winter now—except no snow to speak of.

A soft rumble beside me told me Denny was out. Gone.

I slid out of his embrace but lay awake for a while, worried about

Delores . . . worried about Florida . . . and Carla . . . and Carl . . . and Chris. . . . I realized I'd practically committed myself to this *quinceañera* thing for Amanda . . . and Stu was moving in on Saturday—really, truly moving into my house! Well, upstairs, but still . . .

I could feel my own heartbeat pick up a little. If I wasn't careful, I could work myself into a stew and lose half a night's sleep. Or I could pray. Pray instead of worry—well, *that* was sure enough biblical! I was tired of my "Be with Delores, bless Florida, take care of Carla" prayers though. Maybe I could pray some Scripture, like Nony did so often.

I clicked on my bedside light with one eye on Denny . . . he didn't move. I found my Bible and was going to hunt for the "Be anxious for nothing" passage in the New Testament; instead, my Bible fell open to where I'd been reading in Isaiah.

"Fear not . . ."

Okay, why not? Quietly, so as not to wake Denny, I began to apply the verse in a low whisper: "You say not to fear, God, because You have redeemed me! You have called me by my name—Jodi, 'God is gracious'—because I am Yours."

"Delores—she's Mine too . . . and Florida and Carl . . . and Stu. I am redeeming them; I've called them by name; they are Mine."

Whoa! I wasn't sure if the verse scrambled right there on the page or if I was hearing a Voice in my head. Yet my prayer felt electric. *That's* why I didn't have to fear! All the people I cared about—and, um, even the ones I didn't care about so much—were known by name to God. Even . . . even Hakim, and his mother, Geraldine.

"Okay, God, You know all the people I'm worried about tonight—especially Delores, who doesn't know what has happened to her family in Mexico. But"—I tried praying the second verse—"You promised that when the waters are deep and scary, You will be with us; even when it feels like the rivers are at flood stage, You said they won't overflow or overwhelm us. Well, the waters are pretty deep and scary for Delores right now, but I'm holding on to Your promise that she won't drown, because You are the Lord our God! You are—"

"Jodi?" Denny raised up on one elbow. "What's going on? Are you all right?" He was looking at me with sleep-startled eyes. The echo of my own voice told me I definitely had *not* been whispering.

"Oh. Sorry." I shushed down to a whisper. "Didn't mean to get so loud." I shut the Bible and turned off the light, scooting down beneath the wedding-ring quilt. "I was just praying."

I smiled into the dark.

WE HEARD ON THE NEWS that twenty-nine people died in the Colima earthquake. Delores finally got word through the Red Cross that none of her family members were among them, even though phone lines were down and she hadn't been able to contact them personally.

Amanda, however, was morose at Saturday breakfast as we got ready to help with Stu's move. "I'm glad Delores's family is okay, but *somebody's* family isn't." She nibbled at her toast. "Wonder if the house we built with Habitat for Humanity last summer suffered any damage. Wish our youth group could go back to Mexico right now and help with cleanup or whatever. I mean, we oughta do something besides just *pray.*"

Hm. She sounded just like me when my father used to say, *"Let's pray about it."*

"Maybe there is something we can do. We'll ask Delores. Hurry with your breakfast—Dad's already warming up the car."

Stu had not only recruited the kids to help with her move, but Denny and me too. Though how much good I was going to be with my still-weak left leg was a good guess—and I didn't look forward to looking like a wimp. Maybe I'd just be straight with Stu and offer to tape boxes or something.

Saturday morning traffic was light, so we drove down Lake Shore Drive to the city center, then headed out the Eisenhower Expressway toward Oak Park, the first suburb west of Chicago. Ice was starting to form along the lakeshore, and the miniharbors were empty of the sailboats and cabin cruisers that lined the drive during the summer. We made good time, but it still took us the best part of an hour to get to Stu's house. *Funny,* I thought as we drove up a quiet street and parked in front of a gray, two-story stucco. *I've never been to Stu's house before, and now she's moving out.*

A U-Haul truck was parked in front of the stucco, and to my surprise Carl Hickman was standing at the back beside a big chest of drawers, scratching his head as if wondering how to get the thing into the truck. "Hey, Carl, let me help you with that," said Denny, grabbing one side of the dresser. "Josh, give us a hand."

"Huh. Could use more muscle," Carl huffed. "That girl got herself some heavy stuff up in that crib!"

Amanda and I followed the open door up the front stairs to a second floor apartment. We met Cedric and Chris coming down, each carrying a box. "Set those on the curb!" Stu's voice yelled after them. "We gotta get the furniture in the truck first when the Baxters get—oh, there you are!"

Stu glanced at her watch. She'd said ten o'clock, and it was only five after. I refused to feel guilty. "Yep. Where do you want us to start? Hey, Florida. Didn't know you guys were coming—we could've picked you up."

Florida poked her head out from behind a cupboard, her head wrapped in a red bandana. "Yeah? Five of us plus y'all in that mini-van?" She lowered her voice. "But, girl, you can take me home. That wind nearly killed me today waitin' for the el."

The men came upstairs just then, and Stu put them to work taking down the bigger pieces of furniture—couch, queen bed set, dining room table, chairs. I told her I couldn't do the stairs—not carrying heavy stuff—so she put me to work cleaning out the refrigerator and packing the perishables. Carla was jumping on the bare bed mattress until Amanda took her by the hand to help scrub the bathroom.

"Eew. Nasty." Carla wrinkled her button nose.

"Not Stu's bathroom." Amanda grinned. "She hasn't got big brothers to mess it up. C'mon."

To tell the truth, it was fun working together with Florida and Stu and the kids. And I was glad that Denny and Carl were getting a chance to work together—though I had to admit I was still surprised that Florida got him out of the house. I said so to her when no one else was around.

"Girl, you and me both. But Stu asked him herself—wasn't me. And it was Carl who kicked the boys out of bed this mornin' and got 'em on the el. 'Course they fussed they heads off, an' he got in they faces and said, 'This lady got your sister back; now she askin' us for a little help, and we gonna give it to her.'"

A few other friends of Stu's came by, and somehow we got her entire apartment packed into that truck by noon. Denny and Carl drove the U-Haul by a different route since trucks weren't allowed on Lake Shore Drive, and the rest of us sorted ourselves between Stu's two-door Celica and our minivan. I expected Stu to be the first to arrive, but the boys crammed into her sporty car must've convinced her to stop for food, because when they finally did arrive, they were carrying two buckets of Kentucky Fried Chicken, biscuits, several sides, and a couple of liters of soda.

And then everything had to come back *out* of the truck and up the stairs to the second floor. "Girl, didn't it occur to you to find a *first*-floor apartment?" Florida grumbled.

I stifled a snort. At least *she* said it, not me.

Stu just laughed. "Next month, Flo. And I'll be sure to let you know."

STU RETURNED THE RENTAL TRUCK, letting Josh follow along behind in the Celica so she'd have a ride back. Josh was in seventh heaven driving that thing—but if I was a nail-biter, they'd be down to the quick. *Arrgh!* No way did I want to have to pay for a fender-bender on Stu's car.

Calm down, Jodi. No sense borrowing trouble.

Denny took the Hickmans home while I peeled potatoes and fried some bacon for a big pot of corn chowder. I was glad enough to invite Stu for supper—the neighborly thing to do since her kitchen wasn't set up yet—but I did wonder how often she'd expect to eat with us. Living so close with another Yada Yada sister might be a bit tricky.

Yada—"to know and be known intimately." I stirred the soup pot thoughtfully. That's what the Hebrew word meant when it was used in the Scriptures. Seemed like a good name for us when we were only talking about meeting every other week. *But how intimately do I really want to "know and be known" by Leslie Stuart?*

I dumped two cans of creamed corn into the soup, still musing. There was also the other meaning: *Yadah,* spelled with an H—"to give praise to God." Huh. I was still working on that one too—giving God praise, especially when I didn't *feel* all that holy and thankful.

"Which I guess is the point, Wonka," I said to my four-footed audience, who was patiently hoping I'd drop some bacon bits on the floor. "Let's get *down!*" I turned the kitchen radio to 1390 AM, Chicago's gospel station—Florida's favorite—and turned it up loud.

Denny got home before Josh and Stu did, lifting the lid to the soup pot and all but drooling into it. "I think it's going to snow," he said, spooning some soup into a mug and leaning back against the counter.

I turned down the radio. "Well, at least Stu had decent weather for her move." My antennae told me that Denny wanted to talk—but I didn't think it was about the weather.

He finished the soup appetizer and set the mug down, still leaning against the counter. "Carl Hickman surprised me today."

"Uh-huh. Me too. Last Saturday he was acting like a jerk. Today he's all hard work. Go figure." I sliced some French bread, and got out the butter and garlic.

"Yeah. Thought about it all the way home. And I realized something . . ."

I checked to see if the oven had reached 400 degrees yet, then wrapped the garlic bread in aluminum foil for its trip into the oven. "Realized . . . ?"

"He said Stu called him, said she needed help moving. Funny

thing, I probably wouldn't think to ask Carl Hickman if I needed help. Too busy trying to think of ways to help him. But I should have known . . ." Denny's brow furrowed.

I stood there with the oven door open, the heat making a clean getaway. "Known what?"

"Guys don't want to be helped. They want to be needed."

14

It was odd to see Stu's sporty two-door next to our mini-van in the garage the next morning when we got ready to leave for church. The Bennetts had been true urbanites and took public transportation everywhere, so we'd had the two-car garage to ourselves. Denny had just pushed the button to open the wide door when Stu came bopping into the garage, wearing a dressy, red wool coat and matching red scrunch hat over her long blonde hair. "Hey, great, I caught you guys! Mind if I ride with you?" She slid open the side door of the minivan and climbed in. "No sense taking two cars to the same place. Parking's terrible on Morse Avenue."

And that was that. The Baxters had just become a family of five on Sunday morning.

Stu's chatter filled the few blocks to Uptown Community—how much she liked the apartment . . . how glad she was that she didn't have to live in an impersonal apartment building . . . how excited she was to begin her new job with DCFS next week. By the time Josh let us off by Uptown's front door, I was quite relieved to melt into the clumps of people surging up the stairs to the second-floor meeting room.

Florida and the kids were back—*yea, God!* I gave her a big hug— then realized only Cedric and Carla were with her. "Chris?" I asked. She rolled her eyes and grimaced. My heart sank. Like father, like son?

Peter Douglass was back too—hadn't seen him since the first Sunday in January. Rick Reilly, guitarist in the praise team, was leading worship today, so Peter and Avis were sitting together on the other side of the room from us. Couldn't help watching them out of the corner of my eye. Peter, looking dapper in a dark gray suit and open-necked black shirt, whispered to Avis from time to time, while she tried to stifle a laugh. Florida must've been watching them, too, because she poked Denny and me from the row behind us just as we stood for the opening song. "Can't you guys invite those two over for dinner or somethin'?" she whispered at us.

Denny and I both grinned. If Peter Douglass intended to court Avis Johnson, he was going to have to pass muster with her Yada Yada sisters—and then some.

So after worship, Denny and I hustled over to where Avis and Peter were greeting several Uptown folks and edging their way toward the door. I gave Avis a hug. "Say," Denny said to Peter, "we'd like to invite you for Sunday lunch sometime soon. You too, Avis."

I could swear Avis rolled her eyes at me without moving a muscle. Peter glanced at her as if looking for a cue, but she was suddenly looking somewhere else. "Uh . . . I'm not sure when I'll be visiting next. Been taking in services down at Salem Baptist on the south side."

"Now that's a big church!" Denny said. "Reverend Meeks, right?

I've heard a lot about him—would like to visit sometime."

Peter Douglass looked amused. "Not too many white folks do. I'm sure you'd be welcome, though."

This conversation was veering down another trail. "About Sunday lunch," I jumped in. "It doesn't matter when. Next week, two weeks, three—just let us know so we have something on hand besides tuna fish. We'd really like to have a meal together." I smiled big at Avis, my meaning clear: *You too.*

YADA YADA MET AT MY HOUSE that evening, but we got a late start because everybody had to tromp upstairs to see Stu's new apartment. That gave me a minute to pull Delores aside for a huddle with Denny. "I know we promised you an answer about the *quinceañera* this weekend," I told her, "but . . . are you sure you want to go through with it? Since you still haven't heard from your family after the earthquake, I mean."

It was an honest question this time, not just a last-ditch attempt to get out of it. Denny and I had had time to talk over our options for the *quinceañera* that afternoon, and even though we had finally agreed to the possibility of a modest party, we both had this one reservation about going ahead.

Delores's eyes brimmed even while her warm smile pushed her cheeks into rounded dumplings. *"Gracias.* Thank you for thinking of us. But . . . life must go on, *si?* I'm sure I will hear from them soon. So . . ." She dabbed at her eyes with a tissue, still smiling. "What do you want to do?"

"Well, okay. If you're sure." I held up my hand, ticking off on my fingers. "Pastor Clark says we can use the big room at Uptown on a

Saturday. And he's okay with José's band—just gotta have everything cleaned up by Sunday morning, of course. And maybe Yo-Yo can get us her employees' discount on a cake from the Bagel Bakery."

Delores beamed. "What about the service? A prayer of blessing? Communion?"

"I don't know. Denny? What do you think?"

Denny pulled his eyebrows together. "I'd like to give that some serious thought. The more I think about this, the more I like it—a public recognition of my girl becoming a young woman. It could be—oh." He cleared his throat. "Hi, Amanda."

Amanda in search of a snack had appeared in the kitchen doorway. "What are you three whispering about?" she asked suspiciously. "Mrs. Enriques?" Suddenly her face broke into a grin. "You're going to let me have a *quinceañera*, aren't you? Thank you! Thank you! *Gracias!*" She threw her arms around her father's neck, then Delores's and mine in quick succession.

"Uh, Amanda?" I untangled myself from her chokehold. "Don't get ahead of yourself. And you interrupted. Give us a few more minutes, okay?"

She grabbed the cordless and flew back into her bedroom, probably to call José. Well, we hadn't denied it.

We could hear the Yada Yada sisters clomping back down Stu's front stairs and coming into our entryway, talking and laughing. Delores laid a hand on my arm. "*Un momentito.* Edesa and I would like to make a dress for Amanda, a special dress for her *quinceañera.* You will let us do this, please?"

Denny and I exchanged glances. A dress was one thing I'd been worried about, but we didn't want this party to be a big expense for the Enriques family. Yet I could tell Delores meant it, and I didn't want to offend her.

"If you . . . oh, Delores." I wrapped my arms around her. "Of course. Thank you. That will be *very* special."

The two of us hustled back to the front of the house, while Denny took himself into our bedroom with a book for the duration. It was times like this I wished we had a larger house with a family room or finished basement or *something* where the rest of the family could hang out when the living room was in use. Oh, well. Maybe in another life.

"We have a lot to thank God for tonight," Avis said, as the Yada Yada sisters settled on the couch and the various chairs around the room. "Also a lot of concerns that need our prayers." She seemed back in her usual form. The pain and uncertainty I'd seen when she'd talked about her cousin that day must be banished to some deep place in her spirit. Did she regret letting me see her doubt—or was it anger?—at God's silence?

I took in the room at a glance—was everyone here tonight? Yo-Yo camped on a floor cushion per usual . . . Adele overflowed a straight-backed chair from the dining room, her arms crossed as if saying, *Maybe I'm here, maybe I'm not* . . . Hoshi and Nony, our two "internationals," sat on the couch on either side of Stu . . . Florida . . . Ruth . . . Delores . . . Edesa . . . hmm. Only eleven. Someone was missing.

"But before we begin our praise and prayer," Avis continued, "we promised last time to answer Yo-Yo's question about baptism. I think it was, 'What's blood got to do with it?'" That got a laugh. Even Avis grinned.

"Yeah." Yo-Yo nodded her spiky hair. "What Florida said about washing in blood. I mean, that is *so* weird."

"It's a good question, and I'm glad you asked." Avis began with the Old Testament concept of a blood sacrifice to atone for the sins of the people. "Sin separates us from God and leads to death," she explained. "The blood sacrifice of an unblemished lamb was God's temporary provision, a substitution, making a way for His people to be reconciled with God. Yet it was only temporary. All along He planned to send His Son to be that perfect sacrifice, to take our penalty for sin on His own body. That is what Jesus's death on the cross was all about—taking the punishment for our sin, so that we can be reconciled with God. He spilled his blood, He died a cruel death—and then God raised Him from the dead!"

Yo-Yo's brow wrinkled. "What's that got to do with dunkin' people in the water—that baptism thing?"

I wasn't the only one who smiled. *Oh God, I love Yo-Yo—I really do.* She didn't let any of us get away with platitudes or pat answers. In fact, her questions made me think. Did *I* really understand all the truths I took for granted about my faith?

"Jesus died and was buried in the earth; then God raised Him up to new life. *That's* what we celebrate in baptism. When we go under the water—like being buried—we show that we have died to our old self, proclaiming that our sins are washed away by the blood of Jesus. When we come up out of the water—like Christ's resurrection—we are proclaiming that we have a *new* life . . . eternal life."

"I don't get it. We still die. People dyin' all over the place."

"Yes. This I want to know too." Hoshi leaned forward with sudden interest.

Avis's voice was passionate. "Yes, these bodies will die. But our real selves, our souls, will live forever."

"With a *new* body, thank ya, Jesus!" Florida put in. "Tired of this ol' thang. Mm-hm . . ." She began to hum, then broke out in a song. "Gonna put on my dancin' shoes . . . down by the riverside . . ."

Adele added her full contralto, then the rest of us joined in—
"Down by the riverside!"—and for a few minutes the living room
was rocking.

When Florida and Adele settled down once more, Yo-Yo spoke
up. "Got one more question. What if you don't get baptized? I
mean, what if some terrorist blew up this house right this minute?
What about us who ain't baptized?"

Avis's voice was gentle. "It's not baptism that saves us, Yo-Yo.
The thief on the cross who acknowledged Jesus as the Son of God
was told, 'Today you will be with me in paradise.' Baptism is a matter of obeying the Word of God, which says, 'Believe and be baptized.' Even Jesus was baptized by his cousin, John the Baptist, as a
testimony, uh . . . a public demonstration of his faith."

"Huh." Yo-Yo nodded, her forehead still wrinkled. She had no
more questions.

I wanted to ask, *"So, do you want to be baptized?"* But I caught
myself. *Don't keep rushing ahead of the Holy Spirit, Jodi.*

Avis shut her Bible. "All right? Why don't we begin with some
praise to the Lamb of God, our Savior." And true to form, she simply
began to murmur words of simple praise, inviting others to join with
her.

The praise got pretty loud with Adele back in the group, her
voice carrying us along even when others had paused to think or
pray silently or just take a breath. Yet I still heard the doorbell . . .
ding-dong. The front door.

I looked up—and saw Hoshi's almond eyes fly open, and her
face tighten with fear. Several others, too, opened their eyes and
looked around uncertainly—memories of that Yada Yada prayer
meeting last September suddenly aroused, when a knife-wielding

burglar had been innocently announced by that same *ding-dong*. I heard Avis say, "Sisters, God has not given us a spirit of fear, but of power and a sound mind. Let Jodi take care of it . . ." And she continued to pray.

Let Jodi take care of it . . . great. At least we kept the door locked now during meetings. I headed for the front door and was relieved to see Denny coming down the hall in his slippers—he'd heard the doorbell too. He peeked through the peephole that allowed us to see someone standing on the front porch . . . and grinned at me.

"Just Chanda," he whispered, giving me a peck on the cheek before disappearing.

I unlocked the door and pulled it open. "'Bout time you lettin' me in!" Chanda protested, darting into our entry as she waved a taxi away. "It be only t'ree degrees out dere!" She was grinning as she peeled off her winter jacket and tossed it on the coat tree. "All de sistahs here? Ooo girl, 'cause I gots some hot news."

A taxi? That wasn't like Chanda, who lived close to the bone on her earnings cleaning houses on the North Shore. Guilt nibbled at the edges of my mind—should we have picked her up? But she didn't call or anything . . .

Chanda made a beeline for the living room. Avis was wrapping up the praise time with a closing prayer, and Chanda danced on her feet, hardly able to wait for the "amen." As the Yada Yada sisters lifted their heads, she blurted out, "I won! I won *big*!" And she jiggled her feet and turned around in a little victory dance.

All of us just stared at her. Finally, practical Ruth snorted. "Won *what*, Chanda George?"

Chanda stopped bouncing, but her grin threatened to knock off both ears. "De *lottery*—dat's wot! Don't you all be watchin' de news ever' night? No takers for de big pot, come now weeks and weeks. It be growin' an' growin,' jess waitin' for dat lucky number—till *today*." She thrust up her arms, holding her fingers in a victory salute like a politician on election night. "Hal-le-*lu*-jah!"

I could tell others in the group were having a hard time believing her. I wanted to ask, but it was Yo-Yo who gave voice to our collective thought. "Okay. How much did you win?"

Chanda wiggled her eyebrows. "Don't know yet—dey gotta take out dey taxes an' all dat stuff. But . . . it gonna be a *lot* o' dem zeros!"

15

Could anything be worse than Chanda George actually winning the lottery? Which is exactly what I said to Denny after the last Yada Yada sister had left and we were shutting down the house for the night. "She's not exactly responsible with the money she does have," I fussed, "buying lottery tickets every week with money she can't afford to spend." I opened the back door long enough to push Willie Wonka out for his last pee and shut it quickly before my face froze solid. "I mean, I like Chanda— she's got a good heart. I'll be eternally grateful to her for the day she hauled all her cleaning supplies over here and cleaned house for me after my accident. But—aack! Now she's going to think gambling is her ticket out of poverty."

Denny opened his mouth to say something, but frantic scratching on the back door interrupted the conversation, and Willie Wonka scuttled in, giving us both reproachful looks as he held up first one paw, then the other. I knelt down and warmed up his pads one by one. "Poor Wonka. It's tough being a dog." I looked up at Denny. "You were gonna say?"

He shrugged. "Don't know what to say. It's mind-boggling! But admit it, Jodi, haven't you ever played 'what if'? 'If I had a million dollars, I'd . . .'"

I made a face at him. "Yeah, but that's different. I haven't spent hundreds of dollars—maybe thousands—trying to make that wish come true."

"So, how did the Yada Yada sisters respond?" Denny locked the back door, turned off the kitchen light, then headed through the house, turning off lights. I trailed behind him with Willie Wonka close on my heels like a four-legged caboose.

"Huh! Most of us didn't know what to say either! I think she was a little offended that we didn't go whooping and hollering for joy. Told us we were just jealous. What do you say to *that*? We've never really challenged her about playing the lottery. Avis once said something to me about 'picking our battles'—guess that wasn't at the top of her priorities. Maybe that was a mistake, though."

"Maybe." Denny started turning off lamps in the living room. "I don't like the lottery either. It preys on poor people. Yet if someone is gonna win the lottery, who needs it more than Chanda?" He reached for the last light. "She just better get a good law—"

"Wait a sec." I snatched up a piece of paper from our seen-better-days coffee table. "Don't want to lose Becky Wallace's letter. Stu suggested another visit to the prison—she wants to go next time, so it depends on how soon she hears if Becky put her on the approved visitors list. Maybe the second Saturday in February."

Denny threw up his hands. "Good grief, Jodi! If it's not one thing, it's another. You Yadas keep my life busier than working two jobs!" He snapped off the light, leaving us in a chilly darkness, warmed only by faint streetlight filtering in through the curtains.

"Huh! Did I say anything about you? I can drive. You don't have to go." I sure wasn't going to admit that I'd been on the verge of asking him.

"Really?" His voice trailed after me as I clomped down the hall toward our bedroom. "That'd be great. Because I really can't go the next few Saturdays, even if I wanted to—I've got two games scheduled." His voice took on a tender note. "You up for that long a drive? It's been six months now . . ."

I didn't know. I hadn't planned on driving downstate till he started fussing. I drove all over the city now, but I still hadn't done a road trip since the accident. I didn't want to be mad at Denny, though. Usually he was a trooper when it came to Yada Yada fallout—look at all the work he and the kids had done to move Stu, not to mention a zillion other bumps that had turned our life inside out since I'd first met these women at that conference.

I turned suddenly at our bedroom door, blocking his entry. "Okay, this is the deal." I dropped my voice to a whisper, given that both Amanda's and Josh's bedroom doors were mere feet away. "All Yada Yada talk, persons, and problems prohibited beyond this point. Only one man and one woman allowed. We could even try kicking out the dog."

By this time he was chuckling. Without another word he grabbed me around the waist and pulled me inside the door, shutting it right in Willie Wonka's face.

THE TEMPERATURE hit seven *below* zero the next day, and it warmed up just enough on Tuesday to dump nearly three inches of snow on Chicago. So much for our mild winter. But even the

129

weather took a backseat to the national and international news that week. The TV was on all day in the teachers' lounge at school, and Denny and Josh parked themselves in front of the TV every evening at home. Everybody was following the reports from the UN weapons inspectors in Iraq and keeping an eye on the national election in Israel. On Tuesday night, even Amanda gave up the phone long enough to watch the president's State of the Union address.

"Are we going to war with Iraq?" she asked, alarm pinching her pretty features.

"Looks like it," Josh muttered. His face was dark. Unreadable.

I shared Amanda's alarm. Real war? I'd been barely older than she was when the Vietnam War ended. Both my brothers had been drafted, but the war was over before they got out of boot camp. The world had been plenty rocky during my adult life—the Iran hostage crisis . . . the fall of the Berlin Wall . . . Desert Storm . . . the Oklahoma City bombing . . . and then 9/11—the day of terror. Just not all-out war—not with a son who was now eighteen.

Stu didn't start her new job till the following week, so we heard her working upstairs a lot, getting her new apartment in shape. She came downstairs at least once a day to borrow stuff—a wrench to fix a leaky faucet, a plunger to unstop the toilet, vinegar for some recipe or other, and fabric softener for her laundry till she could get to the store.

"It's not that I mind her borrowing stuff," I told Denny as we loaded the dishwasher after the latest request for any extra hangers we had "just lying around." "But what in the world did she do for vinegar and hangers when she didn't live on top of us?"

Denny lined up the dirty plates in the rack. "She's just lonely."

Was he joking? No, he had that innocent look he got whenever he said something simple and obvious.

"Well. fine. I want to be friendly neighbors. We've simply seen more of Stu in one week than we saw our last neighbors in a year and a half! I mean, couldn't we shoot for a happy medium?"

Denny snorted. "Has *anything* been a 'happy medium' in our life since you women started this Yada Yada thing?" He snapped my behind with a dishtowel and scuttled out of the kitchen before I could retaliate.

What he said lingered in the air as I poured soap in the dishwasher cups and set the dial to *On*. It was true. Nothing much had been a "happy medium" in the past nine months. Seemed like everything had been a big, sticky blend of trauma and deep joy. Funny mix. *Whatever.* One thing for sure—my New Year's prayer for a few months of "dull and boring" must've taken a detour.

AVIS ASKED ME TO STOP IN HER OFFICE after school on Friday to talk about counseling for Hakim. I'd been looking forward to getting home and claiming the tub for a nice, long soak—maybe even going out with Denny to a movie if he didn't get home too late. But I dutifully presented myself in Avis's office and collapsed in a padded chair till she got off the phone.

She replaced the receiver and lifted a questioning eyebrow. "Things okay in your classroom?"

I snickered. "Define *okay*. On Monday, LeTisha threw up all over Britny, and now Britny won't sit next to her—or even close. Kaya and Jade are making some reading progress; hopefully they won't have to repeat third grade. Hakim wadded up his classwork only three times—half of last week's quota. And nobody burned down the school, even though a box of matches fell out of D'Angelo's backpack when he pulled out his take-home folder. Not a book of paper matches, mind you, but a box full of *kitchen* matches."

Avis frowned. "You should have reported the matches to the office, Jodi. We take any kind of physical threat very seriously."

I sighed. "Okay, consider it reported." Even as I spoke, I knew my response didn't sound respectful. "I'm sorry, Avis. It's just that if I reported every little thing that *might* be a problem, half my class would be in your office every week."

To her credit, Avis didn't push it. Instead, she turned to the issue of Hakim seeing the social worker. "I'm having a meeting with Hakim's mother next week to explain why we think counseling would be a positive thing, and so she can meet Ms. Gray." She eyed me closely. "Do you want to be in that meeting?"

"Are you giving me a choice?" I noted Avis's slight shrug. "Um, methinks the question is more like, does Hakim's mother want me in the meeting?"

This time I got a lopsided smile. "Probably not. Though in a situation like this, the teacher is usually present as well."

I leaned forward. "Avis, face it. You've never had a situation like this before. And I think both she and I would be happy if you made an exception. I think everyone concerned could concentrate on what's good for Hakim, and not be distracted by the tension between his mother and me."

She tented her fingers and nodded. I stood to go and then turned back. "About you and Peter coming to Sunday lunch . . ."

Her eyes narrowed warily. "Aren't you rushing things a little?"

I grinned big. "Nope."

"Okay." She sighed. "How about a week from Sunday?"

BY THE TIME I GOT HOME FROM SCHOOL, it was too late for that long soak. But at least it was Friday. *And* the last day of January. The school year was half over—that was something to be thankful for.

I peeled off my jersey wool jumper and replaced it with a pair of comfy jeans and a turtleneck. *Ahhh.* That felt better. Brushing my shoulder-length hair back into a short ponytail, I felt tempted to curl up with a book and a cup of hot tea in the living room recliner, but I knew I should probably figure out something for supper first. In the kitchen, I pulled open the freezer door and assessed the situation: a package of chicken thighs, leftover potatoes au gratin, and a skinned catfish Denny "caught" at Dominick's on sale. None of it looked interesting; all of it looked like work—except the potatoes. What I wouldn't give for big bucks to take the whole family out for dinner every Friday!

Chanda can—every day if she wants to.

Whoa. Where did *that* renegade thought come from? I certainly wasn't jealous of Chanda—was I? Maybe Chanda's winnings. It was just too easy; it didn't seem fair. On one hand Denny was right; she could certainly use the money. But so much? It *wasn't* fair. Denny and I played by all the rules—got married, *then* had kids, worked two jobs, paid off all our school loans, tithed to the church, paid our bills, didn't waste our money on the lottery or foolish schemes—and yet we never really got ahead. The budget noose was just as tight today as twenty years ago.

I shut the freezer door with a *whump* and chided myself. *Jodi Baxter, you're pitiful. You have absolutely nothing to complain about! And you know good and well you wouldn't change places with Chanda George for all the chump change in Chicago.* I pulled out a hunk of cheddar cheese and looked at it with interest. Maybe I'd make something different for a change—baked cheese soufflé with mushroom sauce. Used to be one of the kids' favorites.

With a renewed burst of energy that sent Willie Wonka scurrying out of the kitchen in self-defense, I started chopping cheese, onions, and bread cubes, and whipped up the necessary eggs. By the time Josh and Amanda got home from school, red-nosed from the nippy walk from the bus, the soufflé was in the oven and sliced fresh mushrooms were sizzling in the frying pan. By the time Denny drove into the garage, I had the table set and was tossing up a nice green salad.

"What's for supper?" Denny started to pull open the oven door.

"You'll see. Wash up first." I raised my voice. "Josh! Amanda! Come eat!" I felt pretty smug as I grabbed a couple of hot pads to take out the baked soufflé. A made-from-scratch hot meal on a Friday night was no mean accomplishment.

The back door buzzer was so unexpected I nearly tripped over Willie Wonka turning to see who it was. Stu waved gaily on the other side of the door window. I stepped over Wonka and opened the door.

"You guys haven't eaten yet, have you?" Stu's eyes danced, merry blue lights beneath a warm knit hat and matching neck scarf. "I thought I saw Denny just pull in." She was balancing a liter of root beer and two big pizza boxes with *Giordano's* written in the familiar red script across the top. "Ta-da! Supper! My thank you to the Baxters for all the help you've been this past week!"

16

*P*izza?" Three heads appeared out of nowhere in the kitchen doorway. "All right!" Stu, pizza boxes, and big grins disappeared into the dining room.

Pulling the bubbling cheese-and-bread soufflé out of the oven, I fought down a nasty urge to set the casserole on the dining room floor in full view of present company and let Willie Wonka enjoy . . . and blew out a long sigh. After all, I told myself, setting it on the counter to cool, Stu meant well. She *always* meant well. "Which is just the problem," I muttered to Wonka, who was watching my every move, hoping for something besides dog food for dinner. "She's so darn thoughtful, she tramples all over my plans, and *I* end up feeling like a whiner."

"Jodi? You coming?" Denny's voice was upbeat. "Bring that salad you were making—just what this pizza needs!"

I didn't move. Didn't anybody realize I'd been busting my butt to make supper for them? I considered my choices: Old Jodi response . . . or New Jodi? Did plastering a smile over my annoyance count as

"New Jodi"? Probably not. *Jesus, help me here. I really do feel walked over. But I know she meant to do something nice. And You said 'love covers a multitude of sins'. . . . so give me some of that love right now.*

I picked up the salad and took a deep breath. The cooling soufflé was starting to sag—wouldn't make very good leftovers. Wonka might get it after all.

God came through, and I was able to enjoy the pizza and root beer, in spite of my neglected soufflé. Josh took off after supper to catch the Jesus People band playing a gig somewhere, and Denny and I left Stu playing chess with Amanda—who for some odd reason had "nothing to do" this particular Friday night—and walked down to the Heartland Café for mocha decaf cappuccinos. The Heartland was a favorite hangout in the Rogers Park neighborhood—just a few blocks down our street, stubbornly unchanged from its birth in the sixties, still offbeat, still good food, still a fun place to hang out. Not being totally self-effacing, I told Denny how I felt when Stu had bopped in with her surprise supper, "after I'd mustered up the energy to actually cook on a Friday night!"

To his credit, Denny apologized for being oblivious to my efforts. "Though you have to admit, Jodi," he added, "Friday night is usually catch-as-catch-can, so I didn't realize you'd gone to any trouble."

"I know." I cupped my cold hands around my cappuccino. "That's what was hard. For once I *had*—and Stu upstaged me."

He grinned. "Yeah. It's hard to compete with Giordano's."

"No," I shot back, "it's hard to compete with Stu."

"That's what you think this is—a competition?" I shifted under his scrutiny. "Jodi. It was just a misunderstanding. Tell her to let you know next time!"

"Right," I said glumly. "Then she'll feel bad that I didn't appreciate her surprise."

I knew that look on Denny's face—now *he* was getting annoyed. "Know what?" he said, slapping the table. "Let's talk about something else. Spring vacation—why don't we take the kids to visit my folks in New York? We didn't get a vacation last summer—it'd be fun to take a road trip."

A ROAD TRIP . . . THAT WOULD BE FUN. New England in springtime. Even if it did mean visiting my East Coast in-laws, who still made me feel like a stray Denny had brought home on a whim.

I chuckled, making the soapy bubbles of my bathwater dance like a field of dandelion fuzz. It was Saturday morning, and I was finally getting my long soak in the tub. I'd even found some strawberry bubble bath and dumped in the whole thing.

The senior Baxters tried hard; they really did. But the only time they'd visited us when we first moved into the city, they passed up our invitation to come to Uptown Community Sunday morning and instead found a nice upper-crust mainline church somewhere on the North Shore to attend. Didn't bother me—I was just as glad not to have to worry about their reaction to our rag-tag congregation—but it hurt Denny.

I sighed, and the bubbles danced once more. Did God mind if I used my bath as prayer time? Decided it counted as "pray without ceasing" and let my mind wander over my heart concerns . . .

Amanda's quinceañera—God, I hope we're doing the right thing. She's pretty excited. Denny says he's going to take her out for milkshakes this weekend and talk about the "service" part—some idea he's got . . . And

Hoshi—as far as I know, God, she still hasn't heard from her parents. Have they truly disowned her because she became a Christian? That must hurt so much—and yet, she has a quiet stubbornness that seems determined to see this through. But, Lord, soften her parents' hearts to at least talk to her again . . . And what's up with Josh, Lord? He seems more interested in hanging around Jesus People on weekends than doing college visits—and he's gotten so political! Sheesh! Maybe it's good; maybe not. I don't know . . .

The bubbles of my bath were fading away, and I saw the scars on my body from the surgery to remove my damaged spleen and from the rod they'd inserted into my left thigh. Scars . . . would they eventually fade? Or would they always remain as a reminder . . .

A reminder of what? Of my stupid anger, my failure to be the kind of Christian I thought I was? A constant reminder of the boy who died in front of my car?

A reminder of My grace, Jodi. And a reminder to pray.

Pray?

Yes, pray. I have forgiven you; remember that. You sometimes forget. But the scars can remind you to pray for Jamal's mother, who is still grieving and confused. And for Hakim. Because I put him in your classroom for a reason.

I sat up suddenly, splashing water over the side of the tub and soaking the bath mat. It was like a revelation. *God* put Hakim in my classroom, not as some cosmic joke, but because He is a Redeemer! Didn't the psalms talk about God "redeeming our life from the pit" and "renewing our youth like the eagle's"—or something like that?

I climbed out of the tub, eager now to look up that verse and see what it said. Yes, that's what I would do. Every time I saw these scars, I would pray *that* prayer for Hakim and his mother.

As I toweled myself dry, I heard the doorbell ring and padded footsteps running to answer it. Kinda early for Saturday morning . . . probably Stu wanting to borrow something. But right then I didn't care. I hummed as I pulled on underwear, jeans, a long-sleeved T-shirt, and a fleece vest, then plugged in the hair dryer.

"Mom? Mom!" Amanda's cries were accompanied by loud bangs on the bathroom door. "You gotta come see—it's terrible!"

I turned off the hair dryer. "What's terrible?" Yet she was already gone, footsteps running back to the living room, where I could hear the TV being flipped through channels. Unlocking the door, I ran in bare feet to the living room where Stu, Amanda, Denny, and Josh in various stages of half-dress stared at the TV screen. The news-caster was saying, "—disintegrated over Texas during reentry around nine a.m. this morning. All astronauts on board the space shuttle *Columbia* are presumed dead."

Oh God, no! Not again!

I slowly sank onto the couch, pulling Amanda down with me and holding her close. I'd been only twenty-six years old, an idealis-tic whippersnapper in my first classroom, when schoolteacher Christa McAuliffe accompanied the crew of the space shuttle *Challenger*. My third graders had been so excited to watch the launch on TV, I'd passed out party whistles and kazoos to celebrate. And then . . . the shuttle had exploded during its launch, right in front of our eyes. I was so shaken and the kids so traumatized, I still have no idea how we made it through the rest of that Tuesday.

Amanda was dry-eyed but pale as the TV began giving short bios of the seven crewmembers. Denny had to leave to coach a basketball game between West Rogers High and the Lincoln Park Lions. Josh went out without saying what or where—leaving me to walk Willie Wonka. He was going to hear about *that* later. To tell the truth, though, the walk in the nippy air with the dog was just what I needed to work the kinks out of my unsettled spirit. We headed for Touhy Park, where I unsnapped Wonka's leash and let the old dog nose around the trees and bushes to his heart's content while I sat on a park bench, hunched up inside my winter jacket. My mind didn't know what to think, and I found myself doing stream-of-consciousness prayers for the devastated families of those seven astronauts . . . for Hakim and his mother, who had lost their older brother . . . for Delores, who still had not heard from her family in Mexico . . . for Hoshi's parents, who were probably not as cold and uncaring as they seemed, but hurt and feeling betrayed . . .

A sharp wind off the lake drove Willie Wonka and me back toward the house. Amanda, still in her PJs, was glued to the TV coverage of the shuttle disaster. I brought her some toast and cocoa, but when Stu rang the doorbell around noon, I noticed she'd barely touched it.

Stu handed me our mail, waving a long envelope addressed to her in familiar handwriting. "Heard back from Becky Wallace," she said, trailing me into the kitchen. "She says she put me on her visitors' list."

"Huh. That was quick." I started making a list for the grocery run once Denny got back with the car.

Stu settled herself on the lone kitchen stool, her long hair wound into a loose knot at the back of her neck, showing its dark roots. "Yeah. What do you think—could we go next Saturday?"

Whaddya mean "we"? You're the Lone Ranger with the white horse. I cringed at my insulting thoughts. I did say, "You could really go anytime, you know—you don't have to wait on the rest of us."

Stu looked flustered. "But . . . when you went before, it was a group. I'd like to go with someone who's been to the prison before. Really. I *don't* want to go alone." For the first time since I'd known Stu, she seemed uncertain, even vulnerable.

I softened. I wouldn't want to go visit Bandana Woman by myself either. "Well, I might be able to go next Saturday—Denny can't, I know. The others on the okay list are Hoshi, Florida, and Yo-Yo. Why don't you call them and ask who wants to go?"

Stu slid off the stool. "Thanks, Jodi." She headed for the front door. A moment later she was back. "Amanda shouldn't watch that shuttle tragedy all day. She doesn't look good. Make her clean her room or something."

It was all I could do to keep from rolling my eyes. *Arrgh!* Two steps forward, one step back with Stu. But . . . she was right—as usual. I needed to get Amanda busy.

WHEN I GOT TO SCHOOL MONDAY MORNING, I wasn't sure where the weekend had gone. Sunday afternoon Denny had taken Amanda to the new Steak 'n Shake on Howard Avenue for peach milkshakes and a long talk about her *quinceañera*. When I asked him what they'd talked about, he'd just wiggled his eyebrows. "It's a father-daughter thing. You'll see."

I'd decided to talk to my students about the shuttle tragedy—it'd been all over the TV all weekend. First thing in the morning I gathered them on the Story Rug and told them about my third-grade class seventeen years earlier who had watched a similar tragedy on TV, right in their classroom. "Those children are grown up now, about the age of Ms. James, our student teacher the first half of this year—remember her? They had lots of questions and lots of feelings about what happened to the *Challenger*. How about you? Do you have some questions about what happened to the *Columbia* on Saturday? How do you feel about it?"

What I *really* wanted to do was grab them all in a big smother-hug and tell them it was going to be all right. That more bad things would happen in the world in their lifetime, but God would give them strength to see them through. Because there were lots of good things and good people in the world too . . .

Instead, I let them ask questions—"Did they blow up in the sky and come down with parachutes?" "Why did people let them go in the shuttle if it isn't safe?" "Were they coming back from Mars?"—and answered them as best I could. Then Hakim raised his hand. "Were there any daddies or big brothers on the shuttle that blew up?"

For a moment I was speechless. *Oh God, what shall I say?* I swallowed. Finally I managed, "Yes, I'm sure some of them were daddies or big brothers. Some were mommies and sisters too." I blinked rapidly, afraid I was going to cry.

Hakim stared at me for a long moment, the corners of his dark eyes twitching. Then he said, "I bet their little boys are sad." He got up from the Story Rug, slumped into his desk with its jagged scar, and stared out the window.

17

*F*or one brief moment, Hakim had given me a glimpse into his soul—a glimpse that stabbed like a hot knife into my own. *Oh God! Will it ever stop hurting?*

Somehow I made it through the day, beginning our new math unit on measurements and simple fractions. Chanté and Astrid, budding artists, got assigned to make a temperature chart for the month of February. Each student printed his or her name on a strip of paper that went into a jar to "take the temperature" each school day—all except Hakim, who said he didn't want a turn. Terrell's name came out of the jar to read the thermometer outside the classroom window today. Proudly he wrote down +15 in the Fahrenheit column and −10 in the Celsius column.

No surprises there. February in Chicago.

But I was worried. Was Hakim pulling back into his *I-don't-wanna-and-you-can't-make-me* shroud? And I had to send a report home to his mother this week for the second marking period! I fell back on my rule of thumb—"When in doubt, stall!"—and just left him alone while the rest of the class measured their desks, the window ledge, and the chalkboard with plastic rulers. I noticed Hakim pushed to the front of the group at the worktable when I brought out a package of store-bought cinnamon buns and a table knife, my shameless introduction to fractions. "We're going to divide each one into four parts so we can all have a taste," I said. "Who wants to divide the first one?"

Cornell tried first, ending up with one big lump and three small snitches. Protests went up. "That ain't fair!" "Who gets the big one?" "I ain't gonna eat that little crumb."

Ramón tried next, with equally lopsided results.

Hakim looked disgusted. "Let me do it!" I handed him the table knife. With a swift, smooth motion, he cut the next bun in half, turned it, and cut it in half again. "See?" he sneered. "Easy."

I thought my buttons might pop. "Good job, Hakim. Who wants to try next?"

"No!" several voices chorused. "Let Hakim do it! He makes 'em even!"

Obviously, my eight- and nine-year-olds had more interest in getting a fair share of the cinnamon buns than learning to cut things in equal fourths. I handed the knife back to Hakim. Still plenty of time for fractions.

By the time the school day was over and I'd tied the last scarf and unstuck the last zipper, I was pooped. And I still had all those reports to do so they could get sent in the take-home folders on Thursday. Yet something compelled me to fish in my tote bag for the small Bible I carried, hunting for that verse about being "redeemed from the pit." I finally found it in Psalm 103.

Keeping my finger in place, I walked over to Hakim's desk and squeezed myself into his seat. *Ugh... tight fit.* Sitting in the chair he occupied each day, I murmured the fourth and fifth verses for Hakim: "Oh God, redeem Hakim's life from the pit! Crown him with love and compassion. Satisfy his desires with good things, so that his youth can be renewed like the eagle's!" I blinked back sudden tears. "Yes, Lord, let him fly."

DOING REPORTS FOR THE SECOND MARKING PERIOD took every spare minute that week, so I just said, "Fine, fine," when Stu came downstairs Wednesday evening and said Hoshi had a paper she had to write this weekend, but both Florida and Yo-Yo signed on for the visit to the prison again. "Can we take your car?" Stu asked. "I can squeeze four in mine, but it won't be that comfortable all the way to Lincoln."

"Sure, fine," I said, hoping it was. I'd have to work out logistics with Denny.

I finished the last report at lunchtime the next day and managed to get them stuffed into the correct take-home folders. I had lingered over what to say in Hakim's report. After marking the appropriate boxes in each subject category regarding work completed and work handed in—which showed a need for *lots* of improvement—I added a note: "Hakim still struggles with paperwork but excels when it comes to spatial and conceptual math in his head. Once we discover the key to helping Hakim translate what's in his mind and get it down on paper, this boy will fly. Sincerely, Ms. Baxter."

Hallelujah! That's done. I packed up my tote bag at the end of the day and headed down the hallway. *Maybe now I can start making plans for Amanda's quinceañera, which is*—I had to think about the date—*aack! Only two weeks from Saturday!*

As I passed the school office, a woman who looked vaguely familiar stood at the counter. Business suit, chunky earrings, close-cropped hair, small glasses. I slowed, wondering . . . and then I heard her crisp voice. "Ms. Wilkins-Porter—I have an appointment with Ms. Johnson."

My heart practically surged up into my throat. Hakim's mother! I picked up my pace to get out of sight before the woman saw me. She must be here for the meeting with Avis and the social worker. Why hadn't Avis warned me? But . . . at least she came. *Yes!* I breathed, as I slowed to a normal pace for the half-mile walk back to Lunt Avenue. *Thank You, Jesus!*

I COLLECTED THE TAKE-HOME FOLDERS the next morning. Parents were supposed to sign and return the reports. As usual, half of them would dribble in next week. But Hakim's was back. Curious, I pulled out his report card. Had he given it to his mother?

Must have. There was her signature: *Ms. Geraldine Wilkins-Porter.* Period. No comments. Oh well. At least she hadn't followed through on her threat to transfer him to another school. That alone was no small miracle.

This Friday evening—unlike the previous week—we were back to catch-as-catch-can for supper. Denny had a seven o'clock game, Josh had stayed at school for a debate team practice, and Amanda was getting picked up to baby-sit the Reilly twins.

"Oh! Mom?" Amanda yelled, just as the doorbell rang—her ride. "Can you take me down to Edesa's tomorrow morning? I'm supposed to get a fitting for my dress for the *quinceañera*."

"Wait! Tomorrow?" I trailed her into the front hall as she bundled into her hat and jacket. "I can't. I promised Stu I'd drive down to the prison tomorrow—Florida and Yo-Yo are going, too, so we need a bigger car."

Amanda looked at me, stricken. "*Mo-om!* I have to get a fitting or Edesa can't keep sewing!" She yanked open the door, filling the entryway with cold air. "Oh, never mind. I'll take the el."

"No! I don't want you traveling to the west side by yourself."

"Oh, great. So now what am I supposed to do? You just said you're taking the car all day." She rolled her eyes big-time. "That . . . that robber person is more important to you than I am."

I pushed the door shut, choosing to ignore that last remark. "Amanda, calm down. We'll figure out something. We can . . ." My brain scrambled. Send Josh with her? Ask to borrow Stu's car? No, wasn't going to go there. "We'll drop you off on the way and pick you up on the way back."

She considered my offer. "Guess so. Just don't leave so *early*, like you did last time." Then she was gone.

I locked the door behind her and leaned against it—and that's when it hit me. Not only was Amanda's *quinceañera* only two weeks away, but Peter Douglass and Avis were coming to lunch after church this Sunday! I hadn't sent out invitations, hadn't planned refreshments or decorations for the party, hadn't shopped for food for Sunday—I must've been crazy to agree to drive all the way to Lincoln this weekend!

BUT THERE I WAS, pointing our Dodge minivan down I-55 the next morning after dropping Amanda off at Edesa's apartment around nine o'clock. The fitting wasn't going to take long, so it surprised me when

Amanda didn't balk at not getting picked up till three or four. She'd tossed off something about José teaching her the traditional waltzes. *"Josh has to learn them, too,"* she had said. *"All the* chambelánes *do."*

"Whatcha groanin' about, Jodi?" Yo-Yo's voice from the front passenger seat broke into my thoughts.

"I groaned? Oh, dear." I was hugging the righthand lane, going five miles below the speed limit. Car after car pulled around me and passed. I didn't care. It was my first time driving at highway speed since before the accident. "Just thinking about all the stuff I have to do to get ready for Amanda's *quinceañera* in two weeks."

"What's that you sayin', Jodi?" Florida called out from where she and Stu took up the bench seat behind me. "Speak up so we can hear ya. Y'all decided ta do that *quinceañera* thing? How come we jus' now hearin' about it?"

I did groan this time. "That's the problem, Flo—I haven't even had time to get out invitations, and it's two weeks from today! And I have no idea what to do about food, except—Yo-Yo! Could I order a cake from the Bagel Bakery? A big one?"

"Just send out e-invitations, Jodi," Stu tossed in. "I could show you—or even do it, if you want. No big deal."

Now that sounded hopeful. I opened my mouth to say thanks, when Stu added, "Besides, it's too late for snail-mail invitations. Should have done that two weeks ago."

Arrgh. Why did she always have to stick it to me?

Get over it, Jodi. She's right, you know.

"I know," I said glumly. "But thanks for the e-invitation idea. Might save my butt."

"Well, I knew somethin' was up," Yo-Yo said, "'cause Amanda called Pete and asked him ta be one of her 'chamber-somethin's' for a big party."

I tore my eyes away from the road and gaped at Yo-Yo. "Really? Amanda asked Pete?" My eyes went back to the road, which stretched out on either side of the median like twin lizard tongues, sucking up car bugs. "I wonder how many escorts she's asking?"

Yo-Yo shrugged. "Dunno. Pete seemed pleased, though . . . Huh. Lookit that. Everything looks so dead. Not like last fall when we came down. That was boss." Yo-Yo, who'd never been out of Chicago in her twenty-three years except for the eighteen months she'd spent at Lincoln Correctional herself, gazed hungrily at the flat, frozen farmland on either side of the highway. Probably why she liked to come on these junkets to visit "our thief"—just to soak up a little open space.

"You inviting Yada Yada to Amanda's party?" Flo asked. " 'Cause if you are, I'm cookin'."

"Of course Yada Yada's invited!" I sputtered. "Just haven't got there yet. But I was just gonna have, you know, cake and punch—"

"Aw, Jodi. You need *real* food for a party! Let me round it up."

"And a piñata," said Stu. "Gotta have a piñata for a Mexican fiesta. The kids'll love it!"

"Stu! We're trying to keep expenses down." But I felt a flutter of excitement. A piñata! What a great idea!

"Pooh. They don't cost much. It'll be my birthday present for Amanda's fifteenth."

I giggled. "Fifteen-and-a-*half*, you mean . . ."

By the time we pulled off the highway and rolled up to the guardhouse of the state women's prison, Stu, Florida, and Yo-Yo practically had the entire *quinceañera* planned—and jobs for everybody from Avis to Adele, even though they didn't know it yet.

18

After two previous visits to Lincoln Correctional, I was no longer surprised at the drill. We had to shed our coats and purses, dig stuff out of our pockets, and put it all in a locker. A female guard examined our shoes before letting us put them back on, and then there was the pat-down. Stu pressed her lips into a thin line as the guard told her to stand with feet apart and arms out straight, running an electronic wand up and down her body.

"You flying standby?" I said, trying to lighten things up. Stu said nothing.

We found an empty table in the gray-on-gray visitors' room and prepared to wait. Yo-Yo slid into her customary slouch; Florida—who said she was trying to cut back on cigarettes—kept up a tap dance with her painted fingertips. Stu tried to look relaxed, sitting in the molded plastic chair with one pant leg crossed casually over the other. But I could tell from the constant movement of her hands—winding a strand of long hair around her finger, picking at a spot on the table, brushing nonexistent lint from her fine-knit sweater set—that she was anything *but*.

My attention was distracted by voices at the table behind us. "—'cause it's too crowded. Talkin' 'bout early parole—for sixty, maybe a hundred! Hear that, baby? Mama might be gettin' out early."

I shifted in my seat, hoping I wasn't being obvious but wanting to see who was talking. A thirtyish brown woman with a young child on her lap leaned toward an older woman, graying, tired, across the table. A couple of other kids squirmed in the plastic chairs.

I was so busy eavesdropping, I jumped when a familiar voice said, "Hey. Didn't know you guys was comin' so soon."

Becky Wallace, midtwenties, lean and wiry, stood with her fingers shoved into the front pockets of her tight jeans, her hair tucked inside a red bandana tied snugly around her head. The bandana startled me, because standing in front of us was the spitting image of the junkie who had terrorized the prayer group at knifepoint that night—tight jeans, jean jacket, red bandana—except no wraparound shades to cover her gray eyes, and the sallow skin had regained some healthy color. *"Bandana Woman,"* I'd called her, till we learned her name.

Yo-Yo unfolded herself and grabbed a nearby chair. "Hey, Becky. Sit."

Becky acknowledged each of us as she lowered her lean body into the chair. "Yo-Yo . . . Flo . . . Jodi." She looked Stu up and down. "You Leslie Stuart? The one who wrote me?"

"That's right." Stu stuck her hand across the table.

Becky pulled her fingers out of her jean pocket and shook Stu's hand, squinting her eyes as though trying to recall Stu's face. "Was you at that prayer meetin' I busted up?" When Stu nodded, Becky cussed under her breath. "Huh. Don't remember—just that squinty-eyed lady I cut up . . . an' the big lady with the red 'fro, scared the hell out of me . . . an' that Denny guy who got me on the floor." She glanced around the room. "He ain't with you guys this time?"

"Not today. He's a high school coach—got basketball games today." I smiled. I'd have to tell Denny he was missed at the prison.

Becky shifted nervously in her seat, eyeing Stu again. "So. You said somethin' in yo' letter 'bout wantin' ta help me talk to my baby? How can ya do that?"

Stu was transformed. She leaned forward, forearms on the table, her hands clasped. "I just got rehired by the Department of Child and Family Services, the Rogers Park office. Don't know if I can get assigned to your case, but I could ask for it—if that's all right with you. But even if I don't get the case, I could check out that phone number you were given and see why you haven't been able to make contact with the foster parents. I'll try to set something up."

Becky's eyes locked on to Stu's for a long moment before her eyes fell. "I'd like that. Like that a lot." A tear slid down her cheek, which she brushed away impatiently, as if angry at the weakness it showed. "Hey, wanna thank you guys for sending me all that fancy hand cream and stuff for Christmas. That was nice, real nice." She gave a little laugh. "Made my day, no joke."

"Coulda used some of that nice, smelly stuff when I was in the joint," Yo-Yo complained good-naturedly.

"You could use some of it *now*." Florida picked up one of Yo-Yo's hands across the table. "Look at your hands! So dry they gonna fall right off."

Yo-Yo grimaced. "Can't help it. Gotta wash my hands practically ever' thirty minutes at the Bagel Bakery."

"I'm glad you liked it," I said to Becky. "Stu picked it out, but it was from all of us."

A long, awkward silence yawned between us. Florida tapped. Not knowing what else to say, I asked about the early paroles. "Is it true?"

Becky shrugged. "Yeah, I guess. At least that's the rumor goin' around. They gotta do *somethin'*—this place is way over the population limit. Makes for trouble . . ." Her eyes shifted away from us. "A lot of trouble."

"What about you?" Stu leaned forward again, as if interviewing a prospective client. "Could you get an early parole? Plead hardship! You've got a toddler who needs his mother."

"'Fore he *forgets* you're his mama," Florida muttered under her breath.

"Me?" Becky snorted. "Ain't nobody likely to give *me* early parole—not with a violent conviction." She wagged her head slowly. "Stupid. So stupid . . ."

Yo-Yo spoke up. "Tell us about your little boy. Andy—ain't that his name? How old is he?"

Whether or not Yo-Yo intended to pull the conversation out of its downward spiral, it worked. Becky lifted her eyes. "Andy? Yeah, he's two—named after his daddy. Got a head full o' black curls, big brown eyes. His daddy's black. Don't know what he saw in me, but we sure did make a pretty baby." She laughed, but without real mirth. "Big Andy and I was together for a couple of years—thought we might get married when lil' Andy was born, but"—she shrugged—"didn't happen. An' then the drugs got bad—real bad."

"Do you have a picture?" Yo-Yo seemed genuinely interested.

"Nah. Wish I did. By the time I got busted, I was zoned out." Her shoulders sagged. "Cain't blame nobody but myself. Somebody else raisin' him now. Just wish . . . just wish I could talk ta him now 'n then, so he don't forget me."

"That much is going to happen," Stu said firmly. "If I have to stand by the phone myself."

MY STOMACH WAS GROWLING by the time we collected our stuff and drove out of the prison parking lot. "At least we get to leave," I murmured, heading into the town of Lincoln and the closest food. "Can't imagine being locked in there for *years*."

Stu and I voted for Subway, but Florida and Yo-Yo saw a sign for Hardee's Big Burgers. So Yo-Yo flipped a nickel and the sub sandwiches lost. "Don't take it so hard, Jodi," Yo-Yo snickered. "You won't die from fast food just *once*."

The food was actually tasty, and I was glad we opted to eat in rather than do the drive-through. It was a good time to debrief from our visit—easier to talk facing each other than lined up in the car talking to the windshield. "Funny what she said about wanting to work in the prison garden come spring," I said, trying to keep all the fixin's inside my charbroiled chicken sandwich. "I mean, hard to imagine a hip-hop street person like Becky wanting to *grow* things."

"I like her!" Yo-Yo announced. "I mean, she's workin' on her GED, workin' in the kitchen, readin' books—says somethin' about the lady."

I smiled at *"the lady."* Becky was probably all of two years older than Yo-Yo. But I agreed with her. Becky Wallace off drugs had a lot of drive—*hustle*, Florida called it—to make something of herself. She was even likable, which was an odd way to feel about the person who'd terrorized your family and friends only a few months earlier.

The wind was kicking up as we got back in the minivan with four coffees-to-go, and the clouds looked heavy, like a big belly about to pop. "Say a prayer, sisters," I muttered. "I really don't want to drive in a snowstorm."

I meant just sending up the silent kind, but Florida—who had taken over the front passenger seat—belted out, "Okay, Lord, You heard my sister here. She don't need ta be drivin' in no snowstorm today, 'cause we all wantin' to get home safe to our families. You're a big God, and we know this is nothin' for You. Just hold off on the snow, all right?"

Well, amen. Sure hoped God didn't mind being bossed around by Florida. I pushed the speedometer up to the speed limit, more anxious about getting caught in a snowstorm than driving seventy. Stu and Yo-Yo were talking to themselves in the middle seat, so I told Florida that Avis had actually agreed to come to Sunday lunch at our house tomorrow—*with* Peter Douglass.

"You go, girl! *Somebody* gotta find out whassup with them two. Avis better hold on ta that man, all I can say. Hey—where's Yada Yada meeting tomorrow night?"

"Avis's apartment." Stu answered from the middle seat.

"Odds gotta be somebody's birthday," Yo-Yo added. "We got twelve women an' twelve months. When's your birthday, Stu?"

"March."

"What about you, Florida?"

No answer. Florida was looking gloomily out the window. "Flo!"

"Awright! Next week. But . . ." She turned and glared at all of us. "Don't nobody go doing any birthday thing for *me*. I've had it up to *here* with birthdays for a while. Jus' let me pass this one by in peace."

I glanced in my rearview mirror and caught Stu's eye. *Not likely.*

"Hey, rest area," Florida announced as a blue-and-white sign flew by. "Take a pit stop, Jodi. I've been good long enough. I really *do* need a cig."

No snow so far, but the wind was bitter. I was glad to get back in the car and kept it running while Florida and Yo-Yo hunched up in their jackets and burned down a cigarette each. When they climbed back in, Yo-Yo said, "Did we *really* jump in Lake Michigan on New Year's Day? Glad it wasn't no day like today!"

I couldn't resist. "Speaking of getting wet in Lake Michigan . . ." I glanced over my shoulder at Yo-Yo. "Have you thought any more about baptism since the last time Yada Yada met?"

"Ha. Not till the weather warms up."

That got a laugh from all of us. "But seriously, Yo-Yo," I pressed.

"Huh. I dunno. Don't think I'm good enough yet." She tapped the package of cigarettes tucked in the bib of her overalls. "Still smokin' these things, for starters."

Florida twisted as far as her seat belt would let her. "What's that got ta do with it?"

I saw Yo-Yo shrug in the rearview mirror. "Well, you know, being holy an' all that—no offense, Florida. But, you know, goin' public . . . Pete an' Jerry gonna laugh their heads off, 'cause they know I'm no saint."

"It's not about being a saint, Yo-Yo," Stu said. "It's just a declaration that you want to be a Christian."

"You been baptized?" Yo-Yo asked.

"Well, yeah—when I was a baby."

"A baby!" Yo-Yo sounded shocked. "They dunked you under when you was a *baby*—with no say-so about it? What if you drowned?"

Stu laughed. "Not 'dunked.' In my church they baptized babies by sprinkling them."

"Get outta here!"

I was just as surprised as Yo-Yo—not that some churches baptized babies, but that Stu said "in my church." What church was *that?* In the nine months since Stu had introduced herself in that first prayer group at the women's conference, I had never heard her talk about "her church."

Her family either.

19

Amanda was so high when we picked her up on the way through the city—at the Enriqueses' house in Little Village, not at Edesa's—that she babbled nonstop all the way home. "You should *see* the dress Edesa is making me, Mom! The skirt has all these layers that flounce and sway, kinda white but it shimmers pale blue—and the dance Jose taught me is *so* much fun! The guys are gonna wear white dress shirts and black pants—does Pete have a white shirt, Yo-Yo? . . . Florida! I haven't asked Chris yet if he'd be one of my *chambelánes*—an escort, ya know. Do you think he'd be too embarrassed? I know he's a good dancer—he'd pick up the traditional waltz in a minute . . ."

I did manage to squeeze in a question, like exactly how many *chambelánes* did she plan on having? And didn't that mean she had to have a corresponding number of female attendants?

"Of *course*, Mom! I've already asked Edesa and Emerald—you know, kinda like my big and little sisters—to be my *damas*. And I'll probably ask Patti Sanders—hope she won't get all weirded out. So that'd make it even if I have José and Josh and Pete and Chris . . ."

Even? Unless my math skills had digressed, that made four guys and three girls . . . *Oh, I get it. One of those chambelánes is going to be the Numero Uno escort for Amanda.* And it didn't take an Einstein to figure out who.

When we dropped off Florida, she leaned over and patted my knee. "Good luck, Jodi. You gonna need it." She grinned big. "But we got your back. I'm cookin', remember?"

By the time I dropped off Stu and Amanda and drove Yo-Yo home to Lincolnwood, it was five o'clock when I finally made it to the Rogers Park Fruit Market—the first pit stop in my quest for groceries. "You are late today, Mrs. Jodi!" hailed the Greek owner, who seemed to know all his customers by name.

"Hi, Nick. Got any good buys on meat today?"

"Got any?" He clutched his heart dramatically. "We have the best meat prices in Chicago *every* day. Go, go, see for yourself." He waved me away. "Hello, Mr. Baptiste! How is your mama today?"

I pushed a green plastic grocery cart down the first aisle, picking up carrots, fresh cilantro, and romaine lettuce on the way. The fruit market was one of my favorite haunts in Rogers Park, with its down-to-earth mix of accents and ethnic foods, good prices for fresh vegetables and fruits—okay, not as fancy as the big-box grocery stores, but still—and the same for meat, where I could get *exactly* twenty chicken wings or two pork chops if I wanted, because nothing was prepackaged. Many times I walked out of there with two heavy bags of groceries and only ten or twelve dollars poorer.

Today I pointed to a nice boneless chuck roast, hefted a ten-pound bag of potatoes into the cart, and added a Mexican mango to the usual mix of bananas, lemons, apples, and a grapefruit or two. A good old American pot roast would be perfect for Sunday lunch tomorrow—I could put it in the oven in the morning with potatoes and onions and carrots, and it'd be warm and savory by the time we walked in the door with Peter Douglass and Avis. Everybody liked pot roast, didn't they?

APPARENTLY NOT.

"Help yourself, Peter." Feeling slightly weird calling this distinguished-looking man by his first name, I handed our guest the large, shallow pasta bowl filled to its brim with beautifully browned potatoes, tender carrots, and hunks of sweet onions surrounding the juicy hunk of beef. He smiled, took a polite serving of vegetables, and then passed the dish to Avis.

Oh God! He must be vegetarian!

The fruit salad with mango went over better, along with the hot dinner rolls. But to me, Peter's plate looked too empty. What if he went home hungry? Aack!

Avis and Peter had driven to our house from Uptown Community in his black Lexus. Loaded. My eyes bugged as I'd watched them park across the street. But I liked the way he got out, walked around to Avis's side, and assisted her out of the car. They made a stunning couple. Avis—wearing a black wool coat over her fitted magenta suit, with calf-hugging black dress boots and a faux fur hat—held on to the arm of Peter's gray tweed topcoat as they crossed the street. He must have said something funny, because she tossed her head back and laughed.

I loved seeing Avis laugh.

No one mentioned Peter passing over the pot roast, and he talked easily enough about his business—a computer software company that originated in Philadelphia. ". . . and now I'm here to set up a Chicago branch. By the way, I'm hiring, if you know anyone with a computer background who'd like a job. Lots of room for advancement."

Job? I caught Denny's eye and knew we both had the same thought: Carl Hickman. At the same time my spirit sagged. Peter had said "computer background"—I was certain that didn't describe Carl.

"Uh, I could use a job next summer," Josh spoke up. I'd pretty much gotten used to his shaved head by now, though I did wonder what other people thought when they first met my bald eighteen-year-old. "Don't have any job experience," he added, "but I'm pretty good with computers. I'm a fast learner too."

Okay, smart move. He was going to need money for college.

Peter nodded thoughtfully. "Hm. You're a senior this year, right? I'm basically looking for full-time employees. What are your plans next fall?"

Josh pushed his plate back and shrugged. "Not sure. I applied to U of I—but I'm thinking I might want to wait a year before going to college. Maybe volunteer with Jesus People Ministries downtown. But I'd need a job too."

I rested my chin on my fist so that my mouth wouldn't drop open. Not go to college next fall?! Where did *that* idea come from? Now here was Josh telling Peter Douglass about it before he'd talked to Denny and me!

I stood up. It was time to get dessert. Apple crisp. Surely nobody in his right mind could pass up apple crisp.

Wrong again. "None for me, thanks, Jodi," Peter said, holding up one hand like a traffic cop. "It looks wonderful, but I'm diabetic and need to go easy on the sweets. I'll take some of that coffee, though. Smells great."

I brought coffee—carefully—feeling like a rookie batter who'd already managed to strike out twice. *Sheesh.*

Over coffee, it was Peter who launched the questions. What's this *quinceañera* he'd been hearing about? What a great idea! . . . And he kind of envied Denny's job, coaching high school basketball. "Man! I remember my high school coaches—wouldn't be where I am today if some of them hadn't encouraged me and taught me some discipline. You've got an awesome opportunity to make a difference in kids' lives, Denny." . . . Then, "Tell me about this Yada Yada Prayer Group, Jodi. I've heard Avis's version—I'd like to hear yours."

I blinked, suddenly feeling on the spot. I would've liked to hear Avis's version too! But I found myself telling Peter how this group of women got thrown together randomly at the women's conference, like a college student throwing jeans, underwear, and wool sweaters all into the same load of wash. But somehow we'd hung together, even survived a few trips through the wringer, because we believed in Jesus and we believed in prayer.

"So, let me see if I understand." Peter had taken his suit coat off and leaned back in crisp laundry-pressed shirt and suspenders, cradling his cup of coffee. "You think you are doing something important, maybe cutting edge, being part of a diverse group of women that cuts across class and race and culture."

I was quiet for a moment. Where was *that* question coming from? Did he think Yada Yada was just some effort to be relevant or politically correct? My defenses prickled . . . but maybe it was a good question. *Was* that why I wanted to be part of this group? I looked at Avis, and sudden tears—grateful tears—seemed to fill up my heart.

"I probably had thoughts like that at first," I admitted. "Felt kinda proud of myself being part of such a group—which is dumb, because we all ended up in the group pretty much by accident." Suddenly I had a vivid picture of the drugged-out panhandler on the streets of Rogers Park more than a decade ago who had tried to hit me up for money. And then God had given *that same woman* back to me—"five years saved and five years sober," Florida always said—as one of my best friends, one of my Yada Yada sisters.

"I take that back," I said. "Nothing that has happened in this group, before we met or since, has been an accident."

I looked at Avis through the tears that threatened to smudge my mascara and knew she was reading my heart. "But to tell you the truth, Peter"—my voice wobbled a bit—"I now know that God put me in this group because I need these sisters. The differences in our backgrounds, our cultures, the different ways we worship—they are God's gifts to me. So, yes, it's important—important because God is using Yada Yada to remake my life. Though," I added hastily, "my family will tell you He's not finished with me yet."

"Don't anyone respond to that!" Denny crowed. "It's a trap."

Everyone laughed, even my kids. But to my surprise, Peter Douglass smiled at me.

I hadn't struck out.

STU WAS DOING A DCFS VISIT that afternoon and said she'd go straight to Avis's apartment for Yada Yada, so not to wait for her. That was fine with me, because I wanted to get there a few minutes early and talk with Avis about our lunch with Peter—which meant convincing Josh and Amanda to leave ten minutes early if they wanted me to drop them off at Uptown for youth group on my way. "Or you could walk," I said pointedly, knowing good and well walking over to Morse Avenue at dusk when it was only ten degrees outside was not an attractive option.

I dropped off the kids and still got to Avis's apartment five minutes before anyone else arrived. Her third-floor walkup seemed to sit in the treetops—probably because she left her windows uncovered by blinds or shades, and the last light of the evening filtered through the bare branches of the trees along the parkway into the apartment. Everything had an airy feel—shining oak floors, beige and black furniture, plants hanging in the windows, lots of books and pictures.

"Oh, good," she said, when she'd buzzed me up. "You can help me get the tea things on. I'm running late, for obvious reasons." The magenta suit had given way to a loose tan-and-black caftan over black harem pants.

"Whaddya mean?" I carried a wooden tray of teacups and various kinds of herb tea into the living room and set it on the square coffee table. "You and Peter left our house by three o'clock!"

"Doesn't mean I got *here* by three fifteen." A smile played at the corners of her mouth, but if she was teasing me to ask more, I played dumb.

"What I want to know is . . . why didn't you *tell* me Peter is a vegetarian? And a diabetic, for Pete's sake!—pardon the pun. I would have been glad to fix something else."

She shook her head, every hair and extension tucked tightly into the sculpted braids tight to her scalp. "He wouldn't let me. He doesn't like people catering to how he eats. He thinks people ought to cook and eat like they normally do, and he just eats what he can. Besides, he's not a true vegetarian—he just doesn't eat red meat. It's mostly a health thing—not ideological. He's that age, you know."

I sank down on Avis's couch and sighed. "Yeah, well, I wish I'd known. Felt stupid serving stuff he couldn't eat. Glad to hear he eats chicken and seafood, at least—oughta be easier for you."

She gave me a funny look just as the buzzer rang. "What do you mean, easier for me?"

I couldn't resist. "When you get married, of course."

"Oh, stop!" And she whacked me with a throw pillow as she headed toward the door to let the next Yada Yada in.

It was Stu—carrying a beautiful azalea plant, delicate and pink. "Here," she said breathlessly, handing it to Avis. "Hide this somewhere for Florida. Don't know if everyone got the e-mail I sent last night—only found out yesterday that it's her birthday next week. Jodi, you're always doing those name things. Did you happen to look up what Florida means? Or make her one of your little name posters?"

I groaned. I'd totally forgotten Florida had an upcoming birthday. How could I forget? I'd even had time after Avis and Peter left after lunch to do *something,* except that Denny and I had taken a nap. "Nope," I said weakly, resenting the familiar day-late-and-a-dollar-short demon that twisted my gut. "But I did look up the meaning of her name a while back, and if I remember right, your azalea hits it on the head."

Stu lit up. "What?"

"Florida means 'flowering' or 'blooming'—something like that."

Avis smiled big just as the buzzer rang again. "Well, if that's not just like God."

20

vis decided to "hide" the azalea in plain sight, in the middle of the coffee table. We had nearly a full house of Yada Yada sisters that night—except Adele. "The sistah told to me at church dis mornin' that she has ta stay 'ome with 'er mother," Chanda chirped. "Give me to tell all you."

"Is MaDear sick?" I realized I hadn't seen the thin, birdlike old woman who held court at Adele's Hair and Nails since before Christmas.

Chanda shrugged. "Adele not say. I t'ink she sistah gone away for two, t'ree weeks—someting like that. Adele got de mama all de time."

"If Adele can't come to Yada Yada, we should take Yada Yada to her," Ruth said, giving her head one firm nod.

"I'll ask her," Florida offered. "Gotta get my hair done before Amanda's big party anyway."

A chorus of "Party?" "What party?" followed that announcement.

I groaned silently. The day-late-and-a-dollar-short demon grinned in my gut. "Sisters, you *will* be getting online invitations, but you are *all* invited to Amanda's *quinceañera*—well, you tell them, Delores."

Delores was only too happy to describe the Latino custom of celebrating a girl's fifteenth birthday and to fill in brief details on the upcoming party at Uptown in two weeks.

"An' Stu an' Yo-Yo an' I got jobs for everybody," Florida chimed in. "Don't blame Jodi—she still thinkin' she has ta do everything her own self. But I'm fryin' up some chicken an' a pot o' greens—don't you go rollin' yo' eyes at me, Delores Enriques. We are havin' ourselves a multicultural keen-seen-era, or however you say it—and everybody who's not doin' somethin' else is cookin' too—whatever is your first love. But Jodi, you gotta call Adele yourself an' make an appointment ta get Amanda's hair done that Friday—Saturday mornin' even better if she got a slot."

In a few short minutes, Stu and Florida had covered food, decorations, and cleanup, and got promises from almost everyone that they'd show up. "That new beau of yours, too, Avis," Florida said, wagging her finger at Avis. "If I'm gonna bring Carl, he gonna need a few more black men there. Nony, can Mark and the boys come?"

Nony smiled, her lovely face framed by a cascade of long, beaded braids. "Of course! Well, I'll have to check Mark's calendar, but we will make every effort to be there. What a beautiful idea. A rite of passage is very important in African culture, as well."

Avis moved us on to other prayer concerns. Stu shared about our visit to Becky Wallace the previous day, including the news that a large number of inmates were being given early parole because of the serious overcrowding. "I would like to pray that Becky could get an early parole," Stu said. "Especially because she's got a little boy who needs his mother—or maybe a mother who needs her little boy. She's clean now; I'd like to see her get a chance."

The room was quiet. Good thing, or we might not have heard

Hoshi speak up in her soft voice. "What if we sent a petition on her behalf? I do not know how it works in America, but I learn in my history class that the government listens to its citizens."

Florida snorted. "Huh. Sometimes."

"To serve her time, *that* may be the best thing," Ruth huffed.

Avis said, "An interesting possibility, Hoshi. We should definitely pray about that and ask God if we should send a letter on her behalf."

"Might not make a difference." Yo-Yo shrugged from her seat on a floor pillow. "But what if it did?"

Yeah, I thought. *What if it did? And what if she slid right back into drug hell and held up some other hapless victim at knifepoint? Would we be responsible for that?* Okay, Avis was right—we could at least pray about it. Only trouble was, God had a way of answering Yada Yada's prayers in unexpected ways. What if God answered yes? Then we'd be in a pickle!

"Two more things," Stu added. "I'm trying to add Andy Wallace—Becky's little boy—to my caseload, so I'd appreciate prayer about that. And we haven't done a church visit since . . ." She took a quick survey around the room. ". . . since we went to Delores and Edesa's Spanish church last fall. Isn't it about time we visited the rest of our churches?"

"That so true!" Chanda crowed. "Yada Yada has not come to me church—though it might not be me church too long a time if dey keep askin' me ta give all me winnin's to de Lord's work. Lord 'ave mercy! De deacons, de elders, de pastors—all been by ta see me. An' me, I hain't seen a penny yet. De state sure be takin' a long enough time." Chanda folded her arms and wagged her head in disgust.

I cast a quick glance at Avis, and I swear she almost rolled her eyes. Rather quickly she said, "Anyone else we haven't visited?"

"Well, my church," Stu said, brushing back her hair that had fallen over her shoulder. "That's why I brought it up."

"But you go to Uptown Community," I said, "same as Avis and Florida and me."

"*Now* I go to Uptown, since I met you all. And to be honest, I wasn't going to any church for . . . for a while before I came to Uptown. Yet if our idea is to experience different worship traditions, then it's only fair to visit the church I grew up in as well. Lutheran, in my case. I used to be a member of St. John's Lutheran. I probably still know a few folks there."

So, it was either St. John's Lutheran with Stu, or Paul and Silas Apostolic with Chanda and Adele. I'd been to an Episcopal church with Denny's parents but wasn't sure I'd ever attended a Lutheran church. "Okay," I said. "Let's visit Stu's church. Can we please just wait until after Amanda's *quinceañera*? I'm frazzled enough as it is."

"And not the same day as Yada Yada," Ruth put in. "We go here, we go there the same day—by Monday I'm crazy."

Avis picked up a desk calendar. "All right, that means . . . the first Sunday of March. Actually, that would be a good day. The schools have Pulaski Day off the next day."

I grinned. Chicago was probably the only U.S. city that let kids out of school to honor General Pulaski's birthday in deference to its large Polish community.

So it was decided: A Yada Yada visit to St. John's Lutheran in three weeks.

We let Florida's azalea sit on the coffee table unmentioned all through the prayer time, as we poured out all our thanksgivings and petitions to God. Nony closed out with a wonderful prayer from

John 13, Jesus's prayer that we "would all be one" and that others would know we are His disciples "by our love for one another."

As we opened our eyes, Stu picked up the azalea and presented it to Florida—"Our February birthday girl. Because her name means 'to flower' and 'to bloom.'" A jealous corner of myself tried to rear its head, because Stu was doing "the name thing," which had been my little discovery. But the words of Nony's prayer—that we would all be one—pricked my spirit. *Stuff it, Jodi. What does it matter? Face it: if it'd been just up to you, there would be no "flowering blooms" for Florida tonight!* I squeezed my eyes shut for a brief moment. *Oh God, forgive me. I've got so far to go.*

"For real?" Florida said, taking the flowers almost reverently, her eyes bright. "Flower and bloom? Well, thank ya, Jesus! I'm gonna sit this bit o' hope in the middle of my table and hope some of that bloomin' rub off on my family!"

I WENT STRAIGHT TO THE KITCHEN CALENDAR when I got home to write in Yada Yada's upcoming visit to St. John's—and got a gift straight from heaven. Lincoln's Birthday and President's Day—both holidays in Illinois—fell in the next two weeks before Amanda's *quinceañera*! I did a little jig right there in the kitchen. "Two whole days off, Wonka!" I hooted, dancing in a circle around the poor confused dog. Which meant I might actually have time to do the stuff on my to-do list: shop for a pair of heels for Amanda (who once swore she'd *never* wear "torture shoes"), call the Bagel Bakery about the cake, meet with Pastor Clark and Denny about the "service" part, send out invitations—

Whoa. The invitations couldn't wait for Lincoln's birthday,

which was Wednesday. They *had* to go out tomorrow. I hesitated a brief moment, then picked up the phone.

I could hear Stu's phone ringing faintly upstairs.

"Stu? Hope I'm not calling too late . . . Could I take you up on your offer to help me send out those invitations online? . . . Yeah, tomorrow. Whenever you get home from work . . . Okay. Thanks."

Denny poked his head into the dining room just as I hung up the phone. "You done yet? Let's go to bed."

"In a minute." I grabbed a pad of paper and a pen. "Gotta write down a few names I just thought of who need to be invited to the *quinceañera*."

I had scribbled half a name when I felt the pen being removed from my hand. "Hey!" I grabbed for the pen as Denny held it out of reach with one hand and pulled me out of the desk chair with the other.

"I hate those words," he murmured into my hair, wrapping both arms around me in a body lock.

Struggle was useless. I started to laugh. "What words?"

"'In a minute' . . ."

BY THE TIME I GOT HOME FROM SCHOOL on Monday, I had a decent list of people I wanted to invite to the party: Yada Yada, of course, and their families; Uptown's youth group and leaders, families Amanda babysat for, a few old friends from Downers Grove . . . and I'd better ask Amanda who she wanted to invite. *Huh. Hope they all have e-mail.*

Stu came downstairs after supper that evening and helped me find the e-invitation site on the Internet. The biggest job was entering all the e-mail addresses in the "Send To" box. And—*arrgh!*—everybody did *not* have e-mail. Chanda, for one. Nor Yo-Yo. Didn't know whether some others did or didn't. "Buck up, Jodi," Stu said. "You're going to have to send a few invites by snail mail. Want me to pick up a box for you at Office Max?"

I wanted to say, *"No thanks, I can do it"*—but knew I wouldn't get a chance at the car till the Wednesday holiday rolled around. "Sure. If it's not too much trouble. Not a box of invitations, though—some kind of festive paper I can run through the printer."

THE BAG FROM OFFICE MAX was stuffed in my mailbox when I got home from school the next day. Bright confetti colors all around the edge of eight-by-ten sheets. Perfect.

I was so busy that week checking things off my *quinceañera* to-do list, baking cupcakes for Friday's Valentine party at school, and trying to keep up with my school lesson plans, that I pretty much tuned out the news that glued Denny and Josh to the TV every night. Didn't work, though. What I missed on the TV got rehashed in the teachers' lounge—more conflicting reports about weapons of mass destruction from the UN inspectors . . . more American troops being shipped to the Middle East . . . angry voices denouncing the registration of immigrants . . .

If I thought too much about it, my insides got all twisted. The whole world seemed to be teetering on the brink of terror and fighting over how to fight terrorism—and yet I could walk through a week with my biggest worry being whether we'd have enough food for all the guests who might show up a week from Saturday. By the time I crawled into the recliner on Saturday morning with a mug of fresh hot coffee and my Bible, I was feeling schizophrenic. And helpless. What could *I* do about it?

Pray, Jodi. You can pray.

I almost laughed. My dad used to say that to me as a kid—*"Let's pray about it, shall we?"*—and it always felt like a cop-out. But I knew better now. A small sense of excitement gripped me. Yes. That's what I could do. *"Pray the headlines,"* Avis had encouraged us in worship a few weeks ago.

I brought the recliner back to its upright position with a *thump,* nearly clobbering Willie Wonka on the head with the footrest, and darted out into the cold to get the newspaper off the front porch. For the next twenty minutes, I "prayed the headlines"—prayed for the people of Iraq, even that bully Saddam Hussein, prayed he'd turn around, prayed that war would be avoided, prayed for wisdom for the president, prayed for the sons and daughters in uniform, prayed for Israelis and Palestinians, sons of Abraham living side by side and hating each other, prayed for peace, prayed that terrorists would be disarmed and brought to justice, prayed for the big protests planned around the world today to be peaceful—

Loud voices came from the direction of the kitchen. Amanda and Josh, arguing about something. Reluctantly, I made my way to the back of the house.

"Mo-om! Tell Josh he *has* to be at my *quinceañera* practice this afternoon!" Amanda, still in baggy flannel PJs, banged a few cupboard doors looking for a clean cereal bowl.

"Chill, Manda." Josh shoveled spoonfuls of corn flakes into his mouth while he balanced on the kitchen stool. "I'll be there. I just said I might be late is all."

"You can't be late!" she wailed. "You're my big brother! And you don't know the dance yet!"

I opened my mouth to ask, *"Why late?"* but Denny came into the kitchen just then wearing his jacket and knit hat. "Men's breakfast," he explained, pouring some coffee into a travel cup. "Going to pick up Carl."

The corners of my mouth curled up. "Carl Hickman? How did that happen?"

He shrugged. "Pastor Clark asked if a few of the guys could do some carpentry work around the church after breakfast. So I told Carl we could sure use another pair of hands—and he said okay."

I could almost hear Florida muttering, *"Thank ya, Jesus!"*

"You guys are going to come to the practice today, too, aren't you?" Amanda was still plucking her one-note song. "Da-ad! I'm supposed to do a dance with you!"

Denny looked at Amanda, then me. "Did I know about this?"

I threw up my hands. "Uptown Community at four o'clock. Delores called last night while you were at the game. Sorry, I forgot to tell you."

He leaned over and kissed my ear. "Sorry 'bout the game schedule —kinda screwed up Valentine's Day, didn't it? Can we go out to dinner or something tonight?"

"Definitely!" I opened the back door for him. "It's a date."

"After the practice!" Amanda wailed.

Josh tossed his cereal bowl into the sink. "Dad, wait! Can I catch a ride with you to the el?" He disappeared for thirty seconds, then dashed out the back door, carrying a huge piece of poster board and his jacket tucked under one arm.

"Josh, where . . . ?" I yelled after him.

But he was gone.

21

*D*ENNY DIDN'T GET THE CAR BACK till almost one o'clock, so I really had to hustle to get my errands done by four. His suit definitely needed dry cleaning, so I headed for Devon's Best Dry Cleaners in the middle of Rogers Park's Pakistani/Indian neighborhood. Dozens of tiny shops featuring flowing, feminine attire nestled side by side with restaurants featuring "Spicy Tamarind Soup" and "Lentil Curry." *Might as well scope out a possibility for our dinner date tonight. That'll be fun.*

When I tried to cross Ridge Avenue, though, police barricades prevented any cars from continuing on Devon, and all traffic was being diverted. *What in the world?* Beyond the barricades I could see hundreds of people, bundled up against the cold, many with placards and banners, moving west, away from the barricades. I craned my neck, trying to see what was going on, but a police officer blew her whistle at me and shoveled me into the northbound lane.

Oh, great. I slapped the steering wheel. *Now what?*

I didn't want to waste time driving around looking for another dry cleaner, so I drove home, paged through the yellow pages till I found one on Sheridan Road, and dumped off our clothes, making sure they'd have them done by Thursday.

By the time I stopped at Dominick's for milk and dog food, it was time to get Amanda to Uptown for her practice. Josh wasn't at the house, so we had to leave without him. I was a nervous wreck the first half-hour of the *quinceañera* practice, because he still hadn't shown up by the time Delores called everybody together and began giving instructions. Yet when it was time for the *chambelánes* to escort the *damas* down the aisle, suddenly there he was, cheeks and nose ruddy from the cold, staving off a teary tantrum by the *Quinceañera* herself. I started to give him a piece of my mind, but he hissed, "Chill, Mom. I said I'd be here; I'm here. This isn't the only thing happening in the world, you know." Then he hustled into his place.

Take a deep breath, Jodi. He's here, isn't he? But I wasn't sure I liked this new, cheeky Josh.

Delores walked everybody through the abbreviated service, which I had to admit was going to be really sweet—but I did wonder how much we'd corrupted the traditional *quinceañera* from the formal Catholic mass to a more informal Protestant service. At least most of the guests wouldn't have a clue. At one point Delores turned to Denny and said, "Okay, Papa, this is when you and Amanda do your little ceremony, okay?" and then she moved right on.

"Hey. What's this mysterious ceremony?" I whispered to Denny.

"If I told you, it wouldn't be a mystery, now, would it?" he whispered back.

Arrgh. It'd better not be some practical joke.

Pastor Clark seemed to be getting a huge kick out of the whole thing; he even helped stack the chairs out of the way for the dance practice. José had brought music on a CD to teach the traditional waltz, which involved a lot of clasped hands overhead, spinning of partners, and bowing and curtsies. *"La banda de mariachi* will be here next week, I promise!" he grinned. Everybody was laughing and trying out the steps—even Pete Spencer and Chris Hickman, who threw in a few hip-hop steps just for fun. It *was* funny to see them dancing a waltz in their baggy pants and big athletic shoes with the laces untied—and it occurred to me they might show up in the same attire for the real thing. *Well, so what? It's just a birthday party, not a wedding—thank You, Jesus!*

Josh volunteered to ferry people back home in the minivan so Denny and I could go home and get ready for our belated Valentine's date. Amanda went with him, so I guess she'd forgiven his tardiness. They still weren't back with the car when the front doorbell rang and Stu popped in, darting her eyes this way and that and holding something behind her back. "Is Amanda gone? I want to show you the piñata I found—oh. You guys going out?"

Denny had put on a knit shirt and sport coat, and I was wearing dress slacks, silky blouse, and makeup, no less. "Nah. Thought we'd clean the basement tonight," I said with a straight face.

She laughed. "Okay, okay, dumb question. What do you think?" She brought out a classic piñata, shaped like a burro, decorated with bright lime and yellow and blue paper crinkles.

"Hey!" Denny's eyes lit up. "What a great idea."

"Adorable! Thanks so much, Stu."

"Okay. Shh—don't tell Amanda."

I thought she might leave so we could finish getting ready, but Stu hesitated a moment, then blurted, "You know, if we're going to testify to the parole board on Becky Wallace's behalf, we ought to write a letter right away. We can't wait two weeks between every Yada Yada meeting to make decisions—it's too long!"

Denny frowned. "Uh, did I miss something?" . . . which Stu took for permission to lay out the whole idea of Becky's victims testifying on her behalf, to give her a chance at parole while the powers-that-be were trying to ease prison overcrowding.

Denny shook his head. "I don't know. Her chances are probably slim to none. She pled guilty to a violent crime—and it hasn't even been a year!"

"What could it hurt to write the letter? We'll never know unless we try."

Which was true. I just felt like Stu was pushing. We couldn't run ahead of the whole prayer group—we were *all* victims. Everyone needed to agree to it. And I said so.

Stu threw up her hands. "Fine. But we're not the one sitting in prison separated from our two-year-old child." And she took the piñata and closed the front door behind her with more-than-necessary vigor.

Denny arched an eyebrow at me. "Hmm. Honeymoon over?"

WE DIDN'T STAY OUT LATE since Amanda was home alone—Josh had gone out *again* to some gig that Head Noise was doing—but we did try one of the ethnic restaurants along Devon Avenue. The barricades were gone, and all that was left of the crowds was litter and leaflets skittering down the sidewalks ahead of the wind that bit at our ears and noses. I picked up a crumpled leaflet on the sidewalk in front of Gandhi India, a small corner restaurant on West Devon. *"International Day of Protest Against the War on Iraq,"* the leaflet said.

The fine print also mentioned protesting the "scapegoating" of immigrants and the upcoming deadline requiring Pakistanis in the United States to register with the government.

I stuffed the leaflet in the pocket of my winter coat, feeling uneasy. Maybe this stretch of Devon Avenue wasn't the smartest place to eat after a huge "solidarity" march. "Thought these big antiwar marches usually happened downtown," I murmured to Denny as a waiter seated us at a small table covered with a burgundy cloth, topped with a square of white paper that fit the table corner to corner and burgundy cloth napkins folded to stand up like butterflies at rest. Gandhi India was busy this Saturday night, filling up most of its eighteen small tables with couples, friends, and families. Only an elderly grandmother wore a traditional sari.

Curious—or anxious, I'm not sure which—I looked up at our waiter, a slightly rounded middle-aged man in a white shirt and slicked black hair, as he put a basket of fried bread on our table, crisp and light, with two dips: a sweet-and-sour made with yogurt and a tangy tamarind sauce. "Were there many protesters on the street today?" I asked, too late seeing the cautionary eye Denny sent me. "I, uh, hope it was peaceful."

The man hesitated, probably wondering if it was wise to answer. Then politeness took over. He tipped his head in a slight bow. "Yes, madam. Many thousands of protestors. But peaceful, I believe. We are grateful for this show of support from our fellow Americans. It has been . . . difficult since 9/11."

Now I *was* curious and wanted to ask more questions, but he slipped away, returning ten minutes later with the chicken tandoori and chicken tikki we'd ordered. "Let's not talk politics," Denny hissed at me as the spicy food tantalized our noses. "Not *here*. In fact, let's not talk Yada Yada, not Becky the Bandana Woman, not Amanda teetering between hormones and womanhood. It's Valentine's Day. This is supposed to be romantic—even if I didn't get you a card. Or candy." His dimples deepened with his sheepish confession.

"Day *after* Valentine's," I giggled. "Okay. I didn't get you a card or candy either." But as Denny took my hand and said a brief prayer of thanksgiving for our food ". . . and for the twenty Valentine's Days You've given to Jodi and me," I added, "And, Father, please give wisdom to world leaders and to all of us during these difficult days. We don't want war, Jesus, and we don't want terror either."

Wasn't it just this morning I'd been convicted to "pray the headlines"?

I SAT UP IN BED SUDDENLY, wet with sweat, my heart thumping loudly in my ears. The bedroom was dark—had I heard a noise? I strained to listen. All was still . . . just Denny's soft snoring beside me and the wail of a siren in the distance.

What was it? Why did I feel so frightened, afraid to close my eyes again?

Then I knew what had wakened me. The dream—the same terrible dream that had haunted me since last June. *The torrential summer rain washing over the windshield . . . a sudden face in my headlights . . . that young face, eyes dark and round, mouth wide in a silent scream . . . jerking the wheel, a sickening thump, a pair of headlights from oncoming traffic swerving right toward me . . .*

I squeezed my eyes shut, taking several deep breaths to slow the racing of my heart. Jamal Wilkins—Hakim's brother, Geraldine's son—dead.

Son . . . suddenly my eyes flew open. I hadn't heard Josh come in—had I? What time was it? The red numbers of the digital alarm said 2:13 a.m. *Two thirteen!*

Fear gripping my throat, I slid out of bed and pulled on my robe. Willie Wonka sensed my movements and with a groan got up from his dog basket at the foot of our bed. People up, dog up—that was dog duty, even in the middle of the night.

Quietly I crossed the hall to Josh's bedroom. The door was closed. I turned the handle slowly and pushed the door open past the *squeeeak* till the faint glow from the hall nightlight fell into the room.

A lump in the bed. I crossed the room and laid my hand lightly on the quilt just to make certain. The lump rose and fell slightly beneath my fingers. Josh was home. Josh was safe.

Fear gave way to irritation. Why hadn't he knocked on our door like he was supposed to when he came in? Or had I fallen into such a deep sleep that I hadn't heard him? *Arrgh.* Either way, we had to find something that worked.

I turned to go—*ouch!* My bare toe caught on a corner of something stiff sticking out from under his bed. I bent down and felt around for the offender. Just poster board. I was just about to push it back under the bed when I saw words drawn on it in big, dark letters. Curious, I slid the poster board out from under the bed and carried it into the hall. Even in the dim glow of the nightlight I could read: BLESSED ARE THE PEACEMAKERS.

If I wasn't fully awake before, I was now. I turned the poster over. NO WAR WITH IRAQ.

I caught my breath. Josh had been at that antiwar protest on Devon Avenue this afternoon! Without telling us.

22

*M*y first urge was to barge into Josh's bedroom, flip on the lights like interrogation spots, and confront him with the poster. Mentally I was already yelling, *"Why didn't you tell us where you were going? Who put you up to this? Do you even know what groups sponsored this protest? What time did you get in tonight?"*

A speck of wisdom in my brain woke up long enough to stifle my cannon fodder. *Whoa. Back up.* Okay. At the very least, I needed to wait till morning, tell Denny, and have a sit-down with Josh. *Then* we could ground him for the rest of his natural life.

By this time I was wide awake, so I padded silently into the kitchen, warmed a mug of milk and honey in the microwave, and took it into the living room, lit only by the dim streetlight from outside. I pulled an afghan around my shoulders and curled up on the couch, sipping the warm, sweet milk. Willie Wonka stood in front of me, tail drooping, muzzle in my lap, as if to say, *"Okay. I'm here. Dog on duty—but can't we go back to bed now?"*

"In a few minutes, Wonka," I murmured, stroking his silky ears . . .
but my mind was already spinning off in half a dozen directions. Why
hadn't Josh told us what he was going to do? What was it with my kids
and parades? First, it was Amanda, telling us she was going to the
Mexican Independence Day parade with Edesa—then sneaking off
with José. Now it was Josh, carrying a sign in a huge antiwar protest.
Except, wisdom prompted, *Josh is eighteen—old enough to vote, old
enough to go to war, and old enough to protest against it.*

I swallowed the last of the milk. *But not too old to let his parents
know where he is and what he's doing. We still have rules in this house as
long as he's under our roof.*

In the dark stillness of our front room, the Voice inside my head
said, *This isn't about rules, Jodi. It's about Josh. The main question isn't
why didn't he tell you, but why did he go? Ask him. Have a conversation.
These are tough times. Kids are trying to figure out what's happening to
their world—and if they have any say-so.*

I sat still so long, Willie Wonka gave up and fell asleep standing
up, his muzzle still in my lap. In my head I heard myself telling Peter
Douglass that God was using Yada Yada to "remake my life" . . .
what did that mean at this moment? Remaking Jodi the parent?

If Yada Yada were meeting in my living room right this minute,
they'd encourage me to do first things first: *pray.* Pray for Josh. Pray
for wisdom. Pray to understand. Commit him to God. Not only
that, but they'd pray for our national leaders and pray for our enemies—Saddam was our enemy, wasn't he? Pray for our troops that
might soon be in harm's way. Pray for those who felt compelled to
protest a war that was beginning to feel inevitable, and thank God
that was their right in a democracy.

And so I did. I even got down on my knees beside Willie and

just talked to God. Out loud—mostly to keep me awake. It didn't matter to Willie. He couldn't hear me.

And thank You, Jesus, I added, as I finally tiptoed into Josh's room and slid the poster back under his bed. *Thank You for keeping me from going off half-cocked a while ago.* Maybe what I told Peter Douglass about Yada Yada had some truth, after all.

DENNY AND I DID HAVE A CONVERSATION with Josh later that day after church. Had to admit Denny seemed more surprised that I was calm and rational when I told him about the poster than he did about Josh taking part in the antiwar protest. Josh, too, seemed surprised that we wanted to hear *why* he'd wanted to take part. Relieved, actually. He admitted he had mixed feelings. 9/11 was a terrible thing, and he knew terrorists had to be stopped. Yet some folks at Jesus People had strong questions about invading Iraq—and that made him think. It wasn't just politics, but kind of "What would Jesus do?"

"Who are our enemies? How did Jesus tell us to treat enemies?" Then he added defensively, "But if I'd asked your permission, I'd have had to justify it somehow, and . . . I'm not sure I can. Yet."

Uh-huh. The debater wanted to be sure he had a winning argument.

"Personal enemies and national enemies are two different things, Josh," Denny said.

"Maybe. Though some people make national enemies into personal enemies—it's happened right here in Rogers Park! Targeting innocent people because they *look* Middle Eastern." Our son slouched silently for a long moment, and I remembered the uneasy comment of our waiter at Gandhi India: *"It has been difficult since*

9/11." Josh spoke again, as if thinking out loud. "I know our country has the right to defend itself, but I guess I wanted to at least ask the question: is war the best way to make peace?"

For once I kept my lip zipped and just listened. If I was honest with my mother heart, my primary upset was that a protest might've gotten out of hand—belated worry about my child's safety. Yet Josh was wrestling with the big issues. My heart suddenly swelled with respect for my son. Agree or disagree . . . right or wrong . . . wise or unwise—he was becoming his own man.

We still took away his car keys for a week for not telling us where he'd gone on Saturday.

EVEN WITH THE PRESIDENT'S DAY HOLIDAY on Monday—or maybe because of it—the week leading up to Amanda's *quinceañera* was busy. When I got to school on Tuesday, there was a note in my teacher box in the office asking me to excuse Hakim Porter on Tuesdays and Thursdays right after lunch to meet with Ms. Gray, the school social worker. *Thank You, Jesus,* I thought. But I was a bit unnerved when Hakim said after lunch, "You gonna go with me, Miz B?"

My mind scrambled. "Um, I'll walk you there and pick you up if you want." After the first day, though, he shrugged me off. "I can go by myself."

Just as well. I had my hands full! February was Black History Month, and each class was doing a project for a special assembly at the end of the month. I'd decided to highlight the story of Mary McLeod Bethune since our school bore her name. I took the whole class to the library to use the school computers to see what they could find out about her on the Internet, printed out various articles, and assigned reports. The kids got excited, not even realizing they were learning reading, writing, and computer-research skills along the way. And I loved the facts the kids pounced on:

"Mary McLeod's parents were former slaves, but Mary was born free!"

"Mary was 'plain but smart,' so she was the one who got to go to school."

"When Mary grew up, she went to Moody Bible Institute right here in Chicago because she wanted to be a missionary to Africa, but she couldn't go because nobody had ever heard of a black missionary. She was so disappointed she cried."

I wondered how that would go over in a public-school assembly; still, I determined to let the kids dig up the facts themselves.

At least the all-school assembly wasn't until the following week, so after school one day I stopped at the Rogers Park branch of the Chicago Public Library and checked out all the "readable" books I could find about Mary Bethune. I let the kids take them home overnight, trying not to think about all the fines I might have to pay for missing books. Frankly, I didn't care. Every day hands waved as my third graders eagerly spilled new facts about Mary.

She started a school for five little girls whose daddies worked on the Florida railroad . . .

She had a school motto: "Enter to Learn; Depart to Serve" . . .

She stopped the Ku Klux Klan from burning down her school because she was so brave and she trusted God . . .

She helped people register to vote . . .

She advised President and Eleanor Roosevelt . . .

Her school grew and grew until it became Bethune-Cookman College in Dayton, Florida . . .

"That's where *I'm* going to go to school when I'm big," Kaya announced on Friday when I helped her put on her backpack, stuffed with two books about Mary McLeod Bethune.

I blinked rapidly, but tears slid down my cheeks anyway. Kaya struggled so hard with reading—maybe "Mary the teacher" was just the inspiration Kaya needed to live into the meaning of her name: "wise child."

With all that was going on at school, I barely noticed that the temperature had edged upward the last couple of days. As I walked home that Friday, I realized not one speck of ice or snow edged the sidewalks, sparrows and chickadees chirped happily in the bare trees, and joggers passed me in shorts. *Shorts?!* I checked the back porch thermometer when I let Willie Wonka out after I got home. Fifty degrees! In February!

I smiled. What a gift! Springlike temperatures for Amanda's *quinceañera*. Then I yelped. "Aack! That's tomorrow!"

THE LITTLE BELL TINKLED over the doorway as Amanda and I pushed open the door to Adele's Hair and Nails the next morning. Gospel music welcomed us, as though we'd arrived for a worship service. It was only nine o'clock, but all three chairs were busy already. Adele glanced up, pins in her mouth, and gave a wave with a plastic-gloved hand; next to her Takeisha, the other hairstylist, was coloring an older woman's hair. Behind the third chair, a young man I'd never seen before was using electric clippers to give a middle-aged man a trim. All three stylists wore matching dark green T-shirts with *Adele's Hair and Nails* stitched in white script on the breast pocket.

"The T-shirts look great, Adele," I called over the music as I sank down on the overstuffed couch under the front window and picked up an issue of *Essence*. Amanda headed straight for the plastic-covered cake server on the coffee stand in the corner, which held a stack of tempting sweet rolls.

Adele took the pins out of her mouth and anchored them in the woman's hair. "Takeisha will be with you in five, Amanda." She smiled big, revealing the tiny space between her front teeth. "Ready for your big day?"

Amanda, her mouth full of sweet roll, grinned. "Uhnn-hunnh."

Five minutes later, Amanda was in the second chair and laughing with Takeisha, who was probably shy of twenty-five. Small snips of honey-colored hair began falling to the floor. *Just a trim, Takeisha!* I wanted to shout. But I just flipped the pages of the magazine, not reading a thing.

"What about you, Jodi?" Adele whisked the black plastic cape off her pinned and rolled customer and sat her under a hair dryer. "Those split ends should come off—needs conditioning too."

I grimaced. "I know. Next paycheck."

"Adele!" a familiar voice screeched from the back. "Get me outta this chair! I gotta go to the sto'!"

"Just a minute, MaDear!" Adele yelled toward the back. She stopped beside her customer under the dryer. "That too hot?" She adjusted the temperature. "Okay." She headed toward the back room.

Suddenly snapshots of MaDear clicked in my mind like the old View-Master I used to play with as a child. *Click* . . . MaDear charging toward the front door of the hair salon, complaining loudly about the "rotten food in this rest'runt." *Click* . . . MaDear throwing a hairbrush at Denny and clipping him on the forehead when he came to pick me up after my anniversary makeover. *Click* . . . Adele wrestling her spry little mother into the back room where she spent most of her days. *Click* . . . MaDear tied in her wheelchair with the cloth belt from an old bathrobe to keep her from falling out—or escaping—while Adele worked.

The poor lady just needs to get out and about.

The thought had no sooner entered my head than I called out, "Adele, wait!" I tossed the magazine on the coffee table and scurried after her. "Could I . . . do you think she'd let me take her for a walk? Outside, I mean. It's nearly fifty degrees out there."

Adele hesitated. Was she worried that seeing me would once again raise the specter of that lynching long ago? Suddenly, I was worried too. Why MaDear's confused mind thought Denny was the one who'd done that evil deed, we'd probably never know. Adele and MaDear, Denny and I—we'd all suffered last fall because of her delusion. But Denny's willingness to seek her forgiveness for a crime he hadn't committed had brought a measure of peace to the old lady. And to us. Though I was still pondering Denny's contention that we all need to take responsibility for our nation's racist past.

I opened my mouth to say, *"Maybe it's not a good idea."* But a funny look took over Adele's face . . . like relief. "Would you, Jodi? She'd love it. Better take the chair the first time—she can be a handful if she's on the loose."

I grinned. MaDear on the loose . . . I'd bet she'd been a spitfire in her day.

A few minutes later I headed out the front door pushing MaDear's wheelchair, a lap blanket covering her bony knees, both of us wearing our jackets unzipped. I tossed a wave at Amanda, who was getting her hair spritzed and rolled up by this time. She'd have to sit under the dryer, then get a comb-out and spiffy hairdo for her party that afternoon. I had a good forty-five minutes at least.

MaDear twisted in her chair and squinted up at me. "Does I know ya, sugah?"

I leaned forward and gave her a kiss on her upturned face. "Sure you do. I'm your friend Jodi—remember?" As I pushed her slowly down Clark Street's sidewalk, pausing to window-shop everything from little girls' white communion dresses to the tempting smells of a Pakistani café, I had a brilliant idea.

Yada Yada needed to spell R-E-L-I-E-F for Adele—and her mother—by getting MaDear out of the shop regularly. Wouldn't we do it for our own mothers? But how many of us had mothers in town?

Nope. For most of us, MaDear was it.

23

When MaDear and I got back forty-five minutes later, Takeisha was putting the finishing touches on Amanda's "party 'do"—hair swept up on top of her head, sparkle pins peeking out from under a halo of loose ringlets, wispy tendrils kissing her forehead, ears, and the back of her neck.

Gosh. My daughter was beautiful.

But that was nothing compared to how she looked when she came out of the women's restroom at Uptown Community at five minutes to two that afternoon, wearing the dress Edesa Reyes and Delores Enriques had made. She'd elected Edesa to help her into it behind closed doors. "I want it to be a surprise, Mom."

As we all waited for Amanda to come out, I tried to take in the transformation of Uptown Community's second-floor meeting room. Stu had headed up a decorating committee of Yada Yada sisters, stringing blue and gold streamers in graceful twists around all the windows and hugging the edges of the serving tables, temporarily pushed back against the wall. The piñata dangled from the center of the ceiling, just below a cluster of gently waving streamers like the skinny arms of a blue and gold octopus. Below the piñata, a circle of wide-eyed children lusted for its contents.

Ruth and Ben Garfield had brought Yo-Yo, her brothers, and a cake from the Bagel Bakery. *Happy Quinceañera, Amanda!* it said in blue icing amid sprays of blue and yellow sugar roses. Yo-Yo, dressed in a new pair of wheat-colored overalls, got all flustered when I gave her a thank-you hug.

Florida was busy in the church kitchen, sticking fried chicken into an oven to keep hot and taking covered dishes as people arrived. The entire Hickman family was there, including Carl—would wonders never cease?—who immediately gravitated to Peter Douglass when he arrived with Avis, even though the two men had never met before. In fact, *all* the Yada Yada husbands or "significant others" ended up clumping together like a football huddle: Ben Garfield, short and silver haired; Peter Douglass and Mark Smith, both dressed smartly in expensive suits; Carl Hickman, looking pretty fine himself in a sport coat and tie; and Denny, turned out in his best black suit, which brought out the gray in his eyes and flecks in his hair. He looked almost distinguished until he smiled—and then his cheek dimples gave him away.

José's mariachi band was tuning up when we arrived. One of the musicians—a middle-aged man wearing a short, black, embroidered jacket and matching pants—looked familiar. But I was startled when José said, grinning proudly, "My papa, lead guitarist of our *banda!*" Ricardo Enriques? The only time I'd ever seen Delores's husband was in the hospital room when José got shot—a worried, angry, bump on a log. But tuning his large guitar (a *guitarrón*, I was informed later), he seemed a different man: eyes closed, listening to the notes, coaxing them into harmony.

José continued with introductions of the mariachi band, which seemed to be made up mostly of Enriques cousins and uncles on violin, trumpet, and smaller guitars. "Thank you for coming, for playing," I said, shaking Mr. Enriques's hand, hoping I wasn't going to cry. "It means so much." He simply nodded, but for the first time I saw a smile tip the corners of his mouth before he leaned over the guitar once more.

The room filled up with Uptown youth and their curious parents, youth leaders, a few of Amanda's friends from Lane Tech, Patti Sanders and her family from Downers Grove, and every single member of Yada Yada—including Adele, who must have gotten someone to cover the shop and take care of MaDear. I shot her a grateful smile just as Chanda George charged up the stairs at the last minute with Dia, Cheree, and Thomas—and a *man* in tow.

I tried to keep my mouth from dropping open, but I noticed that Florida, leaning out the pass-through window in the kitchen, made no such effort. The man, somewhere in his early thirties, had braided twists that stuck out all over his head, gold chains beneath an open-necked shirt that plunged halfway down his chest, black leather vest, and leather pants. His eyes took in the room with a quick glance before he hunkered down in the last row.

Florida's eyes met mine. *"Who is that?"* she mouthed at me. I shook my head.

But the real showstopper was Chanda herself. Shrugging off a long wool coat with a fur collar—real or faux, it was stunning—out popped Chanda in a bright red suit, lips red, fingertips red, grinning nonstop beneath a gorgeous black pageboy. It had to be a wig; Chanda's hair had never been that long or straight.

Every Yada Yada sister in the room probably had the same thought: *Chanda must've finally gotten her "winnings."*

"I wanna sit up front with Carla and Cheree!" wailed five-year-old Dia, refusing to sit in the back row.

Chanda rolled her eyes. "Don' you make no trouble," she hissed, but kept her own seat anchored next to the mystery man. I tried to catch Denny's eye, hoping he'd go over and meet Mr. Leather Vest. Just then the door to the ladies' room opened and Amanda stepped out. A collective gasp rippled around the room.

Amanda, cheeks flushed, shimmered from head to toe under the fluorescent lights. The filmy off-white dress was breathtaking—simple scoop neckline, little cap sleeves, but the skirt floated in layers to just below her knees, picking up pale blue highlights as it moved. Spontaneously everyone broke out in applause, sending Amanda's face color into the beet-red zone.

"I think," Delores spoke up authoritatively, "it is time to begin." She lined us up, Amanda and parents, followed by José, her *chambelán de honor*, then pairs of *chambelánes* and *damas:* Josh Baxter and Edesa Reyes, Pete Spencer and Patti Sanders, Chris Hickman and Emerald Enriques. The teen escorts sported white dress shirts, black bow ties, and black pants; the young women each wore a pastel party dress, Amanda's choice. They were simple but lovely—nothing like the fancy tuxedoes and off-the-shoulder floor-length dresses I'd seen in pictures.

Denny and I stood on either side of Amanda, waiting for the recorded music we'd practiced with the previous Saturday. Denny caught my eye behind Amanda's head. "Nice dress," he murmured.

"I know. It's lovely," I whispered back.

"Not hers. Yours," he deadpanned.

I simpered at him. It was the first time I'd had a chance to wear the slinky black number he'd given me for my birthday last fall. But

I promptly forgot his compliment when the music started. Instead of the recording, the deep notes of a solo guitar began picking out the familiar hymn Amanda had chosen: "Jesu, Joy of Man's Desiring."

Was that Ricardo? Downsized from his trucking job, still unemployed after six months, drinking too much, uncommunicative (according to Delores) . . . making sweet music at my daughter's *quinceañera?* I didn't dare look anywhere but straight ahead at Pastor Clark, now sure I would never make it to the front without bursting into tears.

But I did. We did. Somehow.

The music ended, and Denny and I sat down on the front row along with the young attendants—young men on one side, young ladies on the other. As Amanda stood alone before Pastor Clark, he personalized a verse from First Timothy: "Amanda, don't let anyone think less of you because you are young. Be an example to all believers in what you teach, in the way you live, in your love, your faith, and your purity." Our pastor then gave a minisermon on each part of the verse: "Amanda, guard the words you speak . . . the life choices you make also affect those around you . . . grow in Christlike love . . . keep a childlike faith in God . . . treasure purity of mind and body."

I was mesmerized. What a wonderful thing for all these young people to hear.

At the end of the sermonette, Pastor Clark glanced our way. "Denny?" And our tall, gangly pastor sat down.

Denny stood up and walked to Amanda's side. She turned and gave her daddy a brilliant smile as he took her left hand. *This must be what they've been plotting the last couple of weeks.* For a few moments, Denny couldn't speak. He kept swallowing, and the corners of his mouth twitched. Finally he said, "Amanda, I look forward to walking you down the aisle someday and giving up this hand I'm holding to a very lucky man who wants you to be his wife. But that day's not today—"

Laughter tittered around the room, and I heard Florida's voice, "Hallelujah! Ya got that right!" which sparked more laughter. I wished I had the guts to shout, *"Amen to that!"* but I'm sure Amanda was glad I didn't.

Amanda was giggling yet trying to regain a serious look. Denny cleared his throat. "Though today, Amanda, *is* an important day. You are on the verge of womanhood. And I have to admit, you are"—he swallowed again and blinked rapidly—"lovely."

"Say it, Denny!" a masculine voice cried—was that Peter Douglass?—and suddenly everyone was clapping and grinning, even Amanda's *corte de honor.* My eyes blurred, but I couldn't steal Denny's handkerchief as I usually did when I cried in public. *Why in the world didn't I bring some tissues?* Suddenly Stu's hand reached over my shoulder and dropped a pack into my lap.

The clapping gave Denny a moment to recover. Now he was smiling big. "Because I want all God's best for you, Amanda, I am giving you a promise ring to wear." He dug into his suit coat pocket and drew out a silver ring with a stone in it. He glanced sheepishly at the crowded room that now seemed to be holding its breath. "Don't worry—I'm not putting Amanda on the spot. This is something she wants to do." More laughter.

Denny slid the ring onto Amanda's ring finger of her left hand. "This is a *peridot,* the 'evening emerald,' your birthstone. One day you will wear a diamond on this hand. But today, do you accept this promise ring, a symbol of your promise to God to keep yourself pure—okay, let's say it, a *virgin*—as a gift to God and to your future husband?"

For a long second, no one breathed. "I do," Amanda said clearly—then threw her arms around her father's neck.

The entire room erupted around me. I gave up all pretense of holding back tears and dabbed frantically at my now-running nose. Cheers and clapping went on for what seemed like a long, long time. I glanced at Amanda's young male escorts and saw both Josh and José grinning and clapping madly. My heart seemed to flop like a bass on a hook and landed in my throat. *Oh thank You, Lord Jesus, thank You, thank You,* I cried inside, even though I knew good and well it wasn't time to stop praying about the temptations that faced my children—all these children.

After Denny sat down, Edesa read from Psalm 121: "I lift up my eyes to the hills; where does my help come from? My help comes from the Lord"—after which Josh went up to pray a blessing over his sister. Suddenly I had an awful thought. *Their grandparents ought to be here! Did I even send them an invitation?* But I knew the problem was my own resistance: I'd had no idea how meaningful this *quinceañera* would be.

After the prayer, Pastor Clark put a padded chair in the center of the six-inch-high platform at the front of the room and motioned for Amanda to sit there. He arched his eyebrows at Denny and me expectantly.

What? My mind scrambled. *What comes next?* I'd completely forgotten.

Amanda mouthed the word *"Shoes!"* at us. Oh, right! The shoes!

I dug under my chair for the shoebox I'd put there earlier, and Denny and I approached Amanda in the chair. Kneeling down like a subject before the queen, Denny took off the flats Amanda had been wearing, while I opened the box and lifted out the sling-back high heels Amanda had chosen—the traditional symbol, we'd been told, of taking off childhood and putting on young womanhood.

High heels securely in place, Amanda stood with only the slightest wobble and gave Denny and me each a hug before we turned to face the rows of our friends beaming back at us. Avis and Peter, standing side by side, looking for all the world like a couple straight out of *Ebony* . . . Hoshi, all smiles, holding Marcus and Michael Sisulu-Smith by the hand . . . the Hickman family still all in one piece, at least today . . . Adele nodding her approval . . .

Good thing the mariachi band struck up a rousing recessional, because I couldn't say a word.

THE PLATTERS OF CHICKEN, coleslaw, *carnitas* wrapped in corn tortillas, rice and beans, chopped salad, and Adele's greens with smoky ham hocks disappeared in alarming amounts at the table seating Amanda's *corte de honor*, but there seemed to be enough for everybody. The cake was cut to cheers and sticky fingers, then the tables were pushed aside so the dancing could begin.

The *chambelánes* and *damas* lined up facing each other for the traditional waltz as Amanda and José took a turn down the middle. All over the room, younger children watched their big brothers and sisters throw arms up, clasp hands, turn, and swirl to the guitars and trumpet music. Edesa was such a good sport to join Amanda's "court" of teenagers. *Hmm.* Had she had a *quinceañera* when she'd turned fifteen in Honduras?

The traditional waltz was followed by Denny dancing with his daughter, and I thought my face might crack open if I smiled any bigger. José picked up a small Mexican drum and added some smart percussion as the mariachi music got more raucous. Josh came and pulled me to my feet, but I lasted about five minutes before the rod in my leg started aching, so I fell into a chair, laughing.

Carla appeared at my side and tugged on my skirt. "Ms. Jodi?" She crooked her finger as if wanting to tell me a secret. I bent down till my ear was even with her lips. "I want to be queen when I'm fifteen—like Amanda."

I grinned and gave her a hug. "You're already a princess, Carla."

The music stopped long enough for the younger set to be blind-folded and take turns swinging at the piñata with a broomstick amid screams of encouragement. Cedric Hickman whacked it good, and the rain of candies from the broken piñata caused a near riot, but eventually each child had a fist and cheek full of candy.

As the music resumed, I sat off to the side, giving my aching leg a rest, trying to take it all in. Ricardo Enriques played his huge guitar with a big smile and dancing eyes. The man was a musician, not a trucker! . . . Peter Douglass, Mark Smith, and Denny seemed to be in a serious discussion with Carl Hickman in one corner. *Hmm. Wonder what that's all about?* . . . Amanda was dancing—again—with José . . .

I massaged my leg, wishing the pain would go away, but Geraldine Wilkins-Porter's face intruded into my thoughts, as if she had just come up the stairs, taking in our party. The noise around me dimmed, and I imagined standing in her place, watching the party through her eyes. My own heart was full of joy; what was in her heart?

Pain. A hundred times greater than my stupid leg. Her Jamal would never dress up and dance with abandon like these teenage boys, never flirt with his sweetheart. She would never watch him get his high school diploma or start his first job . . . never lecture him about drugs . . . never give away her heart at his wedding or kiss his babies . . .

I sat very still, as if time had stopped in the space around my chair. I expected to feel the familiar fear tighten inside of me whenever I thought of Jamal and Hakim's mother, but it didn't come. Why was I afraid of her? Because she was angry—angry at me because I had killed her oldest son. My fear kept me at a distance, protected me from being consumed by her anger. But wouldn't I be angry too? As a mother I should know! Anger masked our private fears, our sorrows. Beneath her anger, Geraldine Wilkins-Porter was grieving her loss, a loss no parent should have to bear. More than that, I suddenly understood that the armor of her anger made her sorrow somehow bearable, enabled her to get through each day.

I watched Amanda dancing with José . . . watched Josh, his shaved head bobbing side by side with Chris and Pete as they danced to the music. My heart was bursting with gratitude . . . and yet full of sorrow. Geraldine's sorrow—

"Sista Jodee!" Chanda plopped down in the chair beside me. "Mi mon—he's one good dancer! See? Dancin' with Stu."

Startled out of my thoughts, I glanced at Mr. Leather Vest gyrating in the center of the floor. Stu, laughing, was trying to imitate his steps.

"I see. Where did you meet him, Chanda?"

"*Meet* 'im?" She laughed, her spirit light, as though she might just float off the chair. "Dat's my baby's daddy! He's back!"

24

ia's daddy? Back? "Uh, I thought . . . but you said . . ."
Didn't Chanda say her "baby's daddy" had a new girlfriend and they'd gone off on a cruise or something? She'd
been livid, because he was always telling her he had no money for
child support.

Chanda tilted her nose up and sniffed. "Oh, *that*. He got tired of
her, saw what he was missin'. Says he's home for good now."

Oh, please. The guy probably heard about Chanda winning the
lottery and came running. "Chanda, are you sure? I mean, money
can do funny things to people."

Her eyes flashed. "This ain't about no money, Sista Jodee! De
mon is Dia's daddy, after all. Ain't you happy about that?"

"Yes, of course, Chanda! But . . ." I let it drop and instead leaned
over and gave her a hug. "I hope it all works out, Chanda." I wanted
to be happy for her, but I smelled a rat.

The official *quinceañera* broke up around five o'clock, but the kids
still wanted to party. Josh was the only one with a driver's license, so

Denny gave him back his car keys—it'd been seven days anyway. The *Quinceañera* and her *corte de honor* all piled into our minivan and went out for pizza. Minus Edesa, that is, who begged off, laughing, saying she was done being a teenager for a day, *muchas gracias.*

Adele had stayed for a while, but I'd seen her leaving just after the piñata rained candy all over the floor. "Adele!" I'd scurried over and caught her at the top of the stairs. "I was supposed to ask you when I made Amanda's appointment—and forgot, of course. Since your sister's out of town, could Yada Yada meet at your place tomorrow? You know, bring the prayer group to you since it's hard for you to get care for MaDear right now."

Adele nodded, pulling a snug fake fur hat down over her short 'fro, which was growing out to its natural black and silver color. "Stu already told me. Nice party, Jodi. You and Denny have a right to be proud of that girl."

My smile tightened. *Good ol' Stu, covering for me again.* "Oh. Okay. See you tomorrow then."

But I could hardly complain. Stu and Florida and Delores and Edesa—everybody, really—stayed to help clean up after the kids left. But as Avis put on her coat she murmured, "I won't be at Yada Yada tomorrow night, Jodi. Peter, he, well . . ." She looked a little flustered.

"What? You're going to miss Yada Yada for *Peter?* Hey, this *is* getting serious."

"Oh, stop." Avis batted a hand at me, like a pesky fly. "He's giving a dinner for new employees at the Palmer House tomorrow night and asked me to attend with him. Doesn't mean anything." She lowered her voice. "Peter hates social gatherings, doesn't know how to do small talk. He asked me to come for moral support."

I grinned. "Like I said."

WHEN WE ARRIVED FOR WORSHIP the next morning at Uptown, all traces of Amanda's *quinceañera* had disappeared. Chairs were lined up in neat rows, bent in a half circle; Josh was behind the soundboard; and Amanda was wearing jeans again, like most of the other teenagers. Avis was there, but not Peter; Florida and Carla were there, but not Carl and the boys; the music was definitely words-on-an-overhead contemporary; and the temperature outside had dropped a good twenty-five degrees from last week's high of fifty.

Life had returned to normal.

I was so wrung out after our big day that I had considered not going to Yada Yada that evening. But with Avis not coming and the group meeting at Adele's after so many months, it seemed important to get off my duff. Stu offered to drive. Just as well; that meant Josh could drive himself and Amanda to youth group.

"Poor Denny," I murmured, giving him a kiss on top of his head as I left the house. "Home all alone."

"Shh." He clicked the remote volume up a few notches. "Did you hear about that nightclub fire yesterday in Rhode Island?"

I beat a hasty retreat. One look at the pictures of bodies stacked two and three deep in front of a chained exit had already threatened to give me a new nightmare—only days after a similar nightclub stampede had killed nearly two dozen right here in Chicago.

Another good reason to keep my kids' curfew on lockdown.

On the way to Adele's apartment, Stu was abnormally quiet. "Thanks for all your help with Amanda's party," I said, trying to lighten the mood. "The piñata idea was great."

"Oh. Sure." More silence.

I tried again. "What happened when you tried to get reassigned to Becky Wallace's little boy's foster case? Any luck?"

Her face twitched. "Haven't heard yet. Lots of red tape. I don't know—I'm thinking of withdrawing the request."

I stared at Stu as she nosed into a parking space on Adele's block just in front of a fire hydrant. That didn't sound like Stu! When had she ever backed away from a fight—especially with DCFS? I eyed the space behind the Celica as we got out. Looked less than the required eight feet from a hydrant, if you asked me. Which she hadn't.

Adele's first-floor apartment had the blinds drawn in every window, just like the last time we were there. Made me feel claustrophobic. MaDear was parked in a large overstuffed chair with a light blanket tucked tightly over her lap and into the cushions, seemingly oblivious to the stream of Yada Yada sisters collecting in Adele's compact living room.

Seeing MaDear, I remembered my idea that Yada Yada could maybe take turns getting MaDear out and about while Adele was working at the shop. But it might put people on the spot to talk about it in front of Adele and MaDear. *Shoot. I'll probably have to e-mail or call everyone individually.*

As people arrived, everyone gushed about how fantastic Amanda's *quinceañera* had been. "I think," I said, eyeing Delores sheepishly, "we didn't do it up quite as fancy as a traditional Mexican *quinceañera*—I hear *that's* a party."

"Not to worry," Ruth sniffed. "What Denny did? With that promise ring? Made me cry, it did."

"Yeah," said Yo-Yo. "Way cool. Wish my dad had done somethin' like that—if he'd stuck around, that is. But"—she shrugged—"I'm glad Pete and Jerry saw it. They respect Denny."

"Yeah. My kids too. Where's Avis?" Florida flopped into a corner of Adele's couch.

I cleared my throat dramatically. "Out with Peter Douglass. Employee dinner. At the Palmer House."

"Oooo," said Ruth. "Fancy. Went to a bar mitzvah there once."

"What's the Palmer House?" Yo-Yo asked.

I caught my surprise before it surfaced. Yo-Yo had lived in the city her entire life and still never heard of Chicago's premier hotel?

"A Chicago hotel," Adele filled in.

Yo-Yo shrugged. "Oh."

"So who's leading this meeting?" Florida wanted to know.

I half-expected Stu to say, *"We don't need a leader just for a prayer meeting,"* but she didn't rise to the bait. In fact, she hadn't said much since we came in.

"Nony, will you lead us?" Delores asked sweetly.

"Oh, I don't—"

"Nony!" several voices chorused. "You're it!"

I realized I hadn't really gotten a chance to talk to Nony at the *quinceañera,* even though she'd brought her entire beautiful family, all dressed up in the outfits they'd brought back from South Africa. Tonight she was dressed simply in slacks and a sweater, though her hair was still braided in long extensions.

"All right then," she said quietly. "Are we waiting for anyone else?"

"Chanda's not here—did anybody hear from her? Did she need a ride?" I immediately felt guilty, since we lived as close to her as anyone.

"She knows she can call someone," Stu said. "Probably busy with her new man."

"Not exactly new," I offered. "Dia's daddy. He's back."

"What? They still married?" Yo-Yo asked.

I squirmed. Not that I knew for sure, but I never got the impression Chanda had been married to any of her kids' daddies.

"After her money, he is," Ruth muttered. Ha. There it was. Out in the middle of the room. The exact thing we were all thinking.

"Sisters," said Nony gently, "let's not gossip about Chanda. She can tell us what she wants us to know. There are big changes in her life, regardless of what we think about how this money came about. We need to pray for our sister."

Okay. Guess I needed that. God still had some work to do corralling all my thoughts and feelings and judgments and channeling them into prayers. "Thank you, Nony. You're right."

"Who all these people?" MaDear's shrill voice cut into our circle. "Adele? Where you at, girl? Get 'em outta here!"

Adele rose. "You go on, Nony. I'll give her something to do." Adele picked up a jar of buttons and took them over to her mother. "Here, MaDear. Can you find me some black buttons? I need as many as you can find."

"Humph." MaDear dumped the buttons into her lap and started to poke through them.

Sheesh. Adele deserves a medal. She has the patience of Job.

Nony opened her Bible. "I'm reading from Amos, chapter five," she said. Her melodic voice took on an urgency. "Seek good, not evil, that you may live. Then the Lord God Almighty will be with you . . ."

At least it wasn't ye old King James. I quickly turned in my own modern-language translation and tried to find where she was reading. "Hate evil, love good; maintain justice in the courts," she continued. Then she skipped to the end of the chapter. "I hate, I despise your religious feasts! I cannot stand your assemblies! . . . Away with the noise of your songs! I will not listen to the music of your harps. But let justice roll on like a river, righteousness like a never-failing stream!"

Adele's living room was suddenly quiet, except for the *ping, ping* of MaDear's buttons as they dropped into the jar. *What an odd scripture to read.* I reread the last verses in my own Bible. *"I hate, I despise your religious feasts; I cannot stand your assemblies"? What's that about? Aren't we trying to learn to worship here? Does Nony think we're off track, and God is displeased with us?*

I looked up—and saw tears streaming down Nony's face. Someone handed her a tissue. After a few moments, she looked apologetic—and then the tears started again. "I'm sorry, I'm sorry . . . forgive me, but . . . oh, sisters! I don't know what to do!" she wailed. "I sit here in comfort, taking my freedoms for granted, while my people in South Africa are still suffering from years of injustice! I am so blessed—how can I not share my blessings with my own people? Ignorance abounds! Young people, mothers, fathers—all dying of AIDS by the thousands. And yet, I cannot go, cannot ease the suffering in my heart unless I leave my family—because my husband will not go!"

25

No one moved. *Oh God! Where is Avis when we need her?* I had no idea what to say to Nony. I could feel the pain in her heart—but I understood Mark's reality too. He was the breadwinner, he had a good job, and he was doing what was on *his* heart—teaching history to students like Hoshi. To be a Christian professor on the staff of a major university was a ministry in itself.

Florida broke the silence. "Now you know I ain't been a lot of places, but I think I got one thing figured out. People and problems—they pretty much the same everywhere, know what I'm sayin'? Maybe God is callin' you back to Africa, Nony; I don't know. I jus' know what's wrong over there is wrong here too. Maybe you can do somethin' about that while you waitin'."

Nony stared at the floor. When she spoke again, her voice was small, defensive. "I know. But God has given me a special burden for my homeland—"

"Girl, you carry that burden like you gotta carry it all by yourself! An' that ain't the way it's s'posed to be!" Florida started paging through her Bible. "Ain't there some verse in here about lettin' God carry our burdens?"

I knew that verse—but could I find it? I flipped to the concordance in the back of my Bible, but Delores beat me to it. "First Peter, chapter five," she said. "'Casting all your cares on Him, for He cares for you.'"

"The apostle Paul said to 'carry one another's burdens,'" Nony said stubbornly.

Yo-Yo snorted. "What is this, Battle of the Bible?"

I shook my head. "No, 'cause they're both right." My heart ached for Nony; I knew how much she and Mark struggled with this issue. Maybe they just didn't have to be so stuck. "I . . . I know the burden you carry for your people comes from your heart, Nony, and I believe God put it there." Nony's grateful look made me braver. "But you just said you don't know what to do. What Florida's saying is maybe you don't have to be in South Africa to do something about AIDS, or even to help your people. Start now. Here. In Chicago."

"Like 'bloom where you're planted'?" Yo-Yo asked. "Is that in the Bible?"

"Somebody say yes," Ruth jibed. "Then maybe she'll read the Book for herself looking for it!" That cracked the sober silence and got a laugh. Even Nony smiled and blew her nose.

Stu spoke up for the first time. "I know a lot of organizations that could use—"

"I'm sure you do," Adele cut in. "But I think Nony's got the point and needs some time to think about it. Maybe we can all pray on it with you, Nony."

"Yes, please," Nony whispered. "Would you, Adele?"

And so Adele prayed as those next to Nony reached for her hands, a prayer full of compassion for our sister Nonyameko and her longing to "go home" to South Africa, thanking God for the burden He'd put on her heart and asking God to make it plain how He wanted to use her right here, right now. "And, Jesus, show this prayer group how we can help carry that burden with Nony," Adele added. "There's a lot of hurting people out there—plenty enough to go around."

"Amen to that!" said Florida.

Spontaneous praise started to bubble up around the group, even from Nony, but MaDear's piercing voice rose above the rest. "Adele! I gotta pee! Adele!" Her voice dropped to a mutter. "Where is that girl? Cain't never find her when I need her."

Adele scurried over to her mother in the scuffs she wore around the house. "You guys go on—this is goin' to take awhile." She pulled her mother up out of the chair, and mother and daughter shuffled out of the room.

I couldn't believe it! The perfect opportunity had dropped right in our lap.

"Sisters, wait. Before we move on . . ." I leaned forward and in a low voice recounted my experience on Saturday of taking MaDear out for a walk and the idea God had planted in my spirit. "If we all took a turn getting her out, even once a month, that'd be . . . what? Two to three times a week!"

Yo-Yo shrugged. "I could do it once a month."

I nodded. "Some of you live farther away; it'd be a sacrifice . . ."

"*Si,*" said Delores. "But that is what it means to carry each other's burdens. And if we carry it together, it's not such a big burden."

"Offering to sit here at home so Adele can get out in the evening—that would be good too," Ruth added.

And so we decided. We conspired not to tell Adele, but we

agreed to coordinate somehow so we didn't all show up at the shop the same week. I expected Stu to offer—but it was Hoshi who raised her hand.

"I will keep the calendar for all," she said in her ever-better English. "It is my honor to be able to serve someone's mother since . . ." She looked down at her hands and did not finish. But Nony, having regained her composure, reached out and laid a hand over Hoshi's. I winced. How easily I forgot the rejection Hoshi felt from her own mother. There had been no letter, no phone call, nothing since that fateful visit when Hoshi had told her parents she had decided to be a Christian. The same visit when Hoshi had brought her mother to the Yada Yada Prayer Group, and we'd all been terrorized by Becky Wallace—the Bandana Woman—who'd wanted our money and jewelry to support her heroin habit.

By the time Adele came back with MaDear, we were talking about whether to write a letter to the parole board at Lincoln Correctional Center on Becky Wallace's behalf. A few sisters admitted frankly they'd forgotten about it and hadn't been praying about what to do.

Yo-Yo cradled her knees with her arms. "Yeah. It's easy to forget the dudes in prison—outta sight, outta mind."

"Dudette, in this case," I said in jest, but no one laughed.

"What do you think, Yo-Yo?" Stu prompted. "You spent time in prison. Wouldn't you have been grateful for early parole?"

"You bet! 'Cept I wasn't at Yada Yada the day the chick robbed all you guys. The victims . . . you the ones gotta decide if you wanna step up to the plate. This is just as much about you as about her."

Silence again, except for the *ping, ping* of MaDear's buttons. What did Yo-Yo mean exactly, that this was "as much about us" as about Becky Wallace? *Arrgh!* Why did Avis have to be absent tonight? We could use some of her wisdom about now.

But she wasn't. *Grow up, Jodi. Be honest about your own thoughts and feelings. That's all you can do.*

I didn't much relish looking like a fool, yet I broke the silence. "Okay. I have to admit that my feelings toward Becky Wallace have changed since we've been to see her and talked with her in person. Part of that is knowing she's safely locked up at Lincoln. I get nervous thinking about her back out on the street, in *my* neighborhood. I like her best right where she is."

There. I'd said it.

"Good for Jodi," Adele said. "At least you're being honest. Have to admit, I feel the same way. Haven't been to see this woman, seen too many strung out just like her, don't hold nothin' against her now that I got my ring back—though I really don't want that woman back in my face."

I nearly fell off my chair. Adele Skuggs agreed with *me?*

"Maybe ever'body who was there that night should say what they feel," said Florida. "Get it all out on the table. Then see what God wants ta do with it. Me? You know how I feel. There but for the grace of God goes Florida Hickman—oh! Thank ya, Jesus!" And we waited a few moments while she did some crying and praising. She brushed away tears with the back of her hand. "God gave me another chance, so who am I to stand in the way of someone else getting their chance? I say, let's write the letter."

I could've felt chastised by Florida's answer, but for some reason I didn't. She said we should each say how we feel. I was glad I went first, though, because if I had to follow Florida I probably would've tried to figure out the "right" thing to say.

Ruth spoke up next. "Is asking for early parole the right thing? Is she ready? That's what I'm wondering, it is."

Delores and Edesa passed, since they hadn't been there that night either. All eyes turned to Hoshi.

"My sister," Nony said gently, "if anyone was a victim that night, it was you and your mother." That was the truth. I could hardly imagine subjecting my own mother to what Mrs. Takahashi—a visitor to this country—had been through that night. And the fallout for Hoshi . . . Her parents blamed it all on her forsaking the Shinto religion.

Hoshi nodded thoughtfully. After ten months of Yada Yada, she was still the quietest one among us. She had not wanted to visit Becky Wallace at first—who could blame her!—then surprised all of us by going to the prison a few months ago and telling Becky Wallace that she forgave her. The petition on B. W.'s behalf had actually been Hoshi's idea, but I could sure understand if she was having second thoughts.

"For the last two weeks, I am thinking about sending this petition." Hoshi's voice was surprisingly assertive. "I don't know about 'is she ready.' Maybe that is for the parole board to decide? But what Yo-Yo said is true—this is just as much about us. In Asian culture, we do not focus just on the individual, but on the responsibility of the whole community. So I've been asking myself: Have I really forgiven her? How far does that forgiveness go? What role does my forgiveness—our forgiveness—play in redeeming this woman to once again be part of the community?"

How far does that forgiveness go?

We all looked at each other. Nony said, "I think I have my answer. I would like to sign such a petition or letter or however we want to do it—and then pray over it, commit it to God, whose Word is a lamp unto our feet and a light unto our paths. Because Scripture says that if we commit our works unto the Lord, our thoughts will be established."

"You preachin' now, sister!" Florida crowed. Heads nodded around the circle.

"Then it's agreed?" said Stu. "If so, we should write a letter tonight and sign it while we're all together—this shouldn't wait two weeks till Yada Yada meets again." She jumped up. "Adele? Can I use your computer for a few minutes? I'll just type up something brief, and we can sign it tonight."

"But we don't even know who to send it to," I protested.

But Adele and Stu were already on their way to Adele's bedroom, where she kept her computer. "Details," Stu called over her shoulder.

Again we all looked at each other. What now?

"Let's wait to pray until Stu gets back with the letter," Nony suggested. "Hoshi, do you want to take names of volunteers for—you know." Nony glanced toward MaDear, who was still poking through the buttons. *Ping . . . ping . . . ping.*

I dug out my calendar from my tote bag and volunteered for a Saturday—no way could I baby-sit MaDear during the week, not with lesson plans. But it wouldn't be that hard to add it to my Saturday errands. *Reading . . . would she like someone to read to her?*

Adele and Stu came back in five minutes with a draft of a letter. Stu cleared her throat. "'To whom it may concern: We the undersigned, all belonging to a women's prayer group that was victimized by Becky Wallace'—I'll have to insert her prison number here—'on September 1, 2002, are writing to request that Ms. Wallace be considered for early parole in accordance with the state's desire to reduce prison crowding. Several of us have visited Ms. Wallace on three different occasions and believe she deserves this opportunity to straighten out her life. She also has a two-year-old son who needs his mother. Sincerely . . .' and I left room for our signatures."

"Addresses and telephone numbers too," Nony said.

And so we signed. The only other "victim" not present was Avis. I offered to take it to her at school the next day for her signature and return it to Stu to mail.

"Anything else before we pray?" Nony asked. Stu and Delores waved their hands. "Stu?"

"Just a reminder," Stu said. "We agreed to visit St. John's Lutheran next Sunday. I'll e-mail everybody the address and time, okay?" I grabbed my calendar again and saw I'd already written it in: first Sunday in March.

Delores was next. *"Perdóneme,* I know it's time to pray—but I have the most wonderful idea, and I don't want to forget. Avis and Peter—it's beginning to look serious, *si?"*

That brought knowing snickers and joking comments began to fly. "Whassup, Delores?" Yo-Yo pushed.

Delores's dark eyes were bright with excitement. "Edesa and I, while we sewed the dress for sweet Amanda, thought it would be wonderful to make a *manta* for Avis—a friendship quilt—and give it to her when she gets married."

"When?" I burst out laughing. "Oh, you guys are rushing her now. Shouldn't we wait for an announcement or something?"

Delores shook her head. "Those two, they're past the age for a long engagement. If they decide to do it—*bam!*—two weeks and they're married. We wouldn't have time to put together a quilt."

"I dunno nuthin' about quiltin'," Yo-Yo protested. Murmurs around the room agreed with her.

"You don't have to," Delores said, grinning ear to ear. "Here's my idea . . ."

26

*T*emperatures fell below zero that last week of February—but not before I caught a nasty germ that dehibernated during the previous week's high of fifty degrees, thinking it must be spring. My head tingled and my throat felt scratchy while we practiced for the all-school assembly on Monday, and by Monday night I crawled into bed feeling like week-old garbage.

"You're not going to school, are you?" Denny asked the next morning as I packed my tote bag.

"It's just a cold," I muttered, though staying home was exactly what I felt like doing. But what teacher stayed home just because she had a headache and a scratchy throat? I'd gotten through a lot of school days tanked up on Tylenol and throat lozenges. Besides, this week was the all-school assembly we'd been working on so hard! Not to mention I still had to pick up the petition letter from Avis. She'd been busy all day Monday, and I'd had to leave it on her desk with a note. Stu was probably upset that it wasn't mailed yet; I didn't dare leave it another whole day.

Denny pressed. "Don't forget what the doc said—you gotta be extra careful about colds and flu since they took out your spleen. Maybe you ought to call the doctor."

I'd forgotten about the "be careful" lecture from Dr. Lewinski after the accident. Except for the stiffness in my leg each morning, I'd been pretty healthy since school started. "It's just a cold, Denny. I can't call the doctor and say, hey, I've got a headache . . ." Denny narrowed his eyes at me. I felt too weary to argue. "Okay, tell you what— if I start feeling worse or my nose starts running, I'll come home."

Somewhat mollified, Denny gave me a ride to school, which helped. Yet my third graders must've picked up on my muddleheadedness, because it seemed like I was breaking up fights or yelling at the kids not to yell or counting to five all day. *What I wouldn't give to have my student teacher back,* I moaned to myself, flopping on the couch in the teachers' lounge for five minutes during lunch.

Then I remembered the letter to the parole board and struggled up again. Better see if Avis was around and get it from her while I could.

I stopped in the school office and saw Avis on the phone through her open door. She waved me in, still on the phone, and handed me the letter. I started to leave, but she said to her caller, "Wait—can you hold on a minute?" She put her hand over the receiver. "Jodi. You look awful."

"Thanks a lot."

"You sick? You should go home."

I shrugged listlessly. "Too late to get a sub. Only got a couple more hours. Hakim's got his session with Ms. Gray right after lunch; I'd hate to not be here when he gets back. But thanks for this." I waved the letter. "Stu's got a burr under her saddle to get this off. Not sure what the rush is."

"I'm sorry I missed the discussion and prayer. Talked to Nony last night—sounded like a full evening."

"Yeah." Under normal circumstances, I'd ask how her Palmer House date went, but I didn't have the energy. "Oh. Did Nony remind you about our church visit next Sunday—St. John's Lutheran?"

"Yes. I'm supposed to lead worship next Sunday at Uptown. I can probably trade with someone, though. Shouldn't be a problem."

"Okay." I turned to go.

"Jodi? Stay home tomorrow. That's an order. Tell the secretary on the way out you need a sub." She turned back to the phone. "Peter? . . . Sorry. Had to take care of something. . . . What?" She laughed. "Of course you play second fiddle when you call me at work!"

I suppressed a grin in spite of my headache. Delores was right on the money with that friendship quilt idea.

AS IT TURNED OUT, I stayed home Wednesday and Thursday, with a temperature of 101. I did call Dr. Lewinski, who gave me the usual song and dance: plenty of rest and fluids, call him if the fever lasted more than three days. Avis, bless her, said she'd practice with my class for the assembly.

I half-expected Stu to take over the Baxter household if she knew I was sick—but all she did was pop in Wednesday evening for five minutes to bring me some flowers. "Sorry to hear you're sick, Jodi. Let me know if there's anything I can do, okay?" At the moment I was having a coughing fit and could only nod my head. It wasn't likely I would *ask* Stu—but I was actually disappointed she didn't show up with a pot of chicken noodle soup or even sit for a while. Stu wasn't as predictable as I'd thought—in fact, since she'd moved in, she was sometimes downright moody.

But by Thursday evening I felt a lot better. Friday morning my temp was normal, and I made it back to school for the all-school assembly. I was glad I did, because my third-grade class did an awesome job reporting on the life of Mary McLeod Bethune—even got a standing ovation from the teachers and parents who attended. I was so proud of them! . . . until we got back to the classroom, that is. Maybe it was the letdown after the assembly, or because the kids had been confined inside all week because of the sub-zero weather. Or because they'd had two days with a substitute teacher, and it was Friday to boot. Whatever. But I practically had to peel my charges off the wall and tie them in their seats to get anything done that afternoon.

I finally gave up trying to review simple fractions, took them to the gym and ran them around four times, then brought them back to the classroom and read three chapters of *Little House in the Big Woods*. It might as well have been a story about Mars from the blank expressions of kids who had no idea what "venison" or a "butter churn" were.

My headache was back, big-time.

Well, at least it's the weekend, I thought gratefully, fishing the mail from our box on the front porch and letting myself in the door with my key. Gas bill, bank statement, credit card bill, junk mail, junk mail . . . and a fat envelope from Delores Enriques. I was tempted to rip it open, but Willie Wonka wanted out the back door—now!— zero degrees or not. Once I'd popped two extra-strength Tylenol, let Wonka back in, and had a mug of hot tea to warm my hands and throat, I slit open the envelope and pulled out its contents: a square of muslin material about twelve-by-twelve inches, several skeins of colorful embroidery thread, and a sheet of instructions.

"Dear Yada Yada sisters," the paper said, and proceeded to give tips on how to personalize and embroider the enclosed quilt square. *Embroider?* That was daunting enough, but . . . make up my own design? *Sheesh.*

The only thing that made sense to me at the moment was to crawl into bed and pull the quilt over my head.

DENNY AND AMANDA DID THE GROCERY SHOPPING on Saturday—always a risk, because they came home with things like jicama (which I had no idea how to cook) or arugula (way too expensive). I wasn't complaining, though. A day to lounge around the house and drink gallons of hot tea with lemon and honey—hey, the doc said plenty of rest and fluids!—did wonders for my spirit, and probably my body too.

I invited the rest of my family to go with Yada Yada to St. John's Lutheran Sunday morning, but they weren't interested. "Don't think you ought to go either, Jodi," said Denny. "Just stay home and rest."

I considered that for about ten seconds. There was a point when "rest" began to feel like "stir-crazy." "Stu said the service is only an hour," I pointed out, "and I promise I won't go anywhere, do anything, no cooking, no cleaning, no laundry this afternoon—I'll just veg out in the recliner with the TV remote."

"Huh. I'd like to see *that*. Except for the remote. Big game on."

"Besides," I called after him as Denny and the kids headed out the door, "Monday is a holiday. Pulaski Day, remember?" But they were gone.

Stu rang the doorbell at ten thirty, and we drove the twenty minutes to St. John's Lutheran in her sporty Celica. She wasn't very talkative, which was fine with me, because my throat still felt raw—yet I did yell "Stop!" when she almost ran through a red light. A few minutes later I had to say, "You can turn right on red, Stu," when she sat at a red light with her right turn signal blinking and a car beeping behind her.

"Guess I'm nervous," she said, giving me an apologetic grin. "Haven't been back to St. John's for almost two years."

"Why nervous?" If we went back to visit the church we'd left in Downers Grove a year and a half ago, it'd feel like a family reunion.

"Oh, I don't know. Don't want to have to explain anything." She pulled into the parking lot of a large stone church building in one of the older Chicago neighborhoods. Don't know what I expected—Cadillacs and Mercedes? Maybe a few Lincoln Town Cars. But the parking lot was full of Toyotas, Nissans, minivans, and a few SUVs. Nice cars, though not high end.

"People change," Stu said. "It's water under the bridge." She gave a short laugh. "Anyway. It was my idea for Yada Yada to visit here, wasn't it?"

The sub-zero temperatures had warmed up to the high twenties, but we scurried across the crowded parking lot and into the warm foyer of the church anyway. I was wearing nylons and heels, expecting a more "dress-up" church—and was surprised to see a lot of women wearing pantsuits and men wearing slacks and sweaters or sports coats. No fancy hats. Only a few suits and ties.

A man and a woman wearing *Greeter* badges shook our hands and said, "Hello! Welcome!" but didn't ask our names or anything. Nobody seemed to recognize Stu. Florida, Delores, and Edesa were already there, *sans* kids, waving us over. We figured five Yada Yadas were enough of a critical mass to go sit down together in a nice wooden pew with a long, padded seat cushion. We spread out, saving room for others who might come.

I gazed up at the cheerful, vaulted sanctuary. Modern stained-glass windows (no biblical scenes or ancient Latin words) let in bright colorful light, making the church feel warm in spite of the winter outside. Banners hung between the windows, saying things like *Rejoice!* and *Hallelujah!* Organ pipes filled the center of the wall beyond the platform and a beautiful oak pulpit sat off to the side, leaving the platform open except for a couple of oak armchairs with burgundy padded cushions. I was wondering vaguely where the choir sat—or if St. John's had a choir—when Avis, Nony, and Hoshi appeared in the aisle and we all scrunched closer to make room. A few moments later Ruth scooted into the pew behind us, with Adele and Chanda and Chanda's three kids decked out like it was Easter Sunday right on their heels.

I did a quick head count, just as a deep resonant voice from somewhere in the back called out, "All rise!" The triumphant tones of the organ suddenly filled the room like majestic trumpets, and an invisible choir up in the balcony began singing the processional.

All the Yada Yada sisters except Yo-Yo had shown up at St. John's Lutheran.

27

So how was it?" Denny asked, bringing me a sandwich on a paper plate. True to my word, I had come home from church—beating Denny and the kids by thirty minutes, *heh heh*—shed my coat, hat, and mittens, and flopped into the recliner with a box of tissues and the biggest mug I could find of hot tea.

"Short. One hour, start to finish . . . mm, thanks." I sank my teeth into the Dagwood sandwich, piled high with shaved chicken from Dominick's deli (*à la* Denny and Amanda's grocery shopping trip), arugula lettuce, cucumber slices, Swiss cheese (also from the deli), and ranch dressing.

Denny pulled over the rocking chair, obviously not satisfied with my one-word answer. "So tell me."

I chewed another bite of sandwich, wondering where to start. I hadn't had time to process this morning's service for myself yet. I was surprised at the feelings it had brought out in me. But I tried to start at the beginning . . .

When the processional started, little Dia George cried out, "Look, Mama! Birds!" Sure enough, walking behind the pastor—a fortyish man wearing a white robe with a colorful stole around his neck—came a girl and a boy about thirteen or fourteen, also robed, carrying a large brass crucifix and a brass candlestick with two tall, white candles. They were followed by several women holding aloft long, thin poles with large birds and butterflies on the tips, bending and swaying over the heads of the congregation in time to the joyous music coming from the choir in the balcony. My mouth wasn't the only Yada Yada's that dropped open in delight. It was like watching kites—or real birds—dancing in the air over our heads. For some reason, tears darted to my eyes at the unexpected beauty and celebration.

The processional was followed by a liturgical prayer of confession and forgiveness. I'd always assumed liturgical prayers were rote and meaningless. But this morning the words rolled around in my heart and I read them from the order of service as a real prayer . . .

Pastor: "We have spoken ill of others and not been diligent in protecting their good names."

People: "Forgive us, Lord."

Pastor: "We have refused to make peace with those who have hurt us."

People: "Forgive us Lord." . . .

I made sure to stuff a copy of the order of service in my tote bag so I could go over that prayer again.

The congregation sang "What Wondrous Love" from an actual hymnbook, followed by the Kyrie ("Lord have mercy; Christ have mercy") in a singsong chant by the pastor. More prayers, a scripture—all printed in the order of service—and then it was time for "A Word for Children."

The pastor, still in his liturgical robe, plopped down casually on the wide steps leading up to the platform and called all the children to come sit around him, casting all formality aside. Chanda's kids went forward, too, outshining every child there in their frills and finery, the only dark faces in the small crowd of European-American offspring. But all eyes were on "Pastor Bill" as he told the story of the boy who gave his lunch to Jesus—the lunch that ended up feeding thousands and thousands of people. Again tears lurked close to the surface. We used to have a children's sermon back at our church in Downers Grove, and I hadn't realized how much I'd missed it.

"But the biggest surprise," I told Denny, "was the Gospel reading, the story of Mary anointing the feet of Jesus. A drama group did it like a series of tableaus. The reader rang a bell and we were supposed to close our eyes while she read a portion of the story. When the bell rang again, we opened our eyes, and the drama group had arranged themselves in a tableau to depict what had just been read. *Ring*—close eyes and listen. *Ring*—open eyes and see. It was so powerful! I thought the drama group did an awesome job."

Denny nodded. "Sounds effective. Guess I should've gone, huh?"

It was effective ... moving, as well, to see the expressions on the actors' faces frozen in dismay at Mary's "waste" and the compassion on the actor-Jesus's face.

But maybe the most moving part of the service for me was Communion. Several pairs of "ministers"—men and women, all in plain white robes and cloth belts—stood at the front with a cup of wine and a small loaf of bread as row by row, the congregation moved forward to receive "the Lord's body" and "the cup of our salvation." People who had colds or didn't want to drink from a common cup could take a tiny cup from a tray.

For some reason, I felt teary again as I saw my Yada Yada sisters moving forward in the line to receive communion, strangers in the midst of this mostly white, upper-middle-class church ... and I thought, this is the bottom line. Not our differences. Not our color or culture. Not our denominations. But what Jesus has done—for all of us.

Denny stood up. "Well, hope you didn't overdo. Uh . . . mind if I turn on the game?"

I did mind. I wanted to sit there in the quiet and think some more about our visit to St. John's. Because what I didn't tell Denny were the conflicting feelings that had been rising inside since I'd come home.

"That's it? We done?" Florida had hissed in a stage whisper as the pastor, the ministers, the acolytes—or whatever Lutherans called the teenage assistants—all strode down the aisle to the recessional sung by the choir in the balcony. The hands of my watch pointed straight up to noon. Florida fanned her order of service. "Girl, you in trouble at this church if you can't read all this print."

But I'd *liked* reading ahead and seeing what was coming next. I liked getting home with half a day still to go. (Wasn't Sunday supposed to be a day of rest?) I'd been missing hymn singing and hadn't even known it. I even enjoyed some of the liturgy. (Surprised myself.) But most of all, I enjoyed not feeling different from these "white-bread" folks.

Did I dare share these feelings with Yada Yada when we talked about our experience at St. John's? What was I doing at hodgepodge Uptown Community, which hadn't really decided what church tradition it reflected? Did I really belong in Chicago's Rogers Park, the most diverse neighborhood in the U.S.? Even among my sisters of color in Yada Yada . . . who was I really?

Am I just a pretender? A seagull, trying to strut with the peacocks?

DENNY WAS STILL SNORING AWAY at seven thirty the next morning, even though it was a Monday. My teenagers probably wouldn't be up till noon. Josh had taken advantage of the Pulaski holiday and squeaked in by his curfew—but of course that meant I didn't get to sleep till after midnight. At least I got to sleep in an extra thirty minutes. Might've been longer, but Willie Wonka's bladder wasn't on holiday.

Thank you, General Pulaski, I thought, turning on the coffeepot and making a mental note to tell my third graders about the obscure Revolutionary War hero who gave them a day off from school on the first Monday of March—not that I knew much. Maybe I could track down some info about Casimir Pulaski on the Internet.

The coffee smelled wonderful, but I was still on tea, still nursing my week-old cold. The sky was heavy with gray clouds, ready to dump its load of snow or rain. Who cared? A perfect day to . . .

I groaned. A perfect day to get started on my quilt square, that's what. I had no excuse. So what was I going to do? I got out the square of muslin and the skeins of embroidery thread and stared at them. Nothing. Not a single idea.

I picked up the phone and dialed the Enriqueses' number. "Delores! I can't think of anything to embroider on this quilt square. What am I supposed to do?"

Delores sounded rushed. "Sorry, Jodi. I'm heading out the door to work. And pray for Ricardo. The band has been asked to play— how do you say it?—a regular 'gig' at La Fiesta, one of the biggest Mexican-American restaurants in the city. Just on weekends, but I haven't seen him so happy in a long time. It's a start anyway."

"That's wonderful, Delores." I remembered the look on her husband's face as he stroked that big *guitarrón* at Amanda's party. Tender, mesmerizing . . . "Wait! Delores! About my quilt square—"

"You'll think of something, *mi amiga.* Just work your family names into the design so she'll know who it's from—and don't say 'Avis and Peter' on it. We'll save a square for their names and the date when they make an announcement. Have to run. Bye, Jodi."

"When"? More like "if." Delores seemed awfully sure about Avis and Peter.

I heard the shower start up in the bathroom. Probably Denny, creating a sauna that would steam the mirror and peel the wallpaper. But Delores's comment about family names rang a bell. I turned on the computer and waited impatiently for it to boot up. Called up the Internet and clicked on "Favorites." When the name page came up, I typed in the name "Avis."

There it was. "Refuge in battle."

I sat and looked at the meaning of her name for a long time . . . and an idea began to percolate. If only my embroidery skills weren't so lacking!

THE LONG WEEKEND HAD BEEN GOOD for me. I felt nearly recovered from my cold and encouraged that I had an idea for my quilt square. I knew drawing was out—unless I did stick figures. Now that'd be a hoot! But words . . .

Stu dropped in that evening with a big pot of *carboñara* pasta. "Too much for just me," she said. "Thought I'd bring it down to you guys."

Uh-huh. Now that I'm recovered. Go figure. "Thanks. The kids will love it."

She sat down on the kitchen stool and hooked a foot on one of the rungs. "So you had the day off? I should've been a teacher. No such luck for social workers."

She didn't make any move to leave, so I counted out five plates and handed them to her. "Why don't you stay and eat with us?"

"Okay." She got up, added five water glasses to the stack of plates, and took them into the dining room.

"What's happening with Andy Wallace's foster case?" I called after her, wondering how to keep the *carbonara* warm till we actually ate it.

She appeared back in the doorway. "Oh. Guess I didn't tell you. Yeah, they transferred Andy to my caseload. Good news, I guess." She busied herself counting out five sets of knives, forks, and spoons. "Did find out something interesting. The foster parent is Andy Sr.'s mother—a real tiger, they say. Black and proud. She's filing to adopt and wants Becky to lose her parental rights, especially now that she's in prison. Guess the woman has a pretty good case since she's a family member."

"You're kidding. Becky didn't know Andy had been placed with the grandmother? Sheesh."

"Of course, her case would be weakened if Becky got paroled. Even DCFS tries to keep children with a natural parent if possible."

Stu disappeared into the dining room. I sank down on the stool. *Oh God. Forgive me for dragging my feet. Guess Stu was right to hurry up that petition. Might be Becky Wallace's only chance at keeping her son—*

"Know what, Jodi?" Stu was back, looking around my kitchen with a gleam in her studious eye. "Some color would really brighten up this kitchen—something tangerine and yellow with blue trim. What do you think? I could help you paint."

28

Now that my head didn't feel like a lump of cold oatmeal, I tried to do some planning for March—and Stu painting my kitchen was *not* on my priority list. Denny was still talking about driving to New York during spring break, but that wasn't till April. That left March wide open. Good. I needed some extra time to update my lesson plans. We were starting several new units in math, science, and social studies. But, different year, different kids—I needed some different approaches.

Still, maybe I could do something with MaDear this coming Saturday. I checked the calendar to be sure the date was clear and noticed the month of March had two Yada Yada birthdays—Ruth and Stu. *Hm. Makes sense to celebrate them both at the next Yada Yada, which is meeting at . . .* I checked the calendar again. Ha! Ruth's house. That would be a hoot. Knowing Ruth, she'd say, *"Birthdays, smirthdays. Who needs them!"*

I sent an e-mail to Yada Yada—minus Ruth and Stu—suggesting we bring cards for both sisters and offering to make a cake. I even phoned Chanda and Yo-Yo to give them the heads-up, since they didn't have e-mail, though all I got was a busy signal for Yo-Yo. Sent a separate e-mail to Stu saying it was Ruth's birthday, and I was making a cake. Couldn't tell Ruth we were celebrating Stu's birthday, though, since Ruth's came first—she'd know something was up.

Felt proud of myself being so organized after dragging around like an old shoe all last week.

As usual, the school week consumed my time, making it hard to remember my commitment to "pray the headlines." I tried, though, even if I sometimes did it on the run trying to get to school on time. I felt a surge of hope when I heard Iraq had begun to destroy its missiles. Pundits called it too little, too late. Our troops were still gathering in the Middle East, preparing for war. I thought about all those mothers and fathers who were sending their sons and daughters into harm's way—and Josh was eighteen. Not likely he would volunteer, given that protest march. But what if they reinstituted the draft, like Vietnam? "Oh God! Please don't let—"

This isn't just about you, Jodi—or Josh either. Centuries of hatred and violence in the Middle East have left generations of hurting families in their wake.

I hardly needed the Voice in my head to know my prayer was self-centered. It was just too overwhelming. How could I know what to pray? *Oh God, teach me how to pray!* I cried silently, pulling open the front door of Bethune Elementary for the zillionth time and heading for my classroom. *Wait a minute. The disciples said exactly that to Jesus—and He taught them what to pray!*

I'd repeated the Lord's Prayer—King James Version—since I was in the Sunbeam Sunday school class back in Des Moines. Hadn't said it for years, though, mostly because it became rote, and I was into spontaneous prayers. But what if I prayed it like Nony prayed Scripture, personalizing it, applying it to everyday life?

"OUR FATHER, WHO ART IN HEAVEN, hallowed be Thy name . . ."
"Class, please write your name at the top of the sheet I'm hand-ing out and work the five problems on your own." *Oh God, Your name is above every name in heaven and on earth—but You also know each child in this class by name! Draw them to You, Lord! I pray they will feel Your love through me.* "Good job, Ramón! Would you like to show the class how you did that on the board?"

"THY KINGDOM COME, Thy will be done, on earth as it is in heaven . . ."
Another suicide bombing in Jerusalem dominated the evening news. *Oh God! I pray that Your kingdom would triumph over all Satan's dirty tricks in Israel and Palestine—and everywhere in the Middle East.* Denny's eyebrow lifted in surprise when I sat down beside him on the couch to watch the rest of the news.

"GIVE US THIS DAY our daily bread . . ."
On Saturday, I pushed open the door to Adele's Hair and Nails, glad to get inside, out of the spitting sleet. Adele looked up suspiciously from behind the counter. "You don't have an appointment, Jodi Baxter. And you're the third Yada Yada who has been here this week."

I grinned. "Do you think MaDear would like someone to read to her?" I dumped a stack of books out of my tote bag. "What do you think—Bible? Maya Angelou? *The Cat in the Hat?*"

Adele chuckled. "A little of each, I think. Can't promise she'll stay awake, though."

Sure enough, MaDear fell asleep during the Twenty-Third

Psalm. I stopped reading, and she promptly woke up. "You ain't finished, girl! Got two more verses. Go on! Go on!"

Oh God, let Your Word be MaDear's daily bread and feed her spirit. Somewhere deep in MaDear's mind, her memory was clear as fresh spring water.

She caught me skipping a page in *The Cat in the Hat* too.

"*FORGIVE US OUR SINS, as we forgive those who sin against us . . .*"

The light on the answering machine was blinking when I got home Saturday afternoon lugging bags of groceries—later than usual because I ended up reading to MaDear for an hour. (Every time I'd tried to stop, she'd said, *"Read it agin,"* or *"Tha's good, tha's good. What's the next one?"*) I punched the Play button as I unloaded milk, frozen OJ, and a package of chicken quarters. The machine announced, "One new message," then Stu's voice popped out. "Jodi! Guess what came in the mail today?"

I stood in the middle of the kitchen, holding the package of chicken parts, wondering whether to toss it in the freezer or use it to make something for Second Sunday Potluck at church tomorrow.

"A letter from the parole board at Lincoln!" Stu's voice continued. "They're giving us a hearing—two weeks from today! Can you and Denny make it? Good thing Yada Yada meets tomorrow; we can pin this thing down."

The answering machine clicked off, but I just stood there with the package of chicken. The parole board was giving us a hearing? I sank down on the kitchen stool. *Forgive me, Jesus, for having such weak faith. Even wishing the parole board would say no. But . . . what exactly are we getting ourselves into? We've already forgiven Becky Wallace, haven't we?*

Well, yeah, kinda, sorta—but I wasn't sure I knew what the implications were. What did it mean to completely forgive?

There were still consequences, weren't there?

"LEAD US NOT INTO TEMPTATION, but deliver us from evil . . ."
I got up shivering in the middle of the night to put another blanket on our bed—and nearly jumped out of my skin when the phone rang. The glowing digital alarm clock said 4:11. I snatched up the bedside extension, my heart racing. Had to be bad news—my parents? Denny's?

"Jodi?" Yo-Yo's voice was high-pitched, scared. "Hey. Sorry to wake you up, but is Pete over there?"

"Pete? No . . . wait a minute, Yo-Yo."

Denny had risen up on one elbow, but I put my hand over the mouthpiece. "It's Yo-Yo. Go back to sleep." I hustled the phone out of the bedroom and down the hall into the dim shadows of the living room. Willie Wonka's nails clicked on the wooden floor behind me. "What's the matter, Yo-Yo?"

"He never came home last night. That homeboy been comin' in later an' later, givin' me fits. Tonight he never came back at all. I was wonderin' if maybe he stayed over with Josh."

"Haven't seen him. I'll double-check Josh's room." *Not a chance. I'd know if we had an extra body in the house.* I padded back down the hallway, Willie Wonka at my heels, and peered into Josh's bedroom. One lump in the bed. I opened the door wider and scanned the floor. Just the usual mess. I pulled the door shut again. "Sorry, Yo-Yo."

Silence at the other end. Then, "I don't know what ta do, Jodi. Kinda worried."

Kinda? I'd be a total wreck if Josh wasn't home at four in the morning! "Who was Pete out with? Did you try calling his friends?"

"I don't know where he was. He just went out. That"—Yo-Yo blistered my ear with a few choice names in Pete's absence—"thinks he can do anything he wanna do since he turned seventeen. He ain't even a senior yet."

"Oh, Yo-Yo." I wanted to hug her. She was just a kid herself, only twenty-three, trying to raise two teenage brothers. And from stuff she'd said, she'd never had much parenting herself. I felt helpless to comfort her. "Want to pray for him right now, Yo-Yo? God knows where he is."

"You pray, Jodi. I don't . . . I mean, I don't know if God listens to me."

"Of course He listens to you! Why wouldn't He?"

"'Cause I'm not . . . I dunno. Not even sure I'm a Christian. I mean, how can you know when you've made it? Haven't done that baptism thing yet."

Oh, Yo-Yo. "Don't worry about baptism right now, Yo-Yo." After all, it was four in the morning. "Just take my word for it—God listens to you. But if you want, I'll pray for us both, okay?"

Huddled in the darkness and the old afghan on the couch, I prayed aloud, phone clamped to my ear, seeing Yo-Yo in my mind—scared, sleepless, saddled with worries beyond her age. As I prayed, my heart began to lighten. "Steer Pete away from temptation tonight, Jesus, and protect him from all harm and danger. Don't let the evil one snatch him away. We claim Pete for You, Lord . . ."

I'm not sure how long I prayed, but Yo-Yo said, "Thanks, Jodi," when I wrapped it up "in the mighty name of Jesus." "He's prob'ly okay—sleepin' off too many beers at some kid's house or somethin'."

The clock said 4:55 when I crawled back under the covers and pressed my cold feet against Denny's warm ones. Given the possibilities, sleeping off too many beers sounded downright wholesome.

"FOR THINE IS THE KINGDOM, *the power, and the glory, forever and ever! Amen.*"

The Lord's Prayer was still at the forefront of my mind as I dropped off my Crockpot of chicken marengo in the church kitchen the next morning. I was glad to see Avis preparing to lead worship this Sunday. I could use some out-of-our-seats praise this morning, because Yo-Yo had called just as we were making our usual mad dash out the door. Pete had dragged in at five thirty and said he'd been playing pool and hanging out—"Smelling like weed!" she'd yelled in my ear—and "forgot" to call. *Oh, please.* Still, the he's-dead-in-an-alley-somewhere scare was over, and she was mad as a wet cat. Hallelujah! Praise Jesus!

I craned my neck. Huh. Didn't see Peter Douglass . . .

I gave Avis a hug after service. "Peter didn't come? Thought you might bring him to Uptown's infamous Second Sunday Potluck." I grinned sheepishly. "Especially since I made you guys miss it last month with my lunch invitation."

Avis got a funny look on her face. "No, he didn't come. Actually, Peter and I . . . um, we're kind of cooling things right now."

I stared at her, speechless.

"Don't say anything, Jodi. I'll . . . we can talk later, okay?"

Don't say anything? The whole Yada Yada Prayer Group was making a friendship quilt for the two of them, for crying out loud!

29

I managed to not say anything to Florida or Stu, even though Stu rode home with us after the potluck, but I called Delores the minute I got home. "They're cooling it, Delores! Does that mean I don't have to embroider this quilt square?"

"What are you talking about, Jodi!"

"Avis and Peter—she said they're cooling it."

I heard Delores chuckle. "Oh. Do not worry, *mi amiga.* That is to be expected. How do you say it?—cold feet. Did she say why?"

No, she hadn't said why, and I tried to call Avis after I hung up with Delores, but all I got was her voice mail. Humph. She better tell us at Yada Yada tonight—so we could pray, of course.

Yeah, right.

Amanda was hunched over the computer doing schoolwork while I made a birthday cake, but she gave it up for an hour—actually, I bribed her with the mixing bowl and beaters; anything for chocolate—so I managed to make two computer cards for the birthday Yadas, doing the "name" thing. Took me longer than I thought, though, because I had a sneezing fit right in the middle of accessing the Internet and waded through a pile of tissues before I got my runny nose and weepy eyes under control. *Dumb cold better not be making a comeback.* I took a decongestant and a couple of pain relievers for good measure.

Back on the computer, I checked out the meaning of Stu's first name—Leslie—and it came up meaning, "From the gray fortress." *Huh?* What could I do with that? So I looked up her last name—Stuart, which meant "Caretaker." *Hm.* That seemed appropriate, maybe to a fault. But I stuck with the positive and printed out a card that said, *Stuart: Old English for Caretaker. God bless you, Stu, as you make sure that foster kids are taken care of!*

Ruth's name was sweet: "Friend of beauty." In spite of her brusque exterior, Ruth was intensely loyal, just like her counterpart in the Bible. Like the way she'd taken Yo-Yo and her half brothers under her wing. *To Ruth*, my computer card said, *Friend of beauty. A beautiful friend ~ Happy Birthday! Love, Jodi.*

Our ranks were thin at Yada Yada that night—only eight of us. Nony and Florida both stayed home with sick kids, Delores had to work pediatrics at the county hospital, and Edesa was baby-sitting the Enriques kids because Ricardo and José were playing their new weekend gig at La Fiesta. But Adele showed up—her sister was back in town and able to take MaDear on Sundays again—in Chanda's new car. A champagne Lexus. The whole group was standing out by the curb gawking at it when Hoshi and I drove up with Stu.

"What? You didn't bring Denny?" Ben Garfield fussed, giving me a peck on the cheek. "What am I supposed to do while you ladies get holy? I need a beer buddy."

Oh, please. I wasn't keen on Denny being Ben's "beer buddy," so just as well. But I laughed airily and was just about to ask Ben if he'd sneak the cake from Stu's car into the house while we were praying, when he gave me a wink and motioned me to follow him. Ruth was busy taking coats in the living room, so he hustled me through the compact kitchen of their brick bungalow with its single sink and bright mustard counters and opened the door to a tiny utility room. A large bakery cake sat in all its sugary glory on top of the washing machine, boasting, *Happy 39th Birthday, Ruth!*

He pointed to the 39 and snickered. "That gal's been thirty-nine for the last nine years." His large face broke into a mask of laugh wrinkles. "Had Yo-Yo make it. Just give me the high sign and I'll bring it in, candles lit. Better have a fire extinguisher ready."

I groaned silently. I never did get hold of Yo-Yo to tell her *I* was making a cake. Now what? Ben's cake only said "Ruth" and we had two birthdays . . . well, maybe my cake could be for Stu. Not that we needed two cakes.

As I sank into a corner of Ruth's flowered sofa on the tail end of the opening prayer, Avis asked for praise or prayer reports. I wondered if she would say something about "cooling it" with Peter—but knew she probably wouldn't. And suddenly I realized how easy it was for Avis to hide behind being the leader. Yeah, there she went, asking Hoshi how her studies were going at Northwestern and if she'd heard anything from her parents. And then she'd ask someone else . . .

"I write every week," Hoshi said, fingering the delicate oriental scarf around her neck, "and at first all my letters were returned. But lately they have not been returned."

"Praise Jesus!" Chanda threw up her hands. "De parents be readin' dem!"

Hoshi shook her head, the blue-black of her shoulder-straight hair catching highlights from Ruth's table lamp. "I do not think so. Because I got a letter from my aunt this week. She says my mother gives her the letters unopened. But my aunt is reading them and, I think"—a small smile tilted Hoshi's red lips—"telling *mama-san* what I say."

Ruth nodded smugly. "A *yenta*, this aunt is. Good, good!"

Yo-Yo, perched on the arm of the overstuffed sofa, stuck both hands behind the bib of her overalls and grinned. "Now that's bad."

"It is bad? I thought good!" Hoshi looked flustered. "English is so confusing."

Avis smiled. "God is at work, Hoshi. By His stripes we are healed—and that includes our family relationships too."

Yo-Yo, next to me, poked me. "By His stripes *what*?" she asked.

I held up a finger and paged through my Bible to look for the verse Avis had referred to, even as she shifted gears. "Other praise reports?"

Stu waved a long envelope. "This! The parole board is giving us a hearing about Becky Wallace!" She read the brief letter stating the time: two weeks from Saturday.

A stunned silence greeted her announcement, finally broken when Yo-Yo said, "Man! Maybe the Cubs will win the World Series too."

Chanda giggled. "If I live to be t'ree hundred."

"Well." For once Ruth was speechless.

"Lord God Almighty." Adele heaved a sigh and shook her large, gold ear loops. "I never thought . . ."

"But it is what we asked for, correct?" said Hoshi. "You just said God is at work, Avis. For Becky Wallace too."

"Well, yeah." Yo-Yo wagged her head. "But getting a hearing don't mean they actually gonna let her out. Them parole boards can be—"

"Yeah, we know, Yo-Yo," Adele interrupted, squelching Yo-Yo's descriptive language. Chanda snickered again.

I shoved my modern language Bible in Yo-Yo's lap and pointed to the verse in Isaiah about the sufferings of Jesus bringing us peace and healing. She squinted at the passage, then shrugged as if to say, *"Still don't get it."*

"Tell you later," I whispered. For some reason I felt excited to try to explain a familiar scripture I'd always taken for granted. Yo-Yo's lack of "Bible-speak" made me think. I needed down-to-earth words for these truths too.

"Hoshi is right, sisters. God is at work. This is what happens when sisters agree in the name of Jesus and pray together . . . Mm-hm." Avis lifted a hand into the air and closed her eyes. "Jesus! You are a mighty God! All authority—even presidents and kings and parole boards—is under Your dominion. Mm-hm!"

I thought Avis would take us off into a praise meeting then and there, but Stu interrupted. "The point is, who's going to go to this hearing?"

Even though Avis was still "off" praising, the rest of us jumped on Stu's question. Several people bowed out; other names were suggested. The final list included me (it was our house that had been invaded), Hoshi (her mother was the only one wounded by B. W.'s knife), and Stu (because she was spearheading the effort). "What about Yo-Yo and Florida?" I asked. "Maybe all of us who've been to the prison should go."

Yo-Yo grimaced. "I'm an ex-con. Don't think that's an asset. 'Sides, I wasn't even there that night. Not one of her victims. Florida might wanna go, though."

"What about Denny?" Stu grimaced. "Hate to say it, but the parole board will probably take us more seriously if a man goes."

She was probably right. "I dunno. I'll ask him." How did he feel about this anyway? Poor Denny. His life had been a lot more complicated since he got tangled in Yada Yada's briar patch. *God, thank You for Denny. Thank You that he showed up unexpectedly that night . . . that Becky Wallace missed when she lunged with the knife . . .*

I shook that thought out of my brain and reached for a brighter one, even though my brain was starting to feel a little foggy. "Uh, speaking of husbands, Delores told me that Ricardo and José and their band have a regular weekend gig at La Fiesta restaurant downtown. Ricardo still needs a day job, though she says he's happier, drinking less."

Faces lit up around the circle. "Way cool!" said Yo-Yo. "Guess the Big Guy Upstairs likes mariachi music."

I started to laugh but had to stifle a huge sneeze building up in my head instead.

Avis smiled. "A good reminder to keep praying for the men in our lives. Florida's not here, but I know she wants us to keep praying for Carl. Let's include them when we—"

Even before Adele opened her mouth, I knew Avis had walked into her own trap.

"Speakin' of the *men* in our lives," Adele drawled, "isn't it about time you told us what's happenin' with you and Mr. Peter Douglass? You been mighty quiet about his intentions, but we all got eyes, girl. If you can't tell *us*, who you gonna tell?" Unanimous hooting and smart mouths greeted Adele's declaration.

Adele was back, bold and sassy. It felt good.

Avis shot me a *Didn't-I-tell-you-not-to-say-anything?* look, but I shook my head with angelic innocence. The only person I'd told wasn't even there.

The wisecracks simmered away when Avis nodded in resignation. She did not look happy. "All right. To be honest, Peter and I are . . . well, we're letting things cool off right now."

We were getting pretty good at stunned silences.

Ruth frowned. "Joking, you must be! Bad for my heart." Her *yenta*-ness didn't like this at all.

"No. That's it. I'm . . . we're . . . well, still friends. But that's it."

Adele pursed her lips and studied Avis's face. Avis actually squirmed. "I think, Avis, you need to trust us. What's going on? What happened?"

The room got very quiet. Avis blinked rapidly. Out of the corner of my eye, I saw Ben Garfield peek into the living room with a questioning expression. I shook my head imperceptibly.

We waited. Avis took a deep breath. "I . . . like Peter very much. He has brought a lot of joy into my life, especially since . . . since Conrad died. Yet recently he told me . . ." Another breath. "Recently he told me that he has loved me for many years, even while I was married to Conrad. He was Conrad's college friend, you know."

Her words slipped away, but no one spoke. Avis twisted her wedding ring. "I loved my husband very much. I still love him. After he died, when the loneliness was unbearable, I often thought about the fact that he is in heaven, waiting for me." She grimaced, a half smile. "I know, I know. There is no marriage in heaven. And for a while, I did think that maybe God had sent Peter to fill the empty hole in my life. Though now . . . to learn that Peter loved me even while I was married to Conrad makes me feel"—her face muscles tightened—"like I'm committing adultery. Not that there's been any physical intimacy between us—nothing like that. But in the Sermon on the Mount, Jesus said that 'anyone who looks at a woman lustfully' has already committed adultery." Her large, dark eyes flashed. "So I'm supposed to marry a man who's been lusting after me for years, even while I was married to one of his best friends? I don't think so!"

And there it was. We all just stared at her. I blew my nose, trying to clear my fogged up brain. What she said made sense, in a slice-it-close-to-the-bone way. But inwardly, the part of me that loved Avis, that wanted her to laugh again and be loved again, was screaming, *You nitwit! Grab that good-looking man who adores you, who loves God, who's a match for you brain cell for brain cell, and run to the closest preacher!*

It was Adele who broke the silence. "Avis." She said Avis's name like a kid sister who needed straightening out. "Maybe there's somethin' to what you just said; maybe not. It just doesn't sit well with my spirit. If that man loved you all this time, and you just now finding out about it, I'd say he's more of a man than I even figured him to be—and I'd already put him in the top ten of decent men I've met in my lifetime." She leaned back in that Buddha pose of hers, arms folded across her chest. "Seems I recall you remindin' us earlier tonight about agreein' together in prayer. Well, for the record, I'm not agreein' with you yet on this. I will do one thing, though: I will pray on it with you."

Avis nodded, and it was Adele who led us into the prayer time. We poured out all the things on our plate—the meeting with the parole board, Hoshi's parents, Ricardo and Carl needing a job, plus prayers for our sisters who were missing. When I sensed the prayers were winding down—a little sooner than usual, since Avis was pretty muted after her "confession"—I slipped out to Stu's car and got the chocolate cake that had been hiding in the backseat, keeping chilled at least. Chanda was praying when I came back in, giving me time to sneak it into the kitchen, where Ben was waiting. "Didn't know you got a cake for Ruth," I whispered, "but it's okay, because we have two birthdays! Ruth and Stu." I beamed, trying to put him at ease. "A cake for each!"

"Ah! Great solution." He handed me a box of birthday candles. "Stick a few on there, like I did. They can each blow them out."

We could hear the final "Thank You, Jesus! Yes! We thank You!" rising from the living room, so Ben and I lit our candles and carefully carried the cakes through the dining room to the archway leading into the Garfield's tiny living room. "Happy birthday to youuuuu," Ben boomed out—and I nearly dropped my chocolate cake. The man had a deep, velvety voice that could go onstage! But all the Yada Yadas chimed in: "Happy birthday to youuuu!" Ruth's cheeks got pink with embarrassment. "Happy birthday, Ruth and Stu-uuu . . ."

At that exact moment, I felt the stubborn old sneeze I'd been stuffing back into its black hole all evening come sneaking out, bigger and badder than the last attempt to erupt. And holding a cake in both hands, there was not one thing I could do about it. As Ben boomed out the last "Happy birthday to youuuuu" . . . I sneezed all over Stu's chocolate cake and snuffed out the candles.

Literally.

30

So much for my chocolate cake. I felt mortified—but everyone else thought it was hysterical. Especially Ben Garfield. He laughed so hard he almost dropped his cake.

At least there was still plenty of cake to go around. And at least Stu knew she was included in the birthday celebration, especially since all the Yada Yadas had brought cards for her, too, as well as Ruth. She even seemed pleased at my computer-generated card. "Stuart means 'caretaker,' huh? I kinda like that." She struck a dramatic pose, the way we used to play "freeze" when I was a kid. "Stuart . . . the gruff, bewhiskered caretaker, patrolling the grounds of a grand old Scottish castle with his pipe and his dog."

Oh, please.

"Her pipe and *her* dog is correct English, I believe," Hoshi said sincerely.

While Chanda and Stu cracked up at that, I slipped into the Garfields' bathroom to blow my nose and wash my hands, wishing I could take some cold meds *now* and kick this cold before it took up residence in my head again. I opened the medicine cabinet—and the jammed contents spilled out like Niagara Falls. The clatter seemed deafening in that tiny space. *Oh Lord, I'm dead meat,* I groaned, grabbing Dr. Scholl's bunion pads, ear swabs, an old bottle of iodine, and several ancient containers with who-knows-what in them, hoping the rattling bathroom fan had drowned out my fiasco.

A knock on the bathroom door sealed my doom. "You all right in there, Jodi?" Ben Garfield's voice.

I cracked the door. "Sorry. I was looking for some cold medicine. Should've asked."

Ben's grin pushed his cheeks up, nearly closing his twinkling eyes. "I *never* open that cabinet. Everything in it is at least twenty years old—maybe forty! But Ruth won't get rid of anything—'just in case,' you know. Wait here. I'll get you something." His shoulders shook with laughter as he vanished, reappearing moments later with two decongestants, two Tylenol, and a glass of water. I wanted to kiss his big ol' face.

People were shrugging on coats and jackets at the front door when I came out. "Don't you be givin' 'way dat mon, Avis Johnson," Chanda scolded good-naturedly, pulling on a Lord & Taylor leather hat and leather gloves. "Mi hangin' on to my mon dis time."

"Speaking of whom"—Stu slid in on the tail end of Chanda's comment like a sneaky budget amendment in Congress—"when is Dia's daddy going to make an honest woman of you?"

In the split second after Stu opened her mouth, all other mouths closed and a toxic vacuum followed. Chanda's eyes, green with glittery eye shadow, narrowed. "What you meanin' by dat, Leslie Stuart?"

Whoa. Full names. It was as if a bell had rung in a boxing ring.

Stu shrugged. "Well, you said Dia's daddy is back—meaning, I presume, that he's moved in. But is he going to marry you?"

The green eye shadow narrowed into slits. "What business is dat of yours? Dese t'ings take time."

"Maybe we ought to leave this for another—" Avis started.

"No, we into it now." Chanda jutted out her chin. "I know what you all t'inkin' since DeShawn come back. You t'inkin' he just after mi winnin's. But it not like dat. You wait. You see. We gonna make a good t'ing here dis time."

Adele shook her head. "Honey, I hope you're right. I've seen my share of gold-diggers, though, and you're one rich lady right now, as I understand. What *you* need is a lawyer."

Ruth—the only one not swaddled in coat and hat—laid a gentle hand on Chanda's arm. "To be happy is what we want for you, too, Chanda. If he is serious, as you say, he should court you, marry you, *then* move in as the daddy."

Chanda stuck out her bottom lip. "But he's already Dia's daddy—an' my kids need a daddy *now*. We gonna get married, soon as I get me a house, t'ings like dat. Don't want to wait."

"That's what worries us, honey," Adele murmured. "Not to mention you livin' in sin. Don't you read your Bible? You got babies by three different daddies. Don't that say somethin'?"

Chanda's chin went up. "Well, maybe so. At least I didn't get no abortion when I got pregnant wit my t'ree babies. Could've been done wit dat, live free an' easy—but I took responsibility for mi mistakes. Gonna raise my kids and get 'em a daddy, if it be de last t'ing I do!" The green eye shadow was sparkling now.

"I really think this needs another time when—" Avis tried again.

Stu's head jerked up. "Don't go making abortion the worst sin in the world, Chanda George." I flinched. Full names again. Stu's voice raised a notch. "I see a lot of hurting women in my work at DCFS. A woman makes a mistake, gets pregnant, feels backed in a corner. Man leaves, no money, no job, everybody's going to talk—no wonder she considers an abortion! But"—a note of scorn crept in—"a *mistake* is one thing. *Three* mistakes in a row—now, that's something else."

Chanda's mouth dropped and her eyes widened. The tension in the foyer crackled like an electrical short. Sweat trickled down my back, whether from standing so long indoors with my coat on or from stress, I wasn't sure. But just then Adele took a firm grip of Chanda's arm and practically pushed her out the front door. "Avis is right. This conversation needs a sit-down, and I, for one, have to open up the shop at seven a.m. Chanda, take me home in that new chariot of yours."

Ruth's front door shut behind them. All eyes turned to Stu. She pulled her long hair out from under the collar of her jacket and flipped her head to loosen it. "Well, somebody had to say something. Why have we all been dancing around Chanda in ballet slippers?"

BEN'S DOCTORING WAS TOO LATE. I was up half the night sneezing and hacking and trying to breathe, and Denny made the call to Bethune Elementary at six thirty the next morning saying I needed a sub. I crawled back into bed, down in the dumps. One brief week between colds was *not* a good sign. I ached all over. Maybe I had the flu.

Denny called Dr. Lewinski, who said I probably pushed it two weeks ago. He recommended at least three days of bed rest. "There's a nasty Asian flu hitting the States," he told Denny. "Jodi's immune system is weakened without her spleen. She needs to be careful."

Huh. What did he know about careful? I taught third graders for heaven's sake! Colds and flu were part of the job description.

I meekly stayed home the next three days listening to music CDs, working on my quilt square for Avis—*Avis and Peter,* if Delores's faith weighted God's scale—and catching my first glimpse of a robin in our backyard. Would've been bliss if I hadn't felt so rotten. Willie Wonka played the dutiful nursemaid, trailing me from room to room when I was out of bed, watching me with a doggy frown imbedded in his soft brown forehead, and offering his ears to scratch when he thought I needed something to do.

Avis dropped off a new *Songs 4 Worship Gospel* CD. "Keep your praise on, Jodi," she said, breezing in and breezing out again Monday afternoon. I wanted to talk to her about the sparks that flew between Chanda and Stu the other night, but she had a staff meeting.

I skipped some of the exuberant praise songs the first day or two because they made my head throb. Some of the worship cuts were beautiful though. I lay on the couch, stroking Wonka's ears, and absorbing the words like intravenous nourishment. *"There's a lifting of the hands . . . a lifting of the hearts . . . a lifting of the eyes . . . Beyond the hills, to where our help comes from . . ."* I checked the lyric sheet. Some group called Israel & New Breed. I listened to it again . . . and again. So true. *"Our help comes from You . . ."*

Well, Yada Yada was going to need help from God, that was for sure. I kept thinking about what happened Sunday night between Stu and Chanda. On one hand, Stu just said what the rest of us had been thinking. It was true! None of us trusted Dia's daddy, even if he was a good dancer and wore leather. (Or maybe *because* he was a good dancer and wore leather!) But Stu's hackles had really risen when Chanda defended herself about having three kids by different daddies, patting herself on the back because she didn't choose abortion.

Something funny about it all. Almost as if—

I blinked at the notion that pushed its way to the front of my mucus-muddled head. Almost as if Stu was defending *herself.*

STU MUST HAVE TALKED TO FLORIDA about going to testify to the parole board, because Florida called me during the week saying she was good to go, " . . . if Carla not still sick. Saturday after next, right? Well, she oughta be okay by then. 'Less she got that SARS or whatever they talkin' about on the radio."

SARS—Severe Acute Respiratory Syndrome. It was all over the news, at least now that several cases had shown up in the U.S. A few people had come down with what seemed like the flu and died. I rushed to assure Florida. "Haven't heard about any cases involving children . . . ahh-ahh-ahh! 'Scuse me, Flo," and sneezed into the big T-shirt I was wearing. Man! I needed to remember to carry one of Denny's handkerchiefs around with me. Now I had to change my shirt. "Sorry," I sniffled. "Hope Carla doesn't feel as lousy as I do."

"Maybe *you* the one should worry about that SARS thing, Jodi. Didn't the doc say you runnin' around without all your immunities or somethin'?"

Or something. Whatever. So far it was just a cold. I shifted the topic. "So how come you're calling me in the middle of the day? Aren't you at work?"

"Nah. Had to take a couple o' sick days to stay home with Carla. Carl got him a temporary job at some warehouse—security guard or somethin'."

"Hey, that's good, Flo. Sorry you had to miss work, though." I wasn't sure Florida's job paid for sick days.

"Huh. I think it's temporary 'cause his job record's not so hot. Two weeks on a job—then *bam!* he quits. Or gets fired. I ain't complainin', though, 'cause I'm praisin' God for this time with Carla. She's asleep right now, but you know what we been doin'? Reading books! The TV's broke, and she threw a fit at first. Boys too. But I went to the library, an' we been reading *Amelia Bedelia* an' some old American black folktales—girl! I remember my mama tellin' me some o' those tales!—an' that new chapter book about Ruby Bridges you gave her. Carla, she eatin' it up. I . . ." Florida's voice seemed to choke up, and she cleared her throat a couple of times. "Best thing of all, Jodi, is Carla and me all cuddled up in the bed, my arm under her head . . . an' she been callin' me Mama 'stead of Florida."

"Oh, Florida." I could hardly breathe—and this time it wasn't because of my cold.

"He's a mighty good God, Jodi. Mighty good. I think we gonna make it now, hard as it been. If Chris jus' stop disappearin' when he s'posed to be home, an' Carl hang onto that job—oh. I hear Carla. Gotta go." She hung up.

Well. I sure did have something new to praise God for . . . and pray about. As I tossed the cordless on the couch and shuffled toward the front door to get the mail, I caught myself begging God to make it all right for the Hickman family—*everything* all right. Except I knew God didn't usually work that way, tying up all the loose ends in a pretty bow. What I'd been learning from Florida—from all the Yada Yada sisters, for that matter—was more like two steps forward, one step back, a victory here, a seeming defeat . . . but never losing sight that God was bigger than the enemy.

I stepped out on the porch long enough to dig out the mail from our rusty metal mailbox and pick up the newspaper. A front-page headline blared: SHOCK AND AWE! U.S. MILITARY PLANNING HIGH-TECH WAR ON BAGHDAD. I scanned the story with growing dread, not even realizing I was shivering on the front porch in nothing more than my oversize T-shirt and socks, till I heard Josh's voice yell, "Why is the front door open? . . . Mom! Are you nuts? If Dad saw you out there, he'd have a fit!" My son actually grabbed the paper from me and pulled me inside like a bad puppy.

I ignored his disapproval, rifling through the usual assortment of bills and ads in the mail as I followed him into the kitchen. "Whoa! Josh! Look at this!" I held up a long official envelope with Josh's name on it. "Your letter from UIC!" I handed it to him with a grin. "Open it!"

He shrugged, putting down the glass of orange juice he'd just poured for himself. "Okay." He tore open the flap in a jagged tear and pulled out the contents, scanned the letter, and tossed it on the counter.

"What?" My heart flopped. Had they turned down his application? Couldn't be! He had great grades and good test scores. I reached for the letter and read it myself as Josh wandered toward the living room, orange juice and newspaper in hand.

The first phrase leaped off the page: "We are pleased to inform you . . ." Accepted! Josh had been accepted at the University of Illinois-Champaign. "Josh!" I screeched, tearing toward the living room. "This is great! You got accepted by UIC. Congratulations!"

Josh, imbedded in the couch, barely raised his once-again-shaved-bald head from the newspaper. "Thanks. Doesn't mean I'm going to go, though."

31

I counted to ten—make that twenty—and said in a calm-but-really-screaming voice, "Don't throw away a college acceptance willy-nilly, Joshua James Baxter. We need a sit-down—with Dad too." Good grief. I used all three of his names.

"Okay." Josh lowered his eyelids over the top of the newspaper, feigning patience. "It's not like that's news. I told you I might volunteer at Jesus People for a year and get a job on the side."

"Correction. You told Mr. Douglass in our presence. Not the same thing. You—"

The cordless started ringing somewhere in the couch. Josh dug it out of the cushions. "Yo. Baxters. . . . Okay." He held out the phone in my direction. "For you."

I snatched the phone and mouthed at Josh, *"Later."* . . . Then I spoke into the phone, "Hello? Oh, Nony! Hi. Thanks for returning my call." I stalked down the hall toward my bedroom and flopped on the bed, suddenly very tired. "You weren't at Yada Yada Sunday night. Just wanted to see if the boys are any better, and how you're doin'."

"Oh. Thank you, Jodi." Nony's liquid voice had a calming effect on my ruffled spirit. "Both boys are back in school, praise Jesus."

"You and Mark?"

"Oh, we're fine. Mark never gets sick, healthy as a—"

"I didn't mean that. I meant, how are you and Mark . . . you know."

"Oh. That." A brief pause, like a silent hiccup. "We do best not talking about it, putting it in the cupboard, I think you say." I smiled at the phone. *On the shelf, in the cupboard—same thing.* "But God and I," she continued, "we talk all the time about South Africa. Or"— she laughed nervously—"maybe I'm doing all the talking. I think God was speaking to me at the last Yada Yada meeting, though I didn't want to listen."

"Really? I was afraid it wasn't what you wanted to hear."

"It wasn't. But two days ago, I got an e-mail from my brother in Pietermaritzburg—maybe you heard this on the news—"

Not me. Has there been anything else on the news except the buildup of war clouds in the Middle East?

"—the Truth and Reconciliation Commission has been pressuring the South African government to make reparations for victims of apartheid. Nyack says opinion from the international community is vital and is asking me—begging me!—to make the issue known here in the United States. He wants me to lobby Congress, generate letters of support, whatever I can do. The vote is coming up in Parliament in April."

What Nony was saying began to sink in. Her countrymen actually *needed* her here in the United States. "Oh, Nony."

"I know. I'm a little mad at God. This isn't the answer I wanted. Maybe Florida was right, in her own way. My deepest concern is for the orphans of AIDS—still such a burden on my heart! But maybe God has planted me here for a reason."

"For such a time as this." Nony would know what I was referring to, the Old Testament story of Queen Esther, whom God put in the palace of a foreign government to save her people.

"Yes," Nony breathed, so softly I had to clamp the phone tighter to my ear in order to hear her. "For such a time as this." And then, to my surprise, she laughed. "Better pray that the powers that be hold out the golden scepter and give me favor if I'm going to stick my neck out for a hot issue like reparations!"

I WENT BACK TO SCHOOL ON THURSDAY, and with all the catching up I needed to do, the weekend slam-dunked before Denny and I got a chance to talk to Josh about college. And even then it wasn't satisfactory. "Look," Josh said, in that irritating, patient way of his, "I don't even know what I want to study in college yet. Taking a year off isn't that big a deal. It's not like I'm going to be brain-dead if I don't go to UIC this fall."

If it's only a year, I groused to myself.

"And," he went on, "Jesus People really needs more volunteers to help with the Cornerstone Festival this summer. Sound guys, like me. There'll be tons of sound equipment for all the big CCM bands." He was practically drooling.

"But that's just this summer," I protested, but I got a two-millimeter headshake from Denny that cautioned, *"Chill for now."* I thought he was dispensing parental patience, a willingness to not push the issue too fast, too soon—till I saw Denny and Josh head for the TV and turn on a game that was already in its first quarter.

The turkeys.

THE TRIP TO TESTIFY BEFORE THE PAROLE BOARD at Lincoln Correctional was still a week away, and I kept pushing it out of my mind . . . but that third week of March was suddenly swallowed by war—real war. "Shock and Awe." On our TV screen, the massive nighttime bombing of Baghdad looked nauseatingly like pea soup exploding—all green and flickering, big booms, enormous flashes of light, all from a distance. Josh and Denny were glued to the TV. The mood in our house tiptoed on the edges of morose fascination. All Josh said when I called everybody to supper was a snide, "I don't suppose going to college is a big question for guys my age in Iraq right now."

I bit my tongue. Denny prayed a heartfelt prayer at the table for all our troops in harm's way, for the protection of innocent Iraqi civilians, for government officials faced with world-shaking decisions, for a quick end to this war, for true peace in the Middle East. Me, I was struggling with my own "shock and awe." Shock that the United States was at war—but it was all so "over there." So far away. So easily put out of mind . . .

Oh God! Forgive me for being so self-centered. So callous. So easily consumed with what concerns just me and mine. I don't even know how to pray. Terrorism is so . . . insidious. So irrational. Who is the enemy? Is war the answer? Oh God! Help us! Help us all!

Only later that night, lying in bed curled into Denny's comforting bulk, the window cracked to bring cool fresh air into our stuffy bedroom, did I realize that the day of bombs and death over there was also the first day of spring.

DENNY AND I CELEBRATED THE ARRIVAL OF SPRING on Friday evening with our first walk to the lakefront since New Year's Day and the Polar Bear Plunge. We walked hand in hand down Lunt Avenue, past the still-bare trees along the parkway between sidewalk and street, crossed Sheridan Road, and ended up on the bike path along Lake Michigan. By then I was pooped. We found a bench facing the water, and Denny pulled me close. The temperature hung around forty-five degrees, not yet warm, and damp.

We talked about our upcoming trip to visit his parents in New York during spring break . . . about Josh wanting to take a year off before college, but we couldn't *make* him go, could we? . . . talked about Hakim, who had been seeing the school counselor for five weeks and seemed more in control of his emotions but still stumped me when it came to unlocking the brilliance inside . . . did a few updates on Yada Yada: Nony becoming a political activist for reparations, hoo boy! . . . Florida redeeming Carla's stay-at-home illness by reading books and more books . . . Carl Hickman doing temp work as a security guard . . .

But even as we chatted, why did I have the feeling that Denny and I hadn't talked about anything real and personal—soul deep—since . . . since Amanda's *quinceañera*? Even then, I was mostly an observer to his daddy's heart. How did he feel about ending up as an assistant coach this year—again—when he had more experience than the head coach and athletic director at West Rogers High combined? What

269

had kneeling beside MaDear's wheelchair last Christmas and asking forgiveness for the sins against her, taking them on his own soul, done to this man's heart? He rarely mentioned it, except to be glad that Adele had come back to Yada Yada. He hadn't said much about testifying at Becky Wallace's parole hearing either—just agreed to go. He just . . . plugged on. Did his job. Put up with me and all the Yada Yadas. Volunteered one Saturday a month for Uptown's homeless outreach. Loved our kids. Faithful, faithful, faithful . . .

"Denny?" I snuggled closer under the curve of his arm as the lights of the city blinked on all along the shoreline, dressing up the gray lapping water and flat gray sky with sequins of light. "What do you really think about testifying at Becky Wallace's parole hearing tomorrow?"

"Funny you should ask that . . . you cold?" Denny pulled me even closer, wrapping both arms around me.

Yes, I was shivering inside my jacket and wishing I'd worn a hat, but heck, who cared? I could feel the rough stubble on Denny's cheek against my face, the faint leathery smell of his aftershave, and he was going to open up his real thoughts. "I'm okay. Funny, why?"

"Remember Pastor Clark's sermon on the story of Ruth a couple of Sundays ago?"

"Yeah," I snorted. "I've always wondered why couples use that 'your people shall be my people' bit at weddings, when it was said by a young woman to an older woman."

Denny cleared his throat. "Uh . . . right. But I was thinking about Boaz, the 'kinsman redeemer.' Here's Ruth, this foreigner, this young widow, this distant relative by marriage, who suddenly drops into Boaz's life and ends up being his responsibility. By happenstance. He had a choice to marry her or not; nothing was automatic. If he hadn't taken action, Ruth would have remained a foreigner, an outcast, a childless widow, just marking time and space . . ."

I leaned away from Denny's arm and twisted so I could look at him. I almost blurted, *"We're not 'kinsmen' to Becky Wallace!"* But in a flash of understanding, I knew what he was trying to say. Becky Wallace had dropped into our lives—kind of like Ruth and Naomi dropping back into Boaz's life after years in a "far country"—and we had a choice: we could do nothing and let consequences take their natural course, or we could act as her "kinsmen redeemers," helping her to build a new life. At least give it a try.

I shivered. Or shuddered.

BUT THERE WE WERE THE NEXT MORNING at eleven straight up, four of us from the Yada Yada Prayer Group—Hoshi, Stu, Florida, and me—plus Denny, sitting in the hallway outside a conference room at Lincoln Correctional Center after a three-hour drive in a foggy drizzle worthy of the Northwest rain forest. We talked and prayed and sang on the way down, feeling hopeful. Denny shared his thoughts that maybe God had called us to be kinsmen redeemers for one ex-junkie. But Florida brought us down to earth as we waited for our turn with the parole board. "Wonder what they gonna think when we walk in?" she hissed. "Denny an' the Four Floozies or some-thin'? Ha."

I giggled nervously. Indeed. We made up an unlikely bunch. A svelte university student from Japan . . . a short, wiry black woman with a big smile and a long scar still evident between her cheekbone and ear . . . a DCFS social worker with dark roots under blonde hair that was a tad too long and straight for someone in her midthirties

. . . a third-grade teacher and a high school coach, married with teenagers and not a clue how the penal system worked.

At 11:05, the door opened and a female security guard motioned us inside. The room was small, with an oblong conference table. Three people sat along one side—one man and two women. All white. The man nodded at us and motioned to the three empty chairs along the other side of the table. "Uh, we'll get a couple more chairs. We didn't know there would be five of you."

The chairs arrived; we sat. For several moments, no one spoke as the three parole board members shuffled through some pages in front of them, as though they were reading or rereading them. We waited.

"An unusual request." One of the women broke the awkward silence, peering over her half-moon bifocal glasses at us. "I presume all of you signed this letter"—she waved a copy of Stu's letter with our signatures on it—"and were victims of the prisoner in question. Uh"—she squinted at a folder in front of her—"Becky Wallace."

Our heads bobbed. Denny cleared his throat. "That's right."

The woman leaned back in her chair, still peering at us over the top of her glasses, a gold chain snapped to each earpiece and circling the back of her neck in case they dived off her nose. She looked like a spinster librarian, may all spinsters and librarians the world over forgive me. The man, middle-aged, flabby chin, balding forehead, his suit a size too small—now, anyway—tapped a pencil on the table in irritating staccato. The other woman—younger, maybe thirties, with straight, thin, brown hair—looked at us up and down the row as though sorting us into different cubbyholes.

"Tell us," said Woman One, "how you came to be involved in this case."

I sat there, expecting Denny, or maybe Stu, or even tell-it-straight Florida to speak up—until I realized my cohorts were all looking at me. "Jodi's the one first met up with Becky," Florida offered. "Go ahead, Jodi."

I hadn't planned on saying anything, much less being the spokesperson. For a moment, my mouth went dry. This whole thing couldn't depend on *me*. And in the next nanosecond, I realized it didn't. It depended on God. Whatever happened. All we needed to do was put our case on the table.

So I told the story, as briefly as I could, of the day the "Avon lady" appeared at our front door during a Yada Yada prayer meeting, muscled her way into our home, and robbed all of us at knifepoint. Telling the part about Hoshi's mom getting her hand cut was hard, and Woman Two leaned forward and asked Hoshi more about it. The parole board seemed intensely interested in that part of the story and looked at each other when Hoshi said, "But Becky Wallace says she never meant to hurt anybody, and I believe her."

Florida chimed in—I knew she couldn't keep quiet for long— and said we started praying for Becky, being a prayer group and all. And one thing led to another . . . With helpful bits from Denny and Stu, the story got told.

The man shrugged. "So why are you here? Seems like you good folks have done enough."

"Good folks?" Florida sounded highly amused. "Why, we nothin' but sinners, same as Becky Wallace, same as you folks, but God's given us all another chance, and we all think Becky Wallace deserves that chance too. We ain't her victims anymore. We're her friends— maybe the only ones she got. An' since you all got an overcrowding problem here an' gonna parole some folks, might as well ask for Becky. Bible says we don't get 'cause we don't ask. So we askin'."

"Same as you folks"? I winced, sure Florida had stuck her foot in the cow pie there.

The parole board leaned toward one another, whispered among themselves, pointed something out on one of the many sheets of paper in front of them, then leaned back in their chairs.

"As I said, an unusual case," said Woman One, peering once again over the top of her glasses, which by now, indeed, did look like they were going to drop off the end of her nose. "We have never, to my knowledge, paroled a violent offender within the first year of incarceration. However . . ." She shuffled her papers for a moment. *"If* we were to consider Becky Wallace's parole in this case, we would recommend house arrest for the first three months and an electronic monitor. The problem is"—she cleared her throat—"house arrest means confined to one's home. And as far as we can determine, this prisoner has no known address."

And as surely as if a gavel had fallen in a courtroom, our case was dismissed.

32

Out in the hall we just looked at each other. *So much for kinsmen redeemers.* I'd thought I might feel relieved if the parole was turned down—we did what we could, it was out of our hands, maybe for the best and all that—but I felt sad. Sad for Becky, sad for her little boy, who might not even remember his mommy by the time she got out. Sad for the disruption to young lives. Sad for Carla and Florida, who were still trying to reconnect . . .

Florida took a deep breath. "Guess we might as well try to see Becky, long as we're here." Maybe Florida was thinking about Andy. About Carla too.

"Does she know we wrote to the parole board?" Worry lines gathered between Hoshi's arched brows. "Will she ask what happened? I hate to bring her bad news."

Stu fidgeted. "I didn't tell her, unless someone else wrote to her."

Denny had been standing at a window, his back to us, hands in his pockets. But he turned. "Might be good to tell her we tried. Even if it looks hopeless, it could be encouraging to know we stood up for her."

Stu rubbed her temples. "Why don't you guys go without me? I'm getting a migraine . . . think I'll go lie down in the car." She held out her hand for the car keys.

"Cain't you take somethin' for that headache?" Florida eyed Stu suspiciously. "You know Becky will be wantin' to hear somethin' 'bout her Andy—'specially now that you his caseworker."

Stu was already heading back toward the visitors' entrance. "Don't have any news. Every time I've tried to see him, something's come up." And she was gone.

Florida looked at me, then at Denny. "That the same Leslie Stuart who moved heaven and earth to find Carla? Somethin' don' smell right."

STU WAS ASLEEP in the third seat of the minivan, windows rolled halfway down for air, when we got out to the parking lot an hour later, and she slept back there most of the way home. I didn't know she had migraines, but I knew they could knock you out, really scramble your brain.

Denny was right about Becky. She hadn't reacted at first when we told her why we'd come, but after a moment large tears welled up in her eyes. I quickly handed her a wad of tissues—I traveled prepared these days. *"Don' matter . . . don' matter they said no,"* Becky had said, blowing her nose and dabbing furiously at her eyes as if offended by her tears. *"I never expected anything differ'nt."* She'd swiped an arm across her wet cheeks and sniffed. *"But I never 'spected nobody to stand up for me, neither. Means a lot."*

Back in the car, Florida glanced into the backseat. "Too bad Stu didn't go in. She the one who pushed us into writing the parole board. Becky would be glad to know that."

We didn't say any more, because, after all, we didn't know *how* asleep Stu was. Didn't mention that Becky had asked if "the Stuart lady" got hold of her Andy. She was real anxious to talk to her boy. *Uh-huh. Maybe that's what Stu was avoiding.* As far as I knew, she hadn't done anything about Andy yet.

Stu roused as we came back into the city, threading through traffic slowed by the fog and drizzle, and when we pulled up beside Florida's apartment building she suddenly chirped, "Don't forget, Yada Yada at my house tomorrow night. Can't wait for you guys to see what I've done to that plain ol' box."

"You alive back there, girl? We was beginning to wonder," Florida said as she clambered out.

That was the truth. Pinning down Stu's moods these days was like stapling bubbles.

AT LEAST I DIDN'T HAVE TO COMMUTE to Yada Yada this time or set out tea and munchies. Just went out the front door when I heard other Yada Yadas tromping up the front stairs. Stu hadn't come to church at Uptown that morning—maybe sleeping off the aftereffects of her migraine—but tonight she looked positively the Martha Stewart of hostesses. Cheeks glowing with health (or a good makeup job), mood lights highlighting the melon-and-lime color of her living room, tea and coffee and homemade Mexican wedding cookies, the kind soaking in buttery powdered sugar.

Delores was transported. "Oh! Stu! *Delicioso!* Just like my mama used to make." Telltale traces of powdered sugar clung to Delores chin as she smacked her lips happily.

It had actually been several weeks since I'd been upstairs to Stu's apartment—I was either in bed with a cold, or she'd been busy working—so I joined the crowd getting the grand tour. Lots of oohs and aahs at the sea blue and lavender kitchen, decorated with all shapes of baskets hanging on the walls, and Stu's seashell and burgundy bedroom.

The second floor had three bedrooms, just as we did on the first floor. Stu was obviously using one for a study and workspace, complete with sewing machine in one corner, computer desk, and a comfy chair with an afghan. Florida stood in the doorway of the other small bedroom, simply furnished with a double bed, black and gold comforter, a chest of drawers, a small desk, and a braided rug. "A guest room?" she blurted. "Hey, Stu, you want a couple o' young bloods to raise in this room? I'll send the bunk beds."

Stu laughed. "Make it Carla, and it's a deal."

Avis broke into the tour and called us back into the living room. We all seemed to be present and accounted for this time—except Chanda. *Rats. I haven't called her since she got skewered at Ruth's two weeks ago.* Not that there had been much room in my mucus-filled head—what with Josh getting stubborn about college and bombs bursting in the air over Baghdad—to remember noble stuff like calling Chanda.

Adele anticipated the unspoken question. "She wasn't at Paul and Silas this morning either. I'll give her a call this week, see what's up."

I glanced at Stu to see if she owned any responsibility for Chanda not showing up—she'd come down on her pretty hard in Ruth's foyer—but she was pouring tea and making lighthearted comments as she passed cups around. The smugness of the righteous, I guessed. *Yeah, like you got a leg to stand on, Jodi Baxter. Stu was just braver than the rest of us. Said everything I was thinking. Though like Avis said, it didn't seem the right place and time—*

"Speaking of church," Adele marched on, "guess Paul and Silas might survive a visit from Yada Yada. I think we're the last one on the list—might as well be now."

Whoa. I didn't think Adele would ever invite us to her church. Wasn't sure she'd want to own this ragtag menagerie in *public*.

"Yeah, but will Yada Yada survive a visit to Paul and Silas?" Florida grumbled. "They one of them 'baptize in Jesus's name' churches?"

"What's wrong with that?" Stu said. "Everyone should be baptized in Jesus's name."

"No, I mean Jesus's name *only*. If you been dunked in the name of the Father and Holy Ghost too, it don't count. An' the last Apostolic I tried out, I had to wear one of them doilies on my head."

Yo-Yo screwed up her face. "I think I got somethin' important to do that day."

Ruth snorted. "We haven't *said* what day yet."

Adele crossed her arms in Patient Mama mode. "All right, calm down you all. Paul and Silas still has its Apostolic roots, but our present pastor, Reverend Miles, grew up Baptist. Name of the church is actually Paul and Silas Apostolic Baptist. What we call it depends on who you talk to! MaDear, now, still kicks up a big fuss if the usher board doesn't wear white gloves, but Paul and Silas has been influenced by some of the big-name preachers who have Apostolic backgrounds—Reverend Brazier here in Chicago, Bishop Jakes, preachers like that who appeal to a broad spectrum of folks. But to be on the safe side? Wear a dress that covers your knees and a hat if you've got one."

Sounded kinda weird, but I didn't care. I was still amazed that Adele was actually going to take this motley crew to her church. Just hoped I didn't inadvertently do anything to play the white fool.

Out came the pocket calendars. "First Sunday of April?" Stu said, all business.

March had five Sundays, which meant the first Sunday of April was two weeks away. Looked good to me. I flipped to April—and burst out laughing. "Oh, hey! It's Denny's birthday on April first!"

"You kidding!" Yo-Yo looked skeptical. "April Fool's joke, right?"

"I kid you not. He's fair game, everybody, if you want to play tricks. Somebody should get him good, all the stuff he's pulled over the years."

"Okay, sisters, let's move on." Avis corralled the chitchat. "We really need to come before the Lord and get into His presence. Our nation, our world needs us to fall on our faces, and I know we have some real needs among us too."

She was right, of course. I sat back meekly in Stu's round wicker chair, shaped like an upside-down Chinese coolie hat with a fat, lime-colored cushion, and let Avis's opening prayer sweep out the cobwebs and stray thoughts of my mind. "Jesus! Oh, Jesus!" she prayed. "If ever we needed You, we need You now. The nations rage, floods and earthquakes and tornadoes sweep destruction in their paths, our children face pressures and temptations unknown as we were coming up—"

"Say it, sister," Florida groaned. "Oh, Jesus."

Nony had her Bible open to Psalm 27, and she poured some verses into the prayer. "The Lord is my light and my salvation; whom shall I fear? The Lord is the strength of my life; of whom shall I be afraid? . . . I would have lost heart, unless I had believed that I would see the goodness of the Lord in the land of the living. Wait on the Lord; be of good courage, and He shall strengthen your heart; wait, I say, on the Lord."

"Amen and amen!" said Avis. "Hallelujah!"

Florida added her own postscript. "God is God, all by Himself!"

The whole atmosphere of the room had changed. I wanted to remain wrapped in its cocoon, as though all the annoying sickness I'd had so far this spring, my frustration with Josh, the disappointment of our trip to the parole board, even the major traumas of war and terrorism and ethnic hatred that saturated the news, had all been wrapped in a bundle and laid in God's lap. I kept my eyes closed and blew out a long breath. *Oh God, I appreciate this prayer group so much. I need all the help I can get to help me focus all my worries and anxieties and uncertainties on the Source of my strength and my salvation. Thank You, Jesus. I do believe. Oh God, help me when I waver . . .*

Avis was taking note of things that needed sharing for prayer. "We want to hear from the group that went down to Lincoln this weekend . . . Delores has an update on her family in Colima . . . You too, Florida? Okay."

"Don't need more'n a minute," Florida jumped in. "Just throw Carl into the prayer pot. He out of work *agin*, and all this up and down makin' it hard to keep Chris in line." She threw up her hands. "Sometimes I've just had it."

"Humph. Kick him out," Adele grunted. "Needs a wake-up call."

"Oh no!" Delores cried, genuinely distressed. "Your *niños* need their papa, even an imperfect one." Her eyes misted. "Some day it will turn around; you'll see."

"Yeah, well, he's not out yet, but I'm tempted. Go on, go on, Delores, tell us 'bout your family."

Delores nodded. Most of the rubble from the earthquake in Colima had been cleared away, she said, but the rebuilding was going slowly and two of her brothers, their families, and her parents were all living in one house, the one with the least damage. "Seven children and six adults! *Gracias al Dios,* they all survived the earthquake. But there may be a *familia* earthquake if my brothers' families don't get out soon." She rolled her eyes.

Ruth shook her head and fanned herself. "A disaster, that is!"

The good news, Delores continued, was that a group called Project Amigo had offered to help rebuild the damaged homes but was short on funds. "So please pray—"

"Pray?" Yo-Yo yelped. "Sounds like they need cash." She dug into one of the myriad pockets in her denim overalls. "Hey. Five bucks. That's a start, ain't it?" She tossed the bill in Delores's lap.

"Now that girl's got the right idea." Ruth dug in her big, clunky handbag and produced a checkbook. "Who do I make this out to?"

In five minutes, a small pile of cash and checks lay in Delores's lap. Yo-Yo shrugged. "Not much, I guess. Maybe it'll buy a window or somethin'."

"Gracias, gracias," Delores whispered.

"Edesa, you find an address for Project Amigo," Ruth ordered. "Then we send contributions direct." She looked around. "Decided, yes? Our Yada Yada project for a few months." And that was that.

How I loved this group.

Guessed it was time to report on our trip to Lincoln. I opened my mouth, but Adele cut me off. "Hang onto that, Jodi. Avis? You forgot to put yourself on the agenda. Is Peter Douglass still on ice? And don't fuss at me for askin'. This ain't morbid curiosity. Courtship is serious business, and we all prayin' for you two."

Avis cocked an eyebrow. "Courtship, is it? You've all decided?" She sighed. "I'm praying too. Really. Thank you for caring, but . . .

we're still taking a break. I need some time to hear from the Lord, to sort through my feelings, even time to talk to my daughters. So . . . no change. Thanks for asking, though."

I caught Delores's eye. She let slip a tiny grin and pantomimed sewing tiny stitches. *Okaaaay. Keep on making that quilt square, I guess.* Talk about an act of faith.

Hoshi reported on our visit to the parole board. Bless her, she even described Denny's discussion about the kinsman redeemer from the book of Ruth. "Yet they gave us no hope. As I understand it, it is very unusual to parole a violent offender in such a short time. Even if they did, she would have to be arrested at home—"

"House arrest," Stu said helpfully.

"House arrest, with something on the leg—"

"Electronic monitor."

"All right. I see. But she has no house to be arrested to." Hoshi sat back and shook her head. "That is sad. No place to go home to." A strange look passed over her face. I read it: *"Like me."*

Stu cleared her throat and sat up. "Exactly. So I've been doing some serious thinking. And I think there is a way. Becky does have a home. With me. She can come to live with me."

33

*I*t took a second or two for Stu's words to compute, but when they did, I yelped. *"What?!* Becky Wallace live *here?!* You're out of your mind, Leslie Stuart!"

Stu shrugged. "Why? Didn't Jesus say if we have two coats we should give one to the guy who has none? I've got three bedrooms. Becky has none. Same thing."

It is NOT! I wanted to scream. But I was dangerously close to losing it, and I clamped my teeth, knowing I needed time to cool down. But my mind still raged. *Becky Wallace in my house? After what she did here? Over my dead body.*

At least I wasn't the only one who thought it was a bad idea. I heard others, recovering from the initial shock, begin to respond. "Mm-mm. Doesn't sound wise."

"What if she goes back to the drugs? Happens, you know."

"It's not your responsibility to *make* this happen, Stu."

"Just 'cause we forgive her don't mean there ain't no consequences."

"Whatever put such an idea in your head, Stu?"

I rolled my eyes. "Because Stu's gotta ride in on her white horse and be everybody's savior."

Stu winced as if I'd just slapped her. Avis raised her eyebrows at me. *Good grief. Did I say that out loud?* Since when did my tongue get permission to undress my thoughts in public?

I sighed. "I'm sorry, Stu. I didn't mean it." *Liar. Yes, you did.* "It's just that . . ." *Be honest, Jodi Baxter. Can you be real for just one minute?* I sorted through the thoughts and feelings knocking like jagged rocks in my mind and my gut. No one spoke, waiting for me.

I tried again. "It's just that . . ." Renegade tears threatened to spill. "Becky Wallace living in your house feels like Becky Wallace living in my house. She robbed us downstairs, for pity's sake, in this very house! Threatened all of us—could've killed Denny with that knife, the way she lunged at him. What if she'd seen Amanda? She even threatened Willie Wonka!" I was really blubbering now. "It's not fair to ask me to do this. We live here too."

If I thought getting honest would sway Stu, I was wrong. "I'm not asking you to do anything. Besides, I thought you forgave her," she said stubbornly.

"I do! . . . did. I just don't want her living in this house." I grabbed my wad of ever-ready tissues and tried to sop up the mess on my face.

"That it, Jodi?" Yo-Yo bobbed her spiky thatch at me. "You afraid?"

Well, wasn't that obvious? Didn't I just say—?

I corralled my knee-jerk thoughts. Was I afraid? Was I? Honest?

No. Frankly, my fear had evaporated with the prison visits. Bandana Woman the Menace had become Becky Wallace, pathetic single mom on a collision course with herself unless God intervened.

So what was it?

The truth slugged me right smack in the kisser of my attitude. *I just didn't want to be bothered.*

EVEN THOUGH EVERYBODY HAD QUESTIONS about Stu's offer, Nony wrapped a big prayer around it at the end. Especially after Yo-Yo said, "Can't blame ya, Jodi. Taking Becky in would be askin' a lot. Like you guys say, the Big Guy's forgiven me for all the bad stuff I done, but . . . I dunno. Still not sure He'd want the likes of me hangin' 'round heaven, right in His face. Brings down the neighborhood, know what I mean?"

Of course, we all protested. Of course, God wanted the likes of Yo-Yo and the likes of all the rest of us in heaven. That was the whole point! Why else would He sacrifice His own Son for a bunch of sinners?

But what Yo-Yo said bothered me. Burrowed under my skin like a rash that wouldn't go away. All Yo-Yo knew about God was what she saw lived out in us, in the Yada Yada Prayer Group. In me. And what she saw was that forgiveness stopped short if it really cost you something.

I spilled it all to Denny after I came back downstairs and the Yada Yadas had trooped home. The kids had gone to youth group, but Josh had the car, and if José had come up on the el, which he'd been doing almost every week, I knew good and well Amanda would talk her brother into giving him a ride home. At least we had the house to ourselves. Denny had been watching a video, the shoot-'em-up kind he watched when I wasn't around, but he put it on Pause and listened as he always did, watching me, waiting for me to run down.

I grabbed a basket of clean laundry and started to pull out socks. "I got honest," I admitted. "Told Stu what I thought about her savior complex."

The corners of Denny's mouth twitched, a smile he didn't want to acknowledge.

"You know what's weird? When she visited the prison back in February, Stu made a big deal about taking over as the caseworker for Becky's kid—but I don't think she's even seen him yet. It doesn't add up."

Denny reached for the growing pile of socks. "Yeah, but you know DCFS. Miles of red tape."

I shrugged and started folding underwear. "Yeah, maybe. And who am I to talk? 'Cause I don't like what I see when I get honest with myself. I know Stu is the one offering to have Becky come live with her, yet you know good and well we'll end up getting sucked into . . . whatever. And"—I shook my head at the truth—"it just feels like too much *bother*. Makes me feel tired."

Denny opened his mouth, but my confession was on a roll. "And you know what really bugs me? It's such a *righteous* thing for Stu to do. And I don't want her to be righteous about this. Why can't she be flawed and normal like the rest of us?"

Denny guffawed. "Yeah, well. Even flawed, normal people have occasional moments of righteousness. Even you, Jodi." He threw up an arm in self-defense as I whacked him with a pair of clean boxers.

The kids came home, arguing about the summer mission trip possibilities they'd discussed while pulling cheddar cheese, tortillas, salsa, and onions out of the refrigerator for late-night quesadillas. I heard something about "volunteers" and "Cornerstone Festival"—had to be Josh's idea—and Amanda's high voice insisting the need was much greater for day-camp counselors in Pilsen Park.

Pilsen neighborhood. Hugely Latino. Were my kids predictable or what?

I stayed out of it, glad that the options were local this year. No way did I want my kids flying anywhere this summer, even in the States. The U.S. government was insisting the war with Iraq would be over "quickly," but I wasn't buying it. The whole world was beginning to feel like a danger zone.

Which was another reason I didn't want Becky Wallace living in our house. I wanted home to be *home,* not a halfway house for convicted felons.

I WAS BEGINNING TO COUNT THE DAYS until school was out. Not a good sign, since it was only the last week of March. Eight of my third graders were absent with some kind of virus—and sure enough, I caught it. The stomach virus was majorly worse in my book than a cold. At least with a cold I could sip hot tea and nibble comfort foods. This time around there was no comfort to be had. Even my family treated me like I had the plague.

"You have to see the doctor, Jodi," Denny said from a safe distance in the bedroom doorway Tuesday evening. "Take vitamins, build up your immunity—something. This is getting ridiculous."

"Tell me about it," I groaned from the depths of my pillow—three seconds before I made another mad dash to the bathroom. I know I used up a whole bottle of Pine Sol that day just disinfecting the john.

At least this flu turned out to be the twenty-four-hour variety, and I was back in school on Thursday, feeling almost perky. Some of my kids were back, but a new crop was out—including Hakim Porter. Seeing his empty desk, I suddenly felt defeated. Between all the days I'd been sick, all the catch-up work I had to do to keep my class "on task" and "on schedule" to satisfy state requirements, and now Hakim out sick . . . frankly, the progress I'd so confidently promised Geraldine Wilkins-Porter if she left him in my classroom just wasn't happening. What would I say at the next parent-teacher conference—less than four weeks away?

That's the real truth, isn't it, Jodi? Hakim isn't failing. You are.

That thought hung over my head all day like a speech balloon in a comic strip. Still hanging there when I got home and sank onto the couch, nursing my tender innards with a mug of peppermint tea and a banana. Odd thing was, I kept wondering what to do with "the truth." Old Jodi tendency would be: beat myself up over it. *You're a fraud, Jodi Baxter! A miserable failure!* And the cover-up: *How can I come out of this looking good?* New Jodi response: did I have one?

Okay, Jesus, I'm definitely in over my head. Now what? I'm not help-ing Hakim—not the kind of help he needs. I should have realized he needed something more than I can give. Why was it so important for me to help him, anyway? Trying to prove something, I guess—that I'm not the monster Hakim's mother thinks I am—

The bleating ring of the telephone invaded my desperate mono-logue. By the time I got to the kitchen phone, the answering machine had kicked in. "Jodi!" Stu's voice. "My Internet server's down and I can't—"

I picked up. "Hi Stu." Automatic response. Did I really want to talk to Stu?

"Oh! Jodi." Stu sounded taken off guard. "Didn't know you were home from school yet. Was just going to leave a message on your machine."

"That's okay. Yeah, I'm still on the wobbly side of the stomach flu. Came straight home."

"Oh. Sorry. Uh, like I said, my Internet server is down and I can't send any e-mail. I finally got an appointment to see Andy Wallace on Saturday, though. Wondered if you'd send an e-mail for me, ask Yada Yada to pray that it'd work out okay."

What was up with this? Stu usually acted first and praised God later. "Well, sure. Anything particular you want us to pray for?" The phone was silent. "You still there, Stu?"

"Yes. Just . . . pray that it'd work out okay."

"Okay. Got it." I hung up the phone, yet I had an uneasy feeling. It wasn't like Stu to be nervous. Even facing a hostile grandmother. One day she's boldly inviting a recent heroin addict to be her house-mate; the next she's nervous about meeting with a two-year-old foster kid? It didn't add up.

STU HADN'T SAID WHEN HER APPOINTMENT WAS on Saturday, but I heard her go down the back stairs and out to the garage about ten o'clock. Denny had an all-day training session with a new group of suburban volunteers for Uptown's outreach, now that the homeless were back out on the streets and in the parks. I kept the car so I could run my errands.

Still, I was curious how Stu's appointment would go, what little Andy looked like, if the grandmother was willing to take calls from Lincoln Correctional, stuff like that, so I puttered around the house, keeping an ear out for Stu to come back.

Sure enough, I heard footsteps running up the back stairs about eleven thirty. But I was in the basement stuffing dirty sheets and towels in the washing machine and didn't get out to the back porch in time to catch her on the way up. So I punched in Stu's number, cradled the phone between shoulder and ear as I hauled another laundry basket down to the basement and listened to the rings. Four . . . five . . . then the answering machine kicked in. *"Hi! I'm not home right now. Please leave a—"* Annoyed, I pushed the Off button. I was sure I'd heard her go upstairs. Huh. Maybe she came home and went right out again. Or maybe my ears had played tricks on me.

I finished setting the washing machine and decided I couldn't put off my errands any longer. I shrugged into a jacket and gathered up my stuff for the weekly Baxter shopping trip: dry cleaning, grocery list, birthday list, plastic bags to recycle, wallet, car keys—

Footsteps. Upstairs. Walking right over my head.

She *was* there, the jerk. Though in the interest of fairness, maybe she'd been in the bathroom or something and hadn't heard the phone. Well, I'd try again. I punched Redial and waited. Four rings . . . five . . . *"Hi! I'm not home right now. Please leave a message."* Click.

"Forget you," I muttered, grabbing up my stuff and heading out the back door. Okay, I was annoyed. But it could wait. I'd do my errands and then ask how it went with Andy and Andy's grandmother. Not a big deal, right?

I turned on the CD player as soon as I got in the car. Fill the car with praise! I wasn't going to let Leslie Stuart ruin my day. Adjust the car seat . . . check. Adjust the rearview mirror . . . check. Click the garage door opener . . . check. I turned on the ignition, put the minivan in reverse, started to back out of the garage—and nearly backed straight into Stu's silver Celica, parked broadside in front of our garage door, blocking my way.

That does it! I bolted out of the car, out the garage door, up the back walk, and literally stomped up the flight of stairs to Stu's back door. *Who does she think she is? She thinks she can park anywhere, not even answer the phone, because it's all about her!* Well, she was going to answer the door now.

I pounded on her back door with my fist. "Stu! Leslie Stuart! Your car is blocking my way—I can't get out!" *Pound! Pound! Pound!* I listened. No answer.

Okay. Two could play this game. I hustled back down the stairs, ignoring the short stabs of pain in my leg with the rod in it, grabbed the key marked *Stu* from the key rack in the kitchen, and stormed up the stairs again. It had been Stu's idea to exchange house keys "for emergencies." Well, this might not be an emergency, but I knew she was there, her car was blocking my garage door, and no way was I going to let her ignore me.

I inserted the key, opened the door—then hesitated. "Stu! It's Jodi!" I yelled through the kitchen. No answer. Silence. What in the heck . . .?

Stu's ring of keys lay in a jumble on the kitchen floor. A flicker of worry nudged my anger aside. Something was wrong. "Stu!" I called out, checking the dining room . . . living room . . . bathroom . . .

Nothing. Nobody.

Stu's bedroom door was closed. Maybe she was taking a nap. Maybe she was a heavy sleeper. Maybe—

I slowly turned the knob and quietly opened the door. Stu was sitting on the edge of her bed, long hair falling over one shoulder, staring at her lap. On the bedside stand, an empty prescription bottle lay on its side. In one hand, she held a drinking glass, half full of water. In the other, a handful of blue caplets.

I shot into the room and slapped the pills out of her hand. Stu's head jerked up as the pills flew wild. She grabbed at me as I snatched the empty prescription bottle, but I pushed her away, scanning the label. *Zoloft.* An antidepressant.

"How many of these did you take?" I screamed at her. *"How many?"*

34

Stu shrank away from me. "Just . . . just one. No . . . maybe two," she whimpered. "I forgot to take my meds this morning . . . I feel so bad . . ."

"I don't believe you!" Panic bubbled up in my throat. *Oh God, Oh God, what should I do?* Call 911, that's what. I lunged for the phone on her nightstand—but Stu's free hand shot out, grasping my wrist with a surprising steel grip.

"Don't, Jodi! Please!" She dropped the water glass in her other hand, grabbed the phone and clutched it fiercely to her chest. "Don't call an ambulance. I didn't do it! I . . . I was thinking about it, but I didn't! I didn't!" The braided rug beside her bed had broken the fall of the glass, yet I felt water splash all over my shoes.

"I don't believe you," I hissed, twisting my wrist free. "I called up here—twice. I banged on the door. You didn't answer! Something's wrong. You need help." Why was I even arguing with her? I turned and headed for the door. I'd call 911 on my own phone.

Stu came hot on my heels. "Jodi, please don't! I'm okay! See?"

I kept moving, out the back door, down the outside stairs. She clattered right behind me. "Jodi! Jodi! Wait! I can explain!"

I charged through my kitchen door and tripped over Willie Wonka, lying in his usual spot. Stu collided with my back and we both went down, cushioned by Wonka's soft, square body, like a football pileup. The dog grunted heavily and tried to wiggle out from under our tangle of legs and arms.

The ridiculous heap we made was all out of proportion to how upset I was. The feelings in my chest felt ready to explode—either in hysterical laughter or hysterical crying. But as I struggled to get up, Stu's arms clung tightly around me. "Jodi, wait. Please wait. Don't call anybody. I'll tell you."

I hesitated. *Oh God, I don't know what to do!* Then it came to me.

Ipecac syrup. The little brown bottle that sat in our bathroom cupboard in case any little kids ever accidentally chewed on the philodendron or mistook the antihistamine pills for candy. I scrambled to my feet, pulling her up with me. "Come with me," I ordered, hauling her toward the bathroom. To my surprise, she didn't resist. I put the toilet seat lid down. "Sit." She sat.

I stood on the little wooden stepstool—another relic from the kids' younger days—and got down the brown bottle. "Hold this," I barked, feeling like an army sergeant with a new recruit. I dashed back to the kitchen for a tablespoon and a glass of water—thirty seconds, tops—and to my relief she was still holding the bottle, looking bewildered.

"Throw up," I said. "That's the deal. You throw up and I won't call 911."

I knew good and well I was supposed to call poison control or some medical person before giving ipecac, but Stu was no two-year-old and if she'd swallowed anything, it was medicine—not anything acid or toxic like cleaning supplies that would burn coming back up. I poured the dosage into the tablespoon; with the resignation of a cornered stowaway, she swallowed it. I pushed the glass of water at her. "All of it," I ordered. She drank.

We didn't talk. I just sat on the edge of the tub, and she sat on the stool, staring at the floor, waiting. Willie Wonka's nails clicked on the wood floor of the hallway and hesitated outside the bathroom. A neighbor's door slammed. The bathroom window rattled—*boom! ba-da boom! boom!*—as a car with a serious sound system invaded Lunt Street, then faded away.

Within fifteen minutes, it all came up. Afterward I wet a washcloth with warm water and washed her face, feeling a sudden tenderness for Stu I'd never felt before. I knelt awkwardly on the bathroom rug, put my arms around Leslie Stuart, and pulled her close. She leaned into my shoulder and began to cry. The sobs became a wail; her whole body shook within my embrace. But I just held on, murmuring comforting words, wondering. Had I done the right thing?

HALF AN HOUR LATER, I'd gotten Stu back up to her apartment, picked up all the pills that had flown around her room, and was making some peppermint tea to settle her stomach. Denny wasn't due home till late afternoon, but the kids might've wandered in at any moment, and they'd definitely ask questions if they'd seen us entwined in the bathroom. I put two mugs of hot tea on the pert white table that served as a breakfast nook and sat down in one of the matching chairs across from Stu.

"All right. Tell me." My words came out gentle; she gave me a brief smile.

"I thought . . . I could do it," she said in a half-whisper. "I knew what his birth date was, but I prayed about it, I really did, and I knew Yada Yada was praying for my visit." She suddenly squinted at me. "You did send that e-mail for me, didn't you?"

"*Yes*, I sent it! Whose birth date? Andy's?"

She nodded. "When I got his case reassigned . . . there it was. That date. And I wasn't sure I could do it. Becky was counting on me, though, and . . . I knew all the Yadas were wondering why I hadn't been to see him. So I asked God to help me, but—"

"Stu. What in the heck are you talking about? What *about* Andy's birth date?"

Tears welled up in her eyes, and I pushed a wicker holder of paper napkins toward her. She dabbed at her eyes and blew her nose. "His birthday," she whispered. "The same day . . . the same day . . ." Her shoulders began to shake. With a dose of wisdom from on high, I said nothing, just reached out and touched her arm.

She finally took a long, shuddering breath. "His birthday is . . . the same day *my* baby was due. Would be the same age. But . . . but my baby died. I mean . . ." Her voice fell to a mere whisper. "I killed my baby."

It wasn't wisdom that kept me from saying anything this time. *Killed her baby?!* I was so shocked, I could hardly breathe, much less talk.

Now that Stu had said the words, it was as if she'd pulled her finger out of the dike. "An abortion. I had an abortion. Maybe it was a little boy—I don't know. A little boy like Andy. I didn't want to, but what could I do? The jerk left me, dumped me like a rotting carcass when I told him I was pregnant—"

A loud knock at Stu's back door made us both jump. "I'll get it," I told Stu, hastily rising from my chair and spilling my tea in the process. Stu waved me away and mopped up the spilled liquid with a wad of napkins. I could see Josh's shaved head framed in the glass window of Stu's kitchen door.

"Mom!" he said when I slipped out onto the second story porch. "Stu's car is blocking the garage door! I can't get the minivan out, and I want—"

I held up my hand to stop him, stepped back inside and scooped up Stu's car keys, still lying on the floor, and went back outside. Josh's quizzical expression made him look like an overgrown, comic-strip Swee'Pea. "Here. Move Stu's car into the garage. Leave the keys downstairs on the counter. Yeah, yeah, take the Caravan."

He shrugged. "Okay." As my lanky teenager headed down the outside stairs, it occurred to me that I hadn't done my errands yet. Or asked Josh where he was going. It also occurred to me that it didn't matter. Not now.

IF I WASN'T GOING TO CALL 911, I sure didn't want to leave Stu alone for even a minute. I didn't trust her. Wasn't even sure I understood what was really going on. I knew I needed help; I couldn't be her shadow every second. With another person we could spell each other, get some sleep, whatever. I thought about asking Stu whom I should call, then decided just to tell her I was calling Avis. She opened her mouth to protest, but I was getting good with the steely eyed *"This is the way it is, buster,"* and she deflated.

All I got was Avis's voicemail. *Humph. Where could she be?* Now that she'd given Peter Douglass the boot, seemed to me Avis ought to be home staring at her four walls, realizing she'd made a big mistake.

Who else could I call? Chanda lived closest—ha, not likely. Not the way Stu had skewered her a few weeks ago. There'd be no sympathy there. Adele? It was Saturday. Adele's Hair and Nails was surely full of weaves, pedicures, and braided extensions.

I dialed Flo's number, told her Stu was having a meltdown, and asked if she could help me sit it out. Florida didn't even ask what it was about. Just said, "Be there in an hour. But Carl and the boys ain't here. I'll have to bring Carla."

My heart sank. "Carla? I don't think—"

"Carla?" Stu, who'd been slumped on one elbow at the small kitchen table, sat up. "Sure, let Carla come. I'd like that."

I covered the receiver. "Stu, I don't think that's a good . . ."

But she was smiling. I let it drop. If Stu was comfortable with Florida and Carla being here, so be it. Maybe it was a cover, so she wouldn't have to talk about her feelings or what had just happened. *Almost happened.* Or maybe it'd be a good thing. It wasn't as if I really knew what I was doing here. Just knew, for the first time since I'd met Leslie Stuart, that God had crossed our paths, and I needed to walk with her right now.

Turned out, Carla was a good thing. An air of normalcy returned to the second-floor apartment. Carla's short, beaded braids bounced from room to room, then she settled down to play with a set of Russian dolls from Stu's bookcase—ten wooden babushkas of graduated sizes hidden inside one another. While Florida hunted in the refrigerator for something to cook for supper, I took advantage of the distraction to go downstairs, where I discovered Amanda and José eating pita pizzas and watching *Spiderman* in the living room.

"Ahem!"

Amanda sparred first. "Where *were* you, Mom? I would've asked if José could stay to watch a video but nobody was home, and the door wasn't even locked!"

I let it go, even though we had a no-boyfriend-if-an-adult-isn't-home rule. When Denny got home, I gave him a brief rundown of what had gone on upstairs, told him not to ask any questions because I didn't know any answers, and handed him the grocery list. "Would you mind?"

He recovered from the blitz. "Sure. Except the car's not here. Where's Josh?"

Huh. Like I know. Probably down at Jesus People. He'd been hanging out there nearly every weekend. Undaunted, I spied Stu's key ring he'd returned to the kitchen counter. "Here. Take Stu's car. Take Amanda and José. Buy out the store."

"Cool," Denny said—which struck me so funny, I started to laugh. The pent-up emotions of that day suddenly erupted like a Texas oil well, and I leaned against Denny's shirt to stifle my torrent of wet giggles, pointing silently upward at the ceiling, not wanting Stu to hear my hysterical laughter. Denny circled me with his arms till I'd calmed down and wiped my eyes on his T-shirt, leaving black mascara smudges. "You did good, Jodi," he murmured into my hair. "Go back upstairs. I can handle the Alamo down here all by myself."

FLORIDA HAD PUT TOGETHER A TACO SALAD from Stu's pantry and refrigerator, and Carla kept us entertained with her new repertoire of vampire jokes. Carla: "What do you get when you cross a snowman with a vampire?" Three ignorant adults: "We dunno." Carla: "Frostbite!" Laughter punctured the tension, and supper almost felt like a party.

Later, while Florida and I cleaned up the kitchen, we could hear Stu reading Shel Silverstein's *Where the Sidewalk Ends* to Carla in the front room with much giggling at the silly poems. "Maybe I overreacted," I murmured, loading the dishwasher while Florida tackled the dirty pots in the sink. "Stu seems okay."

"Nah. What you told me 'bout how she was actin' this morning? She shouldn't be alone. We're okay, Carla and me. Don't have church clothes with us for tomorrow, but I did grab some clean underwear." She smirked.

Stu appeared in the kitchen doorway just as we gave the counters a last swipe. "Carla's asleep. I put her in the spare bedroom. Hope that's okay."

"Good," Florida said. "Now we're goin' to talk." She steered Stu toward the living room. To my surprise, Stu didn't resist but curled up in one of her wicker basket-chairs while Florida and I took the futon. The fading daylight outside the front windows filled the corners of the room with shadows, leaving the three of us in a small pool of lamplight.

"You carried this too long by yourself, girl," Florida prodded. "Get it off your chest. We're listening. An' God already knows about it; no surprise to Him."

The hours of just hanging out, giggling at dumb jokes over taco salad, and putting Carla to bed seemed to give Stu the needed strength to bring the dreaded memories into the light. It was a common story, yet strangely peculiar coming out of Stu's mouth. All my stereotypes of "Ms. Perfect" crumbled as she spoke, and in their place was a wounded, vulnerable woman, opening her soul and letting it bleed.

She'd been dating the guy for several months, someone she met through a friend. Said she didn't know for sure what had happened that night—they'd gone to a singles' nightclub, had some drinks, woke up the next morning in her apartment—until she skipped a couple of periods and the home pregnancy kit tested positive. When she told the boyfriend she was pregnant, "He just disappeared," Stu said, her forlorn features betraying the sense of abandonment. "I couldn't prove I'd been date raped, couldn't face telling my family, couldn't bear raising a child alone. I'd seen too many single moms trapped, struggling, ending up on welfare. And I . . . I was embarrassed. I was thirty-two, for heaven's sake! I've got a master's degree! How could I let this happen to me? I'm smart, I'm educated, I'm supposed to be helping people who make dumb mistakes!" Stu's eyes glittered for a brief moment, and then her shoulders slumped. "So I . . . I told myself I had no choice. But I cried for days. Everyone wondered what was wrong. To cope, I . . . I shut everybody who knew me out of my life. Distanced myself from my family, stopped going to St. John's, quit my DCFS job, took a real-estate course, moved, started a new life. Put it out of my mind. Proved to myself I could survive one mistake and start over. But . . ."

She picked at a loose thread, lost in her thoughts. Florida and I exchanged glances but said nothing. Stu looked up. "Then I heard about the Chicago Women's Conference last May. I was so *hungry* for something—I didn't even know what." A wry smile twisted the corners of her mouth. "Ended up in this crazy group of women. The Yada Yada Prayer Group! Don't know why I stayed. You were all so . . . so . . ."

"Weird," Florida finished. "Uh-huh. Thought the same about you." I stifled a giggle, but Florida plunged right on. "It was God who called us into this here prayer group and gave us that name,

Yada Yada, even when we didn't know it had all sorts of God-fearin' meanings. Called each one of us by name too—Jodi, here, been helpin' us with that. Called you, Stu. Called you by name and said, 'I'm puttin' that Leslie Stuart in Yada Yada, 'cause they need her. An' she needs them.'"

Florida's hopeful words raised goose bumps on my arms, but Stu began shaking her head, and the tears welled up again. "No . . . no . . . I ruined it! Ruined my name. 'Caretaker,' Jodi said . . . but I didn't . . . I didn't . . ." Stu rolled herself up into a ball and gulped air between sobs. "I didn't take care of my baby!"

Florida shot off the futon and pulled Stu's flaxen head against her small chest. "Jesus! *Jesus!*" Her own brown face was wet with tears. "Now we *know* Your blood done already covered this terrible pain in Stu's life. You came to take the sin and the pain and cover it with Your own. An' Jesus, we know You've got that baby in Your hand right now. You've called that baby by name too. He . . ."

Florida stopped. "Stu. Did you name that baby?"

Stu shook her head between Florida's strong hands. "No. I . . . told myself it was just a blob of tissue—you know, so I could go through with it."

"Stu, now you listen to me, girl. Somewhere in the Bible it says God *knows us* even before we was born, still inside our mama's womb. An' somewhere else God says, 'I called you by name, you are Mine!' Hear that? Your baby belongs to God, and nothin' you did changes *that*." Florida held Stu at arm's length, eye to eye. "So we goin' to name this baby, an' give him back to God, where he's already safe and waitin' for you when you get to heaven. What name you want?"

Stu shook her head, bewildered. "I don't know." She looked at me, pleading. "Jodi, you're good at this naming business. You pick a name. For a boy. I just know in my heart it was a boy." The tears kept running—her nose too—and I handed her another wad of tissues. But a light had come into her eyes.

My mind scrambled. What did I remember about the meaning of boys' names? Biblical names. *Isaac?* No, that meant "laughter." Not so good. *Jacob? Matthew? David?*

Yes.

I knelt down beside Stu and took her hands, which were busy wadding the damp pile of tissues. They stilled under my touch. The moment felt sacred, and I could hardly find my voice. But I whispered, "His name is David. It means . . . 'Beloved.'"

35

The three of us cried a lot and talked until late. Then we tucked Stu into her bed and fell out ourselves—Florida in the double bed with Carla, and me on the futon with an afghan. In the middle of the night, I woke up confused and sweating. I felt overwhelmed by loss. Someone had died! But who?

Oh God. *Stu's baby. David. David Stuart.*

And . . . *Jamal Wilkins.*

I struggled upright under the afghan, which had knotted itself around my body, pulled my knees up to my forehead, and wept. I wanted Denny—needed Denny to hold me. Yet Denny was downstairs, out cold and oblivious, no doubt. God was here, though . . .

God is gracious. That was the meaning of my name. *God is gracious . . . God is gracious.* "My grace is sufficient," Jesus said. Did I believe that? I laid back down on Stu's futon and imagined crawling up in God's lap, a lap already cradling a baby named David and a teenager named Jamal. And Stu. And Florida and Carla. All on God's lap. And God had His arms around us all.

I DIDN'T THINK STU WOULD BE UP FOR GOING TO CHURCH the next morning, but Florida just said to her, "We're goin'." We let her take *one* antidepressant, and I took the bottle with me as I hustled downstairs to take a quick shower and change out of my sweats—and discovered José eating breakfast cereal with Denny and Josh. I blinked and counted noses. The shower was running in the bathroom—Amanda no doubt, unless there were more gremlins hiding in the woodwork I didn't know about.

"Good morning, *Señora* Baxter," José said politely. I burbled something I hoped sounded like "Hi," but I was so startled, I probably sounded like I was gagging. I shot Denny a look that said, *"What's the meaning of this?"*

Denny chewed placidly. "Gotta drop José at the el on the way to church. You play drums at Iglesia this morning, José, right?"

José nodded and poured another bowl of cereal. *"Sí."*

Florida and Carla rode with Stu in her Celica and I rejoined my family, feeling as if I couldn't be gone twenty minutes, much less twenty hours, without *something* going amiss. "Thought you said you had the Alamo covered," I hissed at Denny as we trailed Josh and Amanda up the stairs at Uptown.

"I did." Denny leveled his eyebrows at me. "Gotta trust me, Jodi. Tell you about it later." His tone also said, *"Don't push me."*

I pressed my lips into a firm line, but they fell open when we reached the second-floor meeting room—and there was Peter Douglass, urbane and handsome as ever, sitting by himself on the far side, halfway back. My head swiveled. Avis was huddled with Pastor Clark; she must be worship leader today. Florida and Stu, who had arrived before we did, saw me staring at Peter and grinned. Florida pumped her fist surreptitiously. *Yes!*

Denny immediately headed over to Peter Douglass, and the two men spoke and nodded, as if agreeing to talk more after service. When Denny came back, we sat behind Florida and Stu, and I noticed Stu dabbing at her eyes throughout the entire service. But I also noticed that when we sang the Israel Houghton song, *"We worship You, for who You are . . . You are good! All the time! All the time, You are good!"* Stu lifted her hands and her face upward—the first time I'd ever seen her worship like that.

Now I was the one who needed the tissues.

"YOU FIRST," I told Denny, wrapping my hands around a double decaf cappucino at the Heartland Café while we waited for our nachos grandes. Denny sipped the head off an iced mug of beer—the first beer I'd seen him drink in months.

I'd been so exhausted after church that I took a long nap. Denny had finally shaken me awake at five o'clock. "Jodi! You'll be up all night if you don't get up. C'mon. We're going out. You and me. Oh—Avis called. I said you'd call her back. *Later.*"

Yeah, I bet she did. She'd caught me after church and said, *"Stu's pretty weepy. What's going on? My caller ID showed you called yesterday."*

"Uh-huh, big stuff. You can either ask her or I can fill you in. But"— *I jutted my chin in Peter's direction, who'd been cornered again by Denny, and grinned wickedly—"only if you fill me in, sister."*

Now I looked at Denny across the "naturally stressed" wooden table of the Heartland's sidewalk café, still enclosed till the weather warmed up a bit more. I was curious, but the steam I'd felt when I'd first seen José at our breakfast table had dissipated. *"You gotta trust me,"* Denny had said. *And Me,* the Holy Spirit had echoed in my spirit. Hadn't God been at work all weekend on the second floor? Had to spill down to the first floor of our house too.

"Okay, me first." Denny shrugged. "I took Amanda and José grocery shopping, like you said. At the fruit market the kids threw a couple of cans of *salsa verde*, some cornmeal, and a package of corn husks into the cart, and José promised to show us how to make authentic Mexican chicken tamales."

"You're kidding. Amanda helped cook?"

"Uh, well, she found the salt and stuck the corn husks in some warm water to soften." He grinned. "Wasn't exactly the cooking breakthrough we've been hoping for. But José knew what he was doing."

"Amazing," I murmured. "José can cook."

"I think he's had to do a lot of things as the oldest of the Enriques brood. Working mom, blue-collar dad who's gone a lot driving trucks—you know. But José and I had a good talk; he kinda opened up. Amanda, bless her, pulled back and just let José and me talk. I was kinda surprised—ah! Here's the nachos."

A blue-jean clad waiter put a huge plate of corn chips covered with beans and melted jack cheese on the table between us. Lettuce, tomatoes, salsa, and sour cream toppings made the plate look like an ad for the Rocky Mountains. We each pulled out a crisp corn chip loaded with stringy cheese and spicy beans. "So what else?" I mumbled between crunchy bites.

Denny washed down a spicy mouthful with the last of his beer and signaled the waiter for another. *Okay, two,* I told myself. *Don't get your tail in a knot, Jodi. Two beers in how many months? Not a big—*

"He wants to go to college," Denny said.

"College!"

"Uh-huh. Said playing together in the mariachi band has been great for him and his dad lately—they'd never been close before. But he doesn't want to end up driving trucks. He asked if I thought he could get into U of I."

Had to admit I was surprised. "Ironic, isn't it? Josh gets accepted at U of I and blows it off. José's only fifteen and he's already hot to go. Go figure." But I squinted at my husband. "So how does this add up to José sleeping over last night?"

Denny allowed a rueful grin. "We talked so long, suddenly I realized it was eleven o'clock and Josh wasn't back yet with the car. José said he'd catch the el, but my conscience wouldn't let me send a fifteen-year-old out of my house at that hour—even a street-smart fifteen-year-old—so I called Delores, said I was keeping him overnight and would send him back in the morning. I put him in Josh's room and made Josh sleep on the couch when he came in. Amanda just said okay and went to bed."

"Oh. Why didn't you just say so this morning?"

Denny leaned toward me. "Because you need to learn to trust, Jodi Marie. Me, God, your friends, your kids—for your own sake. You can't be Mama of the World all the time. The job's too big." He leaned back. "You were where you were supposed to be last night, and so was I. So . . . can you tell me what's going on with Stu?"

The loaded corn chip on its way to my mouth paused in midair. Denny was right. He had trusted *me*. Stepped in and covered for me last night, didn't ask questions, just believed me when I said I needed to be with Stu, even though it meant abandoning my errands, my chores, my house—even his bed. *Trust.*

I FILLED DENNY IN as best I could on everything that had happened yesterday. As we walked home hand in hand, hunched in our jackets against the damp end-of-March chill, I said, "Maybe Stu comes across so Ms. Perfect all the time because she *needs* to—to prove to herself and to God and everybody around her that she's really okay." *Like you, Jodi,* said the Voice in my head. That Spirit of God Voice that made me get honest with myself. "Like me," I confessed. "Trying to keep it all under control. Except, you're right. I can't. It's God who's got it all under control."

Denny put his arm around me and gave me a squeeze. We were almost at our front door when Denny stopped. "Okay, announcement. I know how I want to celebrate my birthday."

"Birthday?" I faked. "What birthday?"

"Uh-huh, I know. April Fool's. But I'm serious. It's kinda last minute, but talking with José last night triggered something in me. You and Florida were there for Stu yesterday when she needed you—and you have the Yada Yada thing that's been going on all year with the sisters. Yet circling Yada Yada are a lot of young men—like José, and Yo-Yo's brothers, and Florida's boys, and even Chanda's oldest—what's his name?"

"Thomas—she says it 'To-mas.'"

"Yeah. And Josh. And Nony's boys."

We stood out on our front sidewalk. I had no idea where Denny was going with this, but I could read the intense lines in his face in the dim streetlight.

"Okay, don't laugh. For my birthday, I'd like to have a Guys' Day Out—maybe next Saturday—and invite all the other Yada Yada husbands, and include the boys, say twelve on up. 'Cause I was thinking, I'm turning forty-four and do I just go along, doing the same-old same-old? But talking to José last night, I realized these teen guys need encouragement. And we dads—'Yada Yada guys,' through no fault of our own—we need encouragement too. So, I dunno, just thought a day together, playing, eating, talking—whatever. Mentioned it to Peter Douglass this morning. He thought it sounded like a great idea."

"He's not a Yada Yada husband."

Denny threw back his head and guffawed, his dimples deep. "Not yet!"

36

IDN'T KNOW WHY I WAS SO TIRED. I knew the emotional marathon with Stu took the starch out of me, but I thought that long Sunday afternoon nap would fix me up. But I barely dragged through Monday—not as prepared as I should have been either. The kids sensed it and bounced haphazardly through the day, like pinballs knocking into each other and missing the scoring holes.

"Uh, tough day at school?" Denny stood in the living room doorway when he got home, gym bag in hand. He had ample clues. No supper on the table; nothing in the oven; Madame Baxter sprawled in the recliner with her feet up—way up.

I let the recliner down with a thump, sending Willie Wonka scrabbling before he got pinned by the footrest. "Sorry. Just pooped is all. Kids home yet? Maybe we could just have waffles or something." *Frozen waffles,* I'm thinking.

"Jodi." Denny loomed beside the chair, hands on his hips. "Make an appointment with Dr. Lewinski *this week.* Understood?"

I nodded meekly. I didn't feel sick this time, just tired, but I could probably use a checkup. What I was really worried about was Denny's birthday—tomorrow! The business with Stu had derailed my shopping over the weekend, leaving me totally unprepared. To pull something together now would take energy that had skipped town.

I splashed water on my face, made a cup of strong coffee, and set the table while Denny whipped up waffles—from scratch. "Show-off," I muttered at his back. He waved me off. The kids were late—debate team and Spanish club—but at least the days were stretching longer, and they got home while daylight still visited the city.

A knock at the back door made me jump. "Stu!" I said, opening the door. "You okay?"

She looked me up and down with a practiced eye. "Could ask you the same thing, girlfriend." *Girlfriend.* First time Stu had ever called me that. "Uh, I came down to get my meds," she said. "Don't want to bother you in the morning."

I held up a finger and disappeared to my bedroom. When I came back, I put one pill into her hand. She frowned. "Humor me," I said. "One week, then you can have 'em back."

Her eyes sparked for a brief second, and then she shrugged. "Okay, if it keeps you happy. But I really am okay." She smiled, but her eyes held sadness. "God is good . . ."

". . . all the time." I gave her a hug. For some odd reason, I actually believed it. And if God was good, all the time . . .

"Uh, Stu? Maybe you should go ahead and write to the parole board and say Becky Wallace does have an address she can be paroled to. This one."

Stu's eyebrows shot up like McDonald's golden arches. Even Denny turned from the waffle iron and stared at me.

"*What?* It's all about redemption, isn't it? God giving us second chances? And redemption involves some risk—did for Jesus, anyway. Okay, I know I'm not very good at it, but I *am* trying to live like Jesus."

Stu eyed me warily. "I thought . . . well, after this weekend, I thought you'd think I was too touchy about little Andy to be any good to Becky."

I had thought that very thing. But I shrugged. "Maybe just the opposite. Now that God is healing that part of your past, maybe you are the perfect person to do some good for Becky. And Andy."

Tears welled up in Stu's eyes. "Oh, Jodi." She hugged me long and tight. "Thank you."

I knew I'd probably get cold feet about my rash righteousness, but as Stu said bye and backed out the door, I went after her. "Oh! Stu! One more thing . . ."

DENNY SPENT MOST OF THE EVENING on the phone lining up his Guys' Day Out. Weatherman said temps would hit the eighties on Tuesday—unless he was pulling an April Fool's joke—so maybe, Denny figured, it'd still be warm enough by Saturday for an afternoon of basketball on one of the outdoor courts. "Geezers" versus the "Young Bloods." Followed by lots of Giordano's pizza delivered to Uptown Community and some "guy talk."

"Dad, Dad." Josh laid a patronizing hand on his father's shoulder. "You got your health insurance paid up?" He grinned wickedly. "We're gonna eat you alive."

Denny's ear was red, but he looked positively beatific when he finally got off the phone around nine. "They said yes! Carl . . . Mark

. . . even Ricardo! Bringing their boys. Oh yeah, Ben Garfield too. Said he'd root for the Geezers from the sidelines, and he'll bring Pete and Jerry. No answer at Peter Douglass's place. Maybe I'll try Avis." He started to dial.

I snatched the phone from him. "If he's *not* at Avis's, you're being presumptuous. If he *is* at Avis's, he sure isn't there to get 'guy' phone calls."

"Oh." Denny grinned. "Guess you're right."

I'd perked up enough after waffles and ice cream—Denny's menu—to plan an actual dinner for his birthday tomorrow, but all the oomph was gone now. I headed for the bedroom. "You might want to ask DeShawn, too, if you're gonna ask Chanda's Thomas," I called back over my shoulder.

THE WEATHERMAN WAS *NOT* FOOLING! April 1 hit the magic eighty degrees, sending schoolkids across Chicago into spasms of premature summer bliss. I walked home, grinning at the jump ropes, roller blades, scooters, and bikes that suddenly appeared, like Christmas in April. I made myself some strong coffee to keep me out of the recliner and cut up vegetables for one of Denny's favorite meals: marinated shishkabobs. I'd managed to find a pot roast with only a little freezer burn in the freezer last night, and the beef chunks had been marinating all day. The rest was a snap: mushrooms, pineapple chunks, hunks of onions, and green peppers.

Stu smuggled a couple of prearranged bags into the house and helped Amanda string crepe paper in the dining room, while I blew on the damp coals in the grill out back. If Denny was surprised to see Stu at his birthday supper, which we ate outside on the back porch, he hid it behind a welcoming grin. Denny and Josh managed to find something to compete about, like how many food items they could string on the shishkabob skewers before stuff fell off into the coals. *Men. Sheesh.*

Birthday dessert was an ice-cream cake from Baskin-Robbins—thanks to Stu, who picked it up for me—and a lumpy, brown paper grocery bag stapled shut with a glut of curlicue ribbon. "What's this?" Denny said suspiciously, eyeing it as if trying to see through the tough brown paper. He pulled open the stapled top, pawed his way through the ribbon, and peered inside. "What in the—?" He pulled out a bottle of champagne, entwined with a fat carrot, stalk of celery, a small zucchini, a few fresh green beans, and a rutabaga, all tied to the bottle with curly ribbon.

I pointed at the rutabaga. "Nice touch, Stu."

"Okay. I give up." Denny turned the bottle around and around, eyeing the raw vegetables. "I know it's April Fool's Day, but I don't get it."

"That's you!" I crowed. "Denny—real name Dennis—derived from Dionysus, the Greek god of wine and vegetation."

Josh hooted. Amanda and Stu were both laughing. I grinned at the quirky look on Denny's face. "I looked up the meaning of your name last night, and Stu, thank you very much"—I gave her a poke—"picked up the champagne and veggies."

"Oh." Denny shrugged. "Well, then. Let's break out the bubbly!" He held the bottle aloft. "But, uh, what am I supposed to do with these raw veggies?"

"Stew," I said, pointing at the few leftover hunks of beef, onion, and three mushrooms left from the shishkabobs. "You're cooking tomorrow."

DENNY'S BIRTHDAY turned out low-key and fun, but the rest of the week really dragged. Correction: *I* really dragged through the rest of the week. Just couldn't seem to get on top of the tiredness I felt. Plus my ears itched, and a low-grade headache hugged my head like a too-tight baseball cap. At least Dr. Lewinski had a cancellation Friday afternoon. Spring break was only a week away, and I wanted to feel chipper for our trip to New York. Last thing Denny's folks needed was ammo to cluck about "poor Denny's" lackluster wife from Iowa.

Got back in the car after my appointment and sat for a while. *Humph.* I could quit worrying. The New York Baxters wouldn't be seeing anything of Jodi Marie. But what was I going to tell Denny?

Didn't have to worry about that either—not for a day or two anyway. Denny was so cranked up about his Guys' Day Out that he didn't even remember that I'd had an appointment with Dr. Lewinski. At least I had time to figure out what to do.

"Can you do your grocery shopping in the morning, Jodi? I need the Caravan all afternoon and evening. Told Chanda I'd pick up Thomas and her boyfriend—what's his name again?"

"DeShawn."

"Yeah, him too, if he'd like to join us. She said she'd ask, but I haven't heard back. Looks like we lost our warm weather, though. Shoot. Maybe I could get permission to use the small gym at West Rogers High—yeah, that's it. No sweat. Hm, better double-check with Giordano's about those pizzas. Don't want ten hungry teenagers on my hands and *no food*." Denny rolled his eyes in mock horror, not especially aware that he'd mostly been talking to himself.

I did a basic grocery shop and picked up the prescription for the ear infection doc said I was working on and probably explained why I'd been feeling so run down. The antibiotic would take care of it in a few days. But that wasn't what I dreaded telling Denny. Still, I had the afternoon to figure it out. Amanda was baby-sitting; Willie Wonka and I had the house to ourselves—a perfect time to finish working on my quilt square for Avis.

DENNY AND JOSH DIDN'T GET HOME till after nine that evening. I'd zonked out on the couch watching Dick Clark host *The Best of the Bloopers,* but I sat up when I heard my own "Geezer" and "Young Blood" raiding the refrigerator, wiped the drool off my face, and tried to look halfway intelligent by the time they tromped into the living room.

"Hi, guys." I clicked off the TV. "How was—"

"Wait, Mom! Turn it back on. Was that *CSI: Miami?*" Josh hunkered down on the other end of the couch and stuffed a sandwich into his mouth.

I stuck the TV remote behind me. "Not on your life, buster. Not till I hear about your Guys' Day Out."

"It was great, wasn't it, Dad?" Josh said, chewing and talking at the same time. "Okay, now turn it on. Never mind, I'll get it." And the scoundrel got up and turned on the TV the old-fashioned way, with the On button.

I gave up on Josh, but I hauled Denny back into the kitchen just before he sank into the recliner. "Denny! C'mon. Tell me about it. Did DeShawn show up?"

"Nope. Chanda made some lame excuse, though Thomas said he never came home last night." Now Denny was chewing and talking. "Frankly, Thomas didn't seem to mind—kinda latched on to Peter Douglass since they were both solo."

"Peter! Really?"

"Uh-huh." Another mouthful of sandwich. "Oh, yeah. Thomas said he wants to be called Tom now."

To hear Denny tell it, the Geezers whupped the Young Bloods—for about thirty minutes of play at West Rogers High's small gym. Then the Young Bloods took the lead and stayed there—for two games. "Even with all those shorties!" Denny groaned in mock despair. "Tell you what, Jodi. I was proud of Josh and Pete and José—Chris Hickman too. They kept cycling the younger guys in on a regular basis, so everybody got to play."

Denny made himself another sandwich. "Didn't you guys get pizza?" I asked, eyeing the Dagwood-size creation.

"Yep. Got two pieces, I think. That was hours ago." The second sandwich seemed to fuel Denny's willingness to re-create the Guys' Day Out, because he launched into the "guy talk" after the pizza. "I was thinking Mark Smith would be the man to get the guys talking—you know, being a teacher and all that. Yet I think the boys were intimidated by all that education and fancy title. Turned out Peter Douglass—sans suit and tie and soaked in sweat—was *da man.* He just kept asking questions: what video games they liked to play, what they liked—and didn't like—about school, what teachers were good, what teachers were lousy. Pretty soon the kids were so eager to talk they kept interrupting each other. But then Peter asked each of the Geezers—sheesh, we'll never live that name down now—to just tell the guys our own stories. What's been tough, what's been important, what we'd do different. Man!" Denny's eyes got a bit wet. "It was powerful stuff."

"Even Ricardo Enriques? I mean, did he actually *talk?*"

"Yeah, he did. He seemed powerfully moved that the rest of us wanted to listen. And Mark . . ." Denny stopped chewing. "Dunno. I might have gone out on a limb there."

"Limb? What limb?"

"Well, Mark actually told the guys—kinda half-joking about it—to think twice before marrying a girl from outside the U.S, or they'd be arguing about where to live the rest of their lives."

Ah. "And you said . . .?"

Denny swallowed his last bite and licked mustard off his fingers. "Well, nothing right then. But later, while Mark and I were taking out the garbage, I opened my big mouth and said, 'Know what, Mark? When I see Nony, I see a woman who's dying inside by inches. Have you ever thought about taking a sabbatical from Northwestern and taking the family to South Africa for a year or two? God put that fire in her for a reason.'"

My mouth dropped. "You didn't! I mean, you did? What in the world did he say to that?"

Denny shrugged. "Not much. Just gave me a funny look and muttered something like, 'Not that easy.' Still, glad I said it. Been thinking it for some time." My husband stretched his shoulder muscles and groaned. "Bet I'm going to be sore tomorrow." He stood up. "Mind if I finish up *CSI* with Josh?"

I shrugged. "Sure." Though I still hadn't told him what Dr. Lewinski said. "Uh, one more thing."

He turned at the hallway. "Yeah?"

Denny looked like a big overgrown kid standing in the doorway, still in his sweats. Face tired but eyes warm and satisfied with his successful outing. Dimples framing the slight smile on his lips. No.

This had been a great day for Denny and the guys. My news could wait. "Uh, just wanted to remind you that Yada Yada is visiting Adele's and Chanda's church tomorrow. Wanna come?"

He rolled his eyes and laughed. "I think I've had enough stimulation for one weekend! If the guys do it again, we'll have to call it the Bada-Boom Bada-Bing Brotherhood or something." He disappeared down the hall, still chuckling.

The Bada-Boom Bada-Bing Brotherhood. Good grief.

37

The first Sunday of April rolled in an hour early—the day Chicago and most of the rest of the country switched to Daylight Savings Time. One less hour of sleep. But I made sure we changed our clocks this time because I didn't want to show up an hour late at Adele's church. Not that that could happen, since I rode with On-Time Stuart the next morning—though when we pulled up a few car lengths from the square brick building, I felt a little embarrassed at the thought of climbing out of her sporty Celica in a neighborhood that seemed like a photo op for urban blight.

"Uh, why don't we park around the corner and walk back?" I suggested.

"'Cause I want to keep an eye on my car, that's why! C'mon."

The church sign said, *Paul and Silas Apostolic Baptist Church*. Huh. There it was, just like Adele said. "Uh, do you see any other Yada Yadas?" I peered anxiously through the windshield at the assorted people gathered around the entrance to the compact church building. Several older men—older than me, anyway—in black suits, white shirts, and narrow black ties stood on the steps and in the double doorway, shaking hands with people. Little boys chased each other in dark pants and button shirts—until a nearby adult cuffed the closest scamp upside the head. Frilly dresses and last year's Easter hats adorned a bevy of little girls. All the women, young and old, wore dresses. And hats. Not a pantsuit in sight. Not a white face either.

Oh, dear. Adele had given us the "dress code," so at least I was wearing a proper skirt. But I didn't have a single hat to my name, and I didn't think one of Denny's handkerchiefs pinned to my head would pass muster.

"There's Adele and MaDear . . . Avis and Florida too." Stu locked the car and hustled across the street to the cluster of Yada Yada sisters. I had to wait for two low-slung cars to rumble by, their sound systems so loud my teeth rattled, before I caught up to her.

MaDear, shuffling behind her walker, peered from under an ancient black hat wrapped in netting and sequins with a puzzled frown. "Do I know you?" she said, squinting at Florida. "Bessie's girl, ain'tcha. Girl, you gotta quit runnin' around and get yo' behind to church mo' often. An' where's yo' hat?" With a shake of her head, she allowed two of the black suits to assist her up the steps to the door of the church.

"Bessie's girl, hmm?" Avis stage-whispered. "Been running around, my my."

"Watch yourself, now," Florida came back.

Adele smirked. "Come on; I'll run interference."

Didn't know what she meant by "running interference" till we got to the inside door. A greeter holding a basket smiled at us.

"Welcome to Paul and Silas. This your first time? Bless the *Lord!* Just help yourself." She held out the basket, which was full of small, lace head coverings with a hairpin stuck in each one.

"That's all right, Sister Berry." Adele waved her off. "These are my guests . . . I spoke to Reverend Miles."

My bubble of relief was immediately pricked by Avis's effort at unity. "It's all right. I don't mind." She took one of the lacy circles and pinned it on the top of her neat French roll.

Oh, thanks, Avis. But I, too, dipped into the basket, just as glad Denny and the kids had elected not to come. I'd never hear the end of *this.*

"Can't say I didn't try," Adele muttered and led the way into the sanctuary.

I started to follow Adele and Avis, then realized Stu was heading back outside. I started to call after her, but saw her heading toward Chanda standing at the bottom of the outside steps and wearing a stunning pink suit and wide-brimmed matching hat. Thirteen-year-old Thomas—Tom—looked quite manly in his suit and bow tie; Cheree and little Dia wore matching coats, white frilly socks, and black-patent Mary Janes. Stu said something to Chanda, and Chanda waved the three kids inside while she stayed behind, one hand on her tailored pink hip, to hear what Stu had to say.

Lord Jesus! I sent up a quick prayer. *Pour some grace on that conversation.* Wasn't sure what Stu intended to say, but hopefully it would be oil on the troubled waters stirred up the last time those two had talked. Had to admire Stu taking the initiative before we all tried worshipping together. *Thank You in advance, Lord, for what You're going to do.* I smiled to myself. Definitely a New Jodi prayer.

The sanctuary was not large, maybe room for two hundred with two aisles dividing three sections of padded pews. A row of older women wearing white dresses and wielding cardboard fans sat in a front pew on the right. Must be the "mother board," though I wasn't clear exactly what that meant. Should've asked Adele to brief us white folks a little more.

Chanda and Stu slipped into the pew behind us just as a young man in a blue and gold choir robe sat down at an actual piano—no electric keyboard—and pounded out several strong chords. As if on cue, the congregation rose, a flower garden of multihued hats and clumps of brown male heads. I took the opportunity to glance around. Nony, wearing an African-print head wrap, sat a few rows back, along with Delores, Edesa, and a wide-eyed Hoshi, "doilies" on their heads. No sign of Ruth or Yo-Yo.

No sign of "Dia's daddy" either.

Two lines of blue-and-gold choir robes started down the aisle, stepping slowly to the music, swaying side to side, filling the room with the proclamation: *"We've . . . come . . . this . . . fa-ar by faith! . . . Lean-ing on . . . the Lo-ord!"*

The words of the old spiritual still echoed in my heart as the service progressed. *("Can't turn arou-ou-ound, We've come this far by faith!")* Two hymns from the pew hymnals were interspersed by two choir numbers (A and B selection), and a testimony time that went something like, "I praise God on today for my salvation, because He's brought me a mighty long way!" and "I coulda been dead, sleepin' in my grave, but He woke me up this morning in my right mind, praise Jesus!" and "I want to give honor to God who is the head of my life, and I'd like to say I'm glad to be in the house of the Lord one more time."

The elderly Reverend Arthur Miles III, wearing a black robe

with a white stole, came in from a side door halfway through the service and sat in an oversize chair, nodding his head to the B selection and the testimonies. But when he got up to preach, I was surprised at the strength of his voice. His sermon, titled "The Blood's Cleansing Power," required two glasses of fresh water and a dry hand towel for mopping sweat off his face and neck. I was fascinated by the old-time preaching, the singsong voice, as he preached from the book of Leviticus about the "sin offering" required—a blood sacrifice—when a person broke God's law. The sermon crackled with electricity between the pulpit and the pews—practically after every phrase. "Preach it, pastor!" "You said it!" "My Lord!"

An impassioned altar call for "salvation, rededication, repentance, or church membership" closed out the service while the choir swayed and sang softly, "Just as I am without one plea . . ." *Oh my.* It'd been a long time since I'd heard that hymn. We didn't have altar calls at Uptown Community, though Pastor Clark had his own ways of inviting sinners into the kingdom. *"Just as I am without one plea . . ."*

Why had it taken so long for *me* to come to Jesus "just as I am," without a lot of excuses?

I had a sudden, un-Jodilike urge to shout, *"Thank You, Jesus!"* that God had brought me this far, even though it had taken a terrible accident—an accident that had taken my spleen and the life of a young boy—to open my eyes to a basic fact: I was just a sinner, saved by grace. But I kept my mouth shut and my hands clasped in my lap. Didn't want to find myself swept to the mourners' bench, surrounded by the deacons.

I'd come this far by faith—but not that far.

After the service, we stood in the foyer, shaking hands and ignoring the stares of giggling children who seemed quite puzzled why a mishmash of beige and brown visitors had come to their church with "Sister Skuggs" and "Sister George." I must have been asked ten times if I enjoyed the service. I nodded and smiled and said yes, which was mostly true—though I'd gotten pretty rattled when a woman started screaming and jumping and crying during the B selection, prompting the "mothers" to surround her in a protective circle, fanning judiciously.

"Oh girl, that took me back!" Avis said, as she and Florida walked Stu and me across the street to our car. "I cut my teeth singing A and B selections in the choir. And the mother board—mm-mm. Still anchoring the black church." She gave me a sly smile. "Maybe we need a mother board at Uptown Community."

"Girl, ain't nobody old enough at Uptown," Florida snorted, "'cept you." She grinned at Avis. "You got a white dress?"

"Now *you* watch yourself, girl," Avis warned, but she and Florida walked off laughing.

As Stu and I piled into her Celica and pulled out of the parking spot, I couldn't help feeling trapped in my own skin. Paul and Silas's service didn't take *me* back—except for "Just As I Am." Wasn't sure I'd ever be able to "get down" with my black sisters. Or Latino sisters either, for that matter. Not really.

But the processional song ("Traditional Spiritual," the bulletin had said) kept running through my mind, edging its way into my spirit:

> *We've come this far by faith*
> *Leaning on the Lord!*
> *Trusting in His Holy Word*
> *He's never failed us yet! We're singing . . .*

Ohhh-oh-oh-oh-ohhhhh-oh-oh-oh-ohhh!
Can't turn around
We've come this far by faith.

Now that was true. True for me, true for Florida, true for Hoshi, true for Stu—true for all of us in Yada Yada.

Can't turn around
We've come this far by faith.

DENNY AND THE KIDS had already snagged some lunch by the time we got home, Josh had gone off to play some basketball, and Amanda was on the phone in her bedroom. "Good time?" Denny asked, leaning against the doorjamb between dining room and kitchen as I put together a fried-egg sandwich.

"Yeah. Interesting. Pretty traditional Black Baptist, I think—except for wearing that doily on my head." I gave him the eye. "Do not snicker; do not pass Go; do not collect two hundred dollars. The old guard takes the head-covering thing seriously."

I took my sandwich into the dining room and slumped into a chair. Wasn't sure I felt hungry. Maybe I needed a nap instead. But I dutifully bit into the wheat bread.

"Oh!" I mumbled, my mouth full. "One really good thing. Stu apologized to Chanda before service. Said God was dealing with her about the sin in her own life, and she had no business pointing fingers."

One of Denny's eyebrows went up. "Really? Stu did that?" He nodded thoughtfully. "Amazing."

"I know. It takes guts to own up to your own sins." I swallowed a bite with difficulty and put down my sandwich, my own words ringing in my ears. *It takes guts to own up to your own sins . . . to ask forgiveness of the person you've sinned against.* Guts I seemed to lack when it came to facing Geraldine Wilkins-Porter, the mother of Jamal Wilkins and Hakim.

"Jodi? Jodi!" Denny's voice cut into my numb thoughts. "Are you okay?"

"Uh . . . yeah. Sorry." I pushed the sandwich away.

Denny looked at me funny. "Ohmigosh, Jodi. I totally forgot to ask about your appointment with Dr. Lewinski on Friday. What'd he say?"

I hesitated.

"What? What'd he say?"

I smiled gamely. "Don't worry. I'm okay. He did some blood work, stuff like that. Says I'm kinda run-down, but nothing serious. Yet. But he's not surprised I've been sick a lot this spring. I don't have as much immunity with my spleen gone, you know. Thinks I *really* need to be careful with all the SARS cases cropping up in the U.S. Told me the surgeon general just issued a quarantine for all SARS patients to keep it from spreading."

Denny's brow puckered. "Which means?"

I sighed. He wasn't going to like this. "Which means he doesn't want me to travel to New York over spring break. Told me to stay home, avoid big crowds, get lots of rest." I could read dismay registering on my husband's face. "But I've been thinking about it all weekend, Denny. I think you and the kids should still go. Without me. Really!"

38

*D*enny called a family meeting that night after the kids came home from youth group. But we could hardly get a word in edgewise. The kids had chosen to volunteer at the seven-day Cornerstone Music Festival over the Fourth of July as their mission project this summer. Excitement dripped from their pores. There'd been a big debate that night about inviting non-Uptown kids to join them at Cornerstone as part of their mission. "You know, like Yo-Yo's brothers and José—kids who've done stuff with us in the past," Amanda explained.

Uh-huh. I could see why the debate. Pete and Jerry Spencer were basically likable pagans, while José Enriques was a church kid with a Christian family. Who needed Cornerstone more? But who would be a responsible volunteer? On the other hand, if José went along, would Denny and I need to go along as chaperones?

I stifled a groan. I didn't need another "I Survived Cornerstone" T-shirt.

Denny finally put a lid on the Cornerstone babble and told the kids what Dr. Lewinski had said. That shut them up—for about two seconds. "But Mom!" Amanda wailed. "You don't look sick to me."

"I'm not, exactly. Just not up to par. Doctor doesn't want me to risk picking up a nasty bug, especially with the SARS epidemic gathering momentum."

Josh cut to the chase. "Does that mean the trip is off?"

Denny cleared his throat. "Well, that's what we need to talk about."

"Absolutely not." I glared at Denny. "It just means I'm not going with you."

"Oh." Relief and guilt tussled on Amanda's face. "It won't be the same without you, Mom."

"Won't be the same without you either. All the phone calls will be for *me*, no punk rock—Christian or otherwise—blaring from your bedrooms, no dirty underwear cluttering up the bathroom. And the mint-chocolate-chip ice cream will actually still be in the fridge the day after I buy it." *Not to mention I'll be as lonely as a single sock. But hopefully not as useless.*

So that was that, though Denny still looked dubious. As the kids disappeared into their rooms to finish up homework before bed, Denny turned on me. "Wait a minute. Didn't the doc say to avoid crowds? You *knew* that, Jodi—and yet you went to this Paul and Silas church in the city today! Isn't that a crowd of strangers?" He rolled his eyes in frustration. "What's up with that? What if you get sick while we're gone?"

I shrank in my chair. Guilty as charged. It hadn't even crossed my mind.

THE WEEK WAS SHORT, SCHOOLWISE. A Professional Development day on Friday gave public-school students a head start on their spring break, and my traveling trio decided to take off early Friday so they could be at the Baxter grandparents' for Palm Sunday. But it also meant only four days to wash clothes and pack three people for nine days, get the minivan tuned up and tires rotated, and make sure the car was packed with all the necessities to function without Mama Bear along—snacks, paper towels, wet wipes, first-aid kit, water jug.

Might have gone without a hitch if the U.S. Army hadn't pushed into Baghdad and claimed control of the city by midweek. But it was almost impossible to keep everybody on task when images of jubilant Iraqis toppling an ego-size statue of the dictator were being shown over and over again on national TV.

Stu caught me in the basement stuffing a load of jeans and sweats into the washing machine the night Baghdad fell, muttering dark threats because Josh hadn't signed up for his SATs yet. "Jodi Baxter! What are you doing washing Josh and Amanda's clothes at their age? In your condition!"

I bristled. She made it sound like I was nine months' pregnant or nine months shy of kicking the bucket. "They do their own wash . . . sometimes. But tonight they're all glued to the TV. And I'm *fine.*"

"Right. You're fine. So doggone fine your family's going off to New York and leaving you home to 'rest.' Here. Let me do that, and you go upstairs and get those two teenage misfits off their butts and down here."

Sheesh! Who was Leslie Stuart to tell me how to run my family? Except, dang it, she was right. I snorted. "Tell you what. I'll do this and *you* go upstairs and get my two misfits off their duffs. That'd shock 'em." I started to giggle . . . and then I started to cry.

"Hey. What's wrong? I'm sorry—"

"No, no, I'm okay. Really." I wiped my face on a dark T-shirt and stuffed it in the washing machine. "Just feeling sorry for myself.

Nine days without Denny and the kids feels like . . . like pulling isolation for bad behavior at the county jail."

"Hey. I'll be here. Do you want to have dinner together or something next week when I get off work? I could cook one night, you the next, something like that." She smiled ruefully. "Fact is, I'm in isolation all the time."

I stared at her in the dim light from the swaying bulb overhead. "Sheesh, Stu. What a jerk I am. Spoiled, too, I guess."

She shrugged. "That's okay. I'm used to it. But I wouldn't mind the company."

"Sure. That'd be great." Suddenly the week ahead didn't seem like such a black hole.

Stu poured a capful of detergent and dumped it on top of the jeans. "Speaking of jail, I wonder what's happening with the parole board? I sent that letter, like you said."

"You did?" *I said that?* "Well, uh, that kind of thing takes time. They've got lots of parolees to consider."

"Yeah, guess so. But I was thinking that maybe some of us should make another visit. Maybe this Saturday?"

I shook my head. "Count me out, Stu. Denny had a fit that I went to Paul and Silas after the doc said to avoid crowds. I'm sure Lincoln Correctional would be off the list. But you could ask some of the sisters who are already on the visitors' list."

DENNY AND THE KIDS TOOK OFF early Friday morning in the Dodge Caravan, trying to beat the morning rush hour. After the invasion of Baghdad, the terrorist alert level nudged up to orange— but what did that mean? Nothing to Josh and Amanda. Yellow, orange, red—nothing short of a nuclear bomb on Chicago would have stopped them heading for New York with CD players, earphones, and duffel bags. I did barricade the back door with my body, and the four of us stopped long enough to hold hands in the kitchen and pray for "traveling mercies," as my dad used to say. Then kisses and hugs and wet licks from Willie Wonka . . . and they were gone.

Me—I had to go to school as usual. I thought about using Dr. Lewinski's order to avoid crowds as an excuse to ditch Professional Development day, but I realized that wouldn't fly since I already mingled with these teachers and staff on a day-to-day basis. Besides, it was required. However, just before leaving the house, I made a rash decision and clipped Willie Wonka's leash to his collar. He needed a walk, and he could just walk to school with me. If Avis didn't like it, she could send me home. Poor Wonka was so pooped by the time we got to school he curled up under my desk and snored through the whole day. Avis never even knew he was there.

My third graders would have loved it. An old dog at school!

True to her word, Stu brought supper Friday night—Chinese takeout. Then she spent most of the evening on the phone finalizing the trip downstate to the prison the next day. Turned out that only Yo-Yo and Hoshi could make it. Carla was still spending every other weekend with her former foster parents, but *this* weekend she was home. As Florida put it to Stu: "No way I'm gonna be gone and Carla end up wishin' she was at their house, see what I'm sayin'? Carla an' me—we're goin' shopping for an Easter dress."

That Saturday our two-flat could have doubled for an abandoned ghost town. I cleaned out two closets, washed all the bedding in the kids' rooms, played all the gospel CDs we owned, decided against calling my parents (they'd want to know why I wasn't on my way to New York with Denny and the kids; no reason to get them all worried), called half a dozen Yada Yada sisters just to see "whassup" but got nobody, and finally wallowed my way through a bag of potato chips watching a beat-up video of *Rainman* and finishing my quilt square.

When Dustin Hoffman laid his head on his sassy little brother's chest and murmured, "My main man," I wiped my eyes with my T-shirt and clicked off the VCR. Now what? The house was so quiet I could hear the wall clock tick, but I didn't want more TV. Every station had constant commentary coming from Iraq. Ambushes, pockets of resistance, more terror threats . . . I shuddered. Nothing clean or quick about this war.

Pray, Jodi. Praise! Praise? Well, why not? As I walked around the house picking up stray stuff, I prayed out loud for Denny and the kids. I prayed for our soldiers in Iraq. I prayed for the Iraqi people, and even public enemy Saddam Hussein, still on the loose. I prayed for Stu and the others driving back from Lincoln, for Becky Wallace and her little boy. For Avis and Peter, for a job for Carl Hickman, for Hakim and his mother . . . and when I ran out of people to pray for, I put on a Gary Oliver CD and let myself go, dancing and swirling and singing along to "House of the Lord" and "More Than Enough." Willie Wonka didn't care. Slept right through it, as a matter of fact. No one else was around to bother. I hiked the music up a notch. Just me and God . . .

The phone rang. Had been ringing for some time, I guess. I snatched the handset just as the answering machine picked up. "Jodi!" It was Stu. "Could you turn down the music a bit? My dishes are rattling up here."

"Oh! Hi, Stu." I punched the Off button on the CD player. "Didn't know you were home. How'd it go?"

"Amazing. Can't talk now 'cause I got an emergency foster case I gotta take care of. Just to say this much—Becky Wallace is on the list for early parole!"

I WAS DYING TO HEAR MORE about Becky Wallace, yet I had to wait till Stu and I were on our way up to Nony's house for Yada Yada the next evening. Figured if I could go to work, I could go to Yada Yada—no new faces there either. Besides, Delores had called and said she was collecting the quilt squares. Time to get them sewn together and quilted, she'd said. Still seemed premature to me, but . . . whatever. At least mine was done. Boy, did I feel smug.

"So tell me what happened at the prison yesterday," I said as Stu turned north on Sheridan Road.

"Whoa. Don't you want to wait to hear from Yo-Yo and Hoshi too?"

"Can't wait. Tell me now."

Stu snorted. "Okay, okay. I didn't plan to say anything to Becky about writing the parole board, because, you know, I hadn't heard anything back. Whole thing was a shot in the dark. So we'd been talking about five minutes in the visitors' room when Becky blurted out, 'I'm on the list.'"

"She said, 'I'm on the list,' just like that?"

"Yeah. The list of early parolees! She was told she was being released to her 'home address on Lunt Avenue,' but she was kind of in shock. 'I don't know any address on Lunt Avenue,' she said. Well, she threw a couple of f-words in there, but that was the gist."

I laughed nervously. "What did you say? Is she really coming here? When? What about that business with house arrest and an ankle monitor—for how many months?"

Stu grinned ruefully. "Yeah. Guess that's part of it. I was tempted to just let the sheriff drop her off at our house and surprise her, but Yo-Yo kept kicking me under the table, so I 'fessed up. Becky . . ." Stu's voice trailed off as she cruised past Northwestern University along Sheridan Road, and then turned on treelined Lincoln Avenue.

"What? Becky what?"

"Her face got all funny. Maybe she was afraid she'd cry. Or maybe she was angry we interfered. Whatever, she got up suddenly and bolted for the inmate door. We sat there about ten minutes or so, and had just about decided she wasn't coming back—oh, here we are. Tell you the rest later."

Stu had pulled up in front of Nony and Mark Smith's lovely two-story brick house covered in creeping ivy. I started to climb out of the sporty car, but Stu laid a hand on my arm. "Jodi, wait."

I turned back. Her usual self-confident air had disappeared.

"Do you think . . . I mean, should I tell Yada Yada what happened that day, you know, after I saw Andy Wallace? And about— you know—what happened a few years ago?"

I hardly knew what to say. I could tell it'd been healing for Stu to own up to the truth, to let go of her need to be Ms. Perfect. But she was doing that. A few of us knew about the abortion. Did she need to tell everybody? And yet . . . most of Yada Yada had witnessed the heated exchange between her and Chanda the last time we met at Ruth's house. Honesty from Stu would explain a lot. And she was asking me.

I made a stab at wisdom. "It has to be up to you, Stu—you and

God. Accountability is good—Lord knows I'm working on it. Trying to be honest with myself and other people. I just don't think we have to tell everybody everything. You got honest with Florida and me—and Avis knows too. Maybe that's enough. Unless . . ."

"Unless what?"

I sat quietly in the car for several moments, my door wide open, thinking about the sin that continued to dog me, even though I had confessed to God, confessed to my husband and family, confessed to Yada Yada, been loved and forgiven. But I still didn't feel free. I'd said I was "sorry" to Jamal's mother that day in the courtroom—but how did she hear it? That I was sorry it had happened? Sorry she'd lost her son? Sure. Anybody would be. Yet had I ever really *confessed my sin* to the mother of the boy I'd killed? Could she ever really forgive me if I didn't?

I wanted to be free. What was it Jesus said? *"If you abide in My Word, you will know the truth, and the truth will set you free."*

I blinked back tears. "God wants to set us free, Stu. With the truth. Listen to God's whisper in your heart. You'll know what's right to say . . . or do."

Right, Jodi. You know what's right to do. Now do you have the courage to do it?

39

Chanda breezed into Nony's house, dolled up in silky black pants and a big-print overblouse, topped by a cascade of braided extensions. "Girl, you look *good!*" I said, giving her a hug. But the moment I let her go, she made a beeline for Stu and gave her a long hug. Over their heads, I saw Nony's eyes roll up to the heavenlies, and her smiling lips moved silently. Probably thanking God He hadn't given up on this motley crew.

"We need T-shirts that say W-I-P," I whispered to Nony as I helped her take a tray of tea and chocolate-dipped strawberries into the Smith's tastefully appointed family room. The tray had one less strawberry by the time it got there.

"W-I-P?" Nony's excellent command of English seemed stumped.

I grinned. "Work In Progress."

"Yes! Hallelujah." She laughed. "Scripture says we work out our own salvation with fear and trembling."

The chocolate-dipped strawberries didn't last long. Delores and

Edesa had the farthest to come by el, and by the time they got there the plate was empty. I gave Edesa a big hug—the bright-eyed Honduran student had been so busy with college classes, we hadn't seen much of her at the Baxter house lately, even though she was Amanda's favorite Spanish tutor. Delores had a large plastic bag with her and busied herself collecting small, anonymous packages from different sisters when Avis wasn't looking.

I was surprised and delighted to see we had a full hand of Yada Yadas that night. Had expected half the group—at least those with kids in Chicago public schools—to be gone somewhere during spring vacation. "Me, I'm taking my t'ree kids on a Disney Cruise," Chanda crowed. "Leave Tewsday. To-mas, Cheree, and Dia so excited, dem can't sleep, no way."

I cast a sympathetic glance at Florida and Delores. No way could those families afford a Disney Cruise. Wasn't even sure Chanda could, since she'd never told us how much her "winnings" were. But I could have saved my sympathy. Florida lit up. "For real? You go, girl! Someday I'm gonna do that."

"The whole family is going, yes? DeShawn too?" Ruth asked sweetly—but I suspected the question was loaded.

Chanda brushed it off. "Nah, not dis time. Dat mon say he too busy. Some job he doin'." Then she patted me on the shoulder, her large eyes pitying. "Like Sista Jodee. Left home alone while she family do de Big Apple big-time." I pulled my mouth down in a sad clown face, not sure Denny would call visiting his parents "doing the Big Apple big-time." But Chanda had already turned to Avis. "So you, Sista Avis. What you doin' dis week of no school?"

Now *that* was an interesting question. The room suddenly hushed as different ones finished getting their tea and found a seat.

I expected Avis to brush off the question, but she pursed her lips, her smooth forehead knotting into a frown. "I . . . it's a bit of a dilemma, actually." My in-control-and-in-charge principal looked sheepish. "Peter has offered to drive me to South Carolina to see my cousin, Boyd. He's . . . in prison. Death row."

"Avis!" several voices cried, some in shock. "You have a cousin on death row?" . . . "Of *course* you should go see him!" . . . "This is Peter's idea? Bless that man!" And from Ruth: "What's to question? I don't see a dilemma here."

Avis sighed. "Well, you all can pray with me about it. It *is* a dilemma, because we'd be traveling together, several days by car, you know, and—"

"Avis Johnson!" Adele cut her off impatiently. "You worried about your *reputation*? Girl, just get separate motel rooms and don't worry about what anybody thinks. *We* not thinkin' anything." She made eyes around the room. "*Are* we, sisters?"

Yo-Yo snickered and Ruth jabbed her. Avis tossed her hand, as if brushing off a pesky fly. "I'm not worried about what *you* guys think. I'm worried about what *Peter's* going to think. It . . . I still feel disloyal to Conrad, dating one of his old friends, much less taking a car trip all the way to South Carolina with him. I don't want to give Peter the wrong idea."

That did it. Several people jumped in all at once.

"Wrong, schmong. *You're* the one who's got it all wrong, Avis Johnson." Ruth wagged a finger in Avis's direction. "Your Conrad? Happy he would want you to be. Who better than an old friend that he'd trust to treat you right?"

"Don't forget what God said to the prophet Jeremiah," Nony said. "God knows the plans He has for you, plans to prosper you and not to harm you, plans to give you a hope and a future!" That brought several amens and hallelujahs.

"Sister Avis." Delores leaned forward. "Think about your cousin. What an encouragement it would be for you to come see him. Jesus said, 'I was in prison and ye visited me . . .'"

"Yeah. What *she* said." Yo-Yo jerked a thumb in Delores's direction.

"Let's vote!" Stu grinned. "All in favor of Avis going to South Carolina with Peter Douglass say 'aye.'" The "ayes" practically lifted the roof.

Avis's shoulders shook with silent laughter. "Sorry. I have the deciding vote. But I appreciate what you all are saying. Really. And I'm serious about asking you to pray with me, because"—she made a panicky face—"I need to give Peter an answer tonight."

"Then what are we waiting for?" I reached for Edesa's hand on one side of me and Hoshi's on the other. "Let's touch and agree that God will make things plain for Avis." And so we prayed, holding hands around our circle, and the prayers began to flow—not only for wisdom and boldness for Avis, but for "traveling mercies" for Denny and the kids in New York, and Chanda and her kids flying to Florida, and safety for all our kids who were out of school that week, and jobs and MaDear and a quick end to the war in Iraq . . .

Nony's voice lifted on the tide of prayers. "And thank You, Father God, who hears the cries of the orphan and the widow and the down-trodden, that the South African government has agreed to pay repara-tions to victims of apartheid crimes, even though it is only a token . . ."

Her prayer went on, but my eyes flew open, and I saw others around the circle sharing questioning glances. When Nony finally breathed, "Amen," we all jumped in with questions. "Reparations? Really? When? How much?"

Nony was surprised we had not heard about it on the news. The dollar amount was far below what the Truth and Reconciliation Commission had asked for, and some said it was an insult, but Nony seemed grateful that public acknowledgement had been made of the injustices suffered and some reparations given. "It is a beginning, widening the crack in the door of justice."

Hoshi nodded vigorously. "Tell them what you're doing now, Nony."

Nony smiled sheepishly. "You know me, my sisters. I cannot sit on my hands. The United States Congress is considering a fifteen-billion-dollar bill to globally fight the scourge of AIDS. So I'm back to letter writing and making calls to representatives. Such a bill could make a big difference for my country—especially since a third of the money would be earmarked for abstinence education."

"Huh?" Yo-Yo wrinkled her face. "*What* education?"

Edesa, who was closest to Yo-Yo's age, leaned close to her ear and whispered loudly, "Abstinence. No sex. Not sleeping around."

Everybody laughed—except Adele, who started humming a few bars of "What a Mighty God We Serve." A few people picked up on the words, filling in until we were all singing, ". . . Lift your voice and say it: He's a mighty God!"

I had to take a bathroom break—my left leg still got stiff when I sat too long—but when I came back, Stu was telling about the trip to Lincoln Correctional. The group sat open-mouthed and bug-eyed that our "Bandana Woman" was actually getting an early parole—and was coming to live at Stu's house.

"Lord, have mercy," Ruth muttered, fanning rapidly with a piece of paper.

"Becky came back to the visitors' room after she left?" Edesa wanted to know. "What did she say?"

Hoshi picked up the story. "She wanted to know why. *Why* would Stu offer to let a convicted thief live in her house? And Stu told her, 'Because Jesus would.' What is that verse you quoted, Stu?"

Stu seemed embarrassed. "Don't know if I quoted it very well, but the one where Jesus said if we have two coats, we should give one to the person who doesn't have any."

"Yes, that is it. And she started to ask each one of us why we call ourselves Christians." Hoshi's voice softened. "It was the first time I told her the choice I had to make between my parents and following Jesus."

"Yeah. Hoshi gave a good answer. When Becky asked me"— Yo-Yo slouched further down on her chair—"I kinda hemmed and hawed, said sometimes I wasn't sure if I was a Christian or not 'cause I hadn't been dunked yet." Yo-Yo suddenly sat up. "And you know what she said? The nerve!"

"What!" we chorused.

"She said I better get off the fence. I could be a pagan like her or a Christian like these guys, but I better choose."

Adele belly-laughed. "Out of the mouths of thieves!"

The rest of us just shook our heads. Becky Wallace, of all people, telling Yo-Yo to get off the fence. Avis prodded, "And?"

Yo-Yo looked all wide-eyed and innocent. "And what?" Then her grin slipped. "Yeah, yeah, I know what you're askin'. Okay, okay. I've decided. I want to get dunked. You know, baptized. Like Jesus said."

WE HAD A PRETTY GOOD "Holy Ghost Party" the rest of Yada Yada that night, laughing and singing and thanking God that we'd come a mighty long way. Yo-Yo resisted suggestions that she get baptized on Easter—next week!—protesting that it was still only April and the lake was still cold.

"So *now* you worry about jumping in the cold lake," Ruth sniffed. "Seems I remember you doing that Polar Bear Plunge on New Year's Day."

"That was different," Yo-Yo insisted over our laughter. "What I was thinkin' was maybe the first weekend in May—our anniversary." She must have caught our blank faces because she sounded exasperated. *"Duh!* The anniversary of that women's conference thing last year—the weekend we all met, remember?"

Recognition dawned around the room. The first weekend of May. *"Bendiga a Jesús!"* Delores whispered. "Has it been a whole year?"

Everybody started talking at once—till Yo-Yo yelled, "Hey! Can I finish?"

The hubbub died away. "Thank you very much," she said sarcastically. "Anyway, I don't go to no church, you know, I usually gotta work, so I was wondering if Uptown would do the baptizing thing—since four of you Yada Yadas go there already. I kinda like that church, anyway."

"Absolutely, Yo-Yo," Avis said. "I'll speak to Pastor Clark." She glanced around the circle. "If that's all, why don't we close our—"

"Not dat Yo-Yo been showin' up at any other churches when Yada Yada comes to visit," Chanda pouted, ignoring Avis's attempt to wrap up our meeting. "So, what the rest of you sistas t'ink about Paul and Silas last week? What you say, Sista Jodee?"

Oh great. Why is she picking on me? I squirmed, and then blurted, "Okay. I'm glad I went. I especially liked that processional song, the one about 'Can't turn around, we've come this far by faith.' But . . ." I groaned. "I still feel so *white* when I'm in an all-black setting. I mean, I've been around you guys for a whole year, and I still don't blend in."

"You feel so—what?" Florida started laughing so hard she had to hold her side. Her laughter was so contagious we all ended up giggling. Except—what was so funny about what I said? I was just trying to be real.

Florida finally wiped her eyes. "Jodi Baxter, honey girl. Nobody here wants you to be black. God sure don't, or He would have made you that way. Just be your white-bread self—that's fine by me. Most important thing you do is show up. And not runnin' when this racial stuff gets messy. Now that counts for somethin'."

She wagged a finger at me. "We *all* come a long way, baby. Way I see it? We need *all* the sisters in this Yada Yada thing to show off just how big God is. Praise Jesus! We got a good thing goin' 'long as we accept each other for just who we be, takin' those itty-bitty baby steps along the way. Some day we get there . . . Say, Avis. Wasn't you tryin' to close us out?"

40

*D*on't know why I felt so teary after Florida wagged her finger at me. *"Most important thing you do is show up . . ."* Wasn't sure what she meant, exactly, but for some reason she made it sound like it was enough to just *be there,* together, slogging along.

Yeah, I could do that.

Our meeting had run over its usual time and even Daylight Savings hadn't kept darkness from blanketing Nony's genteel neighborhood. Those of us with cars gave rides to those who'd walked from the el. Delores seemed especially pushy to make sure she and Edesa rode with Stu and me down to the Howard Street el station.

"Jodi," she said, as soon as she'd squeezed her "pleasant plumpness" along with the bulging plastic bag into Stu's skinny backseat. "It is true you are home by yourself this week? Not working? Oh, *gracias al Dios!*" she cried happily when I nodded. "You are my answer to prayer!"

Red flags went up. "Uh, in what way? I do have lesson plans I gotta—"

"You can sew, *si*?" Delores leaned forward and lowered her voice, as if the car might be bugged. "I was planning to sew these quilt squares together this week—but with my work hours? *No posible!* And there's no time to lose—not if Peter is taking Avis to South Carolina. Am I right, Edesa?" She leaned back, the plastic bag crinkling and squishing. Edesa just laughed.

I twisted around in my seat as Stu headed down Chicago Avenue toward Howard Street. "Delores! I don't know anything about putting a quilt together. Doesn't it have to be, you know, *quilted*? All those tiny little stitches?"

"No, no, do not worry about that! When the top is pieced, we take it to my friend. She will do the quilting. But she needs at least two weeks! That's why we need to get the squares sewn together pronto."

"But—"

"I'll help you," Stu said, pulling up alongside the el station. "It won't be hard. I did one of these before."

I stared at Stu. *Thank you very much, Leslie Stuart. I was trying to get out of this!* I jumped out of the car and pulled my seat forward so Delores and Edesa could wiggle their way out of confinement. *"Gracias, gracias!"* Delores cried, giving me a big kiss on my cheek and thrusting the lumpy plastic bag into my arms. "I will call you— oh! I hear a train coming. Edesa! Come, come!" And she bustled through the lower-level doors.

"I need instructions!" I yelled after her, but with a wave they were gone.

MY ANSWERING MACHINE WAS BLINKING when I let myself in the back door after saying goodnight to Stu. Willie Wonka rose stiffly from his watchdog post just inside the door and gave me a quick wet-nose greeting, though he obviously had bladder issues in mind. I let the dog outside and then punched the button on the answering machine.

"Hi, Jodi. It's Avis. Just wanted to let somebody know I decided to go see my cousin. Not sure when I'll be back—by next Sunday for sure. Don't want to miss Easter service. Tell the sisters to be praying." *Click.*

"Decided to go see my cousin." I grinned in the dark kitchen. *Decided to spend the week with Peter Douglass is more like it.* Well, visit her cousin too, of course. This was definitely a multilayered thing.

The next message was from Denny. "Hi, Jodi! Sorry we missed you. We're going into New York City tomorrow to see Ground Zero, maybe stay overnight at a hotel and see some of the sights on Tuesday. I've got the cell if you need to get hold of us." A pause. "It's pretty lonely without you, babe. Hope you and Wonka are managing okay. Call me back just to let me know you're okay."

I hit Redial, but all I got was the senior Baxters' voice mail on the other end. Tried the cell too; same thing. Left a brief message both places, yet it wasn't the same as talking to Denny in person. Wasn't the same crawling into our queen-size bed a while later, either. *Only three days down . . . six whole nights to go?* Emptiness stretched like a desert on Denny's side of the bed.

Okay, I knew it was against house rules, but I let Wonka sleep on the bed. Actually, I had to hoist him up there like a crate onto a cargo ship. Once on top of the big beach towel I spread over our wedding-ring quilt, Wonka's eyes closed in doggy bliss. His bulk and soft wheeze were comforting—though he didn't smell as good as Denny.

I'd definitely have to wash all the bedding before Denny got home.

I TRIED TO LAY OUT THE QUILT SQUARES the next day on the living room floor but realized I was definitely in over my head. Besides the embroidered quilt squares from the various Yada sisters, Delores had included squares of a beige, black, and gold leaf print, plus long strips of solid muslin and solid black. At the bottom of the bag was a pencil sketch showing the basic idea: embroidered squares alternating with print squares, solid muslin strips separating blocks of squares, muslin and black strips making a large border.

Gosh, it was going to be beautiful . . . if I didn't ruin it first.

By the time Stu got home from work, I had sewn the first row of squares together—three embroidered and two print—and made a beef and broccoli stir-fry supper for two. We sat on the living room floor with our plates of food, admiring the different embroidered squares done by such different personalities. Nony had done an appliquéd shape of the African continent, with the country of South Africa highlighted in gold-colored cloth. She had embroidered the word *LOVE* in the middle of the continent, and in embroidered script under the Cape of Good Hope: Nony Sisulu-Smith . . . Chanda had embroidered a border of flowers and the words *Best Wishes* in the center . . . Adele had three dancing "sistahs" and the words **YADA YADA** in a rainbow over their heads; just her initials beneath the dancing feet identified her square . . .

Stu picked up my square, which hadn't been sewn yet. "Jodi! I like this. But where did you get the idea?" My insides fluttered as I looked at my hours of work: an angel with brown skin hovered over a circle of stick figures, all different colors. The angel's wings and arms stretched out and around the huddle of stick figures. Over the angel's head was the word *Avis* . . . and below the drawing, I'd embroidered the words: *Refuge in Battle*.

"It's her name. Avis means 'refuge in battle.' I . . . thought it was very appropriate. She's definitely been that to me. To our whole group, I think."

To my surprise, Stu gave me a hug. "That's awesome, Jodi. Makes me wish . . ." Her voice got funny for a moment, but she swooped up another square that had Spanish words embroidered in reds and yellows and orange all over it: *¡Gloria al Dios! ¡Jesús le ama! ¡Bendiciones! ¡Alegría!* "Must be Edesa's or Delores's—hey, let me show you how the strips get sewn on. Not a big deal once you know how."

As Stu hunched over my sewing machine in the dining room, blonde hair tucked behind her ear with the row of little earrings running up the curve, I grinned at her back and made a silent promise: *Someday, Stu, we'll make a quilt for you, and I'll make a square that says 'Leslie Stuart . . . Caretaker.'*"

I PROBABLY WOULD HAVE EXISTED ON COLD CEREAL, toasted cheese sandwiches, and tomato soup all that week if Stu hadn't suggested eating suppers together. As it was, we scarfed down black-bean enchiladas, chicken breasts in mango sauce, and homemade vegetable beef soup before tackling the quilt each evening. Our conversations had been sufficiently low-key and chummy that I dared raise a question.

"Stu, you didn't share about, you know, the abortion and Andy Wallace's birth date at Yada Yada last Sunday. Did you decide not to? If you did, that's okay," I added hastily. "Just wondered."

She shrugged and pushed food around on her plate. "No, I wanted to, but so much was going on, never seemed to be a good time to announce, 'Okay, listen up everybody, I had an abortion.'" She smiled ruefully. "But actually, I'm okay with it. Not that I want to hide it. Just . . . maybe it's something better shared one on one—at least at first. In fact, I called Nony the other night and had a long talk with her. She told me about this program—Rachel's Vineyard or something like that—that does retreats for women who have been wounded by abortion. I'm thinking about doing something like that."

"Oh, Stu. That sounds great."

Stu's features softened, the way mine do after a soothing face rub. "Nony gave me some scriptures to pray, too, when I'm tempted to get down on myself. This one especially: 'The Lord is near to those who have a broken heart, and saves those with a contrite spirit.' I've been praying that one from Psalm 34 every day."

The phone rang—as usual. Denny's once-a-day phone call, perfectly timed to interrupt dinner. He always seemed surprised and delighted that he actually found me at home, "resting" like the doc had said. "You sure you're okay? Not sick or anything?"

"I'm fine. Really. Wonka and I get out for a walk a couple of times a day; otherwise I've been working on this Yada Yada quilt for Avis and Peter, and doing lesson plans for school." I wandered out of Stu's earshot. "Just . . ."

"Yeah? Just what?"

"Nights," I whispered into the phone. "They get awfully long without you."

"I know, babe. Me too." His words were so low and sweet, I wanted to eat 'em with a spoon.

Between Denny's phone calls, suppers with Stu, time to get caught up on my lesson plans for the last weeks of school, and seeing Avis's quilt coming together, my spring break moved along better than I had imagined. Except for one thing . . .

Parent-teacher conferences—coming up next week, the last marking period before the end of the school year. Normally I looked forward to meeting with parents, sharing their children's successes, looking for things to encourage in each one. Yet as I wrote out my reports, a growing sense of dread settled in the pit of my stomach.

What am I going to say to Hakim's mother?

Not just because Geraldine Wilkins-Porter had read me the riot act at the fall parent-teacher conference when she discovered *I* was Hakim's teacher, though God knew my knees turned to jelly every time I thought about it. And not because Hakim had been having any "big" problems. He still startled and delighted me with occasional moments of brilliance, such as the time we took apart our broken electric pencil sharpener, and Hakim put it back together so it would work. And his weekly sessions with the school social worker seemed to minimize his mood swings.

But overall? Hakim was still falling behind the other students academically, especially in reading and writing. I'd practically begged his mother to let him stay in my classroom, so sure I could help him. I hadn't, though—not that much. *So what was that about, Jodi? Why did it feel so important to try?*

IT MEANT MISSING GOOD FRIDAY SERVICE at Uptown, but by late Friday evening, Stu and I had Avis's quilt top pieced together— including a blank muslin square smack-dab in the middle, per Delores's instructions. "Ah, that is for God's timing," she'd chuckled when we'd called to ask why a *blank* square. *Oh, yeah,* I remembered, grinning sheepishly. *A square to embroider their wedding date.*

"Shall I send José up to get it?" Delores asked. But Stu said she had to do a foster-care evaluation down in the city on Saturday, so she offered to drop it off.

That left a long, empty Saturday stretching out before me. Stu would be working, Denny and the kids wouldn't get home till late, and the fresh April day—awash with blue sky, billowy white clouds, and a promising green fuzz busting out on all the trees—was too smashingly beautiful to stay inside and clean another closet.

I pulled on jeans and sneakers and caught Stu just as she was heading for the garage. "Stu! Drop me off at Adele's Hair and Nails, will you? I'm going to take MaDear for a walk."

She frowned at me. "What about afterward? That's a good mile walk back home."

"Stu! I'm not an invalid. I'm so rested I'm gonna rust! I'll be fine. But I won't be fine if I stay inside this house one more day."

"Okay, okay," Stu grumbled and headed the car for Clark Street.

Dropping me off at Adele's Hair and Nails only took Stu five minutes out of her way, and I gave her a wave as the Celica disappeared into the southbound traffic. Gosh, it felt good to be out! The air felt sun-kissed, chasing about on a light breeze. The food vendors were out—a sure sign of spring. Chunky wheeled carts, some with faded umbrellas, sat on the street corners, signs beckoning *Fajitas de Pollo* and *Nachos Grande.*

I grinned to myself as I pulled open the door to Adele's Hair and Nails. Maybe MaDear and I would just have to get some of those nachos.

"Hi, Adele!" I called out, as the door tinkled shut. Adele had a customer in the first chair swathed in a black plastic cape, snipping away at the back of her hair. "Hope you don't mind me just dropping in. Can MaDear come out and play?"

"Hey, Jodi." Adele chuckled. "Sure. Help yourself. She's in the back—Geraldine, honey! You gotta sit still, or I'll cut something you ain't expecting."

I'd been grinning at Adele, but at the customer's name my eyes snapped to the mirror. The startled eyes of Geraldine Wilkins-Porter, Hakim's mother, stared back at me.

"Oh!" I stammered. "Uh, hello, Ms. Porter. I . . . didn't realize that was you." I wanted to back out the door, but my feet seemed nailed to Adele's floor.

Adele looked at me, then back at her customer's startled face in the mirror. "Mm-hm. You two know each other?"

41

*G*eraldine Wilkins-Porter, still staring at me from the wall mirror, took a deep breath and pressed her lips together. I managed a weak smile. "Uh, yes. Her son . . ." I could hardly breathe. The name *Jamal* had almost popped out of my mouth. "*Hakim* is in my class at school."

"Oh." Adele scrunched her eyes at me. Did she recognize the name? Did she put it together with the mother of the boy I'd struck and killed with my car last summer? But—*snip, snip*—she carried on. "Well, feel free to abscond with MaDear. She's driving Corey crazy back there."

Gratefully, I pried my feet forward, found MaDear muttering in her wheelchair near the nail stations, and wheeled her quickly out the front door with a squeaky, "Bye!" Took my sweet time bringing her back too. We window-shopped, stopped at several vendors and got something—flavored ices, nachos, a messy tamale—and only turned back when MaDear fell asleep so soundly from food and fresh air I had a hard time keeping her from tumbling out of the chair.

The bell over the door jingled as I wrestled the wheelchair back into the shop with MaDear a dead weight. Adele left her new customer—a twenty-something getting a weave, praise God—and helped me get MaDear settled in the back room. Then she folded her arms and studied me.

I squirmed. "What?"

"So that was the mother."

I nodded. "Did she, uh, say anything?"

"Uh-huh. Wanted to know how I knew you. So I told her."

"Oh. About Yada Yada?" *Oh dear God. What about Yada Yada?*

All she said was, "Uh-huh."

"Did she say anything about—you know, the accident and her other son?"

"Nope." Adele gave me a once-over with a critical eye, then went back to her weave. "'Bout time you made another appointment, Jodi Baxter. That hair got split ends all over the place. Should do something about those raggy nails too."

I COULDN'T GET HAKIM'S MOTHER OUT OF MY MIND the rest of the day. I hadn't seen her since she'd threatened to take Hakim out of school—though at Avis's intervention she had finally agreed to leave him in my class and allow some counseling to help him deal with the losses in his life. But could I do it again? Meet as teacher and parent and talk calmly about Hakim's progress—or lack of it— with The Accident hanging like a sword of doom over our heads?

I don't even remember the walk home from Adele's shop, just that I got home in one piece, totally exhausted. The mail had come, but I didn't even take it out of the box. I just wanted to fall into bed and drown my anxiety in a good, long nap. Instead I found myself on my knees beside the living room couch. *Pray Scripture, Jodi,* said the voice in my head. *"Be anxious for nothing . . ."*

Yeah, right. About as effective as "Don't scratch it" or "Can't eat just one." Still, I got my Bible and looked up the verse in its context: Paul's letter to the Philippian church, chapter four. I read the passage a couple of times, realizing what a difference the surrounding verses made.

"Okay, God," I said aloud, my voice muffled in a couch cushion, "Paul said I don't have to be anxious, but instead to tell You everything that's on my heart. So I gotta admit I'm really nervous about the parent-teacher conferences next week—and it blows my mind that I ran into Hakim's mother today, at Adele's shop of all places! I really need some wisdom and courage to meet her again. This scripture also says, 'with thanksgiving,' and somewhere else it says, 'in everything give thanks.' Does that mean to thank You that we ran into each other today? I don't know what You have in mind, but I do want to trust You to work it all together for good. And help me fill my mind with everything that's good and perfect and beautiful, like verse eight says, so I don't have room for all the anxious thoughts that—"

"Hey!" yelled a familiar voice from the back of the house. "Anybody home?"

"Denny!" I screeched, launching myself off my knees. I'm sure my dash to the kitchen broke somebody's world record, a startled Willie Wonka hard on my heels.

I HADN'T EXPECTED MY FAMILY BACK so early in the afternoon—hadn't washed the bedding, hadn't fixed supper, hadn't put on any makeup—but nobody complained. Certainly not me. I was so glad they were home, I kept wanting to hug them—which got old pretty quick for Amanda and Josh, who began fighting about who got the phone first. Denny seemed content to sprawl on the couch with one arm around me and an iced tea in his other hand. "Remind me not to divorce you," he murmured into my hair. "I'm not ready to be a single parent."

A waft of English Leather tickled my nose as I snuggled closer. Gosh, I was glad he was home.

Eventually I did have to untangle myself, stick the bedding in the washer, and think about supper. I suggested eating out at Siam Pasta, but the kids groaned. "We're dying for home cooking, Mom!" What mother in her right mind could resist outright flattery?

Over roasted chicken with rosemary, baked potatoes with sour cream, and frozen green beans with lemon pepper—the easy-but-yummy formula—I listened to Josh and Amanda tell how chilling it was to stand on Ground Zero and see all the flowers and notes that people still left every day, honoring the people who had died on 9/11. They had wanted to visit Ellis Island, but the Statue of Liberty was closed for security reasons, and they ended up on Museum Mile along Fifth Avenue.

"Yeah. I wanted to see the Metropolitan Museum of Art," Josh grumbled, "but Amanda bullied us into visiting *El Museo del Barrio.*"

Amanda snapped him with her cloth napkin. "We voted! You lost! Besides, you know you liked it." She turned to me, eyes alight. "It was all this Latino art, Mom—mostly Puerto Rican and Caribbean. *So* cool."

Denny and I exchanged glances. Yep, things were back to normal.

AMANDA RAN UP THE BACK STAIRS the next morning to see if Stu wanted a ride to church, but she came back saying Stu didn't get home till late last night and would be coming later. Fine by me. After missing the Good Friday service, I was eager not to miss any of the Easter worship.

Last year—our first Easter at Uptown Community Church—the entire congregation had hiked to the lake carrying colorful bunches of balloons with "Resurrection messages" attached, then let them go, up, up, till they disappeared in the direction of Cleveland. I'd loved the simple beauty of the celebration and was hoping we'd do it again—though when we Baxters topped the stairs to the second-floor meeting room, the room was devoid of any balloons, color, or any decorations whatsoever. Not even an Easter lily. In fact, the windows shades had been pulled down and the room was quite dim. What in the world . . .?

The room was packed. Figured. The weather guy had said a possibility of rain, yet temperatures were already a pleasant sixty-two degrees, luring even the reluctant out of their stuffy houses and apartment buildings. I poked Denny. "Look." Carl Hickman was there; the whole Hickman family, in fact. Florida was beaming like she'd just won an Oscar. She probably deserved one. Avis was back, too, but I couldn't catch her eye. She was too busy whispering back and forth to Peter Douglass as they sat together on the far side of the room.

The lights went out and we scurried to find a seat. A not-so-young guy I'd never seen before with a short, graying beard and hair slicked over a high forehead sat down at the piano, and the room hushed. With a plaintive, Bob Dylan kind of voice he began:

> *Was it a morning like this*
> *When the sun still hid from Jerusalem?*
> *And Mary rose from her bed*
> *To tend the Lord . . . she thought was dead . . .*

Sheila Fitzhugh, who'd loaned me the slinky black dress last year, came up the middle aisle, doing a sorrowful dance in the role of Mary Magdalene. Then a "Peter" and a "John" joined her as the words of the song beckoned:

> *Was it a morning like this*
> *When Peter and John ran from Jerusalem?*
> *And as they raced for the tomb*
> *Beneath their feet, was there a tune?*
> *Did the grass sing? Did the earth rejoice to feel You again?*

Goose bumps danced on my arms as the window shades flew up and sunlight spilled into the room. "Peter," "John," and "Mary" linked hands and began to dance like the floorboards tickled their feet, the youth group suddenly emerged from the kitchen with the missing balloons, and the bard at the piano raised his voice in triumph:

> *Over and over like a trumpet underground*
> *Did the earth seem to pound, "He is risen!"*
> *Over and over in a never-ending round*
> *He is ri-sen! Hallelujah! Hallelujah!*

The atmosphere in the room had gone electric. Everyone was on their feet, the praise team and Uptown musicians took over, and we sang God's praises in song after song. Everyone had their hands in the air. How could a person just sit when Jesus had conquered sin and death . . . just for us?

I tried to find the guest musician before we all set out for the lake with our balloons, but he must have slipped out. I overheard some folks talking who'd heard the song recorded by Sandi Patty—but this guy, Jim Croegaert, was the original songwriter. "How'd he end up at Uptown Community?" someone laughed. "We're not exactly on the tour schedule for Christian musicians."

"He's local. Lives here in Chicago. A friend of Pastor Clark from his old rock-'n'-roll days."

Old rock-'n'-roll days? Hmm. So Pastor Clark had a *past*—ha! I wrote down the guy's name, hoping he had some CDs.

"Jodi," Florida said, charging up to me. "Peter Douglass got my Carl over there in a corner—don't know what about. You be prayin', you hear? That man needs some resurrection, and my naggin' ain't it." She craned her neck around. "Where's Avis? You think she's avoiding us? There she is. Stu! You come on too." Florida grabbed both of us by the hand and made a beeline for Avis, who ducked behind a gaggle of teenagers with balloons.

"You stop right there, Avis Johnson," Florida commanded, dragging Stu and me the other way around the herd of balloons and blocking her way. "Let's see it."

Avis was trying to repress a grin and feigning innocence all at once. "See what?"

"Whatever you're hiding. Out with it."

Avis started to laugh. Impatient, Florida grabbed her left hand and held it up. "I knew it!" she crowed.

My mouth dropped. Stu whistled. A large diamond engagement ring circled Avis's long, slim finger—the finger where she'd still been wearing her gold wedding band since Conrad's death. Heads turned as the three of us shrieked and tackled Avis with a big hug.

"Oh, thanks," Avis wheezed when we finally let her go. "Remind me not to hang around you girlfriends if I want to keep something quiet or dignified."

Florida snorted. "You got that right. It's our duty not to let you get too dignified—uh-oh, my family's goin' out the door with them balloons. You guys comin' to the lake?"

"Uh, can't." Stu looked at me apologetically. "Gotta go home and start cleaning my stuff out of the guest room." We all stared at her as she pulled a business letter out of her shoulder bag. "This came in the mail yesterday. Didn't get it till this morning." She took a deep breath. "Becky Wallace is being paroled next weekend—to my house."

42

Didn't know which bit of news spun me around more—that Avis and Peter Douglass were actually engaged, or that the Bandana Woman was going to take up residence in this very house. Stu seemed in a slight state of shock—the *oh-God-what-have-I-done* variety—and I volunteered Amanda and myself to help with necessary preparations. But what would Becky need? Toiletries? Underwear? We probably wouldn't know till she got here.

When I hit school Monday morning—refreshed from my stay-at-home week, I had to admit—I noticed that Avis was wearing The Ring diamond-side down to stave off questions and squeals from co-workers. But I did wiggle a moment with her behind closed doors in her office, long enough to ask, "*When*, Avis, when? Don't keep us all in suspense. These things take preparation."

"No," she said mildly, "we want to keep this simple. Get a marriage license and . . . I don't know, maybe have Pastor Clark marry us on a Sunday morning."

"*Sunday morning?*" I tried to keep my screech to a whisper. "Are you guys out of your minds? What about flowers, and bridesmaids, and wedding cake, and dancing for joy?" I let slip a grin. "Hey. All the Yada Yadas could be your bridesmaids."

"Jodi Baxter! *Read my lips.* Simple. Sunday morning. Now," she smiled sweetly, "did you have something school-related you wanted to talk about?"

I sank back in her visitor chair. "Yeah. Parent-teacher conferences on Wednesday. I'm scared spitless."

I WAS GLAD I TALKED TO AVIS. I told her about running into Hakim's mother at Adele's shop on Saturday, about my feelings of failure with Hakim, about realizing the accident still didn't have closure. Not for me, and certainly not for Geraldine—how could I expect that? How did a mother ever get over the death of her child? Much less relate normally to the woman responsible for his death, who just happened to be her only surviving son's third-grade teacher?

Avis didn't try to answer all my questions, but she wrote down some scriptures for me to turn into prayers. I tried out the first one—Proverbs 28:13—as I walked home from school on Monday, past the tiny lilies of the valley pushing up along the sidewalk, praying aloud. "Dear God, I don't want to be the kind of person who covers over my sin. You promised that if I confess and forsake them, I will receive mercy." Yes, I knew I'd received mercy. I wasn't in jail, was I?

On Tuesday, I soaked up the second verse she'd given me from Acts. 3:19: "Lord Jesus, You promised that if I repent and turn to you, that You would send times of refreshing." What a wonderful word—*refreshing*. Like a hot shower after camping in the mud all weekend, or ice-cold water on a muggy August day. Even as I was writing that day's homework assignment on the board, my heart was crying, *"Oh, Lord! Please send that time of refreshing!"*

We had early dismissal on Wednesday to allow for report-card pickup and parent-teacher conferences. The third verse Avis had given me was Galatians 6:2. I just wasn't sure I knew how to pray it with Geraldine Wilkins-Porter in mind. "Jesus, Your Word says to carry each other's burdens, but . . . I really don't know how to carry this mother's burden without drowning in my own guilt and her sorrow." Yet the words stayed with me: *"Carry one another's burdens."*

Praying the Scriptures really calmed my mind and my spirit as parents appeared in my classroom, and I crossed off D'Angelo's mother . . . Ebony's father . . . LeTisha's proud parents . . . a couple of no-shows . . . Ramón's uncle . . . and then there it was: Geraldine Wilkins-Porter's signature on the sign-up sheet.

I stood up from my desk chair as the door opened and Hakim's mother stepped into the room. She hesitated a moment just inside the door, trim and businesslike in a gray suit with a short skirt, and a silky red blouse. Adele had done a smashing job on her hair—tight corkscrew curls all over with just a touch of rusty color in the hair, softening her rather sculptured face. "Please. Come in," I said. She crossed the room and we both sat down, eyeing each other anxiously across my desk. I didn't have a clue what I should say. I hadn't written anything out, hadn't practiced anything. Just prayed.

I pushed Hakim's report card aside and folded my hands to keep them from shaking. Somehow I found the courage to keep my eyes on her face. "Ms. Porter, Hakim continues to show some improvement in reading and writing—but I believe that is his accomplishment, not mine. I've been doing some soul-searching and . . . I had no right to try to keep your son in my class. He's a very likable boy, and I really did want him to stay, but . . ." The words kept coming, words that had been hidden thoughts, pushing themselves into the space between us. "I realize now I was trying to redeem myself in your eyes for what I did by helping your second son. Maybe redeem myself in God's eyes too."

Tears pushed themselves to the brink. I blinked them away, afraid that if I stopped, I'd never find the courage to continue. I couldn't read Geraldine's face—it was guarded, but not hostile. *Not hostile.* That counted for something.

"There are two things I need to say to you. I know I said 'I'm sorry' when we met in the courtroom. I am, deeply, so sorry for your loss. But I need to say much more than that. I . . . I was driving angry that day—angry after a dumb fight with my husband. I wasn't breaking any laws behind the wheel, yet my spirit was wrong, *so wrong* that day. And the next thing I knew your son was dead. For that, I not only need to repent before God, but before you."

The dark eyes across the desk from me were deep and luminous. She didn't interrupt or yell at me or turn away. She was listening.

I swallowed. My mouth was dry. "Second, I never should have expected you to leave Hakim in my class when you discovered I was his teacher. That you did says far more about you than about me. I overestimated my abilities, though. He is not progressing as he should—and as I believe he *can* with the right kind of help. Please forgive me for my arrogance. I know you only want the best for your son—as I should. It was wrong of me to ask you to leave him in this awkward situation. If you want to remove him from this class, I—"

Hakim's mother held up her hand to stop me. Her eyes were dry but bright. "You have had your say. Now let me have mine." She stood and walked over to Hakim's desk, her finger slowly tracing the jagged scar he had dug into the wood with a paper clip. Then she turned back to me.

"I don't know if I can forgive you for killing my son," she said slowly. *(Oh God! To hear her say it like that—"for killing my son"—I can't bear it!)* "I don't know if I'm strong enough to do that. But I have something to say to you too—something I've had to face, even though I haven't wanted to. That day, the day of the accident, Jamal was running against the light, against traffic, with a jacket over his head in a downpour that kept drivers from seeing him. His cousins admit it; the other driver—the one that hit your car—said so too. I couldn't hear it; I wanted to put it all on your head." She took a deep breath. "But my Jamal was also responsible for what happened that day. Not just you."

Her words nearly sucked the breath out of me.

She traced the jagged scar again with a carefully manicured nail. "Hakim likes you, Ms. Baxter. Against all odds, against all the hate that has raged inside me, my son likes you. I couldn't understand it. But then . . ." She looked up. "Then you come waltzing into Adele Skuggs's beauty shop to take her elderly mother for a walk. You. Jodi Baxter. The woman I love to hate!" An ironic smile tipped one side of her mouth. "And my beautician tells me you're in her prayer group—her *prayer group*, for God's sake!—and it was your idea for the sisters to take MaDear out or come in and read to her." Geraldine Wilkins-Porter wagged her head. "When I walked out of that beauty shop, it was a lot harder to think of you just as that pig-headed white woman who killed my son."

I didn't know whether to laugh or cry. *Pig-headed!* Hakim's mother thought of me as "that pig-headed white woman." Well, why not?

Didn't I still think of Becky Wallace as "Bandana Woman"? Both of us had hit on a way to deny the humanity of the person who'd wronged us . . . deny her her *name*.

Geraldine sat down across from me again, and for some reason she started to laugh softly. "Yes, pig-headed. Not very creative, I know. I wanted to call you something worse."

I couldn't help it. I started to laugh, too, my shoulders shaking. "You should have," I gasped. "Yes, a lot worse!" I dabbed at my eyes with a tissue, and when I lifted my head, I realized she was looking at me. Our eyes met and the moment hung in the air.

"Oh, Geraldine. Can you forgive me?" I reached my hand across the desk.

To my surprise she touched my fingers briefly, then pulled her hand back and looked down at her lap. "Maybe . . . maybe someday," she whispered.

I WASN'T SURE EXACTLY WHAT HAPPENED in my classroom that afternoon, except that both Hakim's mother and I had spoken honestly to each other—and we had *touched*. As I gathered up my books and papers after the last parent-teacher conference, I felt . . . light. Like refreshing spring water was bubbling up inside my soul. There it was—that word. *Refreshing*. God was true to His Word. He had sent a "time of refreshing."

I wanted to dance all the way home—except Denny was there in the parking lot to pick me up when I came out of the school building at nine o'clock. "Hey, babe. You okay?" He'd known how anxious I was about this parent-teacher conference.

For an answer, I gave him a long, sensuous kiss on the mouth that left him gasping.

Hakim was still in my classroom the next day, and the next. Well, I had released him if his mother thought it best. But in the meantime, I'd just plug along with my lesson plans for finding the perimeter of rectangles, taking a field trip to the Chicago Historical Society, and using prefixes to change the meaning of words.

Friday evening, Denny had to coach a baseball game at West Rogers High, so I didn't feel guilty skipping out with Stu to do some shopping for Becky Wallace. Stu had decided to make a welcome basket of toiletries like shampoo, body lotion, razors, facial scrub, body mist—even a toothbrush, toothpaste, and deodorant—and we had a blast picking out the stuff. We decided to go with a melon scent for consistency, fruity rather than flowery. Becky Wallace didn't exactly seem a "flowery" sort of woman.

Walking up and down the aisles of Target, Stu went nuts— adding a thick bath towel and washcloth to the cart, a pair of one-size-fits-all slippers, and even a small hair dryer. "Uh, Stu," I said, as she paused by a display case of Timex watches, "you're spending a lot of money here. I don't think Becky expects all this. Giving her an address to come home to is a huge gift as it is."

Stu pursed her lips, passed up the watches, and pushed the cart into the next available checkout lane. "Yeah. Guess you're right. Except, I don't think she'll have much, just coming out of prison. Maybe just the clothes she was wearing that night when she . . . anyway. And don't forget, Jodi. You have Denny and the kids to squander gifts on. Right now, Becky Wallace is the closest thing to family I've got." She shrugged. "I figure, why not?"

WE HAD NO IDEA WHEN BECKY WOULD ARRIVE on Saturday. Some of the Yada Yadas said they'd like to be there to greet her, but

Stu decided there'd be time for that later. Becky would probably appreciate a fairly anonymous reentry into society versus the big-band approach. Stu's house was so clean, a hospital patient could eat off the floor. But she was so hyper, about four in the afternoon I made her put her feet up in our recliner with a big mug of valerian herb tea to calm her down.

After one sip, she made a nasty face. "Ugh! Jodi, what is this stuff?"

"It's . . . an acquired taste. I put lots of honey in it."

She held it out. "Put in lots more."

"Mom." Amanda appeared in the doorway to the living room. "There's a strange gray car double-parked outside our house with its hazards on. Two guys in suits and sunglasses. And . . . that woman."

43

The five of us—Stu, Denny, me, Josh, and Amanda—walked out and stood on the front porch of our two-flat as two men in suits and ties got out of the double-parked car. For some reason, I was acutely aware of the tiny yellow and purple crocuses nodding happily along the sidewalk up to our house, sparrows chirping in the trees, the afternoon sun filtering through a curtain of baby leaves sprouting overhead up and down Lunt Street. As the driver opened the back door, a slim figure wearing tight jeans and a jean jacket slid out of the backseat and stood up, clutching a plastic bag.

As his partner leaned against the car, the other man walked Becky Wallace toward the house, stopped at the bottom of the porch steps, and squinted up at us behind his sunglasses. "One of you folks Leslie Stuart?"

Stu stepped forward. "That's me."

He double-checked the address on his clipboard. "State Department of Corrections. We need to activate the electronic monitor through your phone line." He held out a manila envelope. "And here's a copy of the regulations that apply to a parolee on EM."

We couldn't help it. All eyes strayed to the slight bulge around the woman's ankle under her pant leg. *"Bound" . . . "tied." That's what her name meant.* Becky looked off to the side, as if none of this was about her. Stu walked slowly down the steps, took the papers out of the envelope, and skimmed over them. The man pointed. "That's the phone number of the parole agent. The parolee knows she must call to get permission to leave the premises for any reason." He tapped his pen on the clipboard. "Which apartment?"

Stu led the way inside and up the stairs to her apartment. The four of us Baxters hung around on the porch till they returned about ten minutes later. To my surprise, the man politely extended his hand to Becky. "Ms. Wallace, best wishes. I don't want to see you again." The two men climbed back in the unmarked gray car and were gone.

"Okay," Josh quipped, "breathe, everybody." Laughing a bit nervously, we shook Becky's hand, introduced Amanda and Josh, and made jokes about being "the noisy family downstairs."

"But we'll go back in our cave," Denny joshed, "and let Stu get you settled. Maybe see you tomorrow."

Becky nodded. She still had not said a word. But her dark eyes seemed to take in the whole house—porch, front door, bay window sticking out in front. "You dinnit tell me I been here b'fore." Her tone was accusing.

Stu and I exchanged glances. Denny cleared his throat. "Yes. The night you were arrested."

I WONDERED IF BECKY WOULD GO TO CHURCH with Stu the next morning, but Stu caught a ride with us—alone. "She has to get permission from her parole agent to go anywhere," Denny reminded me.

Stu shrugged. "Besides, she's still asleep. Haven't heard a peep this morning."

Humph. Had Stu checked the bedroom? Maybe she'd split already. *Sheesh, Jodi. The girl is probably sleeping in for the first time in months. In a real bed.* Yet I did feel nervous pulling away from the house with a convicted thief locked inside.

Amanda pumped Stu for details all the way to church. "Did she like the gift basket you made for her? What did she say? What did you guys do all evening?"

"Uh, I *think* she liked it. She looked at all the stuff a long time and said, 'Thanks.' She's probably overwhelmed; doesn't know what to say." Frankly, Stu seemed a little shell-shocked herself. "She did take a long bath last night, though."

No wonder. I tried not to think about gang showers in prison.

On the way home from church, Stu's demeanor had perked up. "Jodi! I've been thinking—what would you guys think about me making a case with DCFS for Andy to come live with his mom? Or at least allow regular visits to her here?"

I couldn't believe it! Becky Wallace hadn't been here even twenty-four hours, and Stu was already thinking about adding Becky's kid to the mix. Four weeks ago she'd nearly lost it just seeing the little guy with the unfortunate matching birth date. My old Stu Alert went off, annoyed at her gotta-fix-everything urgency. Bless Denny, though. He matter-of-factly said, "Might be a great idea. I just wouldn't put it forward till you see if this arrangement actually works out."

Stu nodded. "Yeah. You're probably right. She's gotta be dying to see him, though."

"Well, sure. Work on a visit. But one thing at a time."

Stu actually seemed grateful for the advice, and my annoyance was kicked aside by a smidgeon of appreciation. Maybe all Stu's "grand ideas" weren't just about proving herself to God and everybody else. Had to admit she really did have a heart for redeeming lives.

I breathed a sigh of relief when we got home and the house was still standing, just as we'd left it. I decided against inviting Stu and Becky to have lunch with us, however, trying to respect the new housemates' need to get used to each other and work out the details of living together. "But," I whispered to Stu just before she headed up the back stairs, "why don't you see if you can get her to come downstairs to Yada Yada tonight? She wouldn't have to get permission, would she? Same house, right?"

I CALLED AROUND to tell the sisters we might have a visitor at Yada Yada—emphasis on *might*. Half the group hadn't seen Becky Wallace since the night of the robbery; a few hadn't even been here that night. It would be weird at best to have her sitting with us in the very same room, but I didn't want to shock anybody.

That's how I found out from Edesa that Delores had had a birthday earlier in April and hadn't told anybody. Well, we wouldn't let her get away with *that*. It'd be a good distraction if Becky Wallace actually showed up.

Which she did. I was dribbling a sugar glaze on a lemon bundt cake when Stu and Becky came in the back door, ten minutes early. Becky had on her same jeans, tank top, and jean jacket. "Didn't want to make any grand entrances," Stu murmured to me as they passed through the kitchen. When I arrived in the living room with the tea and coffee, I saw that Becky had chosen a straight-backed dining room chair and edged it backward, just out of the circle. Stu sat on the end of the couch closest to Becky's chair.

Nony and Hoshi were the next to arrive. Hoshi—bless her!—went straight to Becky, said hello softly with a small bow, and sat down in the chair next to her. Nony held out her hand from the folds of a roomy African-print caftan. "Becky Wallace? I am Nonyameko Sisulu-Smith." She courteously poured some tea and offered it to Becky, acting for all the world as if this woman hadn't stolen her wedding ring right off her finger.

So far, so good. But my stomach was still in a knot. Could only guess what Chanda might say. Or Ruth—heaven help us!

God must have been orchestrating the whole arrival, though, because Florida blew in next and hailed Becky from across the room. "Girl, sure am glad to see *you*. How ya doin'? . . . Where's Avis at? I want to see that big ol' ring of hers again. She and Peter didn't elope, did they?"

I looked at Florida, stricken. "They'd better not!" I exclaimed, just as the rest of Yada Yada arrived in rapid succession—including Avis, who was mobbed by everybody who hadn't been at Uptown on Easter Sunday. It was a good distraction—maybe too good, as Becky was basically ignored for a good five minutes. Yet I noticed that Yo-Yo greeted her and sat down on the floor near Becky's feet.

Chanda was the last to arrive, and she beckoned me out on the porch. "Sista Jodee, I bring flowers for her! What you tink?"

"Oh, Chanda!" My mind scrambled. Flowers would be a disaster. "You are so thoughtful—but I think we'll scare her off if we make a big fuss. But—oh! It's Delores's birthday! You could give them to her, do you mind?"

When Chanda and I came back into the living room—*sans*

flowers, which we left on the porch—Avis was untangling herself from the mob and trying to get the prayer time started. As things got quiet, Ruth spoke up from her chair on the other side of the room, acknowledging our guest. "So, Becky. You have come." She hesitated for the briefest moment, then added, *"Shalom."*

"Yes, exactly, Ruth. *Shalom.* We want to welcome Becky Wallace, Stu's new housemate. Becky, we're glad you're here and hope that you experience the peace of God." Avis opened her Bible. "Let's open our time together with some praise from the psalmist."

Oh, smooth, Avis. No mention of the robbery, prison, or anything. Just "Stu's new housemate."

We moved into the meeting as though Becky were not there—reading Scripture, singing a couple of worship songs, opening with some prayer and praise. I could hardly imagine what Becky thought about all this, but when Avis asked for any praise reports, she leaned forward, listening intently. Or she was a good faker.

"Well, I got somethin' to shout about," Florida announced. "Peter Douglass—bless that man! Oh, hallelujah!—he done offered a job to my Carl as his mailroom supervisor." The room erupted with shouts of glee. "Wait, wait, that ain't all! He gets two weeks' job training, room for advancement, and—oh, Jesus! Don't know if I can stand it!—full benefits!" Florida was on her feet, waving her hand in the air. *"Thank* ya! Thank ya, Jesus!"

Carl with a job? With benefits? We'd been praying for months—why was I so surprised? Did I have so little faith? Or had I just pegged Carl as "permanently jobless"?

Florida sat down again, fanning herself with her hand. "You gotta pray for me I don't nag him 'bout this job, though. So afraid he gonna do somethin' dumb and lose it. But job training starts tomorrow, so we'll see."

"Don't worry. He'll do great!" Stu beamed. "You should've seen Carl work the day of my move. Took someone like Peter Douglass to see his potential."

I was so happy for Florida, I wanted to hug her. I wondered . . . maybe the Guys' Day Out had started something.

Nony had the second praise report. Her contacts in Washington had assured her that Congress was set to pass an AIDS bill to fight AIDS globally—"with some of the money earmarked for abstinence education, praise Jesus," she glowed. "Please pray with me, sisters, that this money actually reaches my country of South Africa, before we lose this next generation." Her eyes filled with tears, a mixture of joy and sadness.

And for you, Nony, I added silently. *I know your heart is still in your country.* I would hate to lose Nony from my life, but I found myself praying, *Oh God, if it's in Your will, open the door for Nony to return home—with her whole family.*

"Now you, Avis," Adele ordered. "When this wedding gonna be?"

I thought Avis might be on the spot, but she seemed amused by the question. "Next week."

We all laughed. "Yeah, right." . . . "When, for real?"

"Like I said, next week—for real."

Send a shock through a group of twelve women, and they all react a different way. It was pandemonium for about sixty seconds, but Adele said, "Will you all just shut up? Let the sister have her say."

We shut up. "Thank you," said Avis. "Well, neither Peter nor I want a long engagement or a big wedding. I think we both know it's not the *wedding* but the *marriage* that's important. We"—now she did get embarrassed—"want to get on with it."

I cast an anxious eye at Delores, trying to project my thoughts:

What about the quilt? But her round face was serene. *No problemo* . . . I hoped.

". . . during worship next Sunday at Uptown," Avis was saying. "You are all invited, of course. My daughters and the grandbabies are coming. Otherwise, that's it."

Sheesh. She's actually serious!

Ruth frowned. "Your happiness we want, Avis! But isn't next Sunday the day Yo-Yo wants to be baptized?"

Yo-Yo blinked, like she had just put two and two together. "Uh . . . don't worry 'bout it, Avis. I can do that some other time. August, maybe. When it's hot. Or next year."

Avis laughed. "No, Yo-Yo. That's the whole point! That's why we chose next Sunday. Everybody wants to come to your baptism—right, sisters?" Heads bobbed around the room. "So if Peter and I get married during the service, then everyone will already be there for your baptism at the lake!"

"Oh." Yo-Yo considered that. "So that means I probably gotta go to church with you all."

We all cracked up. Yo-Yo had managed to miss all our Yada Yada visits to each other's churches. "Gotcha!" Florida yelled.

When we'd all wiped our eyes and settled back down, Avis gave me a meaningful look. "Uh, Jodi and Edesa? Don't you have something . . . ?"

Edesa and I split for the kitchen, returning a few minutes later with candles flaming on the lemon cake and singing "Happy Birthday." I hadn't had time to make a card, but after a flustered Delores had blown out the candles, I said, "Delores, do you know what your name means?"

She nodded, even rolled her eyes. "*Sí.* It means, 'Sorrows.'"

"Exactly!" I crowed. "But do I have a song for you!" On our player I had cued an Israel and New Breed CD to the popular Darrell Evans gospel song and turned it up. *I'm trading my sorrows, I'm trading my sha-ame, I'm laying them down for the joy of the Lord!"*

It was the perfect song for Delores. It got all of us to our feet as New Breed—supported by twelve Yada Yadas—belted out, *"Yes Lord, yes Lord, yes yes Lord! . . ."*

In the chair just outside the circle of upraised arms and singing women, I noticed Becky quickly brush a hand across her eyes, as if afraid someone might see.

Maybe it was the perfect song for Becky Wallace too.

44

*T*he answering machine light was blinking furiously when I got home from school the next day—mostly from Yada Yadas buzzing about Avis's wedding. "Ain't she takin' the concept of 'church wedding' a bit too literal?" Florida fussed. Delores left a message that the "quilting lady" broke her wrist, so please pray that the quilt would get done in time, and could I send out an e-mail to that effect? Ruth wanted to incorporate an idea from traditional Jewish weddings "as a surprise for Avis and Peter." Then another message from Ruth: "Cake? A cake she has to have! Should we get one from the Bagel Bakery?"

Sheesh, I thought, scribbling notes so I could erase the messages. *This could get complicated.* Didn't Avis say she wanted to keep it simple?

A knock at the back door interrupted my reading a slew of e-mail messages along the same general thread, plus Yo-Yo's baptism. *(Who's going to bring towels? A blanket? Should we give her flowers afterward? What if it rains?)* Becky Wallace stood at my back door, still wearing the same jeans and tank top she'd arrived in.

"Hey, Becky. Come on in."

She didn't budge. "Nah. Just wanted to know if you want to do somethin' 'bout them flowerbeds." She jerked a thumb at the pathetic flowerbeds that ran the length of the small backyard along both sides. "I could dig 'em up for ya."

"Oh, you don't have to do that!"

"Know that. But I'd kinda like to, if ya don't mind." She shrugged. "Need somethin' to do, an' I got myself on the garden-and-grounds crew at Lincoln a couple of months ago. Learned a few things—didn't get to plant any flowers, though." Her laugh was hollow. "Not that I wanted ta stay longer jus' ta stick in a few marigolds."

"Well . . . sure. Help yourself. Tools are in the garage—I'll unlock the door."

Armed with a long shovel, Becky tackled the weed-choked flowerbeds with the determination of a prisoner-of-war digging an escape tunnel. Willie Wonka seemed fascinated by all the activity and settled on his haunches nearby like a sidewalk supervisor. It took a gulp of faith for me to go about my business inside the house and leave my dog outside with the same woman who'd threatened to "cut him" during the robbery.

Okay, Jesus, I know I'm a little anxious, and I'm probably being silly. I chopped vegetables for a pot of soup with unnecessary vigor. *But we could use a few guardian angels on the job, if You don't mind. One for Willie Wonka too.* I stepped over to the back door and watched Becky working up a good sweat with the shovel. Only God knew what was going on in her mind and her spirit these days. Maybe *she* was anxious about *us*.

And a guardian angel for Becky too, I added.

The phone rang again . . . and continued all week as calls flew back and forth between Yada Yadas about the big weekend coming up. Avis's wedding and Yo-Yo's baptism were briefly overshadowed when the president held a press conference on May first and announced that the fighting in Iraq was over. "Now it is time to rebuild!" I wanted to rejoice, I really did; but something deep in my spirit said it wasn't time to stop praying. I even sent an e-mail to Yada Yada early Saturday morning saying, "Sisters! Keep praying for true peace in Iraq and in the Middle East. Prayer is our battle-ground, and the battle is far from over."

I studied the e-mail a few moments before I hit Send. That was certainly a New Jodi prayer focus—if I practiced what I preached. Already I was tempted to skip my prayer time that morning because of the busy day ahead. Josh had to take his SATs today, Amanda and I both had hair appointments at Adele's Hair and Nails, and Ben Garfield wanted to deliver something to Uptown Community for Avis's wedding—the "surprise." But I managed to squeeze fifteen minutes for prayer between Willie Wonka's first trip to the yard and the first phone call.

It was Yo-Yo. "Hey, Jodi. You said my name meant 'lavender flower,' right?"

"That's right, Yo-Yo. What's up?"

"Oh, nothin'. I was just thinkin' about what to wear tomorrow."

I nearly dropped the phone. Yo-Yo was thinking about *what to wear?* Was it possible she might even show up in a lavender *dress?*

"Mom?" Josh grabbed a banana as he headed out the door to catch the eight o'clock start time for the SAT. "A couple of friends of mine at Jesus People want to visit Uptown Community some-time. Think tomorrow would be okay?"

"Uh, it might be kind of packed tomorrow with Avis getting married, but . . ." I couldn't bring myself to say no to any young person wanting to come to church. "You guys might have to stand."

"No sweat. Oh. Not guys. Girls." And he was out the door.

Girls?

I thought he was gone, but sixty seconds later Josh stuck his head back inside the kitchen door. "Hey, Mom. We usually get you some flowers to plant for Mother's Day, right? Would you mind if we got them early so Becky could get them in the ground rather than make her wait a whole week?"

What could I say? I loved flowers in the yard! I loved the *idea* of planting them myself. Yet the kids knew me too well. Last year half the sets they bought me for Mother's Day died before their little roots ever touched the flowerbeds.

EXCITEMENT WOKE ME that first Sunday of May even before Willie Wonka's bladder did. I lay in the semidarkness, enjoying the stillness of the morning before the day's events took over. A year ago this very weekend, I'd been sharing a king-size bed with Florida Hickman at the Embassy Suites Hotel, where we'd met for the first time at the Chicago Women's Conference. Actually, *not* for the first time, but neither one of us had known it then. The same weekend God assigned me to Prayer Group 26, which we laughingly called Yada Yada, and changed my life forever.

Oh God, You've truly brought us a mighty long way—

I sat up suddenly. What was that noise? I listened carefully then quietly raised the window blind. *Rain!* I sank back onto my pillow in disappointment.

There was nothing to do but get ready for church anyhow. Rain wouldn't stop Avis's wedding—though what was going to happen about the baptism? I put on the coffee and looked out the window into the backyard. At least the Johnny jump-ups, petunias, and zinnias that Becky Wallace had planted yesterday—my Mother's Day gift from Josh and Amanda one week early—were enjoying the good soak.

The clouds still hung low over the city as we headed out the door to church, but at least the rain had stopped. *Maybe . . . just maybe . . .*

We waved at Stu and Becky as they took off in the Celica, having gotten permission from her parole agent to attend church and the baptism—especially when assured that she would be in the company of other members of the household. By the time we parked and got upstairs—twenty minutes early for a change—we barely found two seats together.

Uptown's sanctuary was packed.

To the casual eye, it wasn't apparent that a wedding would be taking place that day. No flowers, no candles—no "surprise" from Ben and Ruth? Just bunches of grinning people in their own version of wedding finery. Avis, introducing her daughters and grandbabies to various folks, was dressed in a creamy suit with a feminine cut that made her look like a double latte, her hair done in braided extensions that swept upward and twisted into an elegant knot on the top of her head. The Sisulu-Smiths were dressed in the exotic matching outfits they'd brought home from South Africa. Chanda and her three kids arrived, dressed like an Easter parade. Except Chanda's face was the inverse of her sunshine yellow suit.

"You okay, Chanda?" I asked.

"T'ree days!" she grumbled. "Dat mon, 'e be gone *t'ree days* wit'out telling me where 'e go or calling home or anyting. I'm fin' his suitcase on de sidewalk in one more minnit—Dia! Quit dat runnin'! Dis be a church, even it don' look like it." And she stalked off.

About time she tossed him out the door. But I felt badly for Dia and Chanda's other kids. *If only DeShawn—*

I was distracted by a female voice calling, "Hey, Josh! We made it!" Must be the girls from Jesus People. Had to admit the green and pink spiky hair, nose rings, and tattoos curling around their necks took me aback. Same with the big hugs they gave Josh.

Oh Lord.

All the Yada Yada families were present in full force—even Ricardo Enriques and José, dressed in the embroidered short jackets and large silver belt buckles they'd worn for Amanda's *quince-añera.* Amanda made a beeline to sit with José, and I let her go. We were just one big family this morning, anyway.

I was worried that Yo-Yo would chicken out because of the rain, but as Pastor Clark announced the opening scripture from Proverbs 18, the Garfields arrived with Yo-Yo and her two brothers trailing behind them . . . and I wanted to burst out laughing.

Yo-Yo was wearing a brand-new pair of lavender overalls.

"The name of the Lord is a strong tower," Pastor Clark boomed, covering my giggle that escaped. "The righteous run into it and are safe." Then the praise team launched into the Don Moen worship song based on that same verse: "The name of the Lord is . . . a strong tower!"

The name of the Lord is a strong tower! What a wonderful theme for Avis's wedding and Yo-Yo's baptism. I'd been thinking of the meaning of Avis's name—"Refuge in battle"—as who *she* was to me and to Yada Yada. But a deeper meaning probably went right along with this proverb: Avis herself took refuge in "the name of the Lord," which probably accounted for her peaceful heart and spirit of praise.

Pastor Clark served Communion as usual on the first Sunday of the month, but as we all settled back in our seats, he still held up a cup and a hunk of bread. "As you all know, we share the sacrament of Communion each month to remember the broken body and spilled blood of Christ as atonement for our sins. There are other sacraments with great meaning for the church—and one of these is marriage, a picture of the relationship between Christ and His bride, the church." In spite of himself, Pastor Clark betrayed the seriousness of his words with a wide grin. "Avis Johnson and Peter Douglass have asked us all to participate with them as they join their lives together in the sacrament of marriage. So if the guest musicians can give us some music, we need a few minutes to get ready."

Avis's and Peter's self-conscious smiles turned to puzzled glances. Obviously, they thought they were just going to stand up, say their vows, and sit down. *Ha! Think again, Avis.* Florida caught my eye across the room and gave me a thumbs-up as Ricardo and José Enriques stood in the back of the room and began picking the tune, "Jesu, Joy of Man's Desiring," on their acoustic guitars. As the music played, Ben Garfield, Ruth, and Delores disappeared into a side room and came out carrying a traditional Jewish *huppah*, which looked very much like a squared-off garden trellis decorated with silk ivy. A collective "Ooooh" from the congregation greeted them as they set it in place and then covered the top and sides with a colorful quilt . . . the friendship quilt.

Avis's mouth dropped open, but she obediently stood up as Pastor Clark motioned her and Peter forward. One of her grandbabies—Conrad's namesake—ran up and gave her a small bouquet of white roses to hold, and he got a big kiss, which he wiped off immediately as he ran back to his mother. Avis and Peter stood under the *huppah* as Pastor Clark gave a short wedding homily based on several "joy" verses, then asked Avis and Peter for their vows. I don't think there was a dry Yada Yada eye as Avis spoke her own words to Peter: "Peter, first of all you are my friend . . ." Tissues came out and noses blew all over the room.

Pastor Clark also asked them to repeat the traditional vows "to love and cherish till death do us part." As Avis and Peter exchanged rings, Ricardo and José came forward with their guitars and serenaded the startled couple with a traditional Latino love song. Another Yada Yada surprise.

Grinning from ear to ear, Pastor Clark finally pronounced them husband and wife. "You may kiss your bride!"

Okay, what happened next wasn't exactly Sunday morning decorum—more like pumped-up fans at a football stadium—and the cheering and clapping and whistles went on for a good five minutes. Peter took advantage of the pandemonium and got in two or three extra kisses.

"Jump de broom!" Chanda cried, conscripting Uptown's janitorial push broom into service. Others took up the chant: "Jump the broom! Jump the broom!" And to my dying day, I'll never forget the poised principal of Mary McLeod Bethune Elementary sailing over that broom on the arm of her new husband as Avis Johnson *Douglass*.

Pastor Clark finally called for a semblance of order long enough to say, "Well, that's half our worship service today. But I've just been told that the sun is out—for the next five minutes anyway." General laughter. "I'd like to suggest we go immediately to the lake for the second half of our celebration—the baptism of Yolanda Spencer."

Yo-Yo ducked as all eyes turned toward her.

"What? Now?" Ruth spluttered. "But what about the wedding cake?" She bustled over to the pass-through window and slid it open. "See? Made special for Avis and Peter. Not so cheap either!"

45

*R*uth was only slightly pacified when assured that we'd all come back to the church for cake. "Just pour some water on Yo-Yo's head," she muttered, "and let's eat." Still, Ben dragged her down the stairs along with the rest of the congregation to pile into cars parked along Morse Avenue and on the side streets. Most of the teenagers elected to walk to the lake since it was only a few blocks to Loyola Beach.

I thought Avis and Peter might sneak away in his black Lexus, but no, there it was in the beach parking lot when we pulled in. Avis had actually done a quick change back in the women's restroom and was wearing a gold-and-black tunic with harem pants and a black shawl—one of her favorite casual outfits. Peter still kept looking at her as if he wanted to eat her up.

It took thirty minutes for everyone to gather on the beach, but the weather was still holding. Billowy thunderheads piled up on the horizon, yet there was no wind, the clouds overhead had broken, and the noonday sun brightened the water to a turquoise green. Seagulls screeched and swooped over the water, then did two-point landings on the sand, probably figuring that "people" equaled "food."

Denny strolled over to talk to Mark and Nony, and Mark seemed easy in his manner. Guessed he wasn't too annoyed at Denny for the "sabbatical" suggestion. But I doubted that he'd told Nony what Denny had said.

Carla ran past me just then, chasing the seagulls, her beaded braids bouncing, making the birds fly up a short distance before they landed again. Carl Hickman squatted down on his haunches, grabbed his daughter as she flew by, and tickled her till she cried, "Stop, Daddy!"

Florida hovered beside me. "See that? I been thinkin' maybe I died and gone to heaven. That man came home every night last week wearin' self-respect like a new suit of clothes. Even Carla feel the difference in our house. Didn't throw a single tantrum all week. Well, okay, one." She pulled on my sleeve. "Hey, they gettin' ready to start."

We all gathered around Pastor Clark and Yo-Yo in her lavender overalls, standing with their backs to the water. Uptown's pastor explained that Yo-Yo was not a member of our church but participated in a prayer group that involved several Uptown members. "Not that it matters," he said. "We don't baptize people into a particular church. We baptize them into the family of God, the universal church of Christ that proclaims Jesus is Lord." He turned to Yo-Yo. "Would you like to say something before we proceed?"

Yo-Yo, shoulders hunched, hands in pockets, stared at her toes as if hoping a pocket of quicksand might swallow her. But she finally lifted her spiky blonde head and managed a quirky grin. "Hey, everybody. Yeah, I wanna thank Ruth and Ben Garfield, you know, for bein' the parents I never really had. Took Pete an' Jerry under their wings 'fore they got too big for their britches."

Yo-Yo's teenage brothers, wearing baggy pants and oversize athletic shirts, got slapped upside the head by a few snickering teenagers nearby.

"An' I wanna thank Yada Yada, all of 'em, for lettin' me ride along with this crazy prayer group all year. Today's our anniversary, ya know . . ." Whatever she said next was drowned out by whoops and hallelujahs and "praise Jesus" from all the Yada Yadas scattered among the crowd at the edge of the water, and our friends and families laughed. But Yo-Yo seemed unfazed and just repeated herself when the noise died down. "An' I 'specially wanna thank Becky Wallace over there . . ." She jerked a thumb toward where Stu stood with Becky, clad in one of Stu's bulky sweaters and a pair of slacks that covered her ankle monitor. "'Cause she ain't patient like these other nice Christian ladies. She tol' me to make up my mind an' get off the fence—either be a Christian or be a pagan like she is."

No! Yo-Yo didn't say that! I shot a glance at Becky, sure she'd be mortified being identified as a pagan in front of a bunch of church folks, even if those *were* her own words. But a grin—the first one I'd seen since the DOC guys dropped her off a week ago; maybe the first one I'd *ever* seen—spread out under the shapeless brown hair. Close behind me I heard Adele mutter: "Get that girl into my shop. That hair needs help—bad."

I strained my ears. Yo-Yo was still talking, her voice almost swallowed by the great outdoors. "Also, Becky's one person who knows what it's like to sit in jail and be free again. An' I guess that's why I want to be baptized today, 'cause we both know being a pagan ain't all it's cracked up to be. I'm tired of my insides bein' in jail, an' I want Jesus to make me free."

"Thank ya, *Jesus!*" Florida shouted, and for half a minute even the teenagers joined the clapping and amens.

Denny slid an arm around me and gave me a slight squeeze. "That girl just preached," he murmured, his voice full of admiration.

Pastor Clark then asked Yo-Yo the baptism questions about confessing her sins and believing that Jesus is the Son of God and accepting His forgiveness because of what He did on the cross. Yo-Yo, never one to follow protocol, blurted, "Yeah, I got it. If not, Avis over there will explain it to me."

It was time to go into the water. Pastor Clark beckoned to Denny, and the two men took off their shoes and rolled up their pant legs. Yo-Yo did the same. Clinging to each other, the trio started into the water. "Aaaiiiieeee!" Yo-Yo screeched, hopping up and down. "It's *freezing!*"

Laughter spread through the crowd, comfortably warm on the shore in our light jackets and sweatshirts. Some of the teenagers and children took off their shoes and waded a few feet into the water, just to prove it wasn't too cold for *them*. But the trio in the water kept walking—up to their knees . . . up to their thighs . . . almost up to Yo-Yo's waist. They finally stopped, turned around, and the two men held Yo-Yo's arms and shoulders in a good grip. Even from the shore we could see Yo-Yo rolling her eyes and making faces at the frigid lake water, though it was hard to hear what Pastor Clark was saying to her. But I caught ". . . in the name of the Father, Son, and Holy Spirit"—and then Pastor Clark and Denny quickly lowered Yo-Yo backward into Lake Michigan and brought her up again, dripping wet.

"Thank ya, *Jesus!*" Florida shouted again, and someone started the group on shore singing, "Tell me, how does it feel to come out the wilderness?" as the trio headed back toward shore.

"Wait!" someone shouted. I was startled to see Becky Wallace pull away from Stu's side and head for the water. At the water's edge, she kicked off her shoes and waded in, heading toward the shivering Yo-Yo. The singing died away as everyone gaped. *What in the world?*

For a nanosecond, I wondered if Becky had figured out a good escape—just head into the water and keep swimming. Or drown the ankle monitor. But she stopped as she met up with Pastor Clark, Denny, and Yo-Yo, saying something and gesturing with her hands. She and Pastor Clark talked intensely for a few minutes. Then the two men looked at each other, and I saw Denny nod.

All four of them turned around and headed back into waist-deep water.

Several of us realized what was happening all at once. *Becky Wallace wanted to be baptized!* Chanda began jumping up and down. "Hallelujah! Hallelujah! Oh, Jesus!" I heard "Glory!" and "Thank You, Jesus!" But Stu caught my eye, and without saying a word, we both kicked off our shoes and waded into the water. That sister needed some sisters around her while she did the bravest thing I'd ever seen—though wading into the water took guts, too. *Ai-yi-yiii!* It was *cold*!

Pastor Clark waited for us until we got there, and to my surprise, Denny stepped aside and beckoned for Stu and me to take his place at Becky's side. She gripped our hands like a lifeline as Pastor Clark said in a loud voice, "Becky Wallace, on your confession of faith and desire to follow Jesus, I baptize you in the name of the Father, Son, and Holy Spirit." And down she went. Back up she came, eyes squeezed shut—but the smile on her face was like its own sunshine.

As Pastor Clark released her, Stu and I enveloped Becky Wallace—thief, felon, ex-con, housemate, sister—in a big, wet hug. With our arms tangled around each other, I had a sudden vision of a *new* meaning for Becky's name, which meant "bound" or "tied." Laughing, I said in her ear, "Becky, you are now *all tied up* in the love of God!" I wanted to say more, but I heard splashing and squeals behind us. Turning my head, I saw half the Yada Yadas wading into the water to hug Becky, grimacing at the cold water.

Chanda was the first to get there. She gave Becky a hug—then to my shock, she dunked herself and her bright yellow Easter suit completely under the water and came up holding her head. "Gonna wash that mon right out o' my hair!" she belted out, as if auditioning for the Broadway musical itself. "Oh Lord, dat mon is *gone* an' this sista is *glad.* I'm free! I'm free!" And she began to jump up and down, splashing the rest of us.

We all started to laugh. The next thing I knew, Stu went down under the water and came up, long hair streaming down her back. She gave me a wet hug. "Oh God, Jodi," she whispered in my ear. "I'm free, too!—from living a lie, from lying to myself. I'm so glad . . . so glad."

I saw Hoshi in the water, hugging Becky Wallace. My heart twisted. I could hardly bear it. Hoshi—who had been rejected by her own family because she chose to follow Jesus—was hugging her new sister in God's family, the same woman who had sent Hoshi's mother back to Japan with a hand full of stitches and a heart full of anger.

Could I forgive like that? *Oh God! Your redemption is so great!*

Back onshore I heard a squeal and saw Peter Douglass sweep Avis into his arms and start wading into the water. "You wouldn't!" she screeched, clinging to his neck, yet he just kept coming, a silly grin on his normally sober features. And then he dumped her in the water.

She came up spluttering—but in half a second, she was splashing him, laughing, and splashing harder. And that's when it hap-

pened. The rest of the Yada Yadas, Amanda and José, Yo-Yo's brothers, the Jesus People teenagers in their tattoos and nose rings,
Florida's squealing kids, Nony in her African-print tunic and head
wrap, and an assortment of other Uptown folks and teenagers—all
in the water, churning up a huge hallelujah water fight! Even Pastor
Clark got a good soaking—and managed to give it back to a few of
the teenagers himself.

Sopping wet, hardly aware of the frigid water, I stepped back as if
watching the scene in the water from a faraway place. What had just
happened here? Two young women had just been baptized.
Redeemed from their own efforts. Set free to be new women. And the
rest of us . . . we were being redeemed too. Florida—turning a new
page in the life of her family. Chanda—seeing "Dia's daddy" for the
faithless moneygrubber he really was. Nony—carrying her vision for
a redeemed South Africa in her heart. Avis—redeemed from the ache
of loneliness she'd lived with since her beloved Conrad had died.

And me. Jodi Marie Baxter. Redeemed to be . . . me! Not the
good girl I thought I was for so many years. Not the hopeless sinner
I discovered myself to be. But the woman God created me to be—
helped along by sisters so different from myself, who weren't afraid
to knock off the rough edges of my pettiness and self-righteousness
and judgmental spirit. Yet who accepted me just for myself.

Already wet, I raised my arms toward the sky, yelled, "Thank
You, Jesus!" and fell backward into Lake Michigan. The cold water
closed over my head. But before I could get my feet under me, I felt
a strong hand pull me up out of the water. I blinked my eyes open.

Denny.

"Lightning," he said. "Storm's coming this way. We need to get
out of the water." He grabbed my hand and headed for shore.

I looked back. The sky had darkened. Jagged bolts of lightning skipped across the horizon. Yes, a storm was coming. So?

The Yada Yada Prayer Group—and the Baxter family—had weathered storms before. And we would again.

Book Club Questions

1. A lot of readers say, "I am *so* Jodi!" Do you identify with Jodi? In what way? Why do you think so many readers identify with her?

2. In chapter 3, Jodi yells at God, "What part of dull and boring don't You understand?" What pressure points do you have in *your* life right now? Have you considered whether God might have a redemptive purpose to "keeping the pressure on"?

3. Do you have a "Stu" in your life—someone who seems to have it all together and makes your best efforts look like a crumb in comparison? How do your feelings affect your relationship? Do you really know this person in her hidden places? What do you think would help you get "unstuck" in this relationship?

4. In what ways do you see Jodi growing and changing since Book One? What do *you* see as the difference in the "Old Jodi" and the "New Jodi" way of responding to situations.

5. The Yada Yada sisters are challenged not just to "believe *in* God," but to "*believe* God." What is the difference? What does that mean to you?

6. In what ways do the various members of Yada Yada "get real"

in this book (or not)? What does "getting real" mean to you? What are the benefits of being more open and honest in your relationships? What might be the downside of doing so?

7. Jodi still carries scars from the car accident—a reminder of her anger and her failure—until she begins to see these scars as a reminder of God's grace and a reminder to pray for Hakim and his mom. What scars (physical or emotional) do you carry? In what way could these scars serve a redemptive purpose or encourage you to pray?

8. What prompted Jodi's confession to the mother of Hakim and Jamal at the final parent-teacher conference? How was it different from her first "I'm sorry" at the end of Book One? In what way was the confession healing for Jodi? For Geraldine? In what ways can confession be an agent of redemption?

9. Reflect on the trauma Becky Wallace inflicted on the Yada Yada Prayer Group—and yet something in their response to Becky drew her into the water of baptism. Has God dropped someone into your life—unasked, unannounced, and even unwelcome? What feelings do you have about this person? Are you willing to consider whether God has a redemptive purpose in mind?

10. How has Christ's forgiveness changed *your* life? (Remember, it cost Him.) How might your forgiveness set another person free? What would it cost you? *How far does that forgiveness go?*

Find out how the Yada Yada Story begins . . .

I almost didn't go to the Chicago Women's Conference—after all, being thrown together with 500 strangers wasn't exactly my "comfort zone." But I would be rooming with my boss, Avis, and I hoped that I might make a friend or two.

When Avis and I were assigned to a prayer group of 12 women, I wasn't sure what to think. There was Flo, an outspoken ex-drug addict; Ruth, a Messianic Jew who could smother-mother you to death; and Yo-Yo, who wasn't even a Christian! Not to mention women from Jamaica, Honduras, South Africa—practically a mini-United Nations. We certainly didn't have much in common.

But something happened that weekend to make us realize we had to hang together. So "the Yada Yada Prayer Group" decided to keep praying for each other via e-mail. Our personal struggles and requests soon got too intense for cyberspace, so we decided to meet together every other Sunday night.

Talk about a rock tumbler!—knocking off each other's rough edges, learning to laugh and cry along the way. But when I faced the biggest crisis of my life, God used my newfound girlfriends to help teach me—Jodi Baxter, longtime Christian "good girl"—what it means to be just a sinner saved by grace.

THE YADA YADA PRAYER GROUP

ISBN 1-59145-074-8

AVAILABLE WHEREVER BOOKS ARE SOLD

BOOK 2

When they get shaken up, The Yada Yada Prayer Group Gets Down

I had never felt so violated! The Yada Yada Prayer Group was "gettin' down" with God in prayer and praise one night when a heroin-crazed woman barged into my house, demanded our valuables and threatened us with a 10-inch knife—a knife that drew blood.

We wondered if we'd ever get back to normal after this terrifying experience. I assumed we would (although "normal" doesn't usually describe the 12 of us mismatched women any-way). After all, we'd been through a lot already as spiritual sisters. This was just one more hurdle to conquer, right?

But then a well-meaning gesture suddenly incited a backlash of anger in the group, forcing us to confront generations of racial division, pain and distrust—and stretching our friendships to the limit. Initially I thought, Surely I, Jodi "Good Girl" Baxter, am not responsible for other people's sins—am I? But a shocking confrontation in my third-grade classroom forced me to face my own accountability, and God used the Yada Yada Prayer Group (and my own husband, of all people) to show me what true forgiveness really is.

THE YADA YADA PRAYER GROUP GETS DOWN
ISBN 1-59145-151-5

AVAILABLE WHEREVER BOOKS ARE SOLD

Your chance to "yada yada" with God

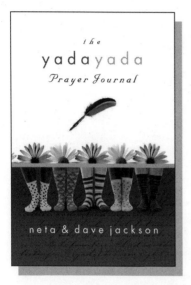

A prayer journal to go with a series of fiction novels? Whoever heard of such a thing! Yet the Yada Yada Prayer Group novels have impacted thousands of lives as these rollicking prayer sisters have inspired a heart-hunger in readers to "yada" (know and be known intimately by) God and each other, and to "yadah" (give praise to) our Lord.

Now you can join author Neta Jackson on a journey that will take you even further into the three books' themes of grace, forgiveness and redemption. Each of these 60 daily devotions include an excerpt from one of the novels, Neta's personal reflections from her heart to yours, thought-provoking questions with relevant scripture and prayer guides . . . and space to respond with your own thoughts, prayers and praise.

Using this journal will not only change you, but may even ready you for the next step: your own prayer group of "Yada Yada" sisters. For Jesus said: "Where two or three are gathered together in My name, there I am in the midst of them" . . . and where Jesus is, something glorious happens!